The Ghost of Neil Diamond

what tradition books
whattradition.com

The Ghost of Neil Diamond

David Milnes

Chapter One

The Karaoke Collection

Amen to all sorrows.

With a few splashes of cold water Neil washed away his sins. He watched them slip down the plughole, one by wretched one. The wrongdoings and wrong turns, the bad debts and bad memories sank beyond the U-bend, and his soul lay empty and prepared. A whiff reached him from the urinals, the stale reminder of that catalogue of men who had fallen short at just this point – the last call, the swan song. Well, forget them, he decided. They had their lives and this is mine. He lifted his aching head to the mirror. This time. Maybe this time.

Two young Chinese – city boys with spiked hair, loosened ties, daytime suits – burst in upon his peace and quiet, banging the toilet door against the wall. They shouted at each other in Cantonese and joked and poked and laughed so hard it doubled them up, slewed how they walked. Neil followed them with scowls of boozy disapproval. They used the urinals quickly, not watching what they were doing, shouting and laughing across the stalls, then left without washing their hands.

These Chinese and their manners, Neil thought, turning back to his sink of sorrows. He remembered an old scare about bar snacks at The Peninsula, The Marriott, The Furama, all the plushest Hong Kong hotels. Fifteen different urine samples, minimum, in a single bowl of crackers. Asia's premier world-class city pissed on inside out.

The toilet door eased shut on its spring, cutting off the lounge once more. He braced himself against the sink, closed his eyes and listened. Mysteries of the oriental night drifted through the broken Xpelair. The clangs of container trucks on the flyover below. The dull, continuous murmur of tyres on concrete. From somewhere a lonesome horn cried out, in the far distance – on the sea perhaps. He winced at that solitary, frightened sound.

While the karaoke machine played, *Sweet Caroline* . . .

Oh, Neil Diamond Nite – when would it ever end? And tomorrow Stevie Wonder Nite. I Just Called To Say I Love You. Stevie Wonder – blind, smiling, chin up against all adversity. And Thursday Marvin Gaye Nite. What's Going On. The late & great Marvin Gaye, gunned down by his preacherman father during a porn film and gone to burning hell. Neil Diamond, Stevie Wonder, Marvin Gaye – all has-beens before the weekend.

Amen to all of them, and to all their sorrows too.

He found his hair band in the mirror and set loose his greying frizz. There was so much of it now it wasn't even funny. Mr Bojangles, the full reprise. He raked and ordered the twists and straggles as best he could, then took a step back so the grey darkened in the mellow mirror light, and the hard lines softened. He turned in profile and looked back at himself with his chin thrust out, haughty and severe, posing as he might have posed for an album cameo, back sleeve, twenty years ago: strong and young and wild.

Now the wild man at forty-eight. Never too late. His hair discreetly hid his thickening jowls, the terrible pear-shape of things to come.

No. Not that . . .

Fare thee well then, *Sweet Caroline*, and all the good times that don't seem so good now.

The lounge felt more threatening, more treacherous, after the healing solitude of the toilets. It was blacker and smokier and noisier than before. He weaved tipsily by pontoons of private booths, edging around the larger parties – Excuse me, excuse me, excuse me, please – and their long glass tables, strewn with empties and peanut bowls, white bowls shining upwards in the darkness, like the whitened Chinese faces rolling up at him, startled, amused, as he passed. Even the carpet he stumbled on was a deep and wavy black shag, hiding all manner of rubbish and insect life. Seaweed. Silverfish. Roaches.

He was still four tables out when the first cry went up.

"Here he comes!"

"Hey! Would you look at that?"

"Oooooh, yeah!"

"I like it!"

"It's all hanging out tonight!"

"Mister Bojangles!"

"He jumped so high!"

"His dog up and died!"

"On a piece of string!"

"It was suicide!"

Please, gentlemen, please . . .

"You letting go tonight, Neil?" Damian teased. "We gonna have some of the ole toons? Where have all the flowers gone? I wonder about that sometimes, you know? Where they all went. Don't you?"

"All the time."

"And where were you the night they drove ole Dixie down? Were you here at the bar? Pissed out your skull?"

"How'd you know that?"

Damian's knavish face smiled up, soft and round and brimful of lewd intent. The mock Teddy boy, cupped in blue velvet, stuck in the middle of his own decade. His grey mullet flowed so smoothly over his collar it must have been curled at the hairdressers' this very afternoon, with heated tongs. He was a curled darling all right. But why was he shielding him from Angel? Or her from him? And why was she rearranging her tight white blouse while he talked? They don't call him big little Damian for nothing, you know.

"You having a good time, Neil? You giving us a turn? Go on, now! Go go go!"

Neil tried to catch Angel's eye, but she was taking a drink, looking the other way.

"Yeah! Go on, Neil! Give us a turn!"

Some new hanger-on, to her right, seconding the motion. A northerner. A Geordie with a stringy, stingy, skew-jawed face, but young, a thirty-something among the pack of grey wolves. Where'd he come from? Trendy black retro glasses. Someone who wanted him out the way as well so he could get closer to Angel in her tight white blouse. A new friend covering the further side. Teamwork.

"Oh, give us a song, Neil!" he whined. "Don't be a meany!" He laughed and looked around for support, pressing his luck. A young loudmouth. "Go strut your stuff, Neil! Let yourself go, why dontcha?"

"He's already let himself go," Damian muttered, and he chuckled and reached for his glass, losing interest.

Neil couldn't take that. He bore down on Damian. Big cock or no big cock, good fuck or no good fuck.

"Why don't you let go a moment, Damian? Hmmn?"

He put his hand on Damian's shoulder and pinched the velvet hard. Damian squirmed under pressure. He grinned and wriggled and pretended to enjoy it.

"Ooooh! Touchy touchy! Touchy touchy touchy!"

Neil watched the grey mullet break up on the blue velvet.

"Touchy-feely!" cried the Geordie.

And they all laughed. Oh, how they laughed.

A squiffy jazz piano, someone just fooling around, signalled the next number. Neil released his grip and gave up the fight. He glanced at the monitor above their table. A song from far, far away, from the mid-sixties, was cueing in at the foot of the screen. Reason to Believe. He knew this song. Knew it only too well. A beautiful song. Tim Hardin. Tim Hardin? Dead at thirty-nine, nursing and cursing his heroin addiction to its lonely, bitter end. Bright colour filled the screen as Neil Diamond himself appeared above the lyrics, his body gloved in a tight red jumpsuit spangled with sequins. The top of the suit was open low, Elvis style. He was stepping downstage with an old-fashioned cable mike in his hand. He flicked the trailing cable step by step on his way down to the audience. The picture looked live, shaky, slightly out of focus. It was late seventies, twenty years old at least. There were fairy lights in silly hearts and bows on every step. An amphitheatre somewhere, on a soft and balmy summer evening. The lightest breeze teased the superstar's hair and it made him look down and smile, that teasing breeze, as he put his hair back in place. Because nothing, absolutely nothing, could ruffle him for a moment tonight.

Neil raised his hand for the mike and drifted off from his party. Cheers and jeers and fleers followed him to the dais near the MC's console where the limelighters did their turns. A waitress came forward with the mike, looking up at him with a sympathetic and motherly smile – These funny grey-haired, long-haired guys – Who did they think they were?

No one quietened down for him. They kept chattering away and wandering about. They bought drinks or slipped off to the toilets, or drifted across to perfect strangers to light their cigarettes. He looked down at his baggy pants – Bojangles, again – and at his shoes, the anonymous loafers in which he'd shuffled into middle-age.

Well, never mind.

He took a breath, a deep breath, then gave them the first line, loud and clear but with a cool restraint, the big feeling under control. The line was a gift to them . . . a love gift . . . for all of them . . .

If I listened long enough to you . . .

And a sudden hush followed. Faces turned his way. He saw a Chinese girl look up, take her cigarette from her lovely mouth, and stare at him. She pulled back her hair from her face. He'd hit the world famous voice full on, the slight crack in it, into which he'd poured some of his own feeling, just a little anger, hurt and heartache, but not too much. He shook his hair free once more, loosening everything up, and stepped towards the nearest table –

You know I'd find a way, you know I would, I'd find a way . . .

A few whoops and cheers for the song but more, much more, surely, for who he was, who he was becoming before their very eyes. He was pulling them in, all of them, no head unturned. He slowed right up for the title line . . . yeah, still looking for that -

Reason to Believe . . .

He glanced across at his table, at Angel. He had the whole table, all the old China hands, looking his way, looking up at him, looking up to him. For a moment they were nice guys and full of goodwill. They forgave him and he forgave them. For a moment they all understood maybe, and understood also that this was nothing to him. He panned round the rest of the lounge. They were coming out of their private booths and jostling for places to stand and watch. Standing room only. He had the whole lounge in the palm of his hand. They thought Neil Diamond had just showed up in person for Neil Diamond Nite. Rather older now and a touch desperate. They thought it was some freakish stunt. Top of the bill. Talk of the town. He stared into Angel's eyes –

You see, someone like you . . .

But she looked away.

So he did too, and drew in the MC – How're you doin',
friend? He beckoned to him, mike held high, little finger
crooked on the mike stem, and he rolled his free hand,
working the rhythm, this way, that way, never too much –

You see, someone like you . . .

And the MC – an ancient Chinese groover, complete with
baseball cap, shades, wraparound smile – why, he took it in his
stride, he wanted in on this too, he wanted a part of this, sure
he did, yes sir, he wanted to own a bit of it, and he looked
about and faked it, tried to play the gathering crowd, he
grinned and nodded and cocked his head as well, and tipped
his baseball cap, No. 69 – yeah, sure, keep it comin', I like
that, keep it comin', yeah . . .

Neil bent low to a table for two and offered the next verse
to a pretty Thai girl. She was too young – centre-parted hair, a
schoolgirl smile, and teenage spots under her make-up.
Impossibly, indecently young. Her Chinese sugar daddy, sixty
at least, sagged in his seat opposite. Two black kiss-curls
strayed down his brow. Neil shut him out completely. He
wasn't part of it. He wasn't even sitting there. It was not that
old lecher's moment. Not yet. This was Neil Atherton's
moment, and Neil Diamond's. It belonged to them. The girl
belonged to Neil Atherton and Neil Diamond now. No, you
can't take this away from me. He cradled the mike in his
fingertips, cabaret style, and gave the girl the whole verse,
gave it all away to her, with passion, line by sacred line.

And the Thai girl smiled and giggled and looked anxiously
to her escort, and her pencilled eyebrows arched helplessly –
What could she do? – as Neil turned away, casting another
glance at his table, his wife, in passing, then on to the jealous
crowd –

Yeah, someone like you . . .

And he kept it going right up to the final refrain, when he raised his fist in the limelight and lent the lyric the most tender parting of his world famous voice, filling each note till it broke and fell worthless into awed silence.

Wild applause. Keep it comin', yeah . . . Let's really hear it. And table thumps, whistles and hoots of amusement. The old magic of performance still there. Encore, encore . . . He opened his arms to the crowd, opened his heart to the crowd, and flung his thankyous to them with kisses and imaginary bouquets. He caught the eye of the ancient MC and won a last lipless smile, a farewell tip of the baseball cap – yeah, sure, he really liked that too, but let's keep it rollin' now, it's Neil Diamond Nite, all night, all right, uptightanoutasight.

Only Angel remained unamused. Under the dim monitor lights he saw her break free of Damian and his young northern friend and sit forward at the table, her chin in her hands, watching him gather in the fading applause, watching him make a fool of himself one more time – just one more time, everybody. She shook her head severely. Her new hairstyle, short, dark, expensive, framed her cold stare. Her new make-up, the hard and bruised look, the look of total experience, wasn't so seductive when she really felt it. It aged her. She was more than late thirties, much more. Tonight she'd caught him up: she was mid-forties or even late forties. The company of people like Damian put years on her too. Why couldn't she see that?

He bowed out and handed the mike to an overweight and very drunken Chinese, who launched into *Song Sung Blue* from where he sat.

Do that, friend . . .

Neil's face and throat were burning. He set out to get a drink but was briefly surrounded, nailed and hailed and buttonholed by drunken fans and jokers. The route to the bar became a gauntlet of shoulder pats and high-fives, and when he finally arrived, there was more jokey adulation from the barflies, perched on their high stools. He waved their quips and taunts away and they turned back to their private conversations.

Then someone came up from behind and tapped him on the elbow.

"Hey there . . . You're really very good, you know . . ."

Neil tried to get a drink but it wasn't easy, despite his new status. He looked back, then down. A Chinese or Eurasian guy, early forties maybe, was staring up at him in a very direct and serious way. He was so short Neil could see his hair-flip laddered all along his pasty scalp. Just another nondescript and forgettable guy, except for a bold statement. A wild Hawaiian shirt. Blue skies and palm trees, brown sugar beaches, girls and cocktails and fancy cars – all the good times were there, spilling down to the crotch of his suit trousers. All the good times were there, and they'd never looked so bad. The man stood with one hand in his pocket, ruffling the baggy shirt. In his other hand he held a full bottle of beer. It was difficult to read his very sober and penetrating expression. Was it really intense, or just dense? His flat features gave nothing away.

Neil nodded curtly – Goodnight, pal – and turned back to the bar.

The mood had passed. Ephemeral as the beautiful song that inspired it, the mood had vanished. He felt a light sweat around his hairline. He was worried about what was happening behind him right now, about the attentions Angel might be encouraging and receiving again. The pack were so shameless, so randy. Especially the older ones and the ugly ones. The old China hands. The desperadoes. He had to return to the table and hold the lid on things. He glanced over his shoulder the other way. There was a merry raising of glasses and interlocking of arms.

He caught the barman's attention and ordered his drink.

The fan spoke up again, tapped him on his cold shoulder.

"You sing so well, you know . . ."

Neil shrugged him off without looking back.

"I mean very, very well . . ."

Okay. Neil looked down one last time. The fan was smiling. It was a smile with absolutely nothing in it, animal, the smile of a monkey.

"If you want to fix up some dates, some bookings," the man said, taking out his wallet, "just give me a call or stop by." He removed a business card. "I think you're terrific. Terrific. I really do. Any time. Open door. Perhaps I can be of service."

He offered the card formally to Neil with both hands and a slight bow. Neil took it with one hand, thanked him, and slipped it into his shirt pocket with his change. He grabbed his beer and left.

Damian passed him on his way to buy more drinks. He made the bottle-up gesture and in reply Neil held up his full one. Nothing about his song, of course, about how good he'd been – such an ungracious guy.

"Who's your buddy?" Angel asked, as he took the seat next to her. Damian's seat.

"What buddy?"

"With the shirt." She glanced at the bar.

Neil followed her glance. The fan had gone. Then he saw a kingfisher flash of the Hawaiian shirt out the corner of his eye, under the Exit sign.

"What did he want?"

Neil didn't care to talk about it but there was warmth in the way she blinked at him, patiently, knowingly, and he did care about that, very much.

"He said he might be able to fix something up. Some dates. Bookings."

"When will you see him?"

"I don't know." He had no intention of seeing the man again but to keep her interest he took the business card from his shirt pocket.

"He gave you his card?"

Neil flicked it on his fingernails, at arm's length.

"Losers can't be choosers, Neil."

He looked at her. She must have had too much to drink to say that, though it didn't show. She reached across and put her hand on his wrist. She squeezed, then pulled his hand closer and drew the card from his fingers. That's all it took. Just one squeeze.

"Elbert Chan," she read, squinting at the name. "Funny name."

"Funny guy. Very funny."

She smiled. She put the card back in his shirt pocket, patted the pocket against his chest, then withdrew her hand.

"Go see him in the morning, Neil. First thing. Go see Elbert."

"I don't know . . ."

"Go see him, Neil. First thing."

"I'll think about it. That's all."

"Well, you think about it hard."

Chapter Two

Elbert Chan

"Variety," Neil said. "Any middle-of-the-roadster. Any guy with two first names. Billy Joel, Elton John, George Michael, Cliff Richard – any of their songs . . . No problem at all . . ."

Elbert Chan's looks, last night so nondescript and forgettable, were distinctive enough under the strip light of his poky office first thing in the morning. His face was very flat, very still, quite imperturbable. His hair-flip was sprayed high and firm for the day ahead. Only his eyes moved, and very slowly, admitting nothing and committing nothing, under their smooth brow.

The Hawaiian shirt had vanished without trace. He wore a cheap, dark business suit.

"Or I could go back a bit," Neil continued, filling the silence. "Classic songs. Bigger artists, better artists. Dean Martin. Frank Sinatra, of course. Tony Bennett. Bobby Darin, maybe. Tony Newley. Any of the old crooners – " Neil laughed briefly after that word. A crooner, you see, Mr. Chan, is one of those singers who – "Anyone you like, really. I'm a musician. I can read music and I sing in key. You've heard my voice. You know what I can do."

Why the stonewall? Where was the flattering fan from the karaoke bar? 'I think you're terrific. Come on up and we'll fix some dates and bookings . . .'

"I'm here today to offer a new act, Mr. Chan. Not spoofs, impersonations, jokes – nothing like that. But classic songs, hits through the ages, done my way. My Way, done my way!" He laughed again at this rehearsed joke but to no effect. "And with respect to the original artist, of course. With dignity. Like last night. No hard rock. That's not it. I'm from a different place, different tradition."

"What tradition?"

"All I need is a band and an entrée, Mr. Chan. Just a small band to back me up. It would be easy. No sweat. That's the business plan."

When Elbert Chan spoke again his voice was without tone. It was without any detectable trace of feeling, of memory, without the vaguest hint of welcome, warmth or sentiment.

"Tony Bennett, you say."

"If you like."

"Frank Sinatra."

"No question."

"Tony Newley."

"For sure."

Neil felt Chan's eyes creep over his lined face, his crinkly grey hair.

"But could you really?"

"Yes, I could. No problem at all."

Chan sat back in his swivel chair. There was a sudden flush of gold: gold tie-pin, phoney gold watch, gold cuff links.

"But could you really?"

"Yes I could."

Then Chan smiled, like last night. That quick, tight smile,

over small and tidy teeth. The smile was so detached it was free-standing, hovering there like some clever executive toy.

"Well, let me tell you something." He seemed to relax now that Neil had played his hand. "I know one or two clubs around here. Just one or two clubs. The American Club, out at Tai Tam, and The Jockey Club, for instance. And The Fanling Golf & Country Club and The Beas River Country Club . . . I know these clubs, and I'm welcome at these clubs. That can't be said for all the members, I might add . . ." A soft, secretive chuckle, after sharing this confidence. "And there's The Pacific Club right here in Kowloon. Very classy. If you want more class go on up to Mid-Levels and drop by The Ladies' Recreation Club. Then you have The Hong Kong Club itself, in the middle of town, but that's somewhat top dollar . . ."

Somewhat top dollar . . .

With a wave Chan directed attention to a sheet of contact numbers hanging on the wall.

"All the best clubs. I know all the right people – the Entertainments Managers, the Food and Beverage Managers, the Sports Bar Captains and so on – at all the best clubs. I mean the very best clubs, period. Forget the other clubs."

Things were looking up. Neil tried to study the list on the wall, as directed, but he was led astray by June's girl, suspended beneath the contact sheet on the same picture hook. She was a fleshy Chinese teenager in a strapless bikini, sitting astride an exercise cycle. Her skin was covered in suntan oil or massage oil that glistened under the studio lights, on her shoulders, her flanks, her thighs. She looked like something edible hooked up there, like a piece of caramelized meat or fruit. She returned Neil's gaze with slippery indifference. What was she doing here, in Elbert Chan's office, on her exercise bike?

The contact list for the clubs caught the light too but in a different way. It was a shiny laminated table, A4 size, suspended on a grey treasury tag. The names of the Entertainments Managers, F&B Managers, Sports Bar Captains and so on were given in full, anglicised in the colonial style – Gavin Fan, Harry Lam, Martin Wong – but the exclusive club names were all crudely cut to fit their boxes. American. Ladies. Beas R. Pacific. Jockey . . . It looked amateurish, the contact list, hanging there on its treasury tag.

"Does your wife sing?"

"What?" Neil swung back. "I beg your pardon?"

"Does your wife sing? She's a looker, isn't she?" Another smile. Those nibbling teeth. "I notice everything, you see. Everyone."

"Why do you ask?"

"Sonny and Cher."

"I beg your pardon?"

Chan blinked slowly. "I'm thinking Sonny and Cher."

"My wife doesn't sing . . ." Neil felt a twinge of guilt, letting Angel be mired in any of this. "She did once. A long time ago. But not now. Definitely not."

"What's her name?"

Neil hesitated, very uncomfortable. "Her name is Angel."

"What does Angel do?"

Neil frowned and hesitated again, letting Chan know he was off limits, then answered quickly. "She works in The Lippo Building. Top of the building. She's a negotiator."

"What does she sell?"

"She sells shipping space, Mr. Chan. Insurance contracts, assurance contracts. My wife is a very intelligent and successful woman, Mr. Chan, but she doesn't sing, you see. I sing."

"Left you behind, eh?"

"I wouldn't say that."

"Just a little, though."

"I wouldn't say that."

Chan looked down to his desk and opened The Neil Diamond Collection CD that was lying there in front of him. Neil had bought it in HMV in Hankow Road on the way in. Something to remind Chan, soften him up, focus attention. I can do any of those songs, he'd said, with quiet authority, tapping the CD on Chan's desk. No problem. No problem at all. But now his boasts about his songs and singers, and Chan's boasts about all his clubs, seemed to have cancelled each other out, to have crossed swords in the air above them and fallen in a useless heap, leaving them nothing to say to each other.

Idly now, Chan removed the sleeve notes from the CD case and flicked through the contents, the biographical material, the titles and lyrics.

"*Store bought woman . . .*" he read, squinting at a song lyric. ". . . somethingsomething store bought woman? What does that mean?"

Neil shifted in his rattan armchair, the only other chair in Chan's seedy office. He had no answer to such a question. Somethingsomething . . .

"What does that mean? Store bought woman. Do you know?"

"I don't know what that line means," Neil admitted. "That particular line."

Chan looked at Neil as if he'd already fallen short.

"But you . . ."

"Yes? . . ."

"Are a store bought woman."

"I don't know what it means. I just told you. Does it matter? . . . Prostitute, perhaps. I don't know."

"You're a store bought woman."

"Oh, that's very funny, Mr. Chan. I've got long hair so I'm a woman. Ha ha ha. You'll have to do better than that or I'm out of here."

"Go ahead."

"What?"

"Go right ahead."

There was a pause. Neil stayed where he was.

"You are what you don't know," Chan said, "and that makes you a store bought woman. Remember that."

Chan glanced again at the lyrics, looking for something else, but then he closed the booklet. Game over.

"You're right," he said. "It doesn't matter."

He flicked the booklet aside.

"Now what was it you wanted again?"

Their eyes locked.

"That's ridiculous," Neil said. "You remember me. You know why I'm here. What's your problem, pal?"

Chan drew his laptop in front of him, his Compaq, and opened the lid. He continued absently, speaking to the screen. "Sure I remember you. Of course I remember you . . . I remember your song . . . Your party . . . Your act . . . Your wife . . . Her friends . . ." He typed something, cocked his head at what he'd typed, frowned at what he'd typed. "I remember your long hair, like a lady . . ." He looked at Neil again, looked at him hard. ". . . And your voice . . . I remember everything, I notice everything, you see . . . and everyone . . ."

His right hand floated high off the keyboard and he began to draw limp circles in the air around Neil's face, white cuff and gold cuff link catching the light. He rolled his wrist as Neil had done last night, this way, that way, never too much, showing he remembered everything. Then his eyebrows arched in mild surprise, his mouth opened and his voice lifted into grating half-song, spread over just two or three thin, flat notes. A mockery of the old Sinatra standard –

She never bothers with people she hates –

He'd started at that moment when Sinatra points at a pretty lady in the audience who 'always comes late'. That moment of revelation when, with a flick of his foot, in time with the bass drum hitting home, Sinatra explains, as Chan explained on his two or three flat notes now –

That's why the lady,
That's why the lady,
That's why the lady,
Is a tramp!

Quiet.

Chan's hand finished its circuit and stopped with his finger pointing at the middle of Neil's forehead, where his gaze steadied, not meeting Neil's gaze – pure bull's-eye – pure bullshit –

"Are you a tramp?"

It was Neil's turn to stonewall.

"Are you a tramp? A gypsy? Mister?"

Neil said nothing. His expression said nothing. Just what *right* . . .? Who the fuck was this guy?

"I need to know these things. How you're fixed, that's all."

Chan stood from his desk and looked down at Neil, then turned his back on him to face the window. From behind, standing up, he was suddenly a slight figure again, in his cheap dark business suit. Neil could have felled him with one punch or kick in the kidneys, then walked straight out.

Go ahead. Go right ahead.

There was nothing to be seen out the window beyond Chan. Half of it was taken up with an air conditioner unit and the rest was covered with pollution deposit, the yellow plaque that settled on every ledge, in every gap, on every shelf in Hong Kong. Chan pointed a handset at the AC unit and the room quietened. Sounds of the traffic below filtered in.

"Reason to Believe," he said, sitting down and facing Neil once more. "That's what you were singing, Reason to Believe by Neil Diamond."

"It's a Tim Hardin song," Neil corrected. "Nineteen sixty-six. Neil Diamond just covered it, like Rod Stewart."

Chan's office chair had an adjustable height mechanism that was racked up to full advantage, and he leant forward now so that his slight torso towered behind the desk. He didn't like being corrected like that. Neil tried to sit up, to get on even terms, but the aged rattan armchair was so low it was impossible to do anything but slump in it, legs outstretched across the grubby carpet.

"Neil Diamond is one of my favourite singers, you know," Chan announced, sharing another confidence. "The Atlantis Bar is one of only two karaoke places on the island that carry Neil Diamond songs." He waved two fingers. "Two that I know of, anyway. The other is in Causeway Bay. But that's somewhat expensive . . ."

A terrible homesickness swept through Neil. He thought of Angel, back in their apartment. She was going in late today. She'd told him to give her a call, let her know how it went. He thought of her washing up or taking a shower, or making herself some coffee, maybe eating a croissant or a Danish in the kitchen, glancing at the wall-phone as she ate, as she drank her coffee. If she could see him here, slumped in this office, see the yellow window – 'Oh my God! What a dump!' – if she could see where he had sunk to, his humiliation – Are you a tramp? A gypsy? Mister? – see all this dirt and triviality –

"Mr. Chan. You said you might be able to fix something up."

"Fix something up?"

"Dates. Bookings."

"Dates? Bookings?"

Chan chuckled at that. He shut the lid of his Compaq and set it aside, leaving the space clear again. Another smile started but he withdrew it with a flick of the tongue.

"Do you remember a sixties' band called Manfred Mann?"

"Mr. Chan, I didn't come here to chat about old sixties' bands."

"Do you remember, We are the Manfreds?"

Neil didn't answer.

"Pretty Flamingo?"

"Am I a pretty flamingo? Is that it? Very funny."

"They were over here, in Hong Kong, just last year. Manfred Mann. They played a string of clubs, then went back via Manila and Singapore – and Bangkok, I believe. For a little whoring in Bangkok, maybe. Manfred Mann. I swear not one of them was under fifty-five. I saw them at The Football Club in Happy Valley. They cleaned up there. They cleaned up everywhere."

Neil began to get the drift and was a little worried by it. He vaguely remembered a news item about a concert at The Royal Albert Hall for Manfred Mann in the not so distant past. Several sixties' bands like that had been enjoying twilight comebacks. There had been a fad in England for this sort of thing. He remembered tv pictures, queues of punters outside The Royal Albert Hall, middle-aged people, bald men in light raincoats, solid, dumpy women, smiling and waving their tickets at the cameras. Angel had laughed: "Hope for you yet, Neil!" But he couldn't see the funny side of it. The very notion exasperated him. All this fuss, pictures on the news no less, when a band like his, full of genuine musicians trying to uphold a cultural tradition, could hardly play for its beer, had to do ceilidhs in village halls, play barn dances, Country Fayres, Show Grounds, Truckfests, Summer FunWeeks for all the Family, and all the bloody rest of it.

"They did a concert at The Royal Albert Hall."

"Did they?" Chan's eyebrows lifted. Neil had said the right thing. "At The Royal Albert Hall? I didn't know that. Big venue. Did they clean up there?"

Neil cocked a smile, got there first. "Did they wash the dishes at The Albert Hall? That it? Yeah, that's a lot of dishes. Lots of dishes."

Chan blinked slowly again, didn't smile. "Was it a hit event, or not?"

"It was a sell-out event. Not so long ago. Last spring, maybe."

Chan nodded. "You see, that's very interesting. Very interesting. So what do you play, Mr. Atherton? What kind of music?"

"Well, what I have in mind, like I said – "

"But what do you play? Normally. What instruments."

Neil took a breath. It had to come out. His one and only, lonely answer.

"Well, first and foremost I'm a folk musician, you see, Mr. Chan. That's what I've always been. That's what I've always done. Folk music. I spent a few years – off and on – with Fairport Convention before coming out here. I had to quit when my wife got this job. You know Fairport Convention? World class. Dave Pegg? Dave Swarbrick? Richard Thompson? Or Sandy Denny, from years back? I recorded several albums with those people. And with other bands. Small bands, big bands. High profile bands. Lots of bands."

Chan tugged his jacket from under his buttocks, then settled back. His disappointment was palpable, filling the office like a break of wind. This was such a long way – oh, such a long, long way! – from Manfred Mann in Happy Valley at The Football Club, and then at The Royal Albert Hall.

"Airport Convention, you say."

"Fairport Convention."

"And you're a folk musician."

"That's right." Time to hold on. Ride it out. "That's right. That's where my real musical interest lies. I did a lot of solo tours too, in the U.K., on the circuit." He leant forward. "Listen, if you happen to have any folk connections up your –"

"Jacksie?"

Neil took a breath, sat back.

"What circuit?"

"Northern England. All the university towns, folk societies . . . and the East Midlands, East Anglia . . ."

Chan waved that away. The northern circuit. Folk societies. The East Midlands. "So what instruments do you play?"

"Viola mainly, but guitar, bodhrán – "

"What's that?"

"It's a drum. A hand drum."

"A hand job."

"It's Irish. An Irish hand drum. And I can play a little harmonica too."

"I get the picture," Chan said. "You're a wandering minstrel. Rags and patches. That kind of thing."

"Oh no I'm not, Mr. Chan."

"You're a one-man band. On the road. Hitching a ride."

"No I'm not."

"Swagman. Billabong. Waltzing Matilda."

"I'm not a one-man band, Mr. Chan."

"Sounds like it to me."

From somewhere Chan had fetched a toothpick and he began making his way round his mouth, one hand discreetly hiding what the other was up to. These Chinese and their table manners, Neil thought, but then he noticed that Chan's hands were cupped around his mouth much like a harmonica player's, and he saw some new mockery, another sly joke at his expense. Or was that paranoia now?

"As it happens, I also led a couple of bands," Neil added, asserting himself.

Between picks, frowning at the bloodied tip of his toothpick, Chan asked: "What were they called?"

"Stone Age Doll, in the seventies."

Chan took a Kleenex from a box on his desk. He wiped his mouth, said nothing.

"We brought out three albums. And in the eighties, Folk Renaissance. Dave Pegg played with Renaissance. For a while."

Chan worked a food particle from his incisors, wiped the toothpick on his tissue, then snapped the pick and rolled it up in the tissue, into a tight ball that he squeezed very hard. He reached out and dropped the ball next to his Compaq.

"Time out."

"What? . . . Excuse me?"

"I have no more time for this today. I'm sorry. Come back another day."

Neil stiffened in the rattan chair.

"When, exactly?"

"Er . . ." Chan raised his eyebrows and his eyes flitted about the room, searching everywhere for free dates, in every grey and shady corner. "Friday?"

"When, Friday?"

"Same time. Why not . . ."

Neil needed to recover ground, to get something definite established here. He wanted to name one or two other outfits he'd played for, such as Pentangle and Steeleye Span – big artillery – but Chan's abruptness had wrong-footed him completely.

Now Chan was standing up, holding out his hand.

"Friday," Neil said, getting out of his seat.

Chan shook his hand across the desk.

"Till Friday," Neil repeated.

But Chan said nothing more.

Chapter Three

Veuve Clicquot

"So, how'd it go?"

Oh dear. Neil refilled his glass, put down the bottle, and leant against her desk.

"Don't get drunk, Neil. That's an order."

Her chair was pushed back. She sat with her champagne glass in her lap and her glass was still full. She held it with both hands, very poised. The bag of clothes, underwear and shoes he'd brought lay in front of her, on her empty desk.

Could he talk about Elbert Chan here? In The Lippo Building? Was someone like that allowed all the way up to the twenty-seventh floor, stepping out the lift in his cheap business suit, with his phoney gold watch, cuff links, tie-pin? Or his Hawaiian shirt? Surely a doorman would head him off. One moment, friend. Just where do you think you're going?

"Well?"

"There's something there," Neil answered to the floor. "Could be good. Could be very good. He has the contacts. But there's nothing concrete. Not yet."

"Why so cagey?"

He glanced at her. "I'll let you know on a need-to-know basis. Okay?"

She had a new, subtle look. Different on-the-town make-up for a new and different kind of party. A blue and silky sulky look about her eyes, professionally applied. Her hair was darker too and styled with a slight wave. She must have had it all done after work, while he gathered up and brought her things. Lacy things. Low, short, risky things. That's why she'd had no time to come home and change, why he'd had to fetch and carry for her. That was the real reason, not what she'd said.

"So . . ." She put her glass on the desk and looked about for her handbag. "You'll be needing your allowance, then . . ."

He'd come all this way with her sexy things, on public transport, for his allowance.

"I'll drink to my allowance."

He emptied his glass again. It was such a heavenly drink.

"Please don't get drunk, Neil. I just told you."

He stared about the smart offices, one hand holding his empty champagne glass, the other in his pocket. He gazed vacantly at the mysterious rows of dark, paperless desk tops with their flat screens and state-of-the-art terminals, their complicated telephones, their cables, clipped and bundled, disappearing down stainless steel hatches in the deep, pinstriped carpet. His gaze sank into the carpet, blurring the pinstripes.

Quite at ease, twenty-seven floors up. And on the next floor they drank only Bollinger, she said.

"You've done so well, Angel," he admitted. "You're a very clever woman. I'm a lucky guy . . ."

He glanced at her but she looked away and pushed her hand through her hair, ruffling its moussed thickness. A new, evasive mannerism. She fetched her handbag from under her chair but she didn't open it.

"And I'm lucky too, Neil." She faced him squarely, handbag in her lap. "I know where I stand in the pecking order. I'm a grafter here. That's all."

"You must be good, though."

"I'm not getting any big ideas about myself."

There was no softening her these days, hardly any humour left at all. He had to respond to her wariness, those implications. "So it's time I got rid of *my* big ideas about *myself*, right?"

She frowned and lowered her eyes to her handbag. He could see, under the cold office light, the thickness of her make-up in the creases of her frown. She was becoming more impersonal towards him by the minute, as if she were dealing with a work problem that kept coming back to her desk by mistake, time after time.

"You have to get a job, Neil." She shook her head as if asking herself why she had to say this to him, again and again and again. "One way or another. Something different. Forget your music. Just forget about it. No one's interested here. Not in that. Try something else. Teach kids the guitar or something. Put an ad in the paper. You can't live off me. Not any more."

"I'll find something. You know that. Something will turn up. Always has, always does. Always." He steadied his gaze across the desks. The champagne had already got to him; such insidious bubbles. "I'm a survivor, remember."

"No you're not, Neil."

He looked down. She met his gaze through narrowed eyes.

"You're not surviving if I'm paying your bills. Come on, now."

Well, no answer to that.

He shoved himself off the desk and moved to the windows and stood there with his empty glass, his hand in his pocket, and stared at the views of Kowloon and the South China Sea, from the top of The Lippo Building.

He heard her get up from her desk and come up behind him. Conciliatory, perhaps. But he couldn't handle a moment of sentiment with her right now, no matter how token. Before she could speak he asked her about the view. The new suspension bridge to the airport was quite wonderful from up here, strung up on washing lines of coloured lights across the sea. She gave him the names of the islands the bridge spanned – from Tsing Yi to Ma Wan to Tsing Chau Tsai, on Lantau . . .

Listening to her, and looking out from her offices in this early evening light, and seeing the dark shadows of the mountains all about, and in the far distance the columns of container ships anchored out there, ships and cargoes that were somehow tethered up here as well, to the desk tops on the twenty-seventh floor, through those bundled cables and stainless steel hatches – seeing all of this and sensing the fabulous wealth lying out there on the South China Sea, and up here, all around him, feeling the boom from which everyone – executive, clerk, salesman and saleswoman – was cutting out his or her slice, before it was too late, feeling the boom, at last, as a physical sensation, Neil had a moment of epiphany this Wednesday evening. Everything became sharper, starker, more black and white. Against this backdrop, and the Central and Western business districts, he felt any hope he had for his career, and his marriage, fade out of view. Little wonder the old China hands, Damian and his gang, shook their heads and laughed – Do you know Mr. Bojangles, Neil? I mean, personally? . . . Do you remember that seventies' hit, Neil -'Gypsies, Tramps and Thieves'? . . . Neil, have you got that old sixties' song anywhere -'King of the Road'? We'd really like to hear that now . . .

Just forget about it. No one's interested here. Forget about the kings and queens of folk, and their retinues and genealogies. Forget Dave Pegg, Dave Swarbrick, Sandy Denny. Forget also that Messrs. Pegg and Swarbrick played at a certain wedding twenty years ago, with Sandy Denny singing too, on a makeshift stage, and with him, and with his young bride, in traditional white, head to the stars, singing her heart out to Judy Collins songs. But forget Judy Collins, and Joan Baez, and Joni Mitchell – all Angel's favourites, once upon a time – forget Judy, Joan, Joni – leave them behind. They're out the frame. Forget Both Sides Now, Amazing Grace, Lonesome Road, The Night They Drove Old Dixie Down, Diamonds and Rust. Forget Liege and Lief. Forget Little Boxes, Where Have All the Flowers Gone?, We Shall Overcome, Blowing in the Wind, Mr. Tambourine Man and a hundred other *million-dollar!* songs that had changed the face of western culture – because none of that matters here. Judy, Joan, Joni, Dylan, Seeger, Guthrie, The Weavers, Tom Paxton, Tim Hardin – dead or alive they are unwanted, they hold no sway here. Forget them. End of story. Teach kids the guitar. Charge top dollar.

But look in every song book, every guitar tutor – Teach kids the guitar, indeed! – and on every other page you'll find them. Dylan. Seeger. Guthrie. Joan Baez. So it isn't true. It can not be true.

He felt a shift beneath his feet as he stared out the glass at the dark and glittering seas. A sway in the building. He thought of the apex of the building – inside, under bows of steel, was a hollow for a vast Jacuzzi, with real rocks, and real plants, and bonsai trees, all set around a bubbling, steaming pool. Angel had taken him up there when they'd first arrived. She'd had to share it. It was unbelievable. Walls all the way around of one-way glass. Pine saunas imported from Sweden, and pine changing rooms, forty floors up. A haven for naturists, Angel had joked, but with a bar, of course. You could see forever up there on a clear day. She'd even hummed the tune.

He was no longer looking at the view beyond the glass, and he wasn't listening. His focus had retracted to his own negative in the window. He looked at his lower body, his belly – too much drowning of sorrows on his own, and then too many comforters in the morning, too many guilty croissants and Danishes for breakfast, after she'd gone to work. He stared at the reflection of his heavy belt, a brassy, military thing he'd always worn on stage in England. A talisman, like the black velvet band he used to tie his hair. But neither had brought a drop of luck for twenty years. In the reflection the belt hung crooked over his crotch. The buckle sagged at a weary angle. There was nothing he could do about it. He'd tried. No matter which way he set it, pulled it, tightened it, it had to sag like that.

He looked up to his face: his grey hair scraped into the ponytail and tied back with the black velvet band. That phoney gypsy look –

> '*Her eyes they shone like diamonds*
> *They called her the queen of the land,*
> *And her hair hung over her shoulder*
> *Tied up with a black velvet band . . .*'

Oh, just forget about it now.

The next evening, Thursday, he was reading Hemingway on the sofa in the living room. *Fiesta*. He had the stereo on low and he didn't notice her come in. Without a word she put down her bag and pressed eject.

"Er . . . I was listening to that."

"Oh really, Neil . . ." She picked up a remote from the sideboard and switched on the air conditioner. "I have just finished work and I'm very tired, I'm weary, and the traffic was awful."

He didn't have air conditioning during the day, only the fans, but she never noticed.

"I've spent an hour sitting in one of those horrid green buses," she said. "I'm going to buy a car. This weekend I shall buy my own car."

He put his book down on the sofa. "Something sporty, maybe?"

"Maybe," she replied, replacing the remote, ignoring him. "I haven't decided."

He sighed and knitted his hands behind his ponytail. "Oh, you haven't been down to the showrooms and seen all the new toys, the new soft-tops and coupés? . . ."

"No, Neil."

He ducked further sparring – didn't want it. He'd been so looking forward to her return this evening, not least because he'd cooked something for her. A French casserole from the recipe book. Something special after last night. She must be able to smell it, but she said nothing. And he'd talk to her about tomorrow, about his appointment first thing with Elbert Chan, even though he didn't believe it would come off. That would bring her over for a while. He stood and went to get his CD.

"No! I don't want that noise in my ears!"

She thought he was going to put it on again in some further provocation – "Angel, I wasn't – "

She bent down in an ungainly way and yanked out the plug at the mains. She brushed past him, rushing on to the bedroom – "I want to swim, I want to relax, I want to go out. I want to live a little. Put it on again when I've gone, if you must."

He hesitated, then followed to the bedroom with a firm step. By the time he got there she'd slipped off her dress and was standing in her underwear looking through her wardrobe.

"Angel. We need to talk."

"No. We don't need to talk," she said into the wardrobe, flicking through blouses, dresses, lacy bits and pieces.

He stared at her body, at the indents of her black silk underwear.

"You can see what's happened," she said. "Anyone can see

what's happened."

He couldn't let that go.

"Angel, you must explain to me sometime how this plutocracy thing works, you know? What it does to you. There is no need to be so mean to me now, when things aren't looking too good. Like you're expecting me to just get up and go if you're hard enough. You were quite a decent sort before you copped out and sold out, I seem to recall."

On that last line she rested her head on the edge of the wardrobe door and her shoulders drooped.

Had he got through?

"Oh Neil. If you only understood how that kind of thing sounds to me now."

He quit the bedroom, found his wallet, picked up his book and left the apartment.

Fiesta had a very dated sketch of a matador on the cover, gravely poised with shining blade, dressed all in black with dashes of sun-dried red and yellow. His skin was dark and swarthy and his long hair was drawn tight and tied behind. The gitano, made good. Neil loved the cover. He loved the book. He'd read it many times. Paris, Pamplona, Madrid in the nineteen twenties – a wonderful, in-between, expat world, so remote and glamorous and clear-skied, so far away from all his bars and dives, hangovers and rows.

Every seat on the Star Ferry was familiar to him, from bow to stern, port & starboard, on both decks of every boat. The beautiful lacquered frames, the neat Formica patch of the seat itself, and the views across every quadrant of the ever-changing seascape – all of it, too familiar. Children scrambled ahead and flipped over the back-rests, making a wonderful clattering sound across the teak decks, like the fall of mah-jong tiles.

He took a seat midships, upper deck.

It was just a habit, this trip, that was all. The best place to blow away a hangover or a bad scene. During the crossing he watched the junks and the barges and liners, or sometimes he read a magazine or a book instead, keeping his head down and his eyes away from the painful glint of the waves and office blocks. The sea breeze flipped his ponytail as he sat by the open window and for the few minutes of the ride he was content.

The trip was too short, though, always too short. This evening in particular he needed it to last longer, after such an ugly scene. And the wind was wrong this evening too. Traces of the ferry's oily fumes, and the fumes of the Jetfoils and Turbo-cats and Star Cruise liners, came in light gusts across the deck. Star Pisces and Star Leo were both docked at Ocean Terminal. He'd read somewhere that during one docking a liner pumped out more pollution than 380,000 cars. It was the kind of fact he liked to store away to share at some point. But she'd caught him out, doing that. He'd offered too many of his nasty facts and figures and snippets of bad news, gleaned from secondhand newspapers and dubious magazines.

"Did you know that in Hong Kong there are nine rats for every human being? Did you know that? You are never more than twelve feet away from a rat. It's a fact. World class city, you know. Full of rats."

"Twelve feet? From a rat?" She grimaced.

"Never more than that."

"Well, I'm not."

"Ha ha ha . . ."

As the ferry shunted off across the harbour he opened *Fiesta* at the closing pages. He knew much of the wistful final dialogue in the cocktail bar of the Palace Hotel by heart. *'Isn't it a nice bar?'* . . . *'They're all nice bars.'* . . . *'Barmen and jockeys are the only people who are polite any more'* . . .

'I like an olive in a Martini.' . . . *'Right you are, sir. There you are . . .'*

He looked up and winced at the evening sunlight, still strong despite the haze, the way it caught a golden block and dulled it to copper in the dusk. He shielded his gaze and stared at the postcard skyline, the shimmering slabs of success. Citibank. Standard Chartered. Bank of China. Banks and more banks. The Lippo Building. Insurance. Assurance. More banks . . .

'I like an olive in a Martini.' . . . *'Right you are, sir. There you are . . .'*

When the ferry docked he waited for the crowd to disperse before drifting from the deck and making his way alone up the ramp. Then he faltered at the top, unwilling to cross the jetty to the return boat. He had an urge to walk ahead into the clean and well-lit subways of the island itself. He'd pop up again into the evening somewhere near The Furama Hotel, The Mandarin Oriental, or The Ritz Carlton. He'd take a lift to a high hotel bar overlooking the harbour and he'd order a Martini there, and ask the barman for a cocktail olive. Ah, but he needed to share that, to be with someone, someone new. The time would come, though, must come, he was sure, when he'd sit in a smart hotel bar and order that Martini, and he would use that line from *Fiesta*, and laugh about it to himself. A private joke. He promised never to have another Martini until that moment. He'd clink glasses with someone and smile, in the high hotel bar. Some lucky girl. Chinese. Beautiful. Cheers.

Then he thought of last night, when she came to bed at 2 a.m. after her special party.

How she pushed him away.

"No, Neil."

He reached out again. Stroked her back. Then she said something else, to make a point, as she settled apart from him and tugged the duvet round her: "I don't like your creepy advances any more."

He couldn't stand hearing that. It didn't need saying and it angered and humiliated him so. He was too much abused, too much left on his own, ignored, set aside. He moved over and persisted, more forcefully, trying to kiss her round the neck –

"Get lost, Neil!"

But he wouldn't get lost. He was carried away. He forced his hand between her legs –

"Fuck off, Neil! Please!" she cried out.

And then he slunk away, without sound or words, a wounded animal. That was too much for him by a long stretch. She moved to the edge of the bed and he got up and tried to read in the living room on the sofa.

Now he turned back through the rusty cagework of the terminus, to the turnstile and the waiting boat.

Chapter Four

Breakfast Meeting

Chan's two receptionists ran a travel agency of some description. Very backstreet. Neil couldn't work out how that connected, but first thing Friday morning they were so busy with a consignment of glossy holiday brochures, so busy flicking through their new brochures and chatting about them and sharing them, they could hardly spare a moment just to tell him that Chan wasn't there.

Only one spoke, and not to him but down to her brochure. After she'd told him Chan wasn't there, she flicked the page to a double spread of a fancy hotel swimming pool. It was a crimson, heart-shaped pool, all new and empty. Neil's hope sank deep in it. She turned and smiled to her friend:

"Isn't that romantic?"

Neil cleared his throat. "Not here?"

"Not here."

"But we had an appointment this morning, first thing . . ."

She shrugged – then her friend shrugged, the one who didn't speak, in exactly the same way, a moment later. Neil caught that out the corner of his eye.

"Do you know when he'll be back?"

"No idea."

"Well, do you know where I might find him?"

The one who spoke looked up. She stroked her shiny

black hair.

"He might be down the street?" Her answer curled up at the end. Nothing inside.

They were far too pretty, these receptionists, Neil considered, and enjoyed far too much of their own company. They were like colourful exotic birds, parakeets, preening themselves in the bare cage of Chan's offices. Of course they had no time for him, with his lived-in face and shabby clothes, his long grey frizz in a ponytail. If he'd strolled in here wearing an expensive business suit and asked for a Club Class ticket to New York for this afternoon – at the very latest or just forget about it, please – their attitude would have been completely different. They'd have slipped their beautiful black hair behind their ears and smiled at him, and spoken softly, and flitted and flirted about. But, as things stood, they couldn't give a monkey's fuck about him.

"Down the street?"

She turned the page. The pool was gone. Then the other turned her page.

"Sure. There's a café where he has breakfast. Next to the Plaza."

Neil nodded, though neither was looking at him.

"Thanks."

He stared from one girl to the other while they continued flicking through their brochures. He tapped the counter a few times, putting a marker down, then withdrew.

He thought he heard them titter as the door closed behind him on its spring. Then just as the lift arrived he definitely heard them laugh, laugh out loud, as the bell tingled and the doors sprang open. He felt foolish to pursue what they'd told him, but after that encounter he had nothing left to lose.

There was indeed a café next to the plaza. It was the kind of place that had long fascinated Neil. In the window lay a row of aluminium trays filled with bubbling meat – lungs, tongues, intestines, gizzards – all in a brown sauce, always the same brown sauce, bubbling around the tips and lips of meat, to whet the appetites of passers-by. The café itself was little more than a corridor decked out with collapsible tables and chairs. The corridor was hot and steamy and stank of boiled meat, garlic, ginger, and a tang of powerful bleach.

Chan sat alone in here, past the counter, under a rotating wall fan. No air conditioner.

He ate with his head bent low over his food. On Neil's approach he didn't stop eating, but he raised a hand and waved to the seat opposite. Neil pulled out the collapsible chair and sat down. Chan continued eating. He rolled up his strips of lung, wrapped them in black seaweed, dipped them daintily in chilli sauce and popped them in his mouth. The smell of the café made Neil queasy and he felt worse watching Chan eat his breakfast. Now Chan left the meat and seaweed and lifted his rice bowl to his face. He fed his twitching mouth with quick flicks of his chopsticks. When he'd finished he sat back and swept an open hand across what was left.

"Want some?"

Neil shook his head. "No thanks."

The reason Chan sat at the end of the café now became clear. The fan was only part of it. A traffic jam outside had left a taxi stuck immediately in front of the door and its fumes were pumping into the corridor, filling it up. The two cooks behind the counter, standing on a platform – two tall cooks, too tall for their platform and their café – completely ignored this new taste in the air. They pretended the fumes didn't offend, didn't exist.

Chan offered Neil nothing else to eat or drink.

He took a sip of tea, then said: "Do you mind if I ask you something personal?"

Neil shrugged. There was little Chan could do to hurt him now, not after last time.

"Do you like Neil Diamond?"

Neil frowned: hadn't they done this? Hadn't they moved on from there?

"Do you like him?"

"Well – "

"Do you like him?"

"He's okay."

Chan shook his head. "I think he's a phoney."

"But last time – "

"I don't care what I said last time."

Neil was about to reply but stopped himself. He nodded wisely instead.

Chan folded his arms.

"If I say I like your voice, what I mean is, I like what you can do with your voice. What you can get away with with your voice. But what I actually like or don't like, and what you like or don't like, or do or don't care about – that just doesn't matter. Golden rule. You see that?" Chan was forceful, but he didn't seem to be puffing himself up or trying to score any points this time. His arms were folded way and his slight body was folded away to one side, in the foldaway chair. The open antagonism of Wednesday's meeting was gone, off the record. He just wanted to talk business this morning. But Neil stayed wary. Chan's features flattened out all feeling, and the bald eyes gave nothing away. Elbert Chan was a subtle and intelligent fellow, Neil reflected – but a snake, no question.

"Let's take a look at what we have here."

Chan unfolded his hands and a rapid, hypnotic sequence of movements followed before he spoke – he rubbed his wrists together, knitted his fingers, rubbed his palms, then flipped his left hand open and picked the index finger -

"We have some years on stage. We can use that."

The steel table between them was no more than two feet across and Neil sat very close to Chan, even though Chan was sitting back, side on to the table. Chan's hands were a child's hands, small and clean and innocent, but the first joints were covered in wiry black hair. Despite the greasy food and greasy table Chan's cuffs were perfectly clean and white and dry. His gold cuff links and gold watch still shone in the steamy light. He picked off his second finger.

"We can play those instruments. Viola. Guitar. Bodhrán."

That was quite a feat of memory, and effortless too. Despite himself Neil felt drawn in, felt a need to tuck himself in, to show willing, to bring himself physically deeper into the ambit of Chan's conversation and his sleights of hand. He wanted to lean forward, but didn't dare. If he so much as rested his hands on the table he knew that last slice of lung and the rice bowl and chilli sauce would all flick up in his face. Chan never touched the table, as if he understood it would collapse in this way, or as if he could make it operate in this way, remotely, if he chose to.

"And you have those instruments to hand, I take it."

A setback. Neil considered lying but thought better of it. "Actually, no. I sold up before we left the U.K."

"You haven't got any instruments?" Chan looked incredulous.

"There wasn't room in the baggage allowance." Neil tried to make light of the problem. "An Englishman always pays his way, you know."

"That may be so, but you haven't got any instruments."

One of the tall cooks came and took the dirty bowls and dishes and wiped the tiny table, but just Chan's half.

"Hong Kong is stuffed full of musicians," Chan said, waving the problem away. "Singers, artists, what have you. It's just a question of turning the right stones. We can get a four piece Filipino band for twelve or thirteen hundred a night. Peanuts. And they're really very competent."

Twelve or thirteen hundred dollars? A hundred pounds? For

a whole band? This was hopeless. Neil really needed to get out of this café and get right away from Elbert Chan and his delicious breakfast and his slippery hands. Why had he come back at all? Why had he allowed himself to be led on by those tittering receptionists? 'Sure. There's a café where he has breakfast. Next to the Plaza.' Why had he followed their directions? Why had he bothered?

Because he was desperate. That was all.

"Like I said, I've got connections with the clubs here in Hong Kong," Chan resumed, folding his hands and sitting in profile again, legs crossed, "and with one or two clubs in Macau and on the mainland. I'm not talking about the good clubs, I'm talking about the best clubs." He avoided Neil's eyes. He kept glancing down the corridor into the street, or at the wall of the serving counter. Now he looked back: "You know how much it costs to join The Pacific Club, here in Kowloon?"

Neil didn't answer.

"It costs half a million Hong Kong to join The Pacific Club, Ocean Terminal, Kowloon. That's how much it costs. Half a million. Then you're on the waiting list."

Chan left a pause for these figures to impress, then looked away at his shiny shoe in the corridor. He flicked his shiny shoe.

Neil felt a tension in his calf muscles. The balls of his feet pressed on the floor.

Let's go. Let's go!

"I know the kind of thing they put on, the kind of thing they like," Chan continued. "They had an Elvis impersonator from London. North London. Very good. Very funny. He doubled his itinerary, doubled his money. They couldn't get enough. Particularly the ladies."

No matter how lightly dropped into the conversation, the mention of an Elvis impersonator alarmed Neil. Impersonators, spoofs, jokers, small-timers, hobbyist entertainers – all of that.

Chan turned back to the table and risked tapping it where the cook had wiped. "Let me tell you about these expat ladies. They play tennis in the morning, in the cool, then they have lunch, and then they sit by the pool. That's it. They do step classes. I mean, step classes. They need their entertainment. The men are just as bad when they've had a bit to drink, and a lot are drunk before you walk on. Some of them are throwing food around. They're telling blue jokes. If they don't like the act they throw food around, and if they do like it they throw food around. It's like that sometimes."

Chan chuckled and stopped there. He looked away as if remembering one such riotous evening, and smiled at the busy cooks chopping, scraping and sweating behind the counter. So the acts he was talking about were there to be pilloried. That was it. Scoff the food, scoff at the act. That was the entertainment.

"Look, Mr. Chan, if what you've got in mind is some kind of spoof, some stupid joke – "

"No no no . . ." Chan immediately went into reverse, waved away the very idea – "Of course not! That's not how I see you doing this. I don't see comedy. Not for you. It wouldn't work. You're a serious man." He frowned earnestly at Neil, leaving no doubt on this point. "I've seen you. I've heard you. For your act, you *are* Neil Diamond. The best. The real thing."

The deal. The sell.

Angel would love this, on the 27th floor.

What's your husband do, again, Mrs. Atherton? He's in show business. Oh really? He's an actor? Not an actor, exactly. No? No. What, then? He's an impersonator. Oh really? Who does he impersonate? Find out at your club tonight.

"You come on stage as Neil Diamond. The whipped hair, all the razzmatazz, the whole bag of shit."

Chan thumbed over his shoulder, towards his office block –

"You go into HMV in Hankow Road. It's full of tribute CDs. It's a growth industry. All the oldies recycled. Frank Sinatra, Tom Jones, The Beatles, Shirley Bassey – all made in China, at a fraction of the cost. And you really can't tell the difference. Same talent. Same for Neil Diamond. He doesn't live here, never comes here. I'd go to his concert but I can't. That's where you step in."

Back in England Neil was a known quantity. A little old-fashioned maybe, a little out of time, out of style, but a known quantity. There were album sleeves with his name on, his cameo, his contributions, his arrangements, his credits.

"I'm not talking about a big market," Chan waved away any pipe dreams of that order. "I'm talking about a niche market. But it's big enough to make a living. Maybe a good living. I'm telling you that you can make a living as Neil Diamond here. You can do that. I've heard you sing and I know you can do that."

"I'm very flattered."

Neil stood up. Thanks for that, Mr. Chan. We got there in the end. He held out his hand, offered his own forced smile – "Thanks for your time. I'll think about it and I'll be in touch."

Without getting up Chan took Neil's hand for a fleeting moment, then snapped his fingers and shouted for his bill.

Chapter Five

Leavin' Leavin' Leavin'

It took a full week for reality to bring Neil to heel and drag him back to Chan's office. Even then he only got there late Friday afternoon, when Chan might have been closed. But he wasn't.

"Sure I'm still interested," Chan said. "And I'm still confident. Very confident."

From an HMV bag Neil pulled out half a dozen brand new Neil Diamond CDs, $420 worth, still in their cellophane. He stacked them in front of Chan in the middle of his desk and squared the stack to face Chan. Actions speak louder.

"Let's talk business," he said, tapping the cover of *The Very Best of Neil Diamond*. "I'm your man. Any of these songs. No problem at all. Let's make a booking. Let's make a call. Let's do it."

"Hold on there, friend." Chan looked up at Neil bearing down on him, tapping his CDs. "Calm down. Take a seat."

Neil hesitated, then stepped back and took his place again in the aged rattan armchair.

"How about The American Club?" It was more a demand than a question.

"They don't want you. Not yet." Chan straightened his tie. "Too up-market. Once you're established they'll come running, no doubt about that. Not in my mind. But at the moment it's too much. Too classy. Do you know how much it costs to join The American Club? In Tai Tam?"

Neil couldn't take any more of that bullshit. "Five million. That puts you on the mailing list."

"Three-quarters of a million," Chan said, without a break. "Three-quarters. Half as much again as The Pacific Club. Then you're on the waiting list. Not the mailing list." Chan leant forward and his eyes became intense and forceful, quite unpleasantly so. "Don't think you know all the answers, Mr. Atherton. You probably don't. Not yet, anyway."

Neil's gaze fell to Chan's desk – for goodness' sake, he didn't want another fight! What was he doing? He wanted a deal! Any deal.

He hadn't taken in Chan's desk on his first visit, but he did now. It was a child's bedroom desk, that's all, in black melamine, from IKEA. Indeed, there was something worryingly amateurish about all of Chan's office furniture, now that he noticed it. The filing cabinet in the corner was a low mobile unit of durable blue plastic, with a single drawer, something for home accounts rather than a busy office. IKEA again. The Anglepoise, cream coloured and old-fashioned, on a stepped plinth, was a secondhand item from a grander office, come down in the world. It struck a tired pose on stretched springs. But surely, Neil thought, bringing his gaze back to Chan himself, who was examining his CDs now, cover by cover, checking the price of each one on the back, surely Chan was for real. In the travel agency outside the girls jumped when he spoke over the intercom. There was no mistaking that. You could feel the place tighten up. Despite his size and his nondescript appearance Elbert Chan had some bedrock understanding of his own worth and importance. He had presence, and that was something Neil was acutely sensitive to these days. Presence. One's presence in the world.

Chan re-stacked the CDs and squared the pile up again in

front of him. "Give me what you know about Neil Diamond," he said. "You've had a week. What have you got?"

Neil eased himself forward in the rattan chair. Actually, he had rather a lot to say now about Neil Diamond. He'd been doing a little research, idling away some daytime hours.

"Where do you want me to start?"

"His birth. Why not?"

"1941."

Chan nodded, looked down at the CD stack.

"My age is about okay," Neil added.

"I'd say so."

"But other things are wrong, I think."

"Like what?"

"My hair."

"What about it?"

Chan took a couple of CDs from the stack, held one in each hand, and examined the pictures of Neil Diamond on the covers. His eyes flicked back and forth from the CD covers to Neil's lived-in face, to his grey frizz in its ponytail.

"You need to dye it, straighten it, that's all. I know a good place."

"What about the outfit?"

Chan picked up more CDs but didn't look at them this time. He shuffled them in their cellophane wraps. He seemed suddenly bored with all of this. It was the end of the day. He still had loose ends before the weekend.

"Black also. With sequins. Like this one." He held up the cover of *The Very Best of Neil Diamond*.

They were interrupted by the telephone. Chan answered in Cantonese. On hearing his caller's voice his manner changed completely.

"Harry! . . ."

He turned his chair, cutting Neil out, and smiled into space while he listened to Harry, then replied affably and obligingly.

He made a little joke and chuckled at it. The conversation and the joke were lost to Neil, but he caught another name. A strange and exotic name.

Chan replaced the receiver and snapped a switch on his intercom: "Bring Iannis in."

The door opened and a squat, very grave looking black guy stepped into the office. The door closed behind him, pulled shut by an invisible and obedient hand. Iannis stood in a baggy Mizuno tracksuit with his shoulders pinned back, full of black pride. The tracksuit was black too, and glossy, but worn around the knees. Neil smiled to himself. An African prince, perhaps, fallen on hard times.

Very stiff, very braced, Iannis did not look Neil's way at all, did not even acknowledge Neil's presence in the office. His eyes – trembling, bulging, hungry eyes – stared ahead at Elbert Chan. His expression was a delicate balance of defiance and appeal.

"LRC," Elbert said.

Iannis frowned. He flared his nostrils and sniffed.

"Ladies Recreation Club. Harry Lam. Sports Bar Captain."

Iannis raised his chin, shifted his eyes from side to side, as if to say – Harry who? What's that got to do with me, man?

"He wants you over there tonight, eight o'clock. B team play-off. It's a start. Can you do it?"

Iannis's frown deepened, as if Harry Lam's request were out of the question. He should know better than to ask such things of Iannis. B team play-off? Are you kidding?

"Can you do it?" Elbert repeated bluntly.

"Well, I'll have to – "

"Can you do it?"

"Sure I can do it."

"Eight o'clock."

Iannis turned to go.

"Iannis?"

Iannis had his hand on the door handle. He looked back over his shoulder.

"No drinking."

Iannis shrugged and left.

Elbert nodded after him. "Things are beginning to roll for that guy, and he's a black in Hong Kong. That's not easy." It was a statement of fact, not sympathy. "We Chinese are very racist, you know," he explained. "But he'll be all right. He's highly marketable."

Elbert picked up Neil's CDs, gathered them all up in his tiny hands. Neil assumed he was about to give them back to him, but without a word he opened the middle draw of his desk and tucked them safely away, embezzled them, and closed the drawer.

"Put me a programme of songs together," he said. "Two forty-five minute sets. Get an outfit sorted out. I'll fix up a band and make some calls. Come back next week and we'll put a soundtrack on your life. That's a promise."

Neil needed to play down his excitement, stall with something. He had a break, then. He had a start. At last. Just like that.

"What about copyright, licences, that kind of thing?"

"Forget that stuff. This is Hong Kong. We don't bother with that here. Neil Diamond's pushing sixty, he won't care. He's got other things to worry about. Health problems, weight problems, cash flow problems, maybe. There's a crack in his pool and he can't afford to fix it. Anyway, let him come out and see us. I don't care. I'll send him a ticket. Business class. First class. I'm sure he'd be amused. He might even be impressed. Forget about that stuff. I'll take care of everything."

Fiesta lay closed, gitano down, on the duvet.

Neil was surrounded by another set of CDs, another $420

worth. Such extravagance lying all over the bed. The inner sleeves were removed and the sleeve notes lay scattered. Shiny pictures of Neil Diamond were cast at curious angles across the duvet. The effect looked almost deliberate, like another CD cover, perhaps: a *Best of Compendia* compendium. The slow and heavy swirl of the fan above the bed made the sleeve notes rise and fall and the images of the sequinned star tremble nervously. Neil took up a booklet close by him and studied it. The CD was from '88, ten years old. The cover picture was a full shot of Neil Diamond standing against an over-rich blue sky – a studio sky – smiling, staring out hard at his would-be impersonator.

The superstar's guitar leant against his jeans and his arms were loosely folded. His clothes were outdoor: a well worn leather jacket (an old friend, no doubt) and, of course, the blue jeans and boots. What was curious about this image was the air of frankness and simplicity it presented. The singer's hair was still long and coarse, backcombed from a balding pate, but it had not been dyed: it was an honest, iron grey. The message was, '*One grows older. Why hide it?*' Here was the aging star at the roadside with his guitar, and he was the troubadour again, hitching a ride back to his roots, or to the next stop on a lengthy tour across America, a tour of discovery, maybe, retracing the steps of some forgotten pioneer, some figure who had long fascinated Neil Diamond personally and whom he could talk about with some authority at interviews along the way. Perhaps the album would be dedicated to that forgotten pioneer, in memoriam. Perhaps there was a movie in it somewhere, or at least a tv documentary. Simplicity, honesty, wisdom – it was all here, on his sleeve. It was a good photograph and this is what troubled Neil. How could this be convincingly impersonated? Wasn't the last laugh truly with Neil Diamond, in that he had created something so close to self-parody that it was inimitable?

But this CD, like all the others, was a successful commercial product. Tens of thousands, hundreds of thousands, millions of people saw it differently, just passed it by, thought it was okay, or thought nothing about it one way or the other. Therefore Elbert Chan was right, there must indeed be a market and he was dabbling in just a tiny sector of that market. A niche. The premise was deceptively simple, syllogistic. Perhaps it was because he was in the position of actually studying this star, of taking him seriously, that he found himself worrying about things which couldn't sustain such anxious scrutiny. People just picked up a CD like this – *The Best of Neil Diamond* – and looked at the back to see which songs were on it. If a song they liked was on it, they bought it. They didn't give the photo a second thought. They certainly didn't buy the CD for the photo on the front. There had to be a cover of some description, and the cheapest and easiest thing was just a studio photograph of the star himself.

But Neil was trying to get closer to the persona with which he had to arrive at some kind of working relationship, and he wanted to understand more. Though a hundred thousand, a million buyers in HMV stores across the world might not give the picture a second thought, nevertheless it reflected something about how the artist saw *himself*. Someone of Diamond's stature would have control over his packaging. This was no teenage wonder who could be wrapped up, drugged up, fucked and forgotten. This was Neil Diamond. He'd been around for thirty years. He'd written hits for every major performing artist around. He'd written film scores. UB40 owed him. As did Elvis Presley. The Monkees.

Neil looked up and stared at a Van Gogh print – dentist's waiting room stuff – that Angel had hung in the bedroom. 'Peach Trees'. But the glass caught the afternoon light and erased the peach trees and instead, where the painting had been, Neil began to see, framed there on the empty glass, an image of himself, of Neil Atherton as Neil Diamond, stepping out on stage . . . But the art of Neil Diamond was not showmanship. It looked like it, but it wasn't that. What Neil Diamond did was more akin to method acting, and that's what was required here. Not some comical spoof or imitation. No no no. Elbert was right. What was required here was a man who could walk on stage believing absolutely in the importance, the quality, the artistry of his songs, his voice and his music. It was serious business. Because that's what Neil Diamond had achieved. A conviction in himself so strong that he could shamelessly present and sell to the world this portrait of the middle-aged troubadour at the roadside.

Neil rolled over and reached for his wristwatch that was propped against one of Angel's new bedside lamps. Blue-grey ceramic lamps. The latest thing. Very stylish. $2000 each. £300 the pair, more or less. His wristwatch was an imitation Rolex from a hawker in Mong Kok. One hundred bucks. Not even a tenner.

Six o'clock. Perhaps Angel was staying in this evening. That would be nice. They needed quality time.

Neil sat up and slipped on his Rolex. He took up the booklet of John Howard's sleeve notes on *The Best of Neil Diamond*. The more he read the less he knew. Writing about what followed the success of Diamond's first number one, Howard said:

'*From there on, Diamond was considered a superstar. His semi-concept album "Tap Root Manuscript" broke new ground. The Marty Paich-orchestrated African themes in 'Soolaimon'. . .*'

Neil had never heard of the "Tap Root Manuscript" and had no idea what the title meant. This kind of thing provoked new feelings of insecurity, irritation, frustration. It was all very well for Elbert Chan, after hearing him sing a cover number in Wan

Chai, to offer him a job impersonating Neil Diamond, but didn't the career of this superstar warrant a little more attention and respect? Surely he should at least know the various phases of Diamond's career, the wellsprings of feeling from which the lyrics and melodies came. What was the "Tap Root Manuscript" and why was it 'semi-concept'? He had no idea. Who was Marty Paich? Same answer. Neil read that the songs of this period arose from a *'recording sojourn in Memphis'*, some time in the late sixties or early seventies. It was a period of huge success for Neil Diamond. He had his first U.S. no. 1 and U.K. hit. He was 29 or 30 years old. It must have been a time of great joy, of champagne toasts, the future must have appeared very bright, as indeed it had turned out to be.

Looking up again to the Van Gogh, into the shiny emptiness of the frame, Neil could see the dust fly from the rear tyres of a Buick sedan. The car came to rest at a roadside cafe a few miles outside Memphis. The chunky doors opened, two men got out, the doors slammed. Neil Diamond and Marty Paich were having breakfast together before going on to the recording studio. Here they would talk about the African themes in *Soolaimon* over Columbian coffee -

"What ever are you doing?"

Angel was standing in the bedroom doorway. She had a hairbrush in her hand, which signified that she was about to go out. She was wearing a pale linen dress that was too young and too tight for her. She must have changed in the bathroom. More privacy. The dress clung like a corset to her midriff and exaggerated her top-heaviness. Neil's eyes defocused. Her breasts, just beneath that thin dress, just a few feet away – yet so untouchable. Whenever he felt desire stir now the feeling came alloyed with clammy defeat. His needs had become as much a pest to him as they were to her.

"What are all these CDs?"

She came forward and picked up one of the insert booklets.

She frowned and let it drop. She couldn't be bothered to find out what all this was about. He could listen to what he liked so long as she didn't have to put up with it. His 'noise'.

"I'm going out," she said, turning to the wall mirror. She brushed her short hair, tugging her head down to one side and wincing at her own heavy strokes. She never bothered to tell him where she was going these days and he wouldn't stoop to ask. He showed his disapproval in his careful silences. She took up a pair of earrings – new, diamond earrings in white gold – that had been lying loose on top of the chest of drawers. She inserted them, hanging her head this way then that, as if her hair was still long. Straightening her dress she turned to view herself in profile a moment. Then she took up her new car keys from the chest of drawers, the MX5 keys on their red enamelled fob, and without turning back to say goodbye, she left.

When he heard the front door close, Neil felt his spirit sink to the place it always sank to when he was left alone again in the apartment. He listened for the sonorous clangs of the lift as its counterweights passed their floor and the car ascended. It was a habit now, listening out for those low, dull, inevitable clangs. They sounded to him like the knelling of distant bells.

"Oh no – no no no – you are not going to do that! No way! Over my dead body! No way are you going to do that!"

It was the first genuine outburst of feeling Neil had seen in months.

An unfortunate coincidence. He had returned from his third visit to Chan's offices, and at the same time she had come back at lunch to pick up some clothes and a bathing costume. She wanted to go directly to some function after work, some pool party at a club.

"You are not going to drag me down! I couldn't bear that! What have you done to your *hair*?"

He was sitting on the sofa and on the coffee table in front of him, among more, new, unopened CDs, was another weightier purchase – *The Neil Diamond Song Book*. Now he leant forward and picked up his CDs, tidying his stuff away, ashamed of it.

"I'm trying to drag myself up, Angel."

"Who is this man? Really, now. This Elbert Chan."

"He's a kind of agent. A businessman."

"An agent?"

"He handles lots of things. Lots of strands. Lots of deals with the clubs. He owns a travel agency as well."

"He's a travel agent?"

He looked at her.

"Elbert Chan is a very intelligent and successful guy, Angel. He has deals with the best clubs. Only the best."

She sat down on their Korean settle beneath the window and tucked her skirt beneath her. That Korean settle. The first thing, the very first thing, they'd bought for the flat when she'd signed the lease. Now she sat there, clutching her car keys tightly in her hand. She stole another glance at him, or rather at his hair, and he looked back at her self-consciously, he couldn't help it, with hooded, defensive eyes – *It's all right for you, with your new friends, your new life, your new car. . . . . .*

On Chan's recommendation he had been to an expensive hairdressers' in the Kowloon Hotel arcade – *Ask For Toni's*. Toni's own hair showed what could be done: it was thickly layered and thrown back, long cockerel style, around his shapeless Malaysian face. Toni smiled continuously for some reason. For a whole hour he smiled, while he trimmed and straightened Neil's grey frizz. Then he dyed it black, the same jet black as the young Neil Diamond. It was Chinese it was so black. The change was dramatic. The new darkness around Neil's face cast shadows, made his lived-in lines deeper, craggier. He was not pleased. When Toni had finished Neil looked up in the mirror to see him standing behind, still smiling, his hand on the back of the chair. Then beneath Toni he saw, staring straight back at him, neither the middle-aged Neil Atherton, nor the young Neil Diamond. He saw an old man with long dyed black hair. Shoulder length black hair. He saw Johnny Cash. The Man in Black. Johnny Cash in his late sixties, walking the line. No, Neil was not pleased. But Toni was pleased. He was still smiling.

"Okay?"

Neil nodded carefully, watching how the hair moved, didn't move.

"Sure?"

"It's great."

The Korean settle was below their largest window, a vast sheet of toughened glass in place of the balcony that extended the more expensive apartments. The view behind Angel looked out over the Shing Mun nullah to the tidy, fresh pink blocks of the newest new-town, Ma On Shan, about three miles away. Theirs was a good view, with the water, Ma On Shan, and the green mountains all around. Pictorial Gardens was noted for its views, the best in Sha Tin. Angel sat in front of the window with her knees together and her shoulders hunched. Neil saw her suddenly as a shrunken figure, diminished against the colourful backdrop of the water and the surrounding mountains. He saw that his new plans, dragged out into the open at last, had taken her back to an understanding of him that she'd wilfully forgotten about. Taken her back to their life in England, modest and provincial, mortgaged to the hilt, his career quietly collapsing around them year by year. Then her gamble. Her bid for freedom. The overseas job, hard fought for and won. Neil sat on the sofa with his wad of unopened CDs in his hands, still in their slippery cellophane. Now he had to fight his corner, and such a corner. She was overreacting, no question.

"I've got to start somewhere."

"It's an end, not a start."

"Just let me give it a try."

"NO!" She closed her eyes and shook her head when she shouted that. "If you are going to do that," she said, still with her eyes shut, "you can get out of my life." She opened her eyes and looked at him. "I mean it. I would rather you loafed all day than did that. You are not going on stage at one of these clubs – clubs my friends belong to – our clubs, my friends, these people who have been so good to me, who have such faith in me, you are not getting up in front of them and humiliating me, Neil."

Neil forced a smile. "Isn't that somewhat bourgeois, Angel?"

But that was Chan's word. He'd used it.

"I am bourgeois. I like being bourgeois. That's me. Okay?"

She stared at him narrowly, peering through the present circumstances to a way ahead. When she spoke again it was impossible to mistake the new resolution in her voice. The high feeling had gone, leaving nothing but a flat determination. "You can't stay here, Neil. It's too much. You'll have to go. It's over. I can face that now. I can say that now."

Neil had been expecting this for some time, if the truth were known, yet he felt mortified hearing the words out loud rather than just echoing idly in his imagination. He felt himself blanche, felt his breathing become shallow. It was over. It was mid June, six months since they left England, so full of expectation – the new life! The new start! – and it was over. She had said that. He was forty-eight years old. He was sitting here with a wad of unopened Neil Diamond CDs in his hands, still in their cellophane, and it was over. He could feel the CD cases slip in his weakening grip. He could feel his pulse against the cellophane.

He sensed that she wanted to go back to what she had just said and say it again and again. She wanted those bold statements out there in front of them, between them, repeated until they became immovable.

He found his tongue. "All right," he said. "I won't do it." He looked down at the floor. "I'll find something else."

"No. It's too late for that. It's over. I meant it. That was the last straw."

He replaced the unopened CDs on the coffee table. His shirtsleeve caught the edge of the pile as he sat back and the colourful cases fanned out. Sections of Neil Diamond appeared this way and that in a jagged collage of reds – the red jumpsuit! – golds, sequins . . .

Neil looked up and tried to smile at his wife. His wife of twenty years' standing. For richer or poorer -

"I'm not going to pursue it, Angel. We'll forget about it. I was wrong. It was wrong of me to ever . . . It was a bad idea."

She held his gaze. "I'll give you till tomorrow morning, Neil."

"Tomorrow morning? Tomorrow morning! What are you talking about? I made a mistake and I'm sorry, Angel . . . Okay?"

"You must go."

He had to find a way of getting her to relent. He had nowhere to go, nowhere to live, for goodness' sake. He had nowhere to go! He'd be out on the street!

Have you got that sixties' song, Neil – 'King of the Road'? We'd really like to hear that now.

Then how about, Gypsies, Tramps and Thieves?

That's why the lady . . .

"Look," he said, and he leant forward once more, but as he did so he felt his long, freshly dyed and straightened black hair fall across his cheeks, and for no reason at all he couldn't put it back, he couldn't at this moment slip his hair back behind his ears or put it away in a loose ponytail or do anything at all about it. It just had to hang there, flat and black and straight. He knitted his hands. "Look," he said again, to the floor, "I'm sorry I upset you. I really am. And you are absolutely right. It was a crazy idea. A mad idea, a bad idea. My sense of proportion must be way off. Shot to hell. Too much time alone. Home alone. I didn't think it through. I should have seen how it would upset you. I don't know what I was thinking of. It was very insensitive of me. And I'm really very, very sorry."

"I'll give you some money," she said, ignoring all the tacit accusations, the slippery appeals and apologies. She wouldn't soften, wouldn't break down. "I'll give you the fare. That's about six thousand dollars. But I'll give you eight. The fare plus a couple of thousand to keep you going."

"You don't know what you're saying, Angel."

"Correction. I do know what I'm saying." She was strong again now, oh yes, and ready to rid herself of the past once and for all. Reinvented lady. "I am saying that you must get out of this apartment. Out of my apartment. And out of my life, Neil."

He picked up *The Neil Diamond Song Book*. He was going to make some dramatic gesture to show her, to prove to her that it didn't matter, by tearing the book to pieces. But it wouldn't do any good and he knew it wouldn't. He held the book between his hands and stared down at the back cover, at the monochrome portrait of the young Neil Diamond, handsome and sure of himself in the late sixties, eyes dark and doey.

"We'll check the flights," she continued. She stood and crossed to the phone. "If it's more I'll give you more. But you must go back. You just don't belong here, Neil. Can't you see that? It hasn't worked out for you. It really hasn't. I'm sorry."

He stood up too. He walked slowly to the window, to where she had been sitting, so that they crossed in the room without speaking, as if in a corridor, and he stayed there at the window, hands in pockets. He stared out the toughened glass to the pink blocks of Ma On Shan, to the mountains on the right and the nullah ahead, and in the distance the open sea. He felt a pricking behind his eyes but he dealt with that. He swallowed hard.

No words would come.

Chapter Six

Mr. Cheung

"You want a room?"

Mr. Cheung wore heavy tortoiseshell glasses. Under their frames his eyes were slow and wary and reptilian. His breath came and went in shallow rasps and smelled of menthol cigarettes.

"You want a room?"

Neil nodded.

"English?"

Neil nodded again. How could he tell?

"Come on in."

With his suitcase in hand Neil crossed the threshold into Mr. Cheung's business, *The Languages and Translation Services Ltd.*, but he went no further.

"Come on in."

There was no air conditioning inside, and he needed air conditioning. The clammy air of the lift and the vestibule followed him into the premises. No fans, even. He was breathing from one long roll of dead air, perfumed now with menthol cigarettes. The roll came out the lift shaft, pumped up by the cabin to the eighth floor, then unrolled into *The Languages and Translation Services Ltd.* That was the ventilation system here.

"Come on in."

Mr. Cheung closed the door gently behind Neil. The latch clicked.

Immediately to the left was a partitioned cubicle. Plywood and Perspex. No beading, no varnish, unfinished, homemade. An elderly Chinese lady (Mrs. Cheung?) sat in the cubicle filling in a ledger on a makeshift desk or shelf. Through the teary Perspex Neil saw endless blue columns in her ledger, filled with characters in blue biro. She was marking out some new columns on the left hand page with an old fashioned wooden ruler, a schoolgirl's wooden ruler. It wasn't long enough for the job. Ahead was a narrow passageway leading to another door, which was closed. Mr. Cheung led Neil away to the right.

A bare corridor, broader and lower than the passageway, ended in a flight of wooden steps and a second door, which was also closed. Everywhere closed doors, changing gauges, abrupt ends, makeshift design. Halfway along the corridor on the left was a desk with a writing stand, a black and silver sign saying 'Reception', and several other ledgers identical to Mrs. Cheung's. One ledger was open in the middle of the desk. Mr. Cheung slipped behind, but before he sat down on his wooden stool he hesitated, stooping there. For no apparent reason he flicked back a page of the ledger, frail and dented with characters and columns, to reveal two other crammed blue pages. Neil watched him as he sat down behind his desk, his eyes on his pages all the time, as if reading there what he ought to do next. Things were so confined that he had trouble with his stool and had to lift himself and knock it this way and that with his heel before he could settle. Neil wondered why Mrs. Cheung hadn't left her cubicle to answer the door. Too busy, perhaps.

He stared about himself in a state of shock. Where was he? Where had he sunk to?

The walls of the corridor were panelled, the floor was

parquet, the partition behind him was of bare plywood, and the short flight of stairs to his right, and the door above it, were all of bare, untreated wood. A smell emanated from all this wood, the smell of a library or study, the smell of scholarship. Yet, apart from the curious ledgers, there was not a book to be seen. There were no scholars. And there was no computer terminal, as there must have been on every other reception desk of every other enterprise in Hong Kong. Neil did not feel that he had stepped into the past though, in arriving at this bizarre, misshapen business. He felt as if he'd stepped into the future and was now standing in the middle of a labyrinthine, wooden mausoleum. The heat and smell and staleness of the place were suffocating.

Then, without warning or announcement, three Chinese schoolboys entered, chattering away earnestly in Cantonese, and carrying heavy stacks of colourful language books. They slammed the door behind them, passed by the lady of the cubicle, Neil and Mr. Cheung, without acknowledging any of them in any way. They took the short steps at the end of the corridor two at a time and disappeared into some darker room or passageway beyond. The door closed smartly behind them on a spring. This noisy, youthful disturbance, no sooner come than gone, did nothing to change the morbid atmosphere of the place. It confirmed it with the power of its contrast.

"I show you room?"

Where had he sunk to?

Neil looked back at his prospective landlord, on his stool. The thin and wheezy, uncertain Mr. Cheung. He was too delicate, too crumpled up in the closed confines of his premises. Yet he had adapted to his surroundings, like a parasite in a vacant shell. A hermit crab.

"I show you room?"

That was where Neil had sunk to: deep inside the curly shell of this man's life. He could say nothing. He was too shocked, too upset by what was at stake here. From his silence and his morose staring about the premises, suitcase in hand, Mr. Cheung apparently detected that he had some reservations.

Oh yes, sir. Reservations, and a reservation.

Mr. Cheung now stood up again. He wanted to skip formalities and move the deal forward to its completion or rejection.

Very well. So be it. Let's get on with it.

Neil stood aside as Mr. Cheung came out from behind the desk again and led him back down to the cubicle, where they turned right and followed the narrow passageway to the first closed door. Mr. Cheung opened this door, switched on the light and invited Neil to inspect the room.

It was a room for instruction, that much was certain. There were some faded posters of Paris, Rome and Madrid, all dominated by the green of trees in springtime, and all very dusty. Apart from these posters the sepia walls of the room were bare. The floor was bare boards, not parquet. There were no books; there was no bookcase or bookshelf even. A large Formica table with a clean but scratched beige surface was set in the middle of the room, and around the table were set a dozen or so collapsible aluminium chairs with black seats and backing. Several more chairs were stacked in a far corner. The room had no window, not even a vent or grille, but there was an ancient fan, a colonial thing, far older than the room itself, mounted centrally. Neil stared up at it. Mr. Cheung switched the fan on. With a reluctant whirr it came to life and they both stared up at it together. The blades accelerated briefly, then settled to a worn-out rhythm.

Neil stepped into the room with his suitcase still in hand, his long, straight black hair bouncing on his collar, and walked round to the other side of the Formica table and faced the wall. To walk into the room in this way would have been a natural thing to do, had he been crossing the room to admire the view

from the window. But there was no window, no view, and
Neil's steps into the room were unsure. He turned and put
down his case. He set his hands on the table and looked up
squarely at Mr. Cheung.

"Where's the bed?"

A shake of the reptilian head.

"No bed? Where do I sleep? Is there another room?"

Again the shake of the head. The tortoiseshell glasses
slipped slightly. The heat of the unventilated room had
brought a sweat to Mr. Cheung's ancient, sallow skin.

"You sleep here." The landlord pointed to the floor.

There was a pause.

"Oh, really?"

Neil couldn't stop himself thinking of the comforts and
luxuries of Angel's apartment in Sha Tin. The soft double bed
where he'd lain listening to CDs or reading magazines, or
reading Hemingway, or the sleeve notes of Neil Diamond . . .
the expensive ceramic lamps; his fake Rolex propped against a
lamp . . . And not just all that, but the work he'd put into the
place, all the decorating and the shelves and doorstops and fans
and so on – and some of it he had done, some of the earlier
decorating work, in a state of quiet excitement, as a labour of
love, following Angel's ideas and whims and changes of heart.
The new start. The pearl of great price. That deeper memory
opened the floodgates. He hung his head in a swoon, a nausea
of homesickness, not only a desperate longing for her
apartment and everything in it but a helpless, useless longing
for all of his past life, which in England had always seemed
safe and secure, if nothing else. Postcards of provincial English
towns flashed through his mind, the towns of his lost circuit in
the north of England, the universities – *FolkSoc Presents Neil
Atherton!!* – and the East Midlands, East Anglia, the shabby
pub rooms, the British Legion clubs, cellar bars, back rooms,
church halls . . . A leaden weight of memories unhinged the

current proposition, that he should sleep here on the bare boards of this classroom in *The Languages and Translation Services Ltd.* Tonight. In this stark, windowless classroom. This very night. It was impossible to accept. But at the same time this room cast other prospects and speculations, such as staying in the notorious Chungking Mansions, the backpackers' haven, in a different light. All things are relative, after all. Yes, he must cling to the money Angel had given him. Cling to it. Clasp it tight to his chest with both hands like a crucifix. This place was a refuge, after all. In fact, all things considered, in the end, when all was said and done, it was really a stroke of luck, wasn't it? Wasn't it? Yes, it was. He had to see it that way. He had somewhere indoors to rest his head. He could last a month or six weeks here, perhaps, if need be. Hopefully it wouldn't come to that . . .

Later the same afternoon he invested in a sleeping bag and a foam camping mattress, his 'bindle', he called it, which Mr. Cheung somehow accommodated behind the reception desk. But apart from the expense of this camping gear his new home cost him nothing at all, except the tip he'd given to the guide who'd brought him up here – a very dark young Indian, a tailor's hawker, who'd virtually accosted him when he'd arrived at Chungking Mansions, case in hand. There was no deposit. He paid his rent of $450 a week in advance and that was it. Mr. Cheung had his passport as security.

He was given no key to the premises. In the evening he would be let in by Mrs. Cheung, and in the morning she would ensure he left early, so that she could air his room for the first class.

From now on he spent his days on the street.

McDonald's was another haven.

A place off the pavement, where every step was negotiated with his fellow pedestrians and the stress of the traffic was only inches from his face. He could concentrate just on what he put in his mouth here. He could feel his sweat dry and his shirt grow cold on his back. He could take his time and eat his French fries one by one. All around him there were Chinese people of all ages. Dumpy grandmothers with their long hair tied back, helping with heavy trays. Tiny, happy, orderly children. Whole family groups of three generations with their laden trays looking around for places to sit. He didn't feel he was holding anyone up, though. He was sitting at a counter for solitary diners that ran round one of the pillars in the place. These pillars, everywhere, supporting the colossal structure of flats and shops above – such weight! – such pressure of concrete, glass and humanity all around!

Blue mirror surfaced the pillar in front of him, the same mirror he found in all the plazas and malls, in the lifts, and the public toilets. The blue rinse in the glass took out the blemishes of his skin, shallowed the creases around his mouth and his eyes, took away all the fight and weariness from his face. In these mirrors even his dyed hair, which worried him continuously, looked okay.

He turned from these reflections to the street outside. The cheap shops of City One, Sha Tin, had only gaudy red Chinese characters, no English names. Everyone was Chinese here. Just the supermarket – Park'n'Shop – and the 'drugstore' – Watsons – were intelligible.

There was a pedestrian crossing immediately adjacent the doors and people were pressed up against the glass waiting for the lights to change. Here stood a random selection of the populace of City One, the old and young and not so young, busy shoppers, entrepreneurs, studious adolescents. The lights changed and the crowd began to cross. Neil watched two schoolgirls in tight skirts and blouses go past the window and tag themselves to the end of the crowd now crossing the thoroughfare. His eyes fell to the girls' knees and thighs. The lights changed again. Now they would have to wait there, just outside the McDonald's window, in full view. After a few moments he turned again to the mirror in front of him and his gaze sank in the fathomless blue glass. The skin of Chinese women, Chinese girls, its beautiful smoothness, blankness, had become something of an obsession to him. Just to think of touching it, touching those calves and thighs and breasts, made him feel his uncleanness, his unshavenness. He looked back to the window. There was a break in the traffic and the girls quickly crossed the street, talking, laughing, escaping.

What would Angel think if she could see him now? Here, close by, in a McDonald's in City One, his French fries finished, his Fillet-o-fish bitten and forgotten in its damp tissue? She would think the operation to sever an old attachment, an unwanted appendage from her life, had been bungled. She'd pass by. For her he had become part of that world that lay beyond the toughened glass in her apartment, or beyond the windscreen, or the train window. As on the Kowloon & Canton Railway, passing through the Lion Rock tunnel from Kowloon to Tai Wai: beyond the window lay a vast swimming pool complex, with islands and kiosks and flumes, and next to that a permanent fair ground, complete with dodgems and Ferris wheel, then a football pitch, a bicycle hire business, a vast government driving centre with cars and vans weaving their way around traffic cones. All these things were strung together by the railway line, to be looked upon by the passengers passing by on their way to Tai Po or Lo Wu at the Chinese border. The swimming pool thrashed with slight, childish bodies, and the cars and vans endlessly wove this way and that in the heat, gently polluting the air of the football pitch and the fairground and the swimming pool with warm, sulphurous diesel. If she'd seen him in City One Angel would have passed him by all right, and later, looking down from the train or from her new MX5, stuck in a jam, she would have thought that somewhere in all of this he was about to take his rightful place. That is what she would have thought. She could forget about him now.

He was about to disappear beyond the glass.

Chapter Seven

Lunch Companion

"I'm an impresario of the secondhand, not the second-rate."

Neil was all in black: black shirt, black denims, black boots, black jacket. His dyed black hair was brushed straight and flat. The cheap City One outfit was a statement – to Chan, to himself – and an unequivocal one at that.

"You said authenticity was important."

"Exactly."

"This is authentic. I'm authentic."

"You think so?"

Neil's careful study of the thoughts and sentiments expressed in the songs had led him to his conclusion and nothing now would dissuade him from it. If he was to have any success in cultivating the right aura on stage for his act he must fill himself to the brim with self-belief. That is why he sat in such a confident, even assertive attitude in the rattan armchair, in his cheap black outfit, and didn't flinch for a moment at Chan's put-downs. An investment had been made in City One, way in excess of the cost of the outfit itself.

The world of Neil Diamond, according to the songs, to the CD sleeves, the rock journals, interviews, song books and the rest, had seemed, at first, naturally enough, a fantasy product. But certain irresistible forces had driven Neil to accept it as a reality, and to believe in it as a world without ironies, where

Neil Diamond, Marty Paich and others actually conversed in the back of the Buick, around the poolside, at the cafe in downtown Memphis; and they said things about themselves and about their friends, about their lovers – endearing things, tender things – to which the songs gave voice. Looked at another way this was an inversion of John Lennon's view of his songwriting career, which he said was worthless. The story of the drug addict in the grounds of his New York home who wouldn't go away until Lennon told him what the songs were about. "Don't worry about the songs," Lennon said. "The songs are just a way of saying I had a good shit today."

And yet Neil Diamond could have said that too. That was the 'star quality' itself – 'I had a good shit today' – 'I shat for a million' – as far as Neil understood that concept. Neil Diamond could have said exactly that and meant it too because he was not stuck with a personality at all. He was a creature of the stage, one whose nature checked and changed itself against the warmth of the surrounding footlights. A few weeks ago it would have been easy for Neil to say, in his puffed up way, that inside this superstar's mind there was nothing but a string of trashy songs, banal melodies, cliché lyrics on the themes of sexual fulfilment, 'lonesomeness', joy, fame, stardom, martyrdom and so on – easy meat for his English scorn. But a judgement like that was becoming increasingly difficult because it required a degree of detachment he no longer felt. The more he identified with his subject the more he was in danger of developing the same weakness, because he sensed his own personality was now on shifting sand. The cheap, thin black clothes felt good, felt real. He was not at all self-conscious in them.

It was a mood, of course, and he knew that too. Now that his domestic circumstances had fallen apart his moods had become more extreme. Outside the shelter of Angel's flat, not to mention her income, he found himself exposed beneath a glare of reality that was intolerably bright and painful. He felt the heat of it on his back like a divine punishment as he walked the streets. He hid from its power on the ferries, in the buses and the subways, in McDonald's; he traipsed through air-conditioned malls trying to escape this angry god that would not be propitiated.

A job, a marriage, a home, day to day social interaction, the props upon which a sense of one's place under the stars is held up, with varying degrees of success, these things he simply did not have any more. And as the days went by his own story, his own life, as he had always seen it, became increasingly worthless and irrelevant.

It was all this, as much as the cheap new outfit, which gave his presence today in Chan's office its intensity, and it was an intensity Chan couldn't possibly understand. The new outfit and his dyed hair and the resolution in his eyes – maybe to Chan these things looked like madness, and maybe that's what they were. Very well. So be it.

Neil pointed at the laminated card of Entertainments Managers that hung lopsidedly now above the naked shoulder of June's girl, its crookedness adding to her insouciance.

"Why not contact some of these people right now? Some of the Entertainments Managers you spoke about, Mr. Chan. I can wait."

"I shall do that." Chan nodded. "I shall contact them. But I'm not going to do it right now. I've got some other things to do this morning, you see."

"Why not now?"

"Because I have these other things to do, Mr. Atherton," Chan said. "I have to chase up some gym equipment that hasn't arrived at The Pacific Club, and then I have to sort out some problems with the travel agency about overbookings, and then I'm doing lunch with a client about some printing business, and so on. Priorities, you see? Mine aren't the same as yours. Have you got a problem with that?"

Neil said nothing and Chan drove the point home: "Now is not the time to ring up my contacts at the clubs. Period."

"I'm ready to go."

"I can see that. I can see you're ready."

"Let's make a call."

"Come and see me in a couple of days and maybe I'll have more time. We'll take another look at things. We'll make some calls. We'll sort out a venue. We'll fix some dates and bookings, like I said."

Neil hesitated as he stepped down, all in black, from Chan's block onto the pavement, and he was jostled straightaway, an impediment to the passing crowd. The people on the pavement had already heard about his unsatisfactory meeting with Elbert Chan, so they ignored him and passed him by. They were on their way to new deals, bigger deals, that would leave him behind. He walked as far as the Plaza and stopped by the blue mirrors at the entrance. He found himself mocked by the lengths he had already gone to – his straight black hair, his black suit, his thin black boots. After his meeting with Chan a staleness clung to his appearance. It came from outside, and it came from inside. He could smell it on his crisp, new black shirt. He could smell it on his breath, a sourness from the pit of his empty stomach. He needed to sit awhile in McDonald's, in that sanitized environment, and suffer his dejection in peace. He needed the comfort of that fierce air conditioning –

"*Hey there!*"

They had met only twice, in passing, at Chan's offices, and on neither occasion had they actually spoken to one another, yet Iannis greeted Neil as an old friend. He stepped right in front of him, arrested him, took him by the shoulder in a powerful grip. His smile was broad and excited, exposing protrusive front teeth, and his bulging eyes were full of anticipation. The eyes surprised Neil, close up. They were tight and unfeeling eyes, swollen with pressure, like miniature sports balls. Everything about Iannis's face was coming out at him, keen to get started.

But on what, exactly?

The eyes roved over Neil's new black hair, his new black clothes from City One. If not for the bulky tennis bag in his other hand Iannis would have gripped both Neil's shoulders and pinned him to the pavement so he couldn't run away. He was about to kick off, kick arse, kick shit -

"Hey there!" he said again, at last, with a derisive laugh. "That's quite an outfit. You just come from Elbert's? From Mr. Chan's?"

Neil nodded.

Iannis's brow puckered. His eyes were half shadowed by the peak of his specialist tennis hat, one of those caps with long flaps at the back and sides to protect the neck from the sun. Neil tried to recall in which of Chan's smart clubs Iannis was working but he couldn't remember. What else was in that expression, that puckered frown? With the shadow from the hat it was difficult to say.

"How is he? Channy Chan?"

Neil was puzzled by the question. "How is he? He's fine. Why?""Good. That's good." Iannis glanced away and nodded, as if he'd found out something of more significance than Neil realized. His hand still rested on Neil's shoulder but the welcoming squeeze had gone. Now it was a restraint.

"So where are you going?"

"Lunch."

"Where?"

Neil shrugged and Iannis's hand fell away at last.

"There's a McDonald's just near here," Iannis said, and he turned and pointed down Nathan Road, to the place where Neil had been about to go. "What about that? I'll join you." He lifted his bag onto his shoulder. "So Elbert's okay. That's good news. Good news."

Conversation on the street was awkward but Iannis persisted, shouting over the heads of the milling pedestrians.

"I had a bust up with Elbert not long ago!" he called out, as if amused at the memory. "I was on my way up there to put things right!"

Neil didn't feel obliged to pursue this. He let the conversation lapse and struck ahead, dodging a queue at a bank machine where Iannis got snagged. Iannis caught him at the crossing that took them over to McDonald's.

"Any shows?"

Neil turned and faced Iannis on this question, which seemed way premature. Iannis's face was shadowed by the bag on his shoulder and by his hat. After a pause Neil said: "Not yet, I'm afraid."

Iannis nodded again and looked across the street, then stepped off the pavement. He was always going to be that one step ahead now, at the very least.

They crossed the road and entered McDonald's. Once they'd paid for their food downstairs they went up to the first floor and squeezed round a table by the window. As it happened they settled at Neil's favourite spot in this restaurant. From here, in the air conditioning, safely behind the glass again, he could enjoy the view of the street life below.

Iannis had a BigMac Meal with an extra apple pie. Neil couldn't have afforded anything like that, even if he'd had the appetite for it. He'd settled for his usual Fillet-o-fish.

"The way you're all dressed up I thought you must have done some work," Iannis prompted between mouthfuls, trying to cover his nosiness with his appetite.

Why this interest, and the need to disguise it? Could it be that Iannis was also waiting? In the same queue? Neil had assumed he was just a sports coach, another dangling strand of Chan's business interests with the clubs, but he was behaving in this edgy way as if he had something personal at stake, as if Neil had jumped the queue in which he too was waiting.

Iannis unzipped his tracksuit top, exposing a white sports shirt with a green motif in the shape of a tennis racquet. Around the perimeter of the motif was written: *ITA: Iannis Tennis Academy*, in a fancy rolling script.

"Let me tell you something." Iannis wiped his mouth with his napkin, reached across the table and tapped his stubby index finger in front of Neil's tray. "I think our Mister Chan is stringing you along, pal. He ain't got nothing for you. He's told you about his clubs? Let me spell out something for you – *Chan's* not a *member* of *any* of those *clubs!* Him and his *clubs!* He buys his drinks with coupons! I seen him! With coupons! He told you about his Entertainments Managers? Forget them. He ain't got no gigs, no shows or nothing."

Neil felt a pricking around his hairline, and at the back of his neck, down his spine.

"Well?" he said, holding on, staying calm. "What's it to you?"

Iannis took a powerful bite of his BigMac, a swig of meat and bread, so that his face bulged with burger.

"Now you tell me something," he said, when he'd swallowed some of his mouthful. "How'd you meet our Mr. Chan in the first place?"

Neil hesitated but decided he had nothing to lose in telling the story, and he felt a need to tell it now, to get it out there. Leaving aside the domestic details he began a brief sketch of his first meeting with Chan at the karaoke bar in Lockhart Road. Iannis nodded and grinned. He knew the whole story already. Of course he did.

"The Atlantis Bar!" he said triumphantly, carried away, and he reached across and tapped the table again. "Same as me!

Same as Deano!"

"Deano?"

"The Hawaiian shirt?" Iannis held his hands wide to get the size of it. "Was he wearing that? Big blue thing?"

Neil hesitated. Swallowed air.

"Yes."

Iannis sat back again, still grinning, even shaking his head and chuckling to himself, but his triumph seemed confused with other feelings that had surfaced quickly behind it, and were rushing him off in the wrong direction. He turned away and stared across the restaurant, and after a few moments the triumph and amusement deserted him, and his mouth sank at the corners.

Neil took a drink, just a sip of Coke, ate his Fillet-o-fish and French fries, and watched and waited, staying calm, holding back, holding on.

He sensed that Iannis had taken a few gambles here. He'd taken a gamble in approaching him in the street and then a further, much more reckless gamble in this conversation. And his gambles had not paid off. Not paid off at all. Iannis had anticipated the name of the bar, The Atlantis Bar – he'd seen it coming and he'd blurted it out – but that had been a mistake, to call the name out loud, and then to bring up the Hawaiian shirt on top of that. Those details had fallen straight through the bottom of the conversation. They'd triggered some mechanism of disillusionment in Iannis. Pennies had dropped through the slot. Heavy, worn, and ancient pennies, that sank a lever, rolled a cam, set the tumblers spinning –

Lemon. Lemon. Cherry.

But Neil didn't have to share that disillusionment, didn't have to be a part of that. Not at all. Not a lemon or a cherry or any other piece of rotten fruit.

When Iannis turned back to the table there was no triumph and amusement left in him. Neil bent to his meal and ate, and let his lunch companion watch him eat.

Silence.

"You haven't met Deano?"

"No . . ." Neil answered, and shook his head. He swallowed his food and wiped his hands on his paper napkin. "I haven't had that pleasure."

"Little ol' wine drinker. Elbert's been stringing him along for more than a year. Deano Mart-ee-n-o." Iannis's mouth stayed circled on the last 'o' for a second or two, then he ate again himself, drank some Coke, and belched behind his hand.

"Castles in the air, pal." He was trying to sound above it all, but he choked on his words now. He could hardly drag them out. "Pure fantasy. Pure bull . . . Pure *bullshit!*"

Food splattered on his tray with the force of feeling in that word bullshit.

Politely Neil looked down at the crowded pavements while Iannis cleaned up.

What stretched before him this afternoon? Another ferry ride? A walk along the esplanade, where at least there was no traffic and the sea breeze offered some relief to the heat, pollution and humidity. Or perhaps an afternoon at the top of the Ocean Terminal car park, squinting at the sunbathers on the decks of an ocean liner, counting the cabins, peering into other people's luxury vacations . . .

So, Elbert Chan was a fraud. That is what he was being asked to understand. Chan was a fraud, a fantasist. Maybe, or maybe not. But either way, he could not wait a year to find out. He could not wait around like Deano, whoever he was. At the same time, though, Neil could not help himself suspecting that these other prospects – Iannis's , whatever they were, and those of this other fellow he had mentioned – were not quite in the same league as his own. Neil found it only too easy to imagine that Elbert Chan, after hearing his voice and seeing him perform, had realized that the other acts in his stable, if

Iannis were anything to go by, were simply not up to the mark, were really too second-rate, to use Chan's own terms. Neil was, after all, a genuine musician. He'd played with big name bands and his own name was down there on the sleeves of the albums in black and white. He knew what key to sing in. He had been a professional performer all his life. Chan's standards had changed, that was all. Neil need not share the facile cynicism of the blunt and greedy Iannis.

"How's the tennis coaching?" he asked. He sipped his Coke, making it last.

Iannis fingered in the last of his bun. "Fine."

"You make enough money?"

Iannis nodded, closed his eyes a moment. "Of course I make enough money. I wouldn't be here if I didn't make enough money."

"So what are you worried about?"

Iannis frowned. He began to undo the first of his apple pies. His stubby fingers had trouble with the packaging, and his haughty, quizzical frown seemed to say he was having similar difficulty getting through to Neil: "What am I worried about? . . ." he repeated, as if amused by the question. He freed the pie at last and ate half of it in one bite. Some of the viscous innards slipped down his chin. "I'm not worried." Neil seemed to have given offence by suggesting for a moment that anything in the world could worry the mighty Iannis. "I just don't like being fucked on by this Elbert Chink. And – " he looked up from the pie and wagged a finger – "I don't actually want to be a tennis coach for the rest of my life. No thank you! I'm fifty years old!" He winced and rubbed his legs under the table, in genuine pain, it seemed. "It's too fucking hard on the knees!" He looked across the restaurant again. His eyes picked out the teenage girls, the young women, the young mothers in the crowd, flitted from body to body, buttock to buttock. "And the women. I'm tired of all these Chink women at the clubs."

"The Ladies' Recreation Club?" Neil had remembered.

Iannis looked at him. "Yeah. The LRC. But it's not just ladies. It's a mixed club. They have me coach all their teams – men's 'A' teams, as well as the ladies' teams. All the ladies' teams. That's when the trouble starts."

"Trouble?"

Iannis nodded.

"What trouble?"

"Oh, you know." Iannis sighed and looked resigned. "You fuck one and they all want it."

Neil fell silent. He turned again to the brightness and busyness of Nathan Road, to the steady rush of commerce and ambition out there. Something in the sheer irrelevance of Iannis's brag made his company oppressive. Neil tried to change the subject again.

"What did you do before you came here?"

Iannis's mouth hung open a moment, sticky with pie. He answered Neil as if he were an idiot. "I was a tennis coach."

"But where did you coach?"

"Dubai." Iannis pulled wide his tracksuit top to expose fully the green motif. Neil hadn't noticed *DUBAI* printed at the bottom of the racquet head. "I had my own tennis academy. I was the first pro from Dubai to compete in the Dubai Open."

Neil sensed that no matter what direction the conversation took it would always run into the buffers of such brags. He remembered the other occasions when he'd met this man: first, Iannis's haughty entrance in Chan's office; second, just the other day, on the cushioned bench in Chan's anteroom, a humped and brooding figure flicking through a stack of holiday brochures, scowling covetously at the glossy pictures of Bali and Thailand – bountiful buffet breakfasts in five-star hotels, beautiful Asian women on golden beaches or in crimson heart-shaped pools, coral life through the bottom of a glass-bottomed boat, all the treasures of the Asian dreamlands . . .

"Look," Neil said, rising, "I have to go."

Iannis glanced up. A fleeting pain creased his eyes and in that moment Neil caught a glimpse of the man's loneliness here. He remembered Iannis's pleasure, his delight almost, at their chance encounter, that heavy hand on his shoulder. He remembered also Elbert Chan's curiously blunt admission – 'We Chinese are very racist, you know'.

"What are we going to do about him?" Iannis asked, opening up his second apple pie. "Our Mr. Chan."

"I don't have a problem with Mr. Chan," Neil said, moving away. He didn't want to get involved. He couldn't get involved. "I'll see you around."

Iannis nodded to himself, as if he'd anticipated that response, and they parted without a goodbye.

Neil felt cheated of a small respite. Though he had come to loathe the food at McDonald's, he still looked forward to meal times as moments of reprieve in his sticky, restless, outdoor days. They were breaks when the sweat dried on his back and his thoughts were his own, when he could get to the bottom of things, or stop and stare through the window in comfort. Iannis had robbed him of this today. Neil had never been fussy about the company he kept and he would have tolerated Iannis's wildness, his mythomania, if it hadn't been for the sexual turn the conversation had taken. Once that had started he'd felt a pressure to move on.

But to where? To where?

A wedge of buses and taxis blocked the way across to Kowloon Park. He felt a wall of heat from it, engine heat, at the edge of the pavement. Behind it the fumes poured everywhere yet stayed where they were. The route left, towards the Star Ferry and open water, was jammed by excavations across the pavement half a block down. He took it anyway and within a few steps was sidelined in a queue against the safety railings. Beneath him, some ten feet below, a slave laboured in a pit of pipes and wires. That man had the only private space around. There was nowhere else to go. Nowhere. Going 'outside' was not going outside. Outside was still boarded up, still under construction. When it was finished it would be just another mall, filled with the heat and waste of all the other malls, lit by lurid light in a hazy ceiling.

He stopped at Chow Tai Fook and scanned the plush cream shelves for Angel's earrings. Her diamond earrings in white gold. How much had they cost? But there was nothing remotely like them at Chow Tai Fook's. Jewellery chain stores were too downmarket for Angel now. Oh, she had plenty now. Plenty.

Plenty of nothing. At the end of Nathan Road he turned and passed the fountains of The Peninsula Hotel, The Peninsula Arcade, all that five-star high style, and he passed it by without so much as a sideways glance. It meant nothing to him. Never had. Not pretty things. Not chic styles. No thanks. And she knew that. But how could she have just dispensed with him? How? How could she have just pushed him out, sloughed him off? How could she do that? Where was the common humanity there?

Christ!

Jesus Christ! What a fucking bitch!

His attitude towards his wife, and to everyone else, come to that, these people all around him, these Chinese, these tourists – Why should he give a monkey's fuck about any of them? Or about *Iannis*, for Christ's sake? – his attitude was becoming more calloused than his musician's hands had ever been, when he'd played protest songs for students, or for the oppressed and hard-done-by, or everybody-fucking-else, played for all the laughing drunks and wasters in pub back rooms, for all the loners and ne'er-do-wells in the British Legion clubs – Oh yes, rather more calloused now.

And not before time. The old free-wheeling, big-hearted

Neil Atherton had been vanquished – fool that he was. In unguarded moments like this, stuck at the kerb, waiting to cross to the Star Ferry terminus – yet again! – his eyes teared up freely with recrimination and unhappiness.

But Elbert Chan had given him a thread of hope that wound him back, more or less every day, through the labyrinth of Tsim Sha Tsui to his poky office; the unfortunate meeting with Iannis had pulled the thread tighter but had not snapped it.

At the terminus Neil negotiated his way through the crowds and tourists, dipping his shoulders, ducking in and out, angrily pushing and shoving through a knot of elderly Americans – 'Hey! Watch out there, pal!' – 'Dja see that guy?!' – 'Pickpocket! Check your bag!' – until he came to the beginning of the esplanade. He stopped at a tiled wall and leant there, taking deep breaths, and stared across the choppy water to Hong Kong Island. What a mystery it was to the common man, he thought, how all that wealth was piled up neatly and securely in those shiny stacks. And in those offices, on the top floors of Citibank, The Bank of China, The Lippo Building, there worked high-flying men and women from America, Europe and Australia, who spent their leisure hours at The American Club or The Ladies' Recreation Club, where they might take tennis lessons with an ex-pro from Dubai, and then enjoy a dinner and cabaret entitled, *A Tribute to Neil Diamond*. His own wife worked up there, with a view of the airport bridge and the Tsing Yi and Ma Wan Islands. His estranged wife, rather. His ex-wife. His ex.

He saw her in his mind's eye standing in her underwear, in the bright bathroom of her apartment, putting on that sulky eye make-up. But the image had come involuntarily. It was not wanted and with no lust to fix it there it faded and disappeared. And then a cloud passed and the skyline shrank and became quite drab. It lost its gold-topped and fancy glitter. It was just dusty cosmetic bottles round a filthy sink.

A dinner and cabaret entitled, *A Tribute to Neil Diamond*. That's where he, courtesy of the impresario Elbert Chan, was to be fitted in to this hustling and avaricious community. Well, if no one else was going to do it, he would. If they couldn't bring on anything better than him, if the only other options were an aging Manfred Mann, Elvis from Edmonton, or Deano Mart-ee-n-o, or Iannis, even, then he would step into that lonely spotlight and sing *Reason to Believe*, *Cracklin' Rosie* and *Sweet Caroline* for all he was worth, and he would chat to the audience, humour the audience, and he'd ask for their requests and dedications, and he'd invite them to take to the floor, where they would dance after their banquets, cummerbunds loose over unfastened trousers. It could be done. He had a rôle, a place. There was no need, after all, to feel these agonizing stings of alienation every time he looked up from the pavement.

The wind blew his straightened, dyed black hair across his Adam's apple and tickled him there, and the light off the water made him tighten his eyes and gave him a headache. He turned away from the tiled wall back into Tsim Sha Tsui, away from idle speculation and reflection – he must produce, he must deliver! He began a search of the stalls around the ferry terminus for the perfect pair of sunglasses in which to impersonate the one and only Neil Diamond.

Chapter Eight

Sammy Davis Jnr.

Chan had been away all week and the girls in the travel agency, his two preening parakeets, had done their very best to help Neil in Chan's absence. Every day, before Neil could get a word in, they asked him where he wanted to go, and whether he wanted business class, club class or first class. They chirped their destinations in turn, one after the other – New York? Paris? Montreal? Brazil? Buenos Aires? Moscow? Chicago? Every day he had to hold up his hand, as soon as he came through the door, to stop them offering endless, useless lists of destinations, ticket options, and possible places Elbert might be. One said she was certain he was in Macau, then the other argued with her, turning to exclude Neil – No no no, he was on the mainland somewhere. Shenzen or Guangzhou, maybe, and then she rolled off a list of other Chinese cities whose names meant nothing and that only stirred up fresh unease. "Do you want a ticket to Guangzhou anyway?" she asked, turning back to him, when she'd finished. "Club class? First class? So you can try and find him on the street somewhere?"

Their superciliousness every day had been discomforting, and this Friday morning, when he'd finally secured an appointment with Chan, he could hardly stop his impatience and irritation spilling out in front of the man himself.

In his office Chan was flicking through brochures that had piled up in his absence. New promotions for local hotspots – Bali, Phuket, Penang – three separate piles.

"Neil Atherton and Neil Diamond haven't been uppermost in my thoughts of late," he remarked, by way of welcome, as Neil took his seat.

Neil moved about in the creaky rattan chair, trying to knot up his anger.

Chan licked a finger, turned a page of *Bali Breaks*.

The only trace of Neil's ambitions left in the office this morning was a pair of wraparound sunglasses he'd bought a week ago. They dangled from his fingertips. They were of another era. They were Stevie Wonder or Ray Charles. Blind men's glasses. When he wore them with his black shirt and black jacket, and his black jeans and thin black boots, the effect was so striking, so complete, he attracted looks and smiles in the street all the time, wherever he went. It was a tough call to respond with any lightness of spirit.

Maybe that's how he should have turned up today. The full effect. Turn it on.

Chan closed *Bali Breaks* and stretched the cover, corner to corner, inspecting it, frowning. He tossed it aside and picked up *Phuket Package*.

Another week had gone by. That was another $450 down the Cheung drain, and another week's meals and plain survival, let alone the money he'd spent in City One the week before, and the $150 or so he'd spent on his fancy sunglasses. Angel's $8000 was almost half gone. Quite literally, he could not afford to hang about like this. He had to make some progress. Iannis's words had become italicized, emboldened in his brain during Chan's absence – '*Castles in the air, pal – Pure fantasy – Pure bullshit!*' '*Chan's not a member of any of those clubs!*'

He could go back to Angel, flat broke, pockets inside out,

confess all, and throw himself on her mercy. She would shell out another fare but she'd see him onto the plane this time. What else could she do? He'd never sunk so low as to doubt that she would bail him out one last time. After all, the fare was small beer to her these days. Peanuts. Loose change.

"Mr. Chan, you agreed last week to contact some clubs. To arrange auditions."

Chan set aside *Phuket Package* and leant back in his office chair. "It won't work like that. There won't be auditions. That's a lousy way to do business. Who said anything about auditions?"

Come to think of it, no one had.

"We're talking shows."

"Yeah, but what shows?"

"No one's on trial."

Chan leant forward again and drew his Compaq across the desk and snapped it on.

"I've been doing a little work on this at home," he said, when the Compaq had warmed up. He scrolled through his menus. "The idea has grown somewhat. Let me show you something." He got up from the desk to connect the laptop to the printer. "What I've got in mind – long term – " he began, tucking in his tie-pinned tie and sitting down again, "is a kind of agency. For doublers. For tribute artists. A new concept. Star Tributes. That's the concept title." He looked up at Neil brightly, cheered by this new dimension. "You see it?"

But Neil didn't see it. He just saw Chan's flat features, the flat mouth, opening and shutting in front of him, and the bald face smiling and nodding at him, as Chan went through his Star Tributes concept. Finally, this Friday morning, the scales dropped from Neil's eyes. He saw Elbert Chan, in his cheap business suit and tie-pinned tie, sitting in his poky office behind his IKEA desk, with his pretentious Anglepoise, with his blue plastic filing cabinet in the corner – he saw Chan for what he was: a charlatan, a fraud, a shyster. He was just stringing him along. Why, he did not know, he could not imagine. But that was it, for sure now.

"Mr. Chan, right now I don't – "

"You look good today, you know. Really good."

Neil knew only too well how he looked this morning: his sleepless eyes and worn-out face, framed by his straightened black hair, had that bedevilled and betrayed cast of the aging rock star. It was unmistakable. No, he didn't look good today. Not good at all. No good at all.

"Today you look good." Chan repeated, nodding. "And that's important. Authenticity. You have to know everything about your subject. I mean everything. You have to do the legwork, the research, go everywhere, search everywhere, chase it all down, climb every mountain, look in every nook and cranny. Do the graft. Do the time. You have a long way to go, you know. A long, long way."

Yeah.

A long, long way.

Thanks, Mr. Chan.

Chan cocked his head and continued to examine Neil's face, as if it were on the cover of another magazine, another *Phuket Package*, that he could stretch corner to corner. Stretch a long, long way.

"You really look the part today. It's quite remarkable. You look like a Rolling Stone. Like Bill Wyman or Ron Wood . . . Or even Johnny Cash!"

Chan laughed at that. Johnny Cash. It was too much.

"Mr. Chan, I don't feel much inclined to sit here and listen to you talk about what or who I look like – which fucked up rock star of yesteryear! – or any new concept or grand design, or about how your plans have grown somewhat! I want the work we discussed before and which you have continually failed to deliver. You said I could play The American Club,

The Clearwater Bay Club, The Pacific Club, The Hong Kong Club itself. But nothing has materialised. I want that work. I could do it and I could do it well. I have a background in live music. I can sing and I can play a variety of instruments. I have told you that. I can read music. I'm a professional and I deserve professional standards of dialogue. I have been fobbed off and I will not be fobbed off again!"

It was quite a speech, and there was a distinct air of premeditation about it.

Three lines appeared on Chan's pale, high brow. They were so new, so short and distinct and symbolic, and they fitted Chan's brow so neatly, it was as if they were lines sketched in by a cartoonist. Quick, short, deep curves to signify utter perplexity and dumbfoundment. They were so deep they pulled down the leading strands of his hair-flip.

Neil had shocked Chan. He'd thrown him. Fazed him.

There was some pleasure in that, but the greater effect was relief. His pent-up feeling was out in the open at last. Cramps in his stomach began to relax. He felt a bubble in his bowel and he badly wanted to break wind. He had to cross his legs to squeeze it back.

"Every time I come up here you have some different story to explain why you haven't contacted these Entertainments Managers – " Neil glanced up at the laminated sheet of names, the misaligned rows of phone and fax and mobile numbers, the Gavin Fans, Harry Lams and Martin Wongs, over the shoulder of June's girl on her exercise bike – "and I am weary of the abuse of my time, my effort and my money. I have already invested a good deal in this project. You know that. And I have studied my subject, the subject you suggested and I agreed upon. But when I tell you about the work I've done, you aren't interested. And you do nothing. Why don't you pick up that telephone right now and arrange something with one of these Entertainments Managers, Mr. Chan? Let me see it's real. Let me hear you talking to one of these guys – " again a nod to the laminated list, which had taken on the significance of an exhibit in a court of law – "about this project. That's what I want to hear. Not about some agency pipe dream. Pick up the phone, Mr. Chan, and make a call!"

Chan's expression had not changed. The three lines on his brow remained, no bigger, no smaller. The lank fragment from his hair-flip fell no further. He was staring at Neil but there was no particular intensity in his gaze. In fact, his eyes looked rather glassy.

"Have you been talking to Iannis?"

"What's that got to do with it?"

"Have you?"

"I had lunch with Iannis about a week ago."

"At the LRC? At The Ladies' Recreation Club?"

"No. At McDonald's. What's that got to do with it?"

"You talk the way Iannis talks."

"I'm not Iannis, Mr. Chan."

"Iannis came in here drunk a few weeks ago and demanded that I advance him fifty thousand dollars in lieu of lost bookings. That's how Iannis talks. He makes demands. Somewhat unreasonable demands."

"I'm not asking for any money, Mr. Chan," Neil said, as the doubts swept in now – just how much had he allowed himself to be swayed by Iannis's remarks? "Only – " Where was his sense of proportion, his equilibrium that he had striven to maintain despite the pressure of current circumstances? Iannis, for goodness' sake. Whom he himself had written off as a wildcard, a mythomaniac. "Only the work that – "

"Let me tell you something," Chan said. It was his turn to make a speech. "Iannis is a very good tennis player. He is a passable tennis coach. He can make a living at that. That's what he is and that's what he does, and we are what we are successful at, right? Now, I have secured some business for

Iannis in that line. But that is not enough for Iannis. Iannis likes to sing and perform. He spends all his money in the karaoke bars. He's one of these drunks that tours Wan Chai as if he's doing a series of private concerts. He has a favourite act. You know what it is?"

Neil said nothing. He didn't want to hear any more.

"Didn't he tell you? . . . No? . . . Well, I'll tell you. Iannis believes he can impersonate Sammy Davis Junior. The late and great Sammy Davis Junior."

Neil held up a hand on hearing this. It was enough. Sammy Davis Junior! It was all he needed to know. It cast Iannis in a new, an awful light. But Chan too raised a hand.

"No. You listen a minute. Let's get it straight about Iannis. Iannis drinks till he's drunk. He tells stories about Sammy Davis, Frank Sinatra, that whole 'rat-pack' scene. He tells stories about Dean Martin – Deano Mart-ee-no, no less – and Shirley Maclaine. Then once he's mentioned the women – "

Again Neil held up his hand, palm flat, in serious protest – he had some idea of what was coming next.

You fuck one and they all want it. Of course they do.

"No no, let me tell you this – you need to hear it. Once he's mentioned the women, he's off and away. That's when the fun really starts. This is what he tells the audience." Chan leant forward. "He tells them he's had sex with Shirley Maclaine."

"Look, Mr. Chan – "

"That's part of the act. He tells the audience that he's had sex with Mia Farrow, too. Me Furrow, he calls her. No respect, you see? That's another part. It doesn't stop there. After a few more drinks it turns out he's balled both of them – Shirley Maclaine and Mia Farrow – at the same time!"

"Mr. Chan, Iannis may or may not – "

"I have seen him and heard him do that. He describes it all in detail, the ménage à trois. The bodies of those ladies, in detail, their private parts – Shirley Maclaine and Mia Farrow.

Me Furrow. He says *they* called it, they called it, mind you, they called having sex with Iannis – the tennis coach from Dubai, remember – 'The Chocolate Sandwich'."

"Okay now. That's clear. So let's – "

"It's really quite offensive. Let me assure you that Iannis is not an impersonator of the late and great Sammy Davis Junior. Iannis should show more respect for the dead. And for the living, come to that. I have succeeded in securing business for Iannis in the rôle of Sammy Davis Junior once and once only. I arranged a forty-five minute slot at The Mariners' Club here in Tsim Sha Tsui about a year ago. I should never have done that. It was billed, *A Tribute to Sammy Davis Jnr.* The Oriana was docked at Ocean Terminal. The club was packed. Sailors and their escorts. Did he tell you what happened that night, by any chance? Did he fill you in on that?"

Neil shook his head. His face was grave. He didn't need to be told. He folded his sunglasses and rested them in his lap. He wished he had never had lunch with Iannis. All the gloom he'd inspired. What a fool he'd been to listen to him, against his better judgement. What a fool, fool, fool.

"They threw food at Iannis."

Iannis. In his baggy Mizuno tracksuit. The ITA. The Iannis Tennis Academy. Dubai. Goodbye.

"All right, all right . . ." Neil waved his hand, conceding everything. He wanted to move on now.

"Fish heads. Chicken wings. You name it. Towards the end someone threw a turd at him."

"Someone threw what?"

"A turd. A human turd."

"*No!*"

"A human turd. Iannis wanted me to pay for the cleaning. 'Look at me!' he said. 'Look at my tux! Look what they did! It's all your fault!' That's what I mean – he makes unreasonable demands. So I'm telling you. You don't dictate to me – I dictate to you. Iannis is a tennis coach. He cannot successfully impersonate the late Sammy Davis Junior. It's a proven fact because I proved it. Period."

"You've made your point, Mr. Chan."

"If anyone is, as you say, a pipe dreamer here, it is you, or it might just be Iannis. I don't know – it's a close call. But it is not me."

"Let's move on, Mr. Chan," Neil said, anxious that the interview would now be drawn to a close and nothing would have been achieved apart from a souring of relations. This visit had already lasted longer than any previous. "Let's move on to what you were saying about the new agency."

Chan rested his elbows on his desk and knitted his small hands, calm and collected once more.

"Iannis got paid this week. Check out his act. You'll find him at The Cosmopolitan tonight. Never fails."

"There's really no need, Mr. Chan. I accept what you say."

"Nothing starts there before two a.m."

"It's really okay. I'm sorry I – "

"Check him out," Chan said, leaning back. "I insist. The Cosmopolitan. Tsim Sha Tsui East. Tonight. Nothing starts before two. He never misses. They have a good set-up there. You could learn something."

"Must I?" Neil knew he owed a concession, but . . .

"I insist. Then come and see me tomorrow morning, Saturday, first thing, and we'll discuss the concept. The Star Tributes concept."

Neil stood up wearily. There were no other options. None at all. He made his concession, then left.

Chapter Nine

At The Cosmopolitan

". . . Michael Aspel has become a nationally known personality on both television and radio. He has presented numerous television and radio programmes, including *Family Favourites, Miss World, Crackerjack, Personal Cinema, Aspel and Company, Ask Aspel, After Seven* and the *Bafta Awards* . . . The title of his autobiography is taken from the punch line of one of his favourite jokes: 'What do you get if you cross a parrot with a lion?' . . . "

Neil flicked to the flyleaf for the date of publication. 1974. Aspel was still in his early forties when *Polly Wants a Zebra* hit the streets.

He turned to the rich colour plates at the centre of the book. First there was a photo-record of the compere in his various rôles. Next, some childhood snaps. Then a wide range of incidental shots of M.A. in the company of a galaxy of tv celebrities and popular music stars of the sixties and early seventies, such as Peter Glaze and Don McLean – and yes, as promised in the index, Neil Diamond. At Swindon's bookshop in Ocean Terminal this was the only volume Neil could find that was in any way connected with his research. It was an odd book to find here. A first edition hardback, fetched down for him from a remote and dusty shelf, that was no less than twenty-four years old. Nearly a quarter of a century. Could it possibly have been here all this time? Were the stocktaking procedures so very lax? Or was it here simply because no one knew quite what to do with such a book, still in pristine condition apart from some yellowing around the edges? Presumably the staff who worked in the store had no idea what the book was about. It might never have been opened before.

Holding his place at the Neil Diamond plate with his forefinger, Neil glanced again at the cover. Michael Aspel's friendly bedroom eyes, his wry and knowing smile, shone out from a picture of an antique tv, while the title of his book was punched out in quirky, irregular fonts, in all the colours of the rainbow around the screen. It was a title and picture that set a tone of light self-deprecation. Here was a celebrity who was definitely not going to take himself, his past, or life in general, too seriously.

Clearly in one way, though, this autobiography was a serious project, the product of months of labour, negotiation, consultation. And here it was, twenty-four years on, surviving on the shelves of Swindon's, a bookseller with pretensions to be just as chic as the exclusive clothes and jewellery shops that surrounded it at Ocean Terminal, Tsim Sha Tsui. Here they had the same creaky deck flooring as in the clothes stores, and a fountain trickled near the entrance of the shop, and soft Mozak, classical Muzak, tinkled from discreetly mounted *Bose* speakers.

Neil opened the book again at the colour plates and stood very still. Don McLean, Peter Glaze, top left, Helen Shapiro bottom left, Neil Diamond opposite, full page. Research. Here he was, doing the legwork. Climbing every mountain. Because he had a long, long way to go. The graft. The Research . . . If someone asked him what he was doing here, in this shop, whiling away this particular hour of his life, that would be his answer. Research. That's what he called it, and what Chan called it. In the early morning hours there would be more Research when he visited The Cosmopolitan to see Iannis's impersonation of the late & great Sammy Davis Jnr. More fact-finding, more detailed assessment and analysis. But in this particular piece of Research, this item, this *Polly Wants a Zebra*, with its blurb, its index and its rich colour plates, and its price tag – $98 – in this Research he had stumbled upon something. This Research had lifted a veil.

How on earth had it all come to this? This wild and misshapen hope that drove him on – to what?

With that question the parrot took wing from the open book, pluming itself from the colour plates, and lifted from his hands and flew about the shop, a streak of blue and green and a wild squawk that tore at the mind, at the heart – *Polly Wants a Zebra Polly Wants a Zebra Michael Aspel Polly Wants a Zebra Neil Diamond Polly Wants a Zebra Polly Wants a Zebra Polly Wants a Zebr*a – until he cried out loud -

"POLLY WANTS A ZEBRA!"

Some tourists – English, plump, bourgeois, literary, leafing through coffee table hardbacks – looked up, stopped and stared. He smiled and nodded to them, and held up the cover of his book. They frowned and moved down the table to the photobooks of Hong Kong.

Neil glanced about the shop, watching the bird flit and squawk and screech.

He felt the incongruities of his life stack up around him, like the books in the bookcases, blocking him in – but no, that wasn't it. That suggested confinement, restriction, which was too orderly, not what he felt at all: he felt fragmentation, disorientation, alienation, as if his personality, his understanding of himself, had been dropped here, in this shop, like a glass figurine, on the polished deck floor, and the shards and opaque lumps of it had scattered across the decking, to be lost beneath this shelf or that shelf, crushed under this heel or that heel.

A hot flush, that he was sure was visible to everyone in the shop, to all the tourists and store detectives, warmed his face, made his scalp itch. He turned over *Polly Wants a Zebra* and reread the blurb, staying perfectly still and calm, but the blurb – *Michael Aspel has become a nationally known personality on both television and radio . . .* didn't help. The words cut loose and span before his eyes like newspaper headlines in some old-fashioned film, spinning up towards the camera, to spell out some drastic change in circumstances.

He shook his head and screwed up his eyes.

Chan should be at his elbow right now to make a pitch for this book, to make him see sense and to make him buy it – *Buy it, Neil. Buy it. Go right ahead. I insist* – and to tell him that what he was doing was right, that the lines he was thinking on were straight and sure, and that this was just another quite reasonable way of passing the time, passing his life, before tonight's even grander event, the visit to The Cosmopolitan, to watch Iannis perform. It all made sense. It added up. It was not the hiss of madness, the squawk of futility.

He glanced about the smart and exclusive bookstore, holding his book to his chest as if considering a difficult passage, something moving, a poem, an elegy he'd just read in it. The English tourists didn't seem to be able to find what they wanted. Should he approach them with this book? Excuse me? Is this what you're looking for? Is this it? Is this the one? *Polly Wants a Zebra*? He might open the book at the centre plates and ask them if they remembered these people in the photos, and then stand there by the coffee table books and chat about Don McLean, Peter Glaze, Michael Aspel and Neil Diamond. Oh yeah, sure, I remember him. He was the one who always . . .

He looked past the English tourists to the Chinese cashier standing behind her counter. She was young and very lovely.

He watched her perpetual smile and her perfect manners, the same for every transaction. If he went up and passed his book across the glass counter she would smile just the same, and put it in a bag and take his $98 without a second thought. But that was wrong, terribly wrong – it was a swindle, a cheat, daylight robbery. It wasn't worth it! Yet he would pay – pay, pay, and pay again! – with some of the few notes that still separated him from the pit. And then his life would intersect with these lives, in the book, at this moment in time, here, on the polished decking, before the pretty cashier.

Neil turned the book over and spread his fingers on the tv screen, and covered Michael Aspel's face with his palm. Worth, of course, had nothing whatever to do with it. He reached for that word too often, and reached up on tiptoe every time, full stretch. He needed to consider the price, not the value, and leave the question of what things were worth to the people who bought them. That was it. Simple as that.

A basic truth, like heavenly light, was settling around him now, on his black hair, on his black jacket, in this shop, and bringing with it serenity and understanding, an end to agitation and anxiety. The parrot had fallen silent. Behind a shelf somewhere it folded its brilliant wings and settled out of sight. It would starve and wither there and crumple into fluff and dust.

All his adult life, throughout the seventies, the eighties, the nineties, as the folk scene retracted to its proper roots, and left him high and dry, Neil had adopted what he liked to call an *alternative* view of things. He'd had a different take on how society worked, and how it worked against him and his kind. Now he understood, standing in this chic shop with this book in his hands, that rather than being a view from above, from some moral high ground, as he'd always supposed, his alternative view had actually been subterranean. Over the years he'd dug tunnels of tortuous argument to undermine pillars of obvious fact, but no matter where be burrowed or where he surfaced, such as here, in this Ocean Terminal bookshop, the pillars remained, and looked exactly the same. Only Angel, and perhaps one or two lost souls in pubs or British Legion clubs, had ever been privileged to join him in a crawl down these meandering tunnels. They'd all pulled back from the lack of light and air down there. And the passage of time, of nearly three decades, had caused no subsidence, until now.

He would have this book. Oh yes. He deserved this book. He would learn from this book, and learn by rote. He would read it at dawn in his cell at *The Languages and Translation Services Ltd.,* and then again at dusk, at the Formica table, turning page after page, before he settled down on the dusty floor on his bindle. He would punish himself with this book, in his cell, and already he felt some comfort in that. With this book he took a pledge. He'd swear by it and he'd swear on it. He'd carry it to the ends of the earth. He'd carry it to the pit.

He took the book to the pretty cashier. He paid for it. $98. The cashier smiled, as she did for everyone. Such a beautiful face. The symmetry of it. Her long, pure black hair tucked behind her ears. Jade teardrop earrings.

"My," she said, with an American twang. "That's dusty, isn't it? . . ."

She was on vacation from university, maybe, doing the job to pay her parents back. Her future, her past, all bright and shiny and up to date.

"Let me clean it for you . . ."

She took a brand new yellow duster from under the counter and he watched as she wiped Michael Aspel's grinning face on the monochrome tv. He watched her flick the yellow duster before rubbing the spine of *Polly Wants a Zebra*. Rubbing the spine up and down. And it was agony for him, this waiting, watching, this transaction. He stood there in silent agony, watching her lovely hands at work on his new book, his pledge, his just deserts.

"There you are."

He thanked her. She thanked him. She looked at him. At his thin black jacket, at his long straight black hair, Chinese it was so black. She smiled again, blankly. Oh my, she might be thinking, Who the fuck are you? She bagged his book. She gave it to him. He left the shop. He walked quickly with his bag through the marbled underground and undersea mall of Ocean Terminal. There was an angry strut in his gait as he swept by the clothes stores and jewellery shops, and left behind all their beautiful shop assistants, swept by all the elegant mannequins bearing down at him from the shop windows. He did not want any of this. He had never wanted any of this. He spurned it and kicked it out of his way. The Tai silk suits, the Tag Heuer watches, the Chanel Store – they held nothing for him. No fascination. No charm. He swept by it all, his dyed black hair bouncing on his shoulders.

Yes, he could cope with the irony of his fate.

The Cosmopolitan was a basement club. There was a long flight of concrete stairs with a ragged red carpet, booze-stained and butt-burned, running all the way down, down, down to the basement. What he really needed was some friend, some happy helpful buddy, who'd keep him away from these places, not insist that he went inside them at two in the morning. *I insist, Neil. Check it out. You'll learn something. I insist* . . . And the concrete steps, which had no railing, were a trial because he'd lashed out at a few angry beers himself this evening, and he was pressed from behind by a group of sure-footed Australians, very loud and impatient –

"Move along, pal!"

"Stand aside, cobber!"

After the Swindon's breakdown he'd needed a few beers to

steady his nerves, but with just one bottle – his first alcohol in weeks – his mood had sunk, and the rest just rolled him deeper into maudlin introspection. What lay ahead? At four or five The Cosmopolitan would close and he'd face dawn on the streets, after a sleepless night. No way home to the Cheungs' at four or five a.m. Of course, they'd think it was all over, he was finished, done for, he'd slipped into the abyss somewhere; he lay face down in some stinking nullah, invisible there, black outfit and black hair fanned out on the oily black water. They'd have gone out for a celebratory meal on the remainder of his rent. Party time. And tomorrow they'd take in another waif or stray and start over.

All wrong, Mr. & Mrs. Cheung, Neil told himself. He'd be back. Oh yes. This very evening. The survivor.

The Cosmopolitan Club was long and low ceilinged, a converted storeroom or car park, now packed with good-timers. Neil bought another beer, leant against the bar and stared around. He felt vulnerable, ill at ease, and too drunk already. The low drum and bass mix seemed to come through the concrete all around, and it stirred him up. He couldn't help it. Rods of sound beat the air closer and closer to his face. His fancy Swindon's carrier bag was a hopeless encumbrance here. Completely the wrong thing.

When he finished his first bottle a couple of gays approached. Europeans with slick hair, tight shirts, tighter jeans. They were keen to buy him another beer, or to buy him something stronger, more expensive. He refused and paid for a second bottle himself, but they wouldn't take the hint.

"What're you reading there, friend?"

"A book."

"Yeah? What is it?"

"A book."

"Let's talk about it."

"No thanks."

They started a clever double act, warmly advising him of what went down here, of some of the grosser goings-on at The Cosmopolitan – "You might see some action later," says one enticingly; then says the other – "Last week a guy pulls down his pants and – "

Oh no. Not that. Neil got up and pushed through them to find a seat on his own away from the bar.

But he couldn't sit down anywhere in this place. There were only stools and to take a stool was too presumptuous. The seats were supported on pairs of pink and shapely plastic legs under short black mini-skirts. Some legs wore fishnet stockings. Some wore Lycra tights. The Lycra caught the slivers of light from the mirror-balls and stretched them into pointed fingers, slipping in and out the plastic thighs. When he looked down, everywhere he looked, the thighs were trapped under the overflowing buttocks of European, Australian and American men, in their Thai silk suits or linen chinos. Mainly older men, middle-aged men, old China hands. Where were Damian and the gang? Where was that ugly Geordie? Everywhere manly calves pegged open shapely female thighs. Soft deck-shoes were locked behind strong pink knees. It was as if an army of prosthetic limbs was on the run but everywhere was ambushed, caught and spun about, trapped beneath the copious buttocks of these men. And tucked deep and tight between those overflowing buttocks were arseholes that had farted and shat on long haul flights to and from every capital in the world. Arseholes that had shat in Hyatts all around Asia, broken wind in conference rooms scented with rosewater, in Macau and Shenzen and Guangzhou.

There was no sign of any karaoke yet. On a raised circular stage at the far end of the dance floor were three Filipino girls. Mischievous spotlights poked at them, seeking out breasts, buttocks, thighs, as they writhed in the car park dimness. The main dance floor was white and lit from underneath, like an ice-rink. It even had a chrome railing all around that you had to duck under or climb over. More mirror-balls shed loose change all over the dance floor. With his bag and beer Neil took his place at the opposite end to the dancing girls, where it wasn't so crowded.

The couples on the floor danced to anything at all. It didn't matter. Nothing mattered. The music was a horrible medley of hits and misses from the charts of the last forty years – the charts of Neil's whole life. They danced to Chubby Checker's *Let's Twist Again* one minute, to Herb Albert or Van McCoy the next, and then to the latest drum and bass mixes. Neil stood at the rail watching the men around him watching the dancers and the girls on stage, and he saw in the men's eyes fleeting slippages and seepages of feeling, glimpses of their own youth glancing off the mirror-balls in the discos of Birmingham, Melbourne, Rotterdam, Albuquerque . . .

He felt uncomfortable here but he knew perfectly well he was not out of place. In his black duds, his thin black jacket, his dyed black hair, he fitted in all right. Just another lonely guy looking for sex. But he did not like fitting in here. The music, with its insistent call to let go inhibition, added to his unease. There was something vibrant and tempting in this scene despite its sordidness. Many of the dancers, the non-professionals, were enjoying themselves, no question. His own music had never led to anything like this. It had always stopped well short, finger-picked to prim and careful arrangements, or strummed to a beat to which set steps could be taken, to which a zip-up boot could be steadily tapped, or a down-at-heel loafer gently turned, do-si-do.

Then the music faded out. Someone cut the current that operated the dancing girls and they stopped moving all of a piece. They came down from their stage with heads bowed, shaking their limbs and flicking their fingers and their flat feet, sloughing off their phoney dance moves. A DJ was speaking to the left but he was invisible behind a large party of Australians, swollen further by the group Neil had met outside, who'd pressed him on the steps. They were a sports team, greeting each other in low ducks and dummy passes, a blur of biceps, bullnecks and slapped shoulders. To Neil, they were far too happy, rude and drunk. Close up they didn't seem so young either. Too many neat moustaches hiding nasal hair. They were laughing now, tossing back their heads and stretching their bullnecks, laughing about nothing, about who had to buy the next round.

When three of them left for the bar Neil could see through to the DJ's platform the other side of the dance floor. The DJ was a longhair, a drug-user or addict, thin and sick. He spoke in English but with such a meld of accents – Dutch or German, South African, American – it was impossible to give him a nationality:

"Ladies and gentlemen," he drawled. "Boys and girls . . . "

With a twist of a dial the club filled with applause – for himself? A little intro-joke? No, it went on too long. It was more as if a superstar had just stepped out on the dance stage, but the stage remained white and empty. Then two vast LCD screens, either side of the dance floor, came hotly alive. The left screen carried the action. Here a carousel of stars really were stepping out on stage, one by one, each holding the screen for a few seconds only, each accompanied by the same surge of applause from the DJ's console. All the ancient kings and queens of popular entertainment were there, interspersed with new faces, and not so new faces. Each star took one step on stage, no more, one confident step into The Cosmopolitan tonight: Nat King Cole, Elvis, Aretha Franklin, Roy Orbison, Frank Sinatra, Gladys Night, George Michael, Neil Diamond, David Bowie, Sting, Robbie Williams – Neil watched them stepping out one by one at The Fillmore East, at The Coliseum, at The London Palladium, or wherever, into The

Cosmopolitan . . . A lucky few were there in consecutive shots, past and present. Mick Jagger leapt onto the stage in his early twenties, trussed up in a harlequin frock coat, wearing a joke top hat, and a moment later he stepped out onto a different stage, from behind a black curtain, in his mid-fifties, with gloomy eyes and saggy jowls. He got the same storm of applause on each occasion. The years had changed nothing.

On the screen to the right of the stage there was an image of an iced cake. The resemblance was so clear it must have been deliberate. The white dance stage on top of the icy white dance floor. A Chinese technician stepped up with a candle for the centre of the cake. His image came into focus on the right screen, at least twice life-size. The camera zoomed in and out as he set up the mike stand and fixed the cable and tested the mike with a few taps, no words.

"Ladies and gentlemen . . . serious business this morning . . ."

The DJ's voice drawled low again and faded out, as if he could hardly be bothered with what he uttered. That seemed to be his special voice act. He dipped his head to the mike, and as he spoke he let his voice drop and fade, and he turned away, as if to speak privately to someone about something more important.

"We're gonna have . . . we're gonna have . . . yeah . . . a good time . . . this morning . . ."

And this was serious business, Neil recognized, as the man said. The first performers were already lined up near the stage. He spotted others deep in the crowd, or pressed up against the railing. Striking costumes, dated hairstyles. But he couldn't see Iannis anywhere. There were a couple of black guys in the crowd, but they were close together, and they were dressed up in the style of The Four Tops – white flared suits and black cravats. There were just the two of them, though. Two Tops.

Naturally enough it had to be The King who started things off, but this was not just another Elvis spoof. He was a very young Chinese with a rich tenor voice and richer aspirations. His hair was long and slicked to one side. His glittering suit was a striking and expensive outfit, but far too loose for his skinny frame. The shoulder pads showed through. The trousers flapped about his thighs and the crotch hung badly, folded in by too many pleats. Still, he'd invested a good deal more than Neil had in his black duds from City One. Neil felt a twinge of anxiety about that. Chan had sent him along for another purpose, perhaps. Check it out. I insist. Take a look at the competition. See the new guys on the block. Young guys. Could be your kids. There's plenty out there waiting, friend.

While the boy sang, the real Elvis delivered the same song, *Blue Suede Shoes*, on the left hand screen. As if conscious of what he was up against, the boy faked a thick-lipped snarl here and there. The camera zoomed close, cropping the boy's mouth and nose and bad teeth – merciless. When he thrust out a foot and twisted his blue suede shoe on the white stage, as if stubbing out a cigarette, people began to titter. The next time he did it they laughed openly, hands coming away from their mouths. He tried to run with the joke and take control of it, twisting and stamping his tiny blue suede shoe again and again, with increasing violence, as the laughter faded all around him. The cameraman cut Elvis from the left screen and replaced him with a giant blow-up of the boy's pointed shoe – *That's all, folks!* – till the song died.

But when it was over he received generous applause. There was goodwill here in the audience, as well as good fun at the boy's expense.

"Not bad," one of the sports team conceded. "Wrong song, though."

"Nice voice, crap choice," someone agreed from behind.

The others drank, didn't comment. Their attention was already focused on the next act.

A big white girl was climbing up now, and on the opposite

screen Gladys Knight appeared. Gladys was looking down, preparing herself, during the trumpet intro of *Midnight Train to Georgia*. This white girl looked nervous from the start and nothing went well for her. Despite her operatic size her voice was thin and reedy, strangled by nervousness, and without the backing singers essential to the song she didn't have a hope. The image of Gladys on the other screen disappeared before she even hit the chorus. Neil understood the format now – the impersonators had to stay the distance, keep up with their star for the whole song. That was the challenge. White Gladys failed early and black Gladys quit the screen. Once you'd failed The Cosmopolitan did what it liked. Their turn. So now an image of a Chinese steam train appeared on the left screen, pulling in at what must have been Peking or Shanghai station in the 1950's. The train stopped there at the platform and blew off clouds of steam while the white girl sang *Midnight Train to Georgia*. A guard with a cap alighted from the engine and waved his flag to someone further down the carriages, then walked away, off the picture. The image of the train stayed there on its own, steam blowing across the platform, right to the end of the song, when it let out a shrill and painful whistle as the singer left the stage.

The next act changed the atmosphere completely.

A beautiful Chinese girl came on, dressed in a silvery sixties' slip that was little more than a nightdress. Her hair was cut in a long slashed fringe – the style made famous by Twiggie and Mary Quant. She delivered a flawless *Downtown*. Petula Clark had to stay on the opposite screen for the whole song. But Petula Clark was ignored, irrelevant. She'd been upstaged. Against her beautiful Chinese impersonator, Clark – in her mid-thirties, in dowdy black and white, 1965, couldn't compete. Not even with her one and only British hit. There was a discipline about this girl's performance that was unsettling to Neil. She already had what

Chan wanted: the looks, the voice and the talent too. She would be perfect for his idea, his Star Tributes programme. It was like watching a mirror image to Clark, except that she was so much prettier and sexier and more exotic. Neil began to see the angle of the market here, its fascination and challenge – taking hit songs and performances, known marketable quantities, and with a fresh young voice and body, upgrading what had gone before, and with a detachment that made it sexy and amusing. This girl's silvery slip stopped just below her underwear. Chan was right. This could really catch on, but only with that commitment to authenticity too. This wasn't just cover numbers.

Maybe this girl was the inspiration for his whole idea. Maybe she'd already turned Chan down. He felt relieved that Chan wasn't there, but then realized, of course, that perhaps he was.

There was thunderous applause for this girl, which rolled on and on even after she'd left the platform, and it seemed to show, to Neil's mind, a respect for her professionalism above all. Particularly given the acts that had gone before. But then the applause faltered, because there was some commotion at the base of the dancing stage. Maybe she'd been mobbed, torn down for her loveliness by some desperado. The camera slipped among the audience, roved around, searching for the action.

And suddenly there was Iannis, more or less on cue. The camera found him and fetched him up on screen. He was in a tussle at the foot of the steps, trying to pull the sleeve of his white tux away from another performer, a Chinese in a red suit with fin lapels. Iannis was pulling too hard, too violently, leaning back, hauling and stumbling, very drunk and out of order.

"Aw, not this guy . . ."

The Australian next to Neil was older and flabbier than his

teammates. His gut hung over the rail. Their coach, perhaps, gone to seed after too many bad results.

"Not Sammy . . . Not Sammy arsehole . . ."

He belched, then turned to speak to someone behind. But he caught Neil's stare on the way round and seemed challenged by it. His baggy, disappointed eyes widened and he took a drink from his bottle, rising to the challenge.

"Why'd they let him on, eh? . . . Hmmn?"

Neil shook his head, looked away. He didn't want a fight. Not about Iannis.

"I'm talking to you."

Neil didn't look back. "I don't know."

"Sammy arsehole."

Neil heard him belch again.

"Friend of yours?"

"Why'd they let him *in*?" someone said from behind. "He's the fuckin pits, man!"

On screen things were getting out of hand – compulsive viewing. The Chinese in red, in fin lapels, still wouldn't let go of Iannis's tux. Iannis had barged in, jumped the queue, wronged this fellow somehow. Suddenly Iannis chopped down hard, really hard, on the grip of the Chinese. The man let go and recoiled in pain. Iannis moved on, passing through easily now, a wave of cowards falling away before him. He stumbled up the steps to the stage, taking his time. The camera doubled back to capture the Chinese guy bent over his hand, genuinely hurt. He held out his broken hand to the cowards all around – 'Look what he did! Look what he did to my hand!'

The neat black figure of Sammy Davis Jnr. was on screen already. He was taking a drink on stage and smoking a cigarette, chatting soundlessly to his audience. It looked like a cabaret in Las Vegas. Caesar's Palace, maybe. High rollers all around. On the right screen Iannis was now on stage as well, struggling with the mike. He broke it from its clip but then lost balance and actually fell down, onto his backside, like a clown, with the cable round his feet.

A roar of laughter went up from the crowd. He untangled himself and stood up grinning, very pleased, and walked around the dance stage gathering in the applause.

Sammy Davis stubbed out his cigarette. The music for *Windmills of Your Mind* was firing up, a full orchestral sound.

Iannis tapped the mike. The taps came out loud and clear but he still did a check:

". . . One, two, three . . . . . . four, five, six . . ." He laughed. " . . . seven . . . eight . . ."

But no one else laughed at that.

"Anyone want a drink?" the coach asked, turning round again. "This guy's fuckin awful . . ."

A teammate cupped his hands:

"Sammy arsehole!"

Neil felt a shudder of shame. This was his lunch companion, the guy he knew, he talked to, and listened to, in McDonald's. Friend of yours?

"Fuckin jerk," said another. "Every fuckin week."

"That's Sammy Davis all right. Same colour and everything," said a fourth.

They all hated him, the whole team.

"Come on," said the coach. "I'll buy."

Iannis brought himself under control and came in with Sammy Davis Jnr., whose voice then dropped away, leaving the show to his impersonator. Sammy Davis even turned, eyes shut, at that very moment when he was muted, towards Iannis's screen, as if he were handing over to Iannis. A fluke in the timing.

Neil looked to the dangling, drugged-up DJ. He stood with his arms folded, grinning, enjoying this.

Sammy Davis's gestures were mild and subtle, leaving his voice to do the work, while Iannis was the other way. The idea of the Windmills had taken hold. When it came to the refrain he made a dumb and patronizing gesture, circling his finger round his ear, showing the motion of the windmills in your mind. At that moment, with a flick of a switch, he lost Sammy Davis. The screen went black and stayed black. Show over. But Iannis didn't care. He was carried away now, giving the song all he had to give. At the next refrain he whirled the mike around on its cable in wider and wider circles, imitating the sails of the windmill in his mind.

"Jerk!" someone shouted from the side, not far off.

Others joined in.

"Fuck off!"

"Get off!"

"What's he *doing*?"

The DJ seemed to be the only person entertained by the performance. He was smiling and shaking his head and covering his eyes as if it were all too much, but then Iannis let the mike slip too far and it hit the floor. The crash of that sound demanded action. The DJ cut the song and bent low to his mike -

"*Windmills of Your Mind*, ladies and gentlemen . . . Thank you . . . "

But Iannis hadn't finished. He wound the mike in and started to strut about his stage, rolling his shoulders to the rhythm of a drunken, breathy patter, delivered too close to the mike -

" . . . ratpack guys, those ratpack guys, swell guys, great guys, buddies on the razzle, on the dazzle, boozin' an' cruisin' an' loosin' in L.A. . . . "

"Yeah," the DJ interrupted at top volume, drowning Iannis with reverb in the low basement dive. "We know . . . We know . . . " He cut Iannis's mike, Iannis's oxygen.

Two bouncers were already on stage hustling Iannis, chasing him around in his white tux. When they caught him

Iannis gave up, didn't resist, and they dragged him off the stage facing backwards, facing his audience, grinning all the way.

Neil went to the toilets.

He hung up his Swindon's bag on the hand dryer button and took the last of the three stalls. The other two were occupied by the black performers in white suits, the Two Tops. They urinated in silence, standing very still and staring straight ahead, as if this were a part of their routine. The one next to Neil finished first. He washed his hands and went to the dryer. When he hit the button there was a loud smack as Neil's bag slipped off and fell to the floor. Neil could see it near his feet, deep in the piss-spray zone. He glanced back at the Top and scowled.

"Er . . . Excuse me? . . . . . . My bag?"

But the Top didn't say or do anything. When he caught Neil's eye he smiled and nodded Hello, as if nothing had happened, as if Neil hadn't said anything, the bag hadn't fallen. He just went on drying his hands. The noise, the bag in the piss-spray – he didn't notice. He just carried on.

"Come on," said the second Top from the door. He wasn't bothering to wash his hands. "We'll lose our slot."

The blower stopped. They left.

When Neil emerged from the smoke and noise of *The Cosmopolitan*, carrying his bare hardback tucked under his arm now, and drifted, after a couple of wrong turns, into the warm soft filth of Nathan Road, on Saturday morning at 3 a.m., he remembered, for no good reason, an early – the earliest? – Simon & Garfunkel album, entitled *Wednesday Morning, 3 a.m.* And remembering this album and its melodies, most of which had been folk melodies, stolen melodies, he had a sudden insight into how vulnerable even the grittiest vision is to romanticism. That title was meant to suggest the bleakness of early risings and departures, of chilly bus stations or railway platforms, the alienation of such places, from which the travelling musician, tired and empty, his guitar case heavy, was about to set forth. These were images with which Neil could well identify, images from his own life, in fact, but they were nothing like a match for how he felt here and now, at the roadside, after Iannis's performance, walking along aimlessly, homelessly, with the rest of the night ahead of him. Out of those other images sprang yet another song, another sweet and hopeful melody, such as *Homeward Bound*, and the chilly bus stations and railway platforms disappeared again.

Just at this moment, though, as he walked down Nathan Road with his book under his arm, beneath the tawdry lights and stony shadows, the alienation the street inspired was unmodifiable. It lasted only a few seconds but it made him stop and stand there by the kerb, in the slipstream of a night bus. And for those few seconds he entered the reality of the place, felt it without the relief of lyrics or melodies, endured it naked and alone in the way the animals of the city endured the heat, grit and pollution in their fur or feathers, night and day without respite, for all their brief lives.

He had never noticed until this moment how music protected him from his feelings. It didn't express his feelings. It displaced all reflection about what he really felt and thought. Concentration bubbled away in a froth of melody. And his own music – with roots, with heritage, serious music, he'd always thought – had served as the wellspring for his faith in the future too, and all his spurious optimism. Folk had to come back, he'd always said. It had always been there. These things were cyclical. Of course they were.

But cyclical in a way he hadn't noticed before.

And yet again, this Saturday morning at 3 a.m., as he drew in a warm lungful of exhaust from Nathan Road, there came another lucky strike. Maybe he too, Neil Atherton, could really make money here, in this fabulously wealthy town. Maybe. Who knows? Visiting the Cosmopolitan had been a good thing to do, a necessary thing to do. Chan had been right about that. Look at the hunger out there, he was saying. There was a crying need for something of a higher order. Like the Petula Clark girl. Not Elvis off-cue in the wrong shoes, not Two Tops instead of Four Tops – and with half the manners, too – but something much more professional, something that someone with his experience, so many years on stage, and his ability, could deliver.

There'd be problems, pitfalls, without doubt. Of course there would. And Chan was not to be trusted, certainly. But who knows what might come of this? And who cared, anyway, what he did?

He crossed the pavement to a bright shop window. It was a cheap jewellery store with roller chains over the glass. Again he scanned the shelves through the chains for Angel's earrings in white gold, knowing for certain that he wouldn't find them here, checking that he wouldn't. A rack of brightly coloured *Swatch* watches on a lonely shelf, the only watches left on display, declared the countdown to dawn. Several grim hours on the streets began here, at this store window. While he stared, from up the street he heard a motorcycle approach. It grew louder, and then, sure enough, just as he knew it would, it slowed and stopped right behind him. The engine idled, revved, and idled again. Neil turned. The policeman stared at him from his saddle, one leather boot on the kerb. Loudspeakers on the bike babbled in Cantonese above the idling engine. Whether they babbled to this particular policeman, demanding to know what he'd found out there, at 3.00 a.m., what he'd stopped to look at, this longhair in black with a book under his arm, or whether they spoke to some other patrol, was an open question. The policeman didn't respond to the radio and after a few more crackles the voice stopped. Quiet. Just the engine. He still stared at Neil.

And Neil stared back, his hands in his pockets. The policeman's face was hidden by the plastic shield of the helmet, and by the chin bracket and microphone. Neil smiled and looked as innocent as he could. He shrugged. Don't mind me, man. I'm no lawbreaker. Not me. Hell no. But still the policeman stared. Neil was conscious of the warm sea breeze coming up Nathan Road from the harbour. A gust tousled his long black hair, blew it across his face.

The policeman killed the engine.

Maybe a night in the cells, then, Neil thought. A free meal, free bed. Things were looking up again.

But the sudden silence after the engine died exposed another sound from down the street. It drew the policeman's attention and he stayed in the saddle. Neil stepped into the middle of the pavement to get a better view himself. There was a struggle sixty yards or so down the pavement. Shouts. Blows. Obscenities. Three men, all in evening dress. Two big Chinese with cropped hair, hotel doormen or nightclub bouncers, and a third man, short and black, in a white tuxedo.

"And don't come back!" shouted a bouncer, as Iannis stumbled away from them, down the street.

"And don't come back!" shouted the other.

"I won't come back!" Iannis retaliated, still walking backwards, tidying up his tux. "Me? Come back? Are you kidding? Go fuck yourselves!"

The policeman started his bike and pulled off down Nathan Road. Neil drifted away and found an underpass a few blocks up. He emerged just a stone's throw from Kowloon Park. Keeping to the shadows he started back towards the harbour. When he came parallel to the police bike he stopped. The bouncers had gone. Iannis was quiet and subdued now, finding documents in his wallet for the policeman. The policeman had his notebook out on his petrol tank and was taking down

Iannis's details. Neil stared across at Iannis, at his slumped frame under his dishevelled tux. He remembered how Iannis had put his hand on his shoulder that first time they met on the street outside Chan's block, that powerful squeeze, and the hunger in his eyes. And when they parted in McDonald's, that glimpse into his well of loneliness.

But Neil would not stop for Iannis. A few weeks ago, maybe, but not now. Iannis could look after Iannis. Neil didn't want to listen to it. Not any of it.

He carried on along the empty pavements, in the shadows, in the warm night, following the trail of the sea breeze to the harbour. But the incident stayed with him, bringing an indigestion of mixed-up feelings, unwelcome thoughts. Back at home total strangers had always felt they could bare their souls to him, that they had a right to share secrets they should not have shared and he didn't want to know about. Secrets of their married lives, their sexual failures and anxieties. On his lost circuit through the northern towns, in the tatty pubs, in the British Legion clubs, in the market towns and fenland towns – Good God! How far away was all that, now? – such talk seemed a part of the evening's obligations. Some wearisome confession come closing time from a disillusioned husband who'd had one too many. The sheepish approach, the squiffy smile, the spare drink, the unfunny, evasive opening remark, even while Neil put his guitar back in its case and packed away his bodhrán.

It was the songs that brought it out, of course, he thought, sinking further, with every tired step, into those dark memories. The ballads and twelve bar blues he played towards the end of the evening never failed, not in those places. Many men drifted in just for that, and skipped the protest folk completely. It was as if he tapped into some parochial well of sadness in those pubs and clubs, some water table of fenland tears. Oh, but there had been too much of it, he knew now, stopping at a corner, adjusting his slippery book under his arm, waiting for an empty taxi to crawl past, there had been far too much of that kind of talk in his life. He'd let in far too many of other people's sorrows, when he'd always had quite enough of his own. They assumed that because he was the free-wheeling musician on tour, he lived and loved without the ties that bound their own lives. But that was laughable. There had been no folk groupies on the East Midlands circuit. Not one. Not a single barmaid.

He slunk down another subway and came out at the esplanade in front of The InterContinental Hotel. There were some benches there, but most were occupied by young Chinese couples, kissing and fondling or talking in low voices. He chose a bench as far away from everyone else as he could and lay down on the seat, his knees up, using his jacket folded around his book as a pillow. It was actually very pleasant out here, with the soft breeze and the sound of the sea below. There were no stars, but the lights of the blocks and ads across the harbour were pretty enough and very bright. Sony. Citibank. Samsung . . . This was all far more appealing, and more comfortable, in fact, than his room at *The Languages and Translation Services* Ltd. Other noises, the chugging diesels of small harbour craft, the fans of the air conditioner units of the hotel behind, reassured rather than disturbed, and he soon found himself drifting into light and forgetful sleep.

Chapter Ten

Star Tributes

With his jacket slung over his shoulder, carrying a Seven Eleven bag for his book, a bottle of water and someone else's newspaper, Neil slouched into Chan's steamy café. It was 9.30 a.m. He'd been awake most of the night, drunk throughout the early hours, and since first light he'd been walking the streets. Half his lifetime ago he might have taken this in his stride, but not at forty-eight. His stride into the café was broken and uncertain, sleeplessness pulled at every limb. He'd tried to catnap on the Star Ferry, in the shade, as if he were a labouring Chinese. Back and forth he went. Useless. The journey was so short he only sipped at sleep, like an alcoholic sipping at some beloved cocktail.

The receptionists had sent him down here to the café. They had given him no lists of exotic destinations today. They'd told him Chan wanted to see him, and as soon as possible. It was urgent. They said Chan had left that message for Neil at their desk. Neil smiled wryly at this news from his tormentors, his harpies, but tired and weak as he was he couldn't stop some flap of hope lifting inside. He was too worn out to hold it down.

Chan's table down the corridor, by the fan, was already taken by someone just like Chan, eating what Chan ate, in the way Chan ate, head down over his food. Same age, same suit, same food. But it wasn't Chan. That was the house speciality – food like that for people like Chan. Chan himself, the only other customer in the place, was seated at a table by the window, tucking into his own meal, head down over his food. Neil was hungry, faint with hunger and fatigue, but not even the plain boiled rice tempted him in this place. Chan lifted his head a moment and waved him over, as he had before, still eating, and gestured to the seat opposite.

"Morning!" he said, between mouthfuls.

Neil draped his jacket over the back of the chair and rested his Seven Eleven bag on the floor, careful to keep the water bottle upright. He executed his movements slowly, making a show of his fatigue. He wanted to fold his arms on the collapsible table and set down his head and close his eyes. Chan's dishes would be upset – 'Hey! Neil! Watch out!' – and the table would fold and he'd fold with it to the floor, and that would be an end of things, for a while.

"You wanted to see me."

Chan nodded vigorously as he rolled a length of seaweed on his chopsticks. With his free hand he felt inside his suit jacket and withdrew a sheet of paper. He passed it over to Neil.

Neil took it but didn't look at it.

It would be fitting, he thought, wouldn't it, after such an awful night, beginning at 2.30 a.m. with Iannis as Sammy Davis Jnr. and finishing derelict on the Star Ferry at dawn, it would be fitting if the break came now. The date. The booking. There would be an order, a justice in that. Tired thoughts in Chan's breakfast café, softened by the steam and stench, opened, chopped, scraped, and boiled away by the two tall cooks.

He took the sheet of paper to himself, off the table, and then below the edge of the table, so that he could unfold it in secret, like a child.

It was not a fax from *The American Club* or *The Clearwater*

Bay Golf and Country Club. On the paper were just a few lines in capitals. Lazy man's typing, big and bold.

STAR TRIBUTES CONCEPT

CABARET CONCEPT

VARIETY = TRIBUTES + COMEDY + STRIPTEASE + MAGIC?
ALL BIG NAMES
AUTHENTICITY
TARIFFS = BAR TARIFFS + DINNER TARIFFS + TICKET TARIFFS?
RIGHTS = TV RIGHTS + MTV RIGHTS?

Oh, Mr. Chan. Please . . . please, please, please . . .

He watched Chan finishing his rice. Each and every grain this starchy morning.

"Let me take you through it," he said, setting his chopsticks in a neat bridge on his empty rice bowl.

Neil folded the paper and set it aside on the table with weak and fluttering fingers. The disappointment was as heavy in his bowels as several kilograms of that clumpy boiled rice. He couldn't move for the weight of it. TARIFFS = BAR TARIFFS + DINNER TARIFFS + TICKET TARIFFS? He thought the collapsible chair would collapse under the weight of disappointment inside him. Outside the steamy window, beneath the trays of bubbling meat on their heated shelves, there was nothing to see but pairs of legs in suits or tights, or bare pairs of female legs, on their way here and there – but on their way somewhere! – and beyond, whenever there was a break in the pedestrian rush, there were the red flanks of taxis or the black polished flanks of hotel limousines, crawling by beyond the glass. All going somewhere.

"Variety," Chan began.

+ STRIPTEASE + MAGIC?

"Not just singing. The idea has grown somewhat, like I said. All kinds of acts. Comedy, certainly. Striptease, certainly. Magic, possibly – depends on the artist. Lots of acts, but with this difference. They're all star turns. All the performers are big names. I mean, big names. Hey – are you listening?"

Neil turned from the window and faced Chan. The bald brown eyes. The hair-flip, laddered again today, with the weight of humidity in the café.

"I'm listening."

"You were right about authenticity all along. From the start. I'll hand you that. You come on stage *as* Neil Diamond."

Why did Chan keep backing down and backing up on this issue? This sacred issue of authenticity. And suddenly Neil saw it. Suddenly he had it. He understood what was wrong with Chan, and therefore with whatever took place between them. He understood where that cultural failure of the imagination came from. It was simple, really. Chan had no sense at all – absolutely none, that is – of his own ridiculousness. It was a total blind spot. Neil, as an Englishman, had been born and bred on sneers and jeers, scorn and ridicule. His sensibility had been tempered in a completely different fire. Not the fire of earnest endeavour, the fire of the will, the fire of striving for success at whatever personal cost. No no no. The other fire. The fire of failure, mockery and humiliation.

"You do the research, you make the whole thing true to life, so that the audience respects your professionalism. Why? Because it's the audience who are in control here – that's what's new. What they say goes. They don't just get the songs, the star has to do whatever they want."

"Striptease?"

"Why not?"

Why not? I'll tell you why not, Mr Chan, because personally I have no desire whatever to take off my clothes and strut about like -

"You can have Marilyn Monroe, Madonna, Marlene Dietrich – anyone – anyone you like. Any lady, any man, any boy, any girl – any time, any place, anywhere, it's a wonderful world they can share. All right? You ready for this?"

"I'm ready."

"Okay. Here it is. Here we go. The act begins with the songs – warm people up, set the tone – then some jokes, patter, audience participation, maybe. Maybe not. But the audience want to see Marilyn or Madonna like they've never seen her before. They've been given flashes on films and tv – bare navels, slit skirts, flashes of thigh, bits of breast – but now they can see more, have more, much more. They call the shots. Male strips too. Presley, for example. British stars – Tom Jones, Mick Jagger, Humperdink, Cliff Richard, Elton John, whoever. And we've got comedy or magic to cool everybody off. We've got Bill Cosby, Robin Williams, Anthony Newley. He's very big here, Tony Newley. Every year he stops at The Excelsior Hotel for a whole fortnight. You can have your stars from any era. We've got them all. Anyone you like. The nostalgia ticket. All worked out in the publicity. You can go for a particular generation. You can have Bob Hope and Bing Crosby. Maybe doing bits out of old films, live on stage. Frank Sinatra, Sammy Davis, Dean Martin – the ratpack again. Shirley Maclaine. The old movies, maybe. DVD backdrops in black and white. Bob and Bing in Road to Morocco. Road to Rio. Road to Mandalay. You can have old and new, mix them up, whatever you want. Michael Jackson and Fred Astaire. The living and the dead. That's what it's all about – having anyone you like impersonated for your personal entertainment. Star Tributes. Some of these acts will do lots, others won't. That's okay. Horses for courses – "

Neil had never heard Chan expounding one of his own ideas. It was extraordinary to listen to. It was hypnotic.

" – we have adult tastes, we have family tastes. With some acts anything can happen. Presley comes on, sings a couple of songs, dances with a woman from the audience. Someone shouts for him to strip off. Music changes. He strips off. No questions asked. You do what you want with the stars. That's what's new. You have more fun that way, much, much more fun – " a smile and a shake of the head at this – "so it'll end up more fun going to a Star Tributes evening and seeing an impersonator than it is seeing the real star! Can you imagine? Think of that. But only if the authenticity is there. That's the key. Otherwise it flops. It dives. Washout. If the authenticity is right the audience gets to see the stars they never had the chance to see, like Marilyn, but with no clothes on. It can't miss. It really can't."

What he was talking about was outrageous. It wasn't Star Tributes, it was Star Travesties, but to Chan it was just a business venture.

It can't miss.

Ah, but it could miss, Mr. Chan. It could. Chan should have a white stick.

Next he described the attractions in commercial terms. There was no capital outlay. All overheads could be hired. There were plenty of spin-off opportunities, rip-off opportunities. A percentage on bar takings and dinner takings as well as door money, bribes. If they discovered some real talent there might be cable tv rights, MTV rights. The show was movable. The cabaret could go from city to city for the price of the plane tickets. A very talented impersonator could do maybe three or four different acts – one economy plane ticket for four different stars! . . . Chan had already compiled his first line-up. It included Neil Diamond, of course.

Neil was too tired to object or concur. Too many kilograms

of disappointment weighed him down. The immovable kilograms. But they were both a little hunched now over the table, head to head, and there was agreement enough in that. Neil pointed a crooked finger at the typed sheet.

"Magic?"

"Magic could be there." Chan nodded. "Magic could be in there. Definitely." His impenetrable earnestness. "Variety. Cabaret. Tariffs on the dinner, the wine, the bar." What came next shocked Neil, but he was more shocked still by Chan's disinterested attitude. "Here's another angle." He glanced out the steamy window, at the army of legs going here and there but somewhere, then bent closer, lowered his voice: "The men and women in the songs are on stage too." Neil could smell his breath: the meat, chilli and garlic. "They perform as well. Tom Jones takes Delilah on. Humperdink takes on that woman from the last waltz. You have Cracklin Rosie and Sweet Caroline come on stage with you, one on each arm. If the audience want them to strip off, they strip off. If they want them to perform lewd acts, they perform lewd acts. Cracklin' Rosie goes down while you sing *Cracklin' Rosie.*" Chan raised his eyebrows. "Cracklin' Rosie cracklin' away down there. How about that? Would you like that? Then you bend the other way and Sweet Caroline licks you out while you're singing *Sweet Caroline*. How sweet is that? Would you like that?"

Neil replied softly to Chan, but with a certainty that made his voice rise on the swell of feeling beneath, but rise in such a way that his definitive statement came out as a lilting question: "I wouldn't be prepared to do those things?" He cleared his throat.

"You wouldn't?"

"I wouldn't perform lewd acts, no."

"Well, we'll see about that. You need time to get used to the idea, that's all."

They both sat back as one of the tall cooks, the same as last time, cleared away Chan's dishes, wiped his place, his half of the tiny table.

From inside his jacket Chan pulled a second sheet of folded paper. Out of nowhere. Chan himself was a magician. Fully paid-up member of the Magic Circle. That came next.

Neil took the paper. It was a list of names this time. They weren't in capitals and the font was so small he had to squint to read them. His eyes were going. Too many bad nights staring up at the ancient ceiling fan and the dusty posters of Paris, Rome and Madrid. Oh, far too many nights like that. But how many yet to come? He was fifty years old in little more than a year. Would he live that long? Watching the ceiling fan. Paris, Rome, Madrid. Or roaming Hong Kong at dawn. Bending the other way for Sweet Caroline.

Would Angel like that? Her boss? Her friends?

Damian and Geordie would love it.

Neil scanned Chan's inaugural line-up. Neil Diamond had some strange bedfellows here.

Bassey, Shirley
Bennett, Tony
Bowie, David
Clapton, Eric
Clark, Petula
Collins, Phil
De Burgh, Chris
Denver, John
Diamond, Neil
Dylan, Bob
Humperdink, Englebert
Jackson, Michael
Jackson, Janet
Jones, Tom

Madonna, Madonna
Sinatra, Frank
Sting, Sting

"There are some surprises here . . ."
Chan didn't reply.
"No Dean Martin? . . . No Sammy Davis Junior? . . ."
Neil noticed that for the first time he had begun to converse on equal terms with Elbert Chan. Perhaps it was something to do with the café, being away from Chan's territory and the twittering receptionists, or something to do with being so tired, maybe, with all his defences down. Whatever its cause, the change was for the better, and he began to feel more confident, more engaged now that he could see how seriously Chan was taking the whole business, even if he didn't care for some of the new angles. He began to feel lucky again. Lucky that he hadn't bought Angel's plane ticket and quit with his tail between his legs. But the good feeling was checked by the list Chan had given him, which he kept scanning up and down. Why these stars in particular? They seemed such an unlikely bunch for any kind of cabaret. And there were so many men.

Neil had a sudden inspiration. "We could have a Sixties' Night. People like Petula Clark, Dusty Springfield, Helen Shapiro, Sandy Shaw, Marianne Faithfull. There was an innocence about those starlets. The cabaret could bring that back."

"Both yes and no," Chan said, as if the idea were old hat. "The lure of that kind of show would be to revisit those stars from the point of view of the nineties' man. To strip them off, rip them off, fuck them on stage."

Neil was about to protest. For him personally this would not have been the lure of such a show at all: he found the idea of these virginal icons being torn down highly offensive. But he didn't protest, because on a moment's reflection he discovered that there was an allure, a vindictive allure, in stripping off the mini-skirts of these starlets. In such a British way they had seemed so frigid and aloof. Closer to home, there was a far more powerful allure in the idea of watching Petula Clark pulling off her silvery slip, lifting it over her head, dishevelling her lovely hair. Who knows what tight, cute, cut-away underwear lay beneath that silver slip.

"I saw Petula Clark last night. At The Cosmopolitan."

Chan nodded. He knew, of course. "I know that act." He sighed, looked away, seemed pained by the reference . . . If only . . . Then he turned back to Neil, to what he had. Neil felt himself measured – the middle-aged, English folk musician, against the lovely, young, Chinese Petula Clark. Chan frowned, folded his hands in front of him, looked down at the table, then to the window. "She's not interested," he said to the window. "Not yet, anyway. She's had lots of offers. She's not for sale." He turned back to Neil, remembering something. "You saw Iannis?"

Neil nodded. "Yup."

"And?"

Could all that be only seven hours away? Sammy arsehole? Whirling the mike about? The difference between night and day. The windmills of your mind.

"I liked the finale best."

Chan began to wrap up the meeting. "Don't think that I'm going to call my managers. I'm not. Like I said, we must have authenticity. You have to *be* Neil Diamond. You have to know his material, his background, his life, his childhood even – everything that's available. You build your stage persona out of that. If you can't do it I'll look elsewhere. I've got to get there first with the right people. This idea's too good, too hot, too close. It's got to be right first time out."

Despite his weariness Neil suddenly found himself panicking, scrambling for something to say. Anything. He couldn't lose out now, not at this stage! He had to get on board, with Petula Clark, with *Cracklin' Rosie.*

"How long have I got?"

"One week."

"I don't need a week. I'm ready."

"You need a week. It's got to be perfect. I want to roll with this. Really roll. Make money. Real money. Not fees. Not wages. Not coins, counters, coupons. Real money. Come to the office next Saturday, first thing. Bring all your kit."

For the rest of that week, every morning, Neil promised himself he would buy a pillow and get his bedding arrangements organized once and for all. He awoke with a crick in his neck that took longer to ease day by day. But once on the street he was too distracted, and come the evening he felt too broke and exhausted to do anything about his bedding arrangements. He told himself he'd be out of *The Languages and Translation Services* Ltd. very soon, for better or worse. The countdown had started, either way. For sure. He felt it in his soul. It was a long, hard, and punishing week. With no one to talk to, as the meandering days dragged by, his spirit sank again, and despite Chan's promises and his sublime confidence suspicions festered. About Chan, about everyone.

But nights were the worst.

His return to *The Languages and Translation Services Ltd.* had taken the Cheungs by surprise. Though they said nothing, they looked at him differently. Their eyes followed him rather than avoided him. They were watching him now, and waiting. He began to suspect they actually lived on the premises, down some corridor where he'd never trespassed. Perhaps they meant to do him harm, precipitate disaster. At night he lay on the classroom floor studying the sounds from behind every wall, of mechanical and human movement. He listened for voices, whispers, but heard none. Just a ceaseless concatenation of lift-shaft clangs, door bangs, furniture scrapes, wall switches going on and off, cisterns emptying, and in any odd moment of quiet, a peculiar dry sound very near at hand, a sound like that of a pencil being dropped on the wooden floor, not once but two or three times, as if deliberately, only a foot or so from his face, from his eyes. What was that?

He had met the elderly Mrs. Cheung only once at night, on the way to the toilet in the early hours, but she had been in evening dress on that occasion, wearing an elegant cheoungsam, and she had smelled strongly of alcohol. She might have returned to the premises after a Chinese banquet for any number of drunken reasons. Perhaps she'd come to seduce him . . .

During that week insomnia worsened night by night, wearing away at his mental equilibrium. He never slept more than four hours at a stretch. His sleep invariably began with dreams of relief from present fears, with images of an unearthly state of innocence back in England, in the green and clear skied landscapes of the East Midlands, images of fields and churches, wolds and fens. Certain features always recurred in these dreams. That lightness and greenness was always there to begin with, then there was a clouding and darkening, a subsiding into images of obscure interiors. In particular, the cellar bars of so many British Legion clubs, which took on a heavy and inevitable symbolism. In one dream, suffused with feelings of dread and anxiety, instead of the shadowy cellar and the drunken faces, the lopsided grins, turning to greet him as he lugged in his viola, bodhrán and guitar cases, he discovered only darkness and emptiness and a smell of loam. The dream always ended with him faltering and stumbling, his instrument cases tumbling before him as he fell to a floor of hard and dusty earth.

His room had never been cleaned or aired for him at any time. Having communicated in broken English to begin with, Mr. Cheung had set up a language barrier to any further assistance or obligation on his part. He scowled uncomprehendingly whenever Neil approached him with a question. He refused to understand Neil's exaggerated mimes for a broom and a dustpan and brush. He shook his head and walked away. It had been still less use appealing to Mrs. Cheung. She never spoke to him in English at all. She always smiled politely and passed by.

But not now. Now she stopped in the corridor and her eyes followed him, and so did Mr. Cheung's – sometimes both of them together – and that affected morale. There was an assumption that, yes, he would soon be off their property, and on their terms, leaving them some rent in hand. This tenancy was the last one a creature negotiated before stepping into a humid and fetid oblivion, and somehow his dark Indian guide from the foyer of Chungking Mansions must have seen that he was ready for it, detected it in the way he stopped and rested his suitcase on the fake marble of the Chungking foyer.

His Rolex had stopped working, though he still wore it at all times. The last few nights of that week he lay awake in his windowless cell for hour upon hour with no idea of the time, no dawn to wait for. If he did fall asleep he awoke moments later in a seizure of panic – his sleeping bag was overrun with cockroaches, silverfish, centipedes, all manner of insect life. The only way to allay these fears was to get up, put on the light and turn his sleeping bag inside out. He never found anything. There were often cockroaches, and very large ones, around the skirting of the room, but they never troubled him. They kept themselves to themselves.

So he lay down again, the bare light blazing above him. With nothing else to look at he stared wide-eyed at the green and dusty posters of European capitals, his eyes flicking from

Paris to Rome, to Madrid, to Rome, to Paris, on an endless circuitous tour. Eventually the knock came from Mrs. Cheung and he would get up, with a crick in his neck, already tired out, to begin his day walking the clammy streets.

But the final night he spent in mellower mood.

His thoughts were drawn up by the swirl of the antique ceiling fan, and spread about until they sank into the soft sediment of his past. You never knew what you'd got till it was gone, as Neil Diamond might have put it. And, inevitably, into these thoughts crept reflections on his marriage. The truth was, he could admit it now, there had been nothing left between them. He couldn't help thinking she'd been right to finish it when she did, and in the way she did. Decisively. The clean break. He even admitted to himself that she deserved another chance with someone else. He imagined some ambitious man in mid-career who'd worked as hard as she had, who'd taken the risks, seen off the competition, found the plum job – hard fought for and won – all of that . . .

In this strange, forgiving mood, he didn't grudge her one jot of happiness. He remembered without regret.

"You've always been very kind, Neil," she had told him quietly, sincerely, during their final conversation, over their valedictory breakfast.

No croissants or pastries that morning. They were both on the sofa with their coffee. He sat leaning forward, his cup and saucer in his hands, while she sat back in the corner of the sofa, at a distance, hands in her lap, her bare feet tucked beneath her, her coffee untouched, placed on the sofa arm. His suitcase was next to the glass coffee table. When she said that to him he leant further forward and put his coffee cup aside. He hadn't drunk any coffee either. There was a film of milky skin on the surface. He was all set to go. To leave her. To leave her apartment . . . All his bags were packed, he was ready to go, and already he was so lonesome he could die, but he wasn't, as she supposed, catching any jet plane . . . His 'things' – all the Neil Diamond paraphernalia – were hidden away in a folded shopping bag in his lap. He was very still and silent, leaning forward on the sofa. He was waiting for a gesture from her, a physical gesture, no more words. But it didn't come. She kept her precious distance. More than anything in the world just then he'd wanted her to put her hand on his back, just to rest her hand on his back. He needed that human contact. Nothing more. But she hadn't done that. She would not touch him. "You've always been very kind, Neil." Nothing else. No physical gesture at all.

If one had a calling in life, even as modest as his, then it made one, in the eyes of the world, congenitally irresponsible – he had always known that and he had always made it plain from the very start he was not cut out for a proper job, mortgage, kids and all the rest of it. No doubt she would find that new partner soon, the mid-career man, if she had not already done so. Perhaps they would have children. Why not? For her there was still time.

Under the swirling fan, in this strange and mellow mood, Neil did not find even this idea, of Angel having a child by another man, particularly provoking. He was no dog in the manger. And from these big-hearted ruminations he turned back to his musical career, and to his slow retreat into the wings of life.

He set aside any feelings of bitterness about the way things had panned out, and concentrated instead on the good times, the highlights of his career. Not only the performances themselves but life on the road, nights on the road, in the back of the van, or driving the van all through the night, all over England. Camping out, sometimes. Always for the summer solstice. June 22nd. And the hours and hours of post-concert talk with his folk brotherhood and sisterhood. The arguments, the left-wing rants and the cut and thrust of ideologies, as they set the world to rights over beer, cigarettes and cheap red wine. He heard them again, old friends, old voices from the past, sometimes soft, sometimes loud, rambling on, drunken quarrellers and morallers, bickering over a camp fire in the wilderness somewhere, unheard by and unknown to anybody else.

Chapter Eleven

A Date, a Booking

"We're on our way," Chan said, first thing Saturday morning. He was glancing over a fax. "We have a date, we have a booking."

Neil was dumbstruck. This news had been so long looked forward to, and this last week had been such hell, and suddenly here it was, the break, just like that, first thing Saturday morning. The opening. His own chance. Long sought for, hard fought for, and won.

"We're at The Mariners' Club in two weeks' time. Next Saturday week."

The Mariners' Club? Neil had only heard The Mariners' Club mentioned in connection with Iannis's disastrous début. Wasn't this one of 'the other clubs' that he'd been told so many times to 'forget about'? An audience of sailors and their escorts, Chan had said.

Sailors.

"The Mariners' Club?"

Chan cocked his head with enviable ease. "Down here in Tsim Sha Tsui . . . You must have seen it. Off Chatham Road."

"Isn't that where Iannis played?"

"That's right. It's where Iannis played."

Typically Chan offered nothing more on that coincidence. To pursue that connection would be, in one of his favourite phrases, mere "failure talk".

"You're second on a two part bill. The main event is a male voice choir." He read from the fax. "'*Dai Aspora. The Only Welsh Male Voice Choir in the Far East!*'" Chan chuckled at that, then looked up smiling. "Don't panic. It's lightweight. Something for the sailors. They have a regular spot at The Mariners'."

"Have you seen them?"

"Yes."

"And?"

Chan shrugged. "It's a choir. They stand on benches."

"But what do they sing?"

Chan sighed and knitted his brows, trying to remember. "Old time stuff. Broadway hits. Oklahoma, South Pacific, Desert Song, Paint My Wagon – "

"Paint Your Wagon."

"Whatever . . . And hymns."

"Hymns?"

"A few hymns."

"They sound awful."

"Why?"

"Disastrous."

It was Neil's second, impulsive expression of doubt. The cartoon frown appeared again on Chan's brow, but only two furrows this time. He looked at the fax, then directly at Neil.

"What makes you say that?"

Neil couldn't answer for a moment. It was obvious, plain as day.

"They've been around for years. They're nothing to worry about. There are lots of expat things like this. There's a barbershop quartet plays The American Club every month. How do you think *Dai Aspora* feel about playing before a Neil Diamond tribute?"

Again, Neil had no answer. He was buffeted between

feelings of elation and fathomless disappointment.

"They won't give a damn. All part of the fun. They're there to entertain. So are you. It's variety night."

The crick in his neck eased suddenly and Neil adjusted his position in the rattan armchair, luxuriating in a new freedom of movement. Surely he could relax now, at last, and allow some excitement to flow. He had a date, a booking. Wherever and with whomever it was. He had a break. From here he could prove himself. He just needed this first opening then he'd soar away. Up, up and away. Off the streets. He'd fly the Cheungs' coop. He leant forward and brushed some imaginary dust from the knees of his black denims. Every night since he'd bought them, whether he'd worn the outfit or not, he'd laid out these denims, and his black shirt and black jacket, flat on the Formica table in the classroom at *The Languages and Translation Services Ltd*. It was a nightly ritual. There was a reverence to it, a gathering together of hopes and fears in the re-laying of creases. Now he felt such observance had been rewarded.

"I want to talk about publicity, then I want to talk about preparation for the act," Chan said, setting aside the fax and getting down to business. "We'll run off some flyers through my printing company. Leave that with me. I'll need to – "

"What have you got in mind for those flyers?" Neil wanted in on every detail.

Chan opened the middle drawer of his desk and took out some of the CDs Neil had left behind weeks ago.

"I thought we'd blow up some of these . . ." He gazed absently at a few covers. "I did a sketch somewhere . . ." Without producing the sketch or making clear which covers he'd chosen, Chan put Neil's CDs back and closed the drawer. "But there are two things I need to discuss with you. Firstly, what title to give the act. That'll go on the flyer. Very important. Secondly, payment for the print job. That's going to include a trip to Macau, by Jetfoil – about $500. I'll have to go myself. No one else can do it. I won't charge over the fare, but altogether the publicity will cost you around $1500, and I'll need that in advance. Before the show."

Er, hold on a minute now . . .

He was going to have to pay Chan? In advance? For the second time this interview, but for entirely different reasons, Neil was utterly dumbfounded. He was going to have to pay Chan? Pay for his own publicity flyers? When was Chan going to pay for anything? All he'd done so far was steal his CDs! So was this a scam after all? Was it some weird and wonderful long-tailed sting – Sting, Sting – to take him for $1500 – or more, maybe, further along the road? Next there'd be $2000 for the band, up front, in advance, before the show. And a few more CDs – just a box set, please, Mr. Atherton. That'll do nicely. Elbert Chan was making it up as he went along. ***Castles in the air, pal! Pure bull!*** Neil could see Iannis's stubby black finger tapping the fax on the desk – *That fax is all about travel bookings, pal. It's about gym equipment. It's the invoice for Bali Break and Phuket Package*. A con, a scam. From the start. Taken, duped, gulled. *It's your own Bali Bust, Ball Breaker, Fuckwit Package, pal, bespoke tailored by Elbert Chan! Paint his wagon, pal! Go on! Hahaha!*

No thanks, Mr. Chan. Paint your own fucking wagon.

"Er . . . Why don't you pay for the publicity, Mr. Chan?"

"This is your show."

"But you're setting me up. You're my agent. You've made the booking."

"None of which I've charged for. As soon as you collect your fee I'm going to need reimbursement. The Mariners' will pay four thousand five – three for you and fifteen hundred for the band. That's for two forty-five minute sets. If things go well we'll talk about a contract."

That was too smooth. He wasn't making that up. $3000 for

his first night? About £250? For two forty-five minute sets? This changed everything. Yet somehow Neil had to skirt around the fact that he simply could not pay for the publicity flyers. Chan would have to take that out of the $3000. Only half left, before he paid off Chan. But he gave a dismissive nod now to Chan's concerns about reimbursement: "You'll get your publicity money. No problem. Where's this sketch? What about the title?"

Chan squeezed back again and opened his middle drawer and rummaged around in there. "I've told The Mariners' this is part of a Star Tributes programme, so that will be there somewhere . . ." The sketch wasn't in the drawer. Chan patted his jacket and whipped it from his inside pocket. Another folded sheet of A4. Chan the magician.

"See what you think. Titles overleaf."

All these bits of A4, filched discards from the printer tray, whipped from his inside pocket . . . Neil unfolded the paper. At first sight the sketch looked like nothing more than some doodlings made during a boring telephone call. Perhaps that's what it was, in fact. There were several crude distortions of Neil Diamond in the poses he struck on the CD covers. Taking up most of the page was the one of the superstar as troubadour at the roadside with his guitar. The figure was clear and the road behind had a rough perspective, but the face of Neil Diamond himself, at the very centre of the flyer, was completely missing. It was just a stark oval void with a few strikes of hair. An egg head. Bald as a coot. Worse was a faceless cameo in the corner where the performer, guitar in hand, pelvis thrust forward, head tossed back, played to a crowd of faceless and even headless figures. Neil found all the missing heads and faces alarming. The sketch had a macabre character. It was as easy to imagine the audience screaming at a scaffold or guillotine, baying for blood, as swinging along.

For goodness' sake, they could do better than this, surely.

With some foreboding Neil turned over the page to Chan's titles:

Star Tributes

1. 'Star Tributes' Presents 'A Tribute to Neil Diamond'.

Neil reread that, rubbing his brow. Then he read the rest.

2. Neil Diamond Impersonator In Concert.
3. Cracklin' Rosie Wouldn't Know The Difference!
4. Sweet Caroline Wouldn't Know The Difference!!
5. I am. I said. Neil Diamond . . .
6. Yours Forever. Neil Diamond . . .
7. Yours very truly. Neil Diamond . . .
8. Yours sincerely. Neil Diamond . . .
9. Would The Real Neil Diamond Please Stand Up. Please?

At first some of these struck Neil as just ridiculous, but the longer he stared at them and imagined them splattered across a flyer, the more credible they became. The one he had most misgivings about was number two. The word 'impersonator' set the wrong tone completely. Both pompous and apologetic. He plumped for the last one but insisted Chan take out that second *Please.* He also indicated that he would like either number three or four – but not both, thanks – to be somewhere near the bottom of the flyer, as a signing off, set at an angle, to lighten the tone. The title 'Star Tributes' right at the top was fine and sufficient to indicate the nature of the evening.

Chan stole a sheet of unused A4 from the printer tray and noted down Neil's preferences. He folded the paper, job done, and rested his biro on top.

"The question of authenticity," he resumed, dragging over his Compaq. "I've been doing some background research."

The laptop was already switched on and the LCD threw a blue and ghoulish light onto Chan's face, making it look like the empty oval from his flyer. "There's a mass of stuff on the internet. Did you know there are half a dozen Neil Diamond impersonators in America, each with his own website?" Some urgent bleeps came from the Compaq as he downloaded the files of these impersonators. Actually, Neil knew all about the competition – American, Australian and European. He'd studied it in some detail, particularly those American sites, in the Kowloon Public Library. Now he imagined these other impersonators jockeying for access, falling over each other in their wigs and sequins to sell themselves to Elbert Chan on-line. Chan talked down to this motley crew as he downloaded their files. "There's this fellow here has a nightclub in L.A. Tony Laprisco. It's all he does. He's top of the bill four times a week! The pictures are remarkable. You wouldn't know the difference. Cracklin' Rosie wouldn't know the difference . . ." Chan chuckled into the screen at this self-serving joke. He was certainly in a buoyant mood this Saturday morning. "How old are you again?"

"Forty-eight."

"Laprisco looks mid-thirties at most. He's the business. Impressive. Really impressive. He could teach you a thing or two."

Neil shifted uneasily at that glib, invidious comparison, and the rattan armchair creaked in sympathy. Chan kept scrolling.

"You know how old Neil Diamond really is?"

"Fifty-seven."

"Ten out of ten."

Chan seemed to have forgotten they had covered this ground, but Neil let that pass. He knew he'd done his homework more thoroughly than Chan could possibly imagine. He knew all those internet pages, all about Tony Laprisco and *The Café Diamond* in Los Angeles. He was a master of all that information. Much of the material on the official Diamond website he knew by heart. Authenticity is everything. He'd always said that.

"So what have you got hold of so far?"

Neil dusted his black denims again.

"I know everything about that man. That's everything. What I don't know isn't worth knowing."

"About Tony Laprisco?"

"About Neil Diamond *and* Tony Laprisco, if you want. And all the rest. The whole pack. The also-rans."

"Really?" Chan looked up from the screen. He seemed amused by the quiet authority in Neil's voice. Neil risked a modest smile himself. The booking at The Mariners' Club had lifted a weight off Chan's shoulders too, no doubt about it. He was so buoyant and confident now, almost excited, and not at all prickly and impatient, as he usually was after just a couple of minutes. There was almost a camaraderie between them now, as if they were in this together at last. They seemed to have moved on from the endless sparring and confrontation of the other meetings.

Neil continued. "I downloaded all that stuff at home ages ago, and I've done plenty of background reading besides." When he said that, Neil enjoyed the idea that Chan would think he spent his days lazing around 'at home', in his apartment somewhere, browsing the web, reading in his study or living room, drinking endless cups of coffee . . . The reality was the public Library, or more recently Tom Lee's music superstore in Cameron Road, where he'd been browsing various Neil Diamond song books. He'd whiled away many a happy hour at Tom Lee's, going through anthologies, memorising songs, reading prefaces written by Neil Diamond, and comments made by other popular music artists about Diamond's 'work'. He'd made his written notes in a spiral flip-pad, flipping over page after page of the chunky pad.

When he'd finished he'd tucked his notes away in his back pocket and pored over his research in McDonald's, flipping back through his notes and quotes, wetting his thumb, learning all the new material by heart. That was the reality. No comfy apartment high in the New Territories. Chan just didn't understand. Didn't get half of it. He didn't know that his very own office, this grubby little room where they sat right now, was, for Neil, like a 'You Are Here' sign on a tourist street map. He spent his life walking between the numbered points of Places to Visit – *The Languages and Translation Services Ltd.*, McDonald's, Kowloon Public Library, Ocean Terminal Car Park, Tom Lee's, the Star Ferry – to and from this worn through 'You Are Here' hole in the middle of the map. You Are Right Here. Nowhere Else. That's All. That's It. That's Your Life.

"Test me," said Neil.

Chan was looking for his biro to make another note but it had rolled away somewhere, off the folded paper. He searched his desk, the middle drawer again. Couldn't find it. "I might do that sometime . . ."

"Do it now. Test me. Go ahead. Go right ahead."

Chan quit his search and looked up at Neil.

"Are you kidding?"

"Test me."

There was more at stake here than what the challenge might expose.

"Okay," Chan said. He went back to the Compaq and scrolled through his files. "You asked for it . . . I have a stack of stuff here I've put together. Let's go back to the *Stones* interview, nineteen seventy-one . . . Read it?"

"Of course I have," Neil answered.

Chan glanced up, then back down at the screen. For a few moments a rash of colour was thrown up by the LCD across Chan's pale face. Colour from the gaudy outfits of Neil

Diamond's strutting impersonators, those loud and garish pictures with which Neil was already so familiar . . . 'Tom Sadge gives you the authentic Neil Diamond Experience . . .' Chan narrowed his eyes at the screen as it flickered and turned white – he'd found the text file he wanted. He read to himself for a moment, then came out with his first question, still reading from the screen.

" . . . Okay . . . In that interview Neil Diamond talks about cover songs . . . He makes reference to a song he's covered and explains why he covered it. So, can you tell me which song that was, who wrote it, and why he covered it?"

Neil didn't even hesitate: "The song was, *The Last Thing on My Mind*. It's by a folk artist – Tom Paxton. As to the reasons why he covered it, I can give you those verbatim."

Chan took his eyes from the screen and his hands from the keyboard. He seemed shocked Neil had come up with any answer at all, let alone this. He sat back and stared at Neil. "Are you kidding me?"

"No."

"Go on."

Neil took a breath.

"'*This is a beautiful beautiful Tom Paxton song, very lovely, very delicate and I really enjoyed singing it and I suppose that's reason enough to record it and that's why I did record it.*'"

Chan didn't say anything. He glanced down at the interview on the screen, checking, then back at Neil. He stared hard at Neil. At last he said, "Now that's impressive. Imagine saying that into the mike. Real low. That's what we're aiming for. That kind of perfection."

Neil nodded. "Once on stage I intend to use Diamond's actual words wherever I can. That's always been my plan."

"That's what I want. Exactly what I want. Now look, I'm going to spray some questions at you about the *facts* of Neil

Diamond's career." Chan's attention was back on the screen, downloading another file. "Let's see how you do."

"Fire away."

"With which company did Neil Diamond sign his first recording contract?"

"Bang Records."

"Who ran Bang?"

"Bertie Berns."

"Name two hit songs Bertie Berns had written or co-written."

"*Twist and Shout. Hang on Sloopy.*"

"Any more?"

"*Here comes the Night? . . . Everybody Needs Somebody to Love?*"

Again Chan looked up. "That's really most impressive, Neil." It was the first time Chan had ever called Neil by his Christian name. "I'm going to call you Neil now because that's how I'm going to think of you. *As* Neil Diamond. It'll help build the persona. To me, you *are* Neil Diamond from now on. Who introduced you to Bertie Berns, Neil?"

"Jeff Barry and Ellie Greenwich."

"Friends of yours?"

"Jeff and Ellie were a couple I knew well in Brooklyn."

"What was their pedigree in the business?"

"They had a string of Phil Spector produced hits."

"Such as?"

"*Chapel of Love, Be My Baby, Da Do Ron Ron, Then He Kissed Me.*"

"What was your first album with Bang?"

"*The Feel of Neil Diamond.* Nineteen sixty-six."

"Okay. Some lesser known names now. Who was Guy Labukus?"

"Guy was a session musician I used on the early recordings. He played bass guitar."

"Do you still use him?"

"No."

"Why not?"

"He's dead."

"Well done . . . Who did we have for percussion on those early recordings?"

"Jack Jennings. Specs Powell."

"How many records have you sold over your career?"

"Over one hundred and ten million."

"In nineteen seventy-six you released three albums. What were they?"

"*Beautiful Noise, Love at the Greek, And the Singer sings His Song*."

"Which of your albums could be described as 'concept'?"

"*Tap Root Manuscript*, nineteen seventy, certainly, and perhaps, *On the Way to the Sky*, nineteen eighty-one."

"What video did you make with Waylon Jennings?"

"*One Good Love*."

"What other videos have you made?"

"*Marry me* and *Neil Diamond . . . Under a Tennessee Moon*."

"Who else featured on *Marry Me*?"

"Buffy Lawson."

"You said Guy Labukus died. When was that?"

"Guy passed away last year."

Chan hung his head a moment.

"I've got to hand it to you," he said, looking up, and for once his smile seemed to mean something. "Your preparation is excellent, Neil. But what about the songs themselves? You know which ones you're doing? You know which order you're singing them in?"

Neil nodded. "The songs," he said, smiling back broadly, openly at Chan for the very first time, "the songs are a piece of piss."

Chapter Twelve

Pop Goes the Weasel

The interruption came just as Neil finished committing to heart *Longfellow Serenade*. Iannis set down his tray of BigMac, Double French Fries and Coke as if he were already disgusted with it. Then he dropped his sports bag by Neil's table, and with it all pretence of politeness and goodwill. Neil set his song book aside to make way for conversation – after the business at The Cosmopolitan they had quite a lot to talk about. A rich vein for discussion and debate there. But without a word, not even a salutation of any kind, Iannis sat down and began to eat. He didn't look at Neil. Instead his eyes locked on the monochrome portrait of Neil Diamond on the back of the song book, a smiling portrait from the early seventies. Iannis sighed and shook his head. Stale booze drifted across the table, mixed with the BigMac's scent of pickle, sesame bun and tepid meat. Iannis didn't seem to be drunk, though. The booze was a trace of yesterday's good time.

He took another bite from his burger and grimaced at the taste. It occurred to Neil that they subsisted on a similar diet, he and Iannis. He didn't like the idea.

"I've had more balls hit at my head, my face, my back, my gut, my butt this week than . . . " But the effort to find a new way to say what he wanted to say was too much. Instead he drank some Coke then ate again before speaking more frankly, with his mouth full: "Those bitches at the LRC can't play tennis to save their fucking fannies."

Last time they'd met it had taken a half hour or so before Iannis had descended to this level but today he was in a truly filthy mood. He scowled at an attendant, a gaunt and spotty teenager, who was struggling past his sports bag with a stack of trays. Then in a rude and childish gesture he stretched across and all but snatched *The Neil Diamond Song Book* away from Neil. He dragged it face down over the greasy table. Without wiping his fingers he picked the book up and flipped it the other way, so that he could sneer at the front cover. It offered a recent colour plate of the superstar in full concert mode, complete with surging and adoring crowd. Iannis scowled at the cover and puffed out his cheeks. He let go a soft belch of booze and burger.

"I never liked this guy."

Neil replied testily: "Well, millions love him. He's sold more than one hundred and ten million albums. That's a fact. A statistical fact."

Iannis raised an eyebrow. "I said I never liked him."

"Well, he thinks very highly of you, I'm sure."

"There was something about him," Iannis continued, ignoring Neil's sarcasm, and lightening his scowl now to a puzzled frown – "There was something about him that – " he stroked away some sesame seeds from Neil Diamond's tanned cheek: it seemed almost an act of kindness – "That didn't add up. He wrote some hits, sure. I remember *Cracklin' Rosie*, *Sweet Caroline*, all that stuff. Good songs. But he never seemed to be out there, you know?" He looked at Neil and there was sincerity in his pressurized, sports ball eyes. He was about to impart some pearl of wisdom and he leant forward earnestly. "With people like Aretha Franklin, Dionne Warwick, Sammy Davis, Ray Charles – with the real stars, the real ones, you felt they were giving their all, you know? They were giving you everything they had. But not with Neil Diamond. He was always playing a part, and he never really made top drawer because of that. Not in my book."

Neil hadn't heard Iannis speak in these measured tones before. He felt more comfortable with the hungover braggart. Where had all the anger gone?

"Take Anthony Newley," Iannis said. He straightened his seat and steadied the song book against the table. "I saw him here at The Excelsior Hotel. Cabaret. A Gala performance. *'An evening with Anthony Newley and Tony Carstairs'*." Iannis stared up a moment at the strip lights of McDonald's, trying to remember some detail of that evening at The Excelsior, with Anthony Newley and Tony Carstairs. His eyes were very red and sore and looked too sensitive to stare into the brightness of the strip lights, but he stared up all the same, as if facing off the cruel light could bring him the memory he searched for, no pain no gain. "It was a cabaret," he repeated, at last, giving up the detail he wanted. "He does it every year. December time. Tony Newley. He sang that big song of his, *Pop Goes the Weasel*. You know it?"

Neil didn't answer. He wasn't in the mood to weigh Neil Diamond against Tony Newley, or any of Iannis's other stars for that matter, all of whom he considered somewhat overrated, as Elbert Chan might have put it.

"I'm not saying I like that song." Iannis leant forward, his arms around Neil's song book. He twisted his Coke cup in his hands, warming to his theme. "It's a kid's song – *Pop Goes the Weasel*. Kid's stuff."

"Of course it is," Neil said.

"Of course it is," Iannis agreed, nodding, looking down, twisting his Coke cup. "Sure it is," he agreed again. "*Half a pound of tuppenny rice, Half a pound of treacle* – pantomime stuff. I'm not saying it's a nice song or an adult song or even a good song." He looked up at Neil. "But Tony Newley really sang it. And he's about sixty year's old. He really sang it out, you know? He gave you everything he had, every last cent, with that song. You could see the veins in his neck come out – " Iannis lifted his head to the cruel light again, shut his eyes and fanned his neck where Anthony Newley's veins had stuck out. "His veins came out here . . . And here . . . You know? . . ."

Iannis stared at Neil, demanding a response.

"It must have been quite an act," Neil offered.

"It was one hell of an act. One hell of an act," Iannis confirmed, nodding vigorously.

A silence fell. Neil had nothing more to say on this subject. The gala performance. He was about to open the matter of The Cosmopolitan when Iannis chuckled. It was a private joke. He shook his head now, smiling to himself, looking down.

"So *why* does the weasel go pop, Neil?" His words were addressed to the floor, and were leaden with bogus ambiguity. "Hmmn?" he looked up again at Neil. "Do you know that? Tell me. Why, Neil?"

"I have no idea."

"No idea?"

"None at all."

"Well, well . . ." Iannis turned away again, weary already with his own pretence. "Nor do I . . . Nor do I . . ." He stared around the restaurant: at the women, the girls, mothers, waitresses – "Who gives a fuck about that?" he demanded loudly, to the restaurant at large. Some diners glanced their way and frowned, mouths full, drinks at lips – 'Steady on, there, Mister! Family restaurant, you know?' Iannis looked back at Neil and stubbed his finger on the table. "But he cared. Tony Newley cared. He looked like he was going to pop himself or top himself if someone didn't tell him why the weasel went pop, or whatever. Passion. That's what it was."

He turned and sat square to the table again and opened *The*

Neil Diamond Song Book. He began flicking through it. He smiled wryly at the titles he recognized, shook his head and muttered their names.

"So have you got a show yet?" Iannis asked, at last, interrupting himself. His sore eyes held the page with studied indifference. "Has our Elbert Chan delivered?"

Neil hesitated, then said: "By the way, I saw your show last Saturday."

Iannis looked up, suspicious. "Oh yeah. Where?"

"The Cosmopolitan."

"That dump."

"Yeah . . . You did, *Windmills of Your Mind*."

"Did I?"

"Don't you remember?" It was Neil's turn to look away across the crowded restaurant. "Then afterwards, after you'd sung that, you started telling everyone about the ratpack scene in L.A." Neil glanced back. Iannis was staring down at the book. "Something about, 'boozin' an' cruisin' an' loosin' in L.A.'? . . . Something like that."

Iannis said nothing but he was smiling to himself. Smiling.

"Then you were dragged off," Neil added.

Iannis looked up, pleased about that. "Was I?"

"You were dragged off by the management. You were awful."

Iannis turned an open palm. He smiled. "Everyone's entitled to their opinion."

"Yeah, well the general consensus of opinion was that you were absolutely fucking awful. A complete waste of time and space."

Iannis grinned and mimicked Neil in a whining falsetto: "Oh, the general consensus of opinion was . . . Bullshit. I got up there. I did it. What have you done? Sitting on your arse all day reading song books!"

Neil sensed that no matter how he put this it would turn out wrong, but he had to spill the beans.

"As a matter of fact I've got a show in ten days' time."

Iannis lowered his eyes to the page, gave nothing away. "Really?"

Neil said nothing more either. If Iannis wanted details he would have to look up and ask for them.

And Iannis did look up. He strained to keep his expression neutral. "So where are you playing?"

"The Mariners' Club. Right here in Tsim Sha Tsui."

"Uh-huh." Iannis lowered his gaze again and tried to hold his indifferent expression. He turned the page. Now he had all the cards. All the cards. This time the gamble had paid off big time. He sighed, left a pause, then, turning another page, he came out with it.

"I played there once."

"I know you did," Neil said quickly. He reached across and gripped the top of the song book. "Excuse me," he said. Iannis held on a moment, then smiled and let the book go. He opened his hands to show Neil had been free to take it back any time.

"Hey, all you had to do was ask. A little politeness, you know."

Neil replaced the song book in its Tom Lee carrier bag. "Elbert told me about that," he said. "About your show." He had his book now and he stood up to leave.

But Iannis laughed at him.

"It's just sailors, pal," he said, still laughing. "The Mariners' Club is just sailors. They're gonna fucking eat you, pal. I mean eat you!"

Neil kept his eyes on Iannis long enough to see this repulsive gesture: Iannis cocked his head on his shoulder, and with his thumb and forefinger nipped, pointed into his open mouth, where traces of half-eaten burger mashed with ketchup, pickle and gherkin were still visible –

"I mean eat you!"

Neil stepped away from the table, with his song book in its carrier bag, taking his time, and eased through the queues to the exit.

Chapter Thirteen

Mack the Knife

The Filipino band were called *Los Reyes*. A six piece outfit, complete with saxophone and trumpet. They met Neil and Chan at The Mariners' Club briefly the day before, on the Friday morning, to go through the song list and to show what they could do with a couple of numbers. There was no rehearsal as such. Neil was disappointed to find they were an all male band, and that most of them were around his age or older, but their competence was without question.

The act was going to lack glamour, though, without any female accompaniment. It was a bit late in the day to tackle this but when the band had gone, over coffee at The Mariners' poolside, Neil put it to Chan anyway. He gently reminded him that they were performing to a crowd of sailors, grown men who'd had no sex for months, except between themselves. Seven middle-aged guys on stage, directly following a male voice choir, didn't do it for anyone, let alone a bunch of guys just off the boat. Variety night? Come on. Chan shrugged his shoulders on this one – it didn't matter. He seemed very tired this morning and his manner had been weary and subdued throughout proceedings. These acts were just an entrée, he said. The sailors would go whoring in Wan Chai afterwards, those who weren't with escorts already. Maybe those who were with escorts too, come to that. If this booking went well they could put in backing singers next time, but it was too expensive for their first night out. Neil tried to press the point but Chan only shrugged it off again. He told him he could hire privately if he wished, but, he warned, such girls, if they looked good, would cost treble the band, because he'd be taking them off the dance girl/escort circuit where they'd normally earn their living. And that would mean paying their pimps, who were all triad. Neil dropped it. He couldn't challenge that insider's understanding.

The Mariners' pool was three floors up. They sipped their coffee and stared across the empty pool to the lush tree tops and the smart apartment blocks all around. Each block was faced with the same fashionable ochre tiling, same as the poolside flags beneath their feet. Neil liked it out here very much. He felt they really were at the start of something, out here on the poolside terrace of The Mariner's Club. But he kept his excitement in check with Chan, kept everything low-key, businesslike, professional, as he had earlier with Mr. Wong, the Entertainments Manager.

He'd expressed some concerns he had about the room – The Compass Room – to Mr. Wong. He'd told Wong that he thought The Compass Room was all wrong, too long and narrow for a cabaret. The place lent itself to people sitting at tables banquet style rather than in circles, so most of the sailors would end up facing each other, not the stage. Too many tables and adjusting your seat would be awkward in the narrow aisles, and that could cause friction, which was the last thing they wanted – fist fights breaking out all over the place. If they *had* to use The Compass Room, table layout was going to need some thought, wasn't it? Wong listened to Neil's complaint, but said nothing in reply. He was a chain-smoking, tubby Chinese, who cocked his head on one side while Neil talked, as if he couldn't quite hear, or couldn't quite believe, what Neil was saying. His eyes – long, sly and lazy – kept closing behind his cigarette smoke while he listened. When Neil moved on to stage arrangements, showing his seriousness, his tenacity – "On the question of stage arrangements, Mr. Wong – " Wong lit another cigarette off the one he was still smoking, even though it was only half burned, and drew long and hard on the new cigarette, sucking in his cheeks and frowning up at Neil. He turned away to stub out the old cigarette in a sand ashtray behind them, while Neil explained what he had in mind. Neil told him he would need an apron of some description, with steps, so that he could come down and get among the audience. Wong looked back at him, his mouth open wide, letting out lungfuls of smoke. "An apron?" He grunted through his smoke. "You gonna do some cookin'?" *Dai Aspora* didn't need an apron, he said, they just had some benches from the gym, so he couldn't have one, and that was that. Neil raised a hand, changing tack, avoiding confrontation. He had another problem and maybe this one was easier to solve. "I think we'll need some drapes for the walls . . ." For Neil the walls of The Compass Room, drab and featureless, magnolia flaking from bubbling plaster, were a sad reminder of the dozens of damp church halls he'd played all over the East Midlands – barn dances, ceilidhs and so on. Bad memories. "How about we hang up some old flags?" he suggested. "Old ships' pennants?"

"Old ships' . . . ?" Wong shook his head in disbelief. "Old ships' what?"

He turned away and resumed conversation with Elbert in Cantonese.

Neil didn't react to the snub. He'd come back to that, to the drapes, the pennants, and some other points. No one going to fob him off at this stage. Too much at stake.

And just thirty-three hours to go.

Chan had had a tough week, it seemed. He was taking his coffee strong and black and he drooped in his white plastic chair at the white plastic table. He stared vacantly at the tree tops and apartment blocks. A light breeze unpicked his hair-flip, and his eyelids had sunk to just above the pupil line. In the hard daylight out here he looked older than he did in his office, as if daylight sapped his power, his presence. He could have been in his fifties, late fifties, out here. It occurred to Neil that this venture – the Star Tributes concept – might really be a very important deal for Elbert Chan. The Big One. A last reaching out for fortune. For real money, as he called it. He'd put a lot of time and energy into this, over and above his other business interests, and he'd exhausted himself.

"Look, are you okay? Are you up to this?"

Chan had expressed doubts about the song list. That's what they were meant to be thrashing out right now, over coffee by the pool, in the third floor breeze, but he seemed to have forgotten.

"I'm tired. Really tired."

"*Sweet Caroline,* then. To start. How about that?"

"Terrific."

"Then I'll move on to something they probably don't know so well. I don't want to waste the big hits. I want to come back to them as and when I need to."

"Sure." Chan stared at the tree tops. "You do that."

"If I find things are flagging and I want to bring a hit forward the band will switch the order around, no problem. The band's great," Neil said, though he'd said it before. "Very professional."

"What's next?"

Neil frowned and followed Chan's gaze into the tree tops. He didn't want to rush this but he felt pressed by Chan's monosyllabic responses. "Either *Soolaimon* or *Solitary Man*."

Chan glanced across. "The first one?"

"*Soolaimon*."

"Never heard of it."

"It's early. Sixty-six."

Chan screwed up his sticky eyes. "That's more than thirty years ago!"

"It's a complete change in tempo. I'd link the two with just one line."

"What's that?"

"This is a song I wrote for a friend of mine, Bobby Darin."

"Bobby Darin?"

"Mack The Knife. Big fifties hit."

"Fifties?" Chan was wide awake now all right, but panicky. "Fifties? You've gone back another decade! Who's *Jack the Knife?"*

"Bobby Darin's a big name."

"Never heard of him. Is he still around?"

"He died young."

Chan winced as if from a blow. "Forget him, Neil. Lose him. They're sailors. Not so much history. They'll think you're making it up."

"But I'm not making it up."

"They'll think you are. That's all that matters." Chan looked away again, to the tree tops. For the first time in any of their conversations he looked crestfallen. He looked depressed.

"I don't like it here," he mumbled to himself.

"Bobby Darin's a big name," Neil repeated. "Just because you don't know him doesn't change that. When I say that name they'll get the idea that the impersonation is for real. That's my challenge. That's the tribute, as we agreed."

"So what's after *Jack the Knife?"*

"Mack the Knife."

"What's after that?"

"I don't sing that."

"You don't?"

"No."

Chan closed his eyes, dry washed his face. "You've lost me."

"That was a song by Bobby Darin."

"I thought you said you wrote it?"

"I didn't. But he sang it."

"Leave him out of it, I tell you!" Genuine anger from Chan – there was too much at stake here for him as well. "Lose him! He's out the frame! Bobby Darin! What do you sing?"

"*Solitary Man*. Or *Soolaimon*, like I said."

"What's next?"

"*Cracklin' Rosie*."

"Okay, okay . . . Now we're talking."

Neil was relieved to have Chan's approval again. "It was number one. If the audience were around then, they've got to know *Cracklin' Rosie*. Even if they weren't around they've got to know it. Still gets played."

"Course it does. Sound of an era. Classic. So how do you introduce that?"

"There's another build up. The band are already playing the melody under what I say . . . *Some come easier than others. I wrote this song in a Memphis hotel room just the day before it was recorded. It went to number one in the land of the free –* "

This show material Neil delivered in a husky American accent in tune with the voice of the songs, and it was impressive, Neil knew it was, more impressive than Chan was giving credit for, in his tired and irritable mood.

" – That's a cue. When I say that, the drummer kicks in, almost as if he's getting impatient, like the audience, like he's on their side, they want to get going together, then I pick up with the band, soft and gentle . . ." Neil quietly sang the opening lines for Chan, waving his finger to the beat above the plastic table.

"Hey. That's great."

Neil stopped.

"You know what you're doing and you're going to deliver. I knew you would. It's going to be terrific."

"After that I do *Longfellow Serenade.* "

"I don't want to hear about that." Chan made a 'cut' gesture with both hands out flat, an inch above the plastic table, very emphatic. "The *Longfellow* thing. That's it. I've heard enough."

Neil was stung but didn't retaliate.

"It's all most impressive. Most impressive," Chan mumbled, staring at the tree tops. "There's just one other matter remaining, then we're ready to go. Action stations."

"What's that?"

"Plan B."

"Plan B?"

Chan repeated it to the tree tops: "Plan B . . . What you do if they don't respond."

"They'll respond."

"If they don't play along. The sailors."

"They'll play along. There's a knack to winning an audience. It's in the timing. I've done it a thousand times. Ten thousand times."

"Okay." Chan looked across at Neil again, with his head on one side now, like Mr. Wong. "But what if it goes wrong? What if they get nasty? What if there are catcalls?"

"I'll ride it out."

"What if they start throwing food around?"

"At me? I'm not Iannis, for goodness' sake!"

"At you," Chan nodded gravely, his insider knowledge coming through again. "And at the band. They're sailors, Neil."

Neil shook his head with absolute conviction. "That's not going to happen."

But Chan persisted. "What if it does, though? What if a

fight breaks out? What if someone throws a turd at you? A human turd. You're in full song. Mouth open wide."

Chan opened his mouth wide, exposing his aging teeth, some jagged lines of amalgam. Neil thought of Iannis in McDonald's, mouth open wide. Eat you, pal. And Wong, just half an hour ago, mouth open wide. Suddenly everybody was doing that to him, turning to him with mouth open wide, drop-jawed, in sheer disbelief. No one believed in him. No one believed he could do this. He took a deep breath.

"That's not going to happen. That's just failure talk."

The waiter came with the bill. Chan passed it to Neil.

"Pick up the tab on this one."

He looked across the pool one last time, then stood up to leave.

"I don't like this place," he mumbled again.

It was rotten luck to run into Iannis, standing around in the park just outside The Mariners', but Neil understood soon enough that luck had nothing to do with it. Iannis had followed them here, he'd stalked them. He had a story to break – and what a story.

He'd spotted a short preview of *Uncut Diamonds* in the 'What's On' section of The South China Morning Post. A certain Tony Laprisco was booked to play three nights at The Excelsior Hotel before flying on to Manila, the next leg on an Asian tour encompassing hotels and private clubs in Osaka, Manila, Jakarta, Bangkok, and finishing at the Mandarin Oriental in Singapore. Iannis could hardly contain his pleasure in passing on the bad news. Neil was naturally alarmed – until he saw the dates of the Laprisco engagement at The Excelsior. They fell the week after his own début.

He dismissed Iannis's ominous story. He told him the Laprisco tour was good news and refused to see it in any other light. The pre-publicity would raise the profile of his own show, and reviews of Laprisco would help Elbert to secure further bookings with other clubs and hotels. It would be very much easier, Neil pointed out, for Elbert (the use of his first name was deliberate) to approach The American Club with Laprisco's success in evidence, as well as his own, than to try to convince the Entertainments Manager from cold. (Particularly if he were anything like Wong, Neil noted to himself.) Laprisco gave them plenty to work with: he was straight out from L.A. where he ran *The Café Diamond*. He was a celebrity of sorts in his own right, able to string together a Far East tour . . .

The ragged triangle of park outside The Mariners' Club, just some concrete flower basins and a few blighted trees – how different these trees looked from upstairs across the pool, with just their lush tops showing! – was called Signal Hill Garden. After the spat with Iannis, Neil felt ill at ease here in Signal Hill Garden. A plaque identified the place as a Children's Playground, but there weren't any children around. None at all. Instead there were a lot of elderly Chinese men chatting and gambling in the shade of the trees. They sat perched on the flower basins, protecting their skinny buttocks from the concrete with bits of folded cardboard. For Neil in his current mood these old men were too relaxed, too comfortable with their lot, too idle and resigned. He scowled round at them all, as Iannis fleshed out the Tony Laprisco tour with his own imaginary details. Neil watched the old men chat and smoke and laugh together, and felt an increasing disquiet. They sat with shirts half open, or even removed altogether, exposing sallow, mottled skin stretched over sunken sterna and bird-like ribcages. Their bodies were decrepit, finished, beaten to nothing by a lifetime's labour. The men were shameless. They didn't care any more. They were too far removed from the hot hard struggle in which Neil was still very much engaged, and in which Chan was still engaged, and this is what obscurely disturbed him.

Furthermore – his eyes flitted up to the blue, concave facade of The Mariners' Club, the other side of Signal Hill Garden – furthermore he did not like sitting around here with Iannis, so close to his first venue, just thirty-two hours from his opening night. He felt superstitious about this. Iannis was too near the knuckle, the bone, the pearl of great price. All this contributed to Neil's impatience. He had been tolerant of Iannis up till now, but with the show imminent he felt the urge to bring him down a peg or two. He remembered Iannis's mouth open wide –

"But what do you think? What do you think? Are they going to eat him, or what?"

Iannis merely smiled and folded up his newspaper.

"They might do," he said. "They might eat him. And Candyman Chan too. For breakfast. If he's not the best. I mean, the best. Remember though, The Excelsior Hotel is not The Mariners' Club." He cast a backward glance at the blue facade of the club and folded his newspaper tight into his tracksuit pocket. "And you – no matter what Elbert Chan thinks – are not Tony Laprisco."

That was enough for Neil. He wanted to tell Iannis who *he* was. A washed up sports coach with a bag of rotten dreams. A drunken loudmouth with a chip on his shoulder. But it was not in Neil's nature to speak his turn that way. He satisfied himself by cutting Iannis, by saying nothing more, not even goodbye, and just walking away from him, leaving him there among the incomprehensible chatter and laughter of the old men in Signal Hill Garden. He crossed the park to Middle Road and walked on without looking back, past the Tsim Sha Tsui Post Office, until he was lost again in the crowds of Nathan Road.

He had walked off briskly and purposefully enough, and had left Iannis behind all right, but it was only twelve noon and he had nowhere specific in mind to head for. He couldn't go back to The Mariners' Club and sort out those details now, not in this mood, not with the brusque and bloated Mr. Wong. Young Indian men blocked his path on Nathan Road, hassling him to buy suits and copy-watches. They loitered in the shady patches of the pavement and in the gaps between buildings, black and invisible until he went by -

"Excuse me, sir . . ."

"This way, sir . . ."

"I've been waiting for you, sir . . ."

"Step over here, sir . . ."

The true misery of homelessness had been half Neil's for several weeks now. He would have preferred to have the room at *The Languages and Translation Services Ltd.* by day and the cooler, emptier streets by night. With this angry and futile thought he was reminded of the tailor's hawker from Chungking Mansions who had escorted him to the Cheungs in the first place. Neil had spent his days criss-crossing these very streets where that man plied his trade, and yet he had never run into him again. Did he dodge and hide when he saw Neil approaching? Was he alarmed by Neil's transformation, his stage outfit and wraparound sunglasses? Or was he amused by that, by the smiles and glances Neil garnered on the street? Or had he moved on to bigger and better things? Or fallen to worse things, to wheeling blocks of ice and tubs of fish between bars and hotels, or selling soft porn in the basements of Chungking?

This afternoon Neil had a fresh apprehension of the underworld of poverty that surrounded him here. Though every day he thought he was on the brink of becoming a denizen of this world himself, he had been protected from any understanding of it by his own feelings of alienation, the last luxury of those about to fall into the pit. He now saw in the dark and soggy eyes of the Indian poor, and in the desensitised resolve of the labouring Chinese – wheeling their barrows of ice, of flattened cardboard, their tubs of dying fish – he saw the weight of the pyramid above them all, the incalculable mass of wealth that rested there shimmering in the heat.

But he was not a part of either world and never would be. His destiny was not to barter or manufacture at the lowest level. His way was to sell a certain talent that he had, not a very fine or worthy talent, to be sure, but a talent that was marketable here nonetheless. He thought he began to understand Chan's unchanging indifference towards him – that natural indifference, because Chan must see him as someone already raised on a litter above the crowd, one who, if he couldn't make it here, deserved not a moment of anyone's time, and Neil felt humbled a moment by an understanding of how much harder it was to sell a copy-watch than a copy Neil Diamond.

Chapter Fourteen

For Those in Peril on the Sea

The laughter from within The Compass Room of The Mariners' Club was unnerving. Over the last six months Neil's ears had been adapting to the sound of Chinese laughter, that started and stopped in orchestrated gusts, but the sailors' laughter from The Compass Room was unruly, dissonant, some of it hale and hearty, some light and false; it was the laughter of bosuns and cabin boys, of second mates and third mates, good and bad mates from all around the world.

Neil sat outside on the patio to the rear of the function room, close to a set of shabby French doors, beneath a dripping air conditioner. Half a dozen pairs of French doors opened from The Compass Room onto the patio. The laughter came through the curtains and the French doors behind him, past the air conditioner, and spilled onto the patio. It echoed off the ochreous poolside tiling and the flat blue swimming pool. The tree tops and the apartment blocks pushed it back. The noise of it hung in the air too long. Time was too drawn out today.

Chan had sent a photographer to take some pictures of Neil in his show outfit at the poolside. Publicity material, he'd said. The photographer had come too early. It looked as if he were squeezing the job in before some unscheduled engagement. In the afternoon heat he had frittered away a roll of film with close-up shots of Neil, or with stylish shots of him leaning on a chair by the pool in his black clothes and his sunglasses, smiling and relaxed; or standing at the other end of the pool, his hands folded before him, looking stern and proprietorial. By the end of the shoot Neil was soaked in sweat and quite drained. The photographer – a very young man, possibly just a school-leaver – was sympathetic and at his suggestion, and with his assistance as interpreter, Neil borrowed some trunks from lost property and treated himself to a gentle, solitary swim in the club pool. He did five lengths of unstrenuous breaststroke, careful to keep his head of dyed black hair above the water. The sight of his long, thin white body and his black hair in the blue pool must have had some special meaning to the photographer's eye, because he went on snapping away for some purpose of his own while Neil swam slowly up and down, enjoying the water. When he got out the photographer finished his film with a meaningless shot of his subject relaxing under a parasol, dressed only in his borrowed trunks. The young man grew friendly and Neil, in a mood to deny himself nothing, accepted an offer of one of his cigarettes, though he'd not smoked for years. The photographer leant on a poolside chair close by Neil and loitered there, smoking, for a minute or so, as if wanting to say something more. But in the end he didn't say anything. He checked his watch, said goodbye, and was gone.

Los Reyes had already arrived. Anthony, the smiling, portly leader of the band, checked the order of the songs with Neil then took his musicians off to the bar for their complimentary drink and sandwich. Neil was hungry too and would have liked nothing better than to sit in the air-conditioned bar and eat a club sandwich, but he couldn't handle the company. Now, above all, he needed to be alone with his thoughts. As an accomplished performer this event should have held no fear for him, and up until today he had felt none. But as the minutes ticked by before his walk to the other end of the patio, to that last set of French doors, to that moment when he would muddle his way through the curtains and up onto the stage, as all of that came closer he felt his confidence ebb away. This was why it was vital to be here on his own next to the venue, listening to the audience in there, so that he could gradually come to terms with what lay ahead. This was how he had always prepared for the big performances back in England. Every night on the *Farewell to Fairport* tour he had hung around backstage, sitting on a spare trestle or loudspeaker, nursing his nerves, chain-smoking, talking down his anxieties. But memories of those days were not mixing with his thoughts right now. He'd banished them to focus on the sounds from The Compass Room: the clinking of bottlenecks against glasses, and the shouts of the sailors, and the gales of laughter.

That laughter.

While he was so immersed, *Dai Aspora* came out and began to assemble on the swimming pool patio. It was an extraordinary sight. A spontaneous assembly of British middle-aged men in central Kowloon, all in dinner suits and cummerbunds, on the swimming pool patio of The Mariners' Club. Neil had not seen so many knobbly faces and bald heads gathered together for more than six months. There were even two men, obviously brothers, with bright red hair. The choirmaster was a short, bespectacled, upper middle-class fellow, the very model of a Rotarian from the home counties. He started arranging the choir with much fuss and joviality at the deep end of the pool, right in front of Neil. The bonhomie of the choir and their master's English humour – "Move over, Steve! You envious fellow!" . . . "Chins up, Vic! Let your superiority show, dear!" – released the dread that had been oppressing Neil's spirit. He felt his shoulders relax, his breathing ease. And this choir played The Mariners' Club regularly, according to Chan, and also had bookings with

Chan's 'better' clubs – The Cricket Club and The Football Club had been mentioned. They were established here. There really was nothing to worry about.

Dai Aspora carried on oblivious to his presence. With great solemnity, the choirmaster stepped onto the diving board.

"Now let me have a look at you, you horrible lot!"

The choir duly squared up in their ranks. They stood with their backs to Neil and with their hands clasped behind their backs. The sight of the choirmaster, in full regalia, looking down sternly from the diving board, he too with his hands behind his back, caused much amusement and many asides, and lightly concluded the choir's preening ritual.

"Well, I suppose you'll have to do!"

The choirmaster stepped down and led the way along the patio towards the last set of French doors. As they passed Neil in single file each member of the choir in turn gave him a nod, a wink, or a "Good evening". Neil returned their greetings, smiling at the absurdity of their repetitions as they filed past. Their English humour and sublime confidence gave him just the lift he needed.

Two waiters emerged from the last patio doors and they held the doors back for the choir to file into The Compass Room. The choirmaster did one final check of the line-up then tagged himself to the end. As the first singers, the red-headed brothers, slipped in through the French doors, a roar from the sailors went up, tables were thumped in merriment, and Neil knew that the evening was going to be a success. The sailors would leave no holds barred. The incongruous idea of following a Welsh Male Voice Choir no longer seemed threatening – on the contrary, it was just the kind of variety that was called for. At that roar from the sailors the portly choirmaster looked back to Neil from the tail end and gave him a double thumbs up. Neil smiled, his eyes lingering on the man's pink, safe, office worker's hands.

The waiters saw *Dai Aspora* inside then went in themselves and shut the French doors behind them. A hush fell in The Compass Room. Neil could hear the choirmaster delivering a few words of introduction in his fruity English tones. There was not a hint of Welsh in his voice. It was more the voice of a benign English public school headmaster. Then there was more laughter, of a less ribald kind, as he wrung a few obvious puns on the origins of the name they'd given themselves – Dai Evans had suggested this and Dai Jones had said that – familiar jokes to many, no doubt, but no less welcome for that. This was an audience that would much appreciate familiarity. Neil heard the beginning of some other anecdote about leeks and rugby and so on, but it was lost under a burst of earthy laughter, perhaps unconnected with the choirmaster's story, from the back of The Compass Room. Distracted, Neil was taken by surprise when the choir lifted into song. In the distance, across the valleys, as it were, a tenor opened and then waves of chorus and descant followed close behind, propelling the music to the very back of the hall. The song was, *I Dream of Jeannie with the Light Brown Hair.*

Chan was right. *Dai Aspora* were no purist outfit here to celebrate the Gaelic tongue and Welsh choral heritage. There was nothing methodist chapel about this lot. After, *I Dream of Jeannie with the Light Brown Hair*, virtually without missing a beat, they quickened the tempo to offer another Stephen Foster favourite, *The Camptown Races.* As Neil listened to the succession of sweet, melancholy strains and lively music-hall or Broadway hits, he was reminded more of *The Cliff Adams Singers* from *The BBC Light Programme* of more than thirty years ago, the stuff of his own childhood; or more precisely the music of George Mitchell's *Black & White Minstrel Show,* with John Boulter, Tony Mercer and Dai Francis. (The tenor in this ensemble compared quite favourably with Boulter, in fact.)

The performance, about forty minutes in all, was soon over. The choir knew they couldn't remain in good voice for very long and knew also, no doubt, that they should leave the stage while their audience wanted them to stay. Better one descant too few than too many. The balance between the cheerful and the maudlin was observed until the very end, when *How Much Is That Doggy In The Window?* – sung with shameless innuendo – was followed by an obvious favourite with the sailors, Lee Marvin's gloomy classic from Paint Your Wagon: *Wandering Star*. Neil thought that was the finale, but it wasn't. The finale came with the encore, and the sailors clearly knew it would. It was a very full-throated rendition of the William Whiting hymn, *Eternal Father Strong to Save*. From the start the audience joined in the chorus, and each chorus was louder, deeper, broader-based than the last –

O hear us when we cry to thee
For those in peril on the sea!

The final refrain came crashing from The Compass Room in a rush of discordant, drunken sentiment as the sailors, in the absence of anyone who loved them to pray on their behalf, prayed to God themselves to be spared a watery grave.

Shortly after, the French doors opened and the waiters came out again. Past them tumbled *Dai Aspora*, flushed and excited from their performance. How much nicer it would have been for them, Neil reflected, to have come out of a stuffy church hall into the cool of an English July evening, as he himself had done so many, many times, rather than from the relative cool of the air-conditioned Compass Room onto this hot and humid patio. They trooped back past him shambolically now, cummerbunds and collars loosened, no order to their procession, all discipline gone. Neil envied them their relief and satisfaction. In just a few minutes, after *Los Reyes*, he would pass through those French doors at the other end, wrestle his way through the curtains and step up to that shallow proscenium stage.

Los Reyes came down from the bar. They looked smart enough, perhaps too smart, too formal, in their dark suits and open white shirts, with their medallions or crucifixes glittering, their hair scraped back from their middle-aged faces, but for a horrible moment Neil thought they'd had too much to drink upstairs. Anthony threw his head back and laughed at something the bass player said to him in Tagalog, and the gesture seemed altogether too extravagant to Neil, sitting tight in his poolside chair by the French doors. But as Anthony approached, adjusting his jacket collar, he became more self-possessed. He drew up a plastic chair, set his foot on the seat and began tuning his guitar. He winked at Neil. "Waste of time," he said, smiling, and he glanced up at the air conditioning unit rattling away above the French doors.

Neil nodded. This was where *Dai Aspora* had a distinct advantage. But Anthony and the band had checked all the technical problems early in the afternoon and, providing the benches had been cleared and everything had been put where they'd instructed, the amplifiers far enough forward to prevent any feedback, guitar cables neatly coiled on top, drum kit out in the centre, not too far back, and providing there had been no tampering with their equipment, it should be just a minute's work to connect and tune up as needed.

"*Sweet Caroline*, right?" Anthony said, bending his ear to the neck of his guitar.

Neil nodded again. "Then *Song Sung Blue*. We'll skip *Solitary Man*." During the afternoon he'd had a change of heart about that song. "I don't want to do that now. Okay?"

"You're the boss."

Anthony took his foot from the chair and stood with his guitar resting on his shoe a moment, looking across the pool.

A long sigh escaped him. He glanced behind at the other members of the band, talking among themselves of other things in Tagalog.

"Let's go, boys!"

Ignoring Neil the band walked up to the other end of The Compass Room. They continued chatting together there, laughing again at the bass player – a tall, loose-limbed fellow, obviously the joker of the band – who was amusing everyone now with some desperate mimicry, making wild and helpless gestures that had the other members of *Los Reyes* doubled up in stitches. They seemed very relaxed – too relaxed, Neil thought, watching them.

Then the doors opened and the waiters came out. The blast of sound from the opened doors, the clinking of cannikins, shouts for beer, the noises of chairs being thrust back and tables thumped, brought *Los Reyes* to attention. The bass player looked anxiously over the shoulders of his comrades, his sense of humour quite gone. The sailors were getting rowdy. Anthony turned and looked back and smiled at Neil, and seemed about to make a sign to him, a sign of reassurance perhaps, but he was interrupted by a sharp gesture from the waiter, beckoning him forward. Words were exchanged, and glances in Neil's direction, then nods of understanding from the waiters. Again they waved *Los Reyes* forward. Anthony stepped up through the French doors, holding his head high, as if resolved to meet his fate whatever it might be – death, dishonour, or both. A moment later they were all swallowed up. The doors shut again behind them and Neil was left alone once more by the poolside.

Then another gale of laughter, bad laughter, presumably as *Los Reyes*, his aging Filipino kings, in their dark suits, white shirts and medallions, mounted the stage. Loose, loud, jeering, drunken laughter. Oh, that laughter.

He remembered Chan.

Just one more thing . . . Plan B.

Plan B?

Forget plan B. They have their lives and this is mine. Neil unzipped his guitar case and removed the $300 Japanese acoustic he'd bought for the occasion. It would be there for effect only. He would strum it now and then, but Anthony's acoustic-electric would carry both rhythm and lead. As he tried the A, D and E7 chords he would need for *Sweet Caroline*, out the corner of his eye he saw that the waiters were outside again, staring his way. He leant over the instrument and adjusted the sixth string that seemed a little flat. Satisfied he could do no more he stood, brushed down his black jacket, and put on his wraparound sunglasses.

He began the walk down to the other end, his thin black boots clicking on the poolside tiles, his jacket billowing, his dyed black hair bouncing on his black shoulders. The moment had arrived. The test. The gauntlet. The trial by ordeal. What a long way he'd come from *Reason to Believe* at the karaoke bar in Lockhart Road – and yet no distance at all.

There it was already: the heavy beat of the introductory chords to *Sweet Caroline*. Approaching the far end of the patio he couldn't help notice how scruffy the waiters were. He gave them a passing but harsh inspection from behind the safety of his sunglasses. Their tuxedoes were stained and shabby and their shoes unpolished. These were old, defeated footmen. And they looked sick. Their ape skulls showed under their greasy black hair, their faces were mottled, and the browns of their eyes had diluted across the whites, as if some circlip of muscle had worn out and given up. Their skin was large-pored and their sagging mouths glittered with gold in the way of the older Chinese, the superstitious Chinese. Soon these men would join their brethren in Signal Hill Garden and idle away their remaining days with light gambling under the trees, sitting on bits of folded cardboard, on the edges of the concrete flower basins. Neil could not forgive them their appearance on his début night, their shabbiness and decrepitude. Their jackets were lopsided and abused, their shoes a disgrace.

In turn, the footmen nodded curtly at Neil and did not smile.

From inside there came the sound of open palms smacking the tables in tune to the chuum-chuum-chuum of *Sweet Caroline*, keeping good time. Yes, the sailors were going to buy it. They were going to love it. Just as he had imagined they would in his richest fantasies. The two dried-up footmen were not part of it. They bore no ill omen. They did not matter. They were withered and hormoneless. To them it was all just noise. But their presence could not diminish the power of the good feeling, the sap on the rise. As Neil stepped past them into The Compass Room he left behind their downtrodden defeat, their shabby clothes and beaten faces. Yes, there was still time, after all. There was still time for Neil Atherton. Forty-eight, never too late. And from here on it was easy. The curtains were not in the way. Nothing obstructed him as he strode across and stepped up onto the stage. He had done this a thousand times before, and now, with that thumping from the audience behind him, which was keeping well to the rhythm Anthony had set up, now, with Anthony's broad smile beaming down at him as he came across the stage, as he nodded and smiled to each member of the band in turn, and as he swung towards the mike stand, his black jacket billowing, now Neil knew he'd backed a winner. He understood Chan's sublime confidence in the project. It couldn't miss. He set his guitar in its stand and broke the mike from its clip all in one sweep, and then he was in full voice, no quivers or shivers, no turning back now.

Some elements in the audience started singing along with him straightaway. Three young men near the front staggered from their seats and began swaying – but not to the beat. They swayed with long, wide, slow hip movements, no rhythm at all, and sang with their heads down, hands clapping. Neil kept glancing back at them – whether they were pissed or taking the piss he couldn't tell. Their sexy young escorts remained seated, tittering at them.

But now there was a sudden shedding of inhibitions all around, an outbreak of shared nostalgia for good times past. Reading the mood to the second, Anthony and the bass player were right behind him, with the big chords for the chorus. And the good times were truly with them now. They had been named, they had been summoned. They were there for everyone to seize, rich or poor, small or tall, lovely or unlovely, the good times were there this evening and they were even better than before. Neil admitted to himself that he'd never felt anything like this on stage in England, no matter which band he'd been with, let alone on his cold and lonely solo tours. Here there was some other force at work. Nothing mattered to the sailors but the rhythm, the song which they all knew, the next beer, the help they could lend each other clearing the tables for a makeshift dance floor. The first number had started a roll and Neil's challenge was to control the momentum.

Later, when he had time to think about it, he was embarrassed by his old attitude to the music of Neil Diamond. He saw a certain snobbery in it, a snobbery underwritten by the dissatisfactions of his own career, such as it had been, and by personal cowardice. Of course the good feeling was ephemeral, and for many down there on the floor it was too drunken and licentious, but it was there nonetheless, a palpable force in The Compass Room at The Mariners' Club, Tsim Sha Tsui, that evening. And it was a force for the good, something there all the time, but hidden beneath codes of social conditioning, of status seeking and status keeping, of sexual attraction and evasion, under all of that there was in most people goodwill, a desire to help, to give, to love, all the time kept in check by suspicion, jealousy, fear and self-doubt. The songs, as Lennon had said, didn't matter. They were harmless things, a nuisance at worst. It was what they released that mattered.

It was during *Longfellow Serenade* that Neil spied Elbert Chan in the audience. He was actually quite difficult to spot. Many of the tables stage right of The Compass Room had been pushed back to the wall and some had been stacked on top of one another to create more space for dancing. Waiters hurried this way and that between the stacked tables, setting down drinks on any surface remaining. Neil saw Chan making slow progress down the side, stopping every few feet to allow room for someone dancing or for a waiter to pass by, or to stop and listen to the person with him, for he was not alone. Accompanying him, never more than half a step behind, was a small, caped, bat-like figure. He held Chan back every few steps, physically taking him by the arm and drawing him close to say something into his ear. This could have been quite natural, someone trying to make himself heard over the noise of the band and the incidental choruses from the audience, but in the attitude of the figure, in his attentiveness, there was a clear intention to say things that were for Chan alone to hear. The pair stopped a few tables from the front. Neil glanced down at them as he sang and nodded and smiled to them. Chan's diminutive figure was further down-sized by the bulk of the surrounding sailors, but the man behind him was altogether more dwarfish and wizened. Sometimes they both looked up at him together, sometimes they were looking into the throng of bodies all around. Chan's friend stood with his arms folded across his chest, his shrunken frame stiff against a stacked table.

Neil was careful to give the next number – the heavily autobiographical, *I am . . . I said* – its full introduction, as he'd discussed it with Chan, complete with all those details of authenticity they'd decided were so important. But he only did that to please Chan, to include him somehow in the evening because he looked so apart from it, standing there in his dark business suit. For some reason – professional detachment? Jealousy, maybe? – Chan didn't seem to want to give him even the most token signal of encouragement or congratulation, though all around was tangible evidence of the evening's success.

Neil's introduction to *I am . . . I said* dragged on. It didn't matter to the crowd, who busied themselves getting drinks and snacks, or going to the toilet, while he talked of the difficulties he'd had in writing this song, how it had come from deep inside, about the move from the East to the West coast and the yearning that was still there to return homeward . . . but in all honesty, authenticity didn't matter any more. The show was going well without further gimmickry or pretence. The people were here for a good time, dancing and singing and letting their hair down, and Neil was here to deliver the music. *I am . . . I said* was not a dance number, and as soon as he started it he felt the evening begin to flag under the weight of the song's self-indulgence. It was during the second refrain that he glanced in Chan's direction to find that both Chan and his guest had gone. Neil felt undermined by their departure. It was galling that Chan had come and gone just when the evening had lost a bit of pace. However, he put that behind him, wrapped up *I am . . . I said* and got on with the next song, the rhythmic and rousing *Red, Red Wine*. That song brought the sailors back to the floor. The bass player set up a reggae beat that dragged in a slow clapping from both dancers and bystanders. Neil enjoyed this simple rock song more than any other he'd played, more even than *Sweet Caroline*, because now he felt in complete control.

The rest of the evening kept up well. There was a natural

trailing off towards the end as people tired and took to their seats again, and sensitive to the change in mood Neil rearranged his song list with Anthony and brought forward a succession of quieter numbers. There were one or two calls from the floor for a return to *Sweet Caroline* or *Cracklin' Rosie,* but these came from a hard core of very drunken young men, those who had been first to their feet at the beginning of the evening. Neil was suspicious of their motives. He made one concession to them with *Soolaimon.* It was another of those songs for which he had scripted an introduction and he did begin it, because it seemed a shame to waste it, but as soon as he opened his narrative a raucous Scot from the drunken contingent leapt to his feet and called upon him to *"Cut the fuckin' shite!"* Anthony heard the attack and struck up the *Soolaimon* rhythm straightaway, volume turned up to drown any further abuse.

It was the only unpleasantness during the entire evening.

Afterwards, Neil bought a drink for Anthony and the band in the bar of The Mariners' Club. He had thought this would be the occasion when he would buy that long anticipated Martini, the one with the cocktail olive, the drink to celebrate new prospects. But the occasion did not warrant it. The au revoir to *Los Reyes* turned out to be unexpectedly stiff and awkward. None of them would accept anything alcoholic. The bass player, so comical and lively earlier, looked tired and depressed. The band was not accustomed to being thanked in this way, and though they tried to smile and be polite, they could not share Neil's sense of triumph and relief over what was, for them, just another night's work, and poorly paid at that.

Chapter Fifteen

Loss of Face

"No one's saying it wasn't any good . . ."

Chan's voice seemed very flat and distant, as if he'd retreated to some position further off in their relationship. A film of deceit covered his brown eyes and they held Neil's for a moment only. Chan was giving nothing away this morning. In fact, he might be taking something back. The third person in his office, the squat, bat-like man whom Neil had spotted at The Mariners' Club the previous evening, didn't want to defer to the judgement just given, grudging though it was. This man shifted now in the rattan armchair, preparing to discharge some forthright and contrary opinion.

Neil had no seat for this meeting. He had parked himself at the side of the office on a stack of boxes for the travel agency. Each box was labelled in stencilled English and slab pictograms with its own Asian dreamland: Indonesia, Malaysia, Thailand, Vietnam, Japan, Philippines . . . Neil sat in silence on his boxes and his mind was in stasis, frozen, no thought could move in any direction.

He had come by, late morning, as arranged with Chan, to discuss the show. There had been a lot of good things to discuss. He had been in a mood of sublime confidence and goodwill, ready to share the spoils of triumph with Elbert Chan, and to share some of the plans he'd already conceived for the immediate future. Over a celebratory breakfast in McDonald's he'd considered carefully, soberly, the business side of this morning's meeting. By now they should have been drawing up the terms and conditions of a contract. Neil had even made a few written notes, in his spiral flip-pad, to organize his thoughts on various clauses: on areas where concessions were possible, on areas where no concessions were possible. Those lewd acts . . . But the notes were still in his back pocket. He was sitting on his flip-pad.

He had asked himself in McDonald's, enjoying his double portion of hash browns, glancing down at the busy street beyond the glass – Wasn't there something of a Hong Kong story here? Wasn't it this will, this endurance and tenacity, he'd asked himself, drinking his coffee, this readiness to take a risk and get up there against all odds, and believe in what you were doing and to hell with what people thought, wasn't it this that fuelled the place? And hadn't he, he'd asked himself, hadn't he woken up a part of all that this morning? The names of those other clubs had begun to light up and glow in his mind: The American Club, The Pacific Club, The Clearwater Bay Golf & Country Club . . . And from there of course there were the international engagements, the reciprocal deals with clubs and hotels all over East Asia, in Osaka, Manila, Jakarta, Bangkok and Singapore . . . He'd travel Business Class or First Class via Chan's travel agency. To the facetious receptionists he'd say – *Yes, please. First class to Bangkok. That'll do nicely. Thank you very much. Wanna come along?* Assuming Star Tributes took shape in the way Chan had described there would be women, at last. There would be the female acts. The Monroes and Madonnas; the Marianne Faithfulls, the Shirley Basseys manqué. They would be sitting next to him on the plane, ordering their sticky cocktails . . . A veritable line-up of femmes fatales, no doubt, and they would be a lot of fun. Oh, they'd have some laughs on the plane, flying from one city to the next . . . And of course there would be one girl in particular, that lovely Petula Clark, who . . .

Everything had been slotting into place.

There had been a niche, after all. Chan had been right all along.

But now Neil sat in silence on the boxes in Chan's office. Some secretion, some protective anaesthetic, had numbed his mind before his disappointment could completely overwhelm him. The disappointment was still there, inside his chest, a physical sensation, like heartburn, keeping his breathing shallow and restrained. The feeling was pointed, sharp, agonizingly sharp. It was a hook, no less, caught in his gullet, and he could not speak until it was disgorged.

He had arrived at Chan's office to find his place in the rattan armchair already taken. There was Chan behind his melamine desk as usual, in his cheap dark business suit, very sober and upright, his brown eyes torpid and slightly hooded, and covered in their new film of deceit. And then there was this other fellow, this short, grim figure in the rattan armchair, whom Chan had introduced as Tony Laprisco. Neil had been so preoccupied with his fantasies of contracts and East Asia tours and femmes fatales that he'd forgotten about the man who had been tagging along at The Mariners' Club.

In the office, this close, Neil could see who Tony Laprisco really was. His face was a mock-up of Neil Diamond's as it had been towards the end of the star's youth. There was a glossy tightness about Laprisco's skin that looked wrong, though. The lines that should have been there, around such cynical middle-aged eyes, were all filled in, so the skin had a baby's smoothness. In contrast to this pallid gloss were the heavy black eyebrows, very dense and bushy, but clipped and nipped and pinched around the edges into neat rectangles. Their seams sagged at the ends with their own weight. The patch of skin between them was picked white and hairless. The rest of Laprisco's face had the uniform and insipid pallor of wax or plastic. In fact, it was exactly that of a puppet. Neil half-expected the light to catch on a set of strings above his head. A dense and crinkly mantle of black hair swept up from his forehead and fell stiffly to his caped shoulders. The cape, collar turned up, partially hid his neck, which had the turkey-wattle of a man in his late fifties, possibly early sixties. There was also an unsightly scar, a dark slit along a lumpy, vertical line in the region of his Adam's apple. The lumps either side of the slit were like fingertips. Childish fingertips holding the wound together from inside.

When at last he spoke he used his voice sparingly, as if his vocal cords might stick or tear at any moment. The Los Angeles accent was stale and flavourless as coffee grounds.

"Forgive me, Elbert," he began, with a dwarfish wave from beneath his cape. "I have to say that what I saw last night was pure travesty. There was no meaning in those songs at all."

Laprisco looked at Neil and tried to pin him down. He narrowed his eyes in an attempt to summon up a cop-show toughness. But there was no threat in any of this. Age and infirmity had eaten away whatever threat Laprisco once possessed. He was a small, weak man, old and shrunken before his time. His high heeled country & western boots jutted out daintily from his shiny slacks and hardly touched the floor.

"There was no meaning in those songs," he croaked, and his puppet head turned from side to side. The mantle of hair moved as a solid piece, like a hood or helmet. "There was no meaning in those songs. None at all by the time you'd finished with 'em, pal. It was just a travesty." Laprisco swallowed hard after all this invective, and the infantile fingers in his throat clutched at his horrid scar. Neil looked for some sign of pain in the puppet face but there was none; all nerve ends had been cauterized long ago.

Neil at last found his tongue.

"The show was a success," he said. "Everyone enjoyed themselves. Everyone had a good time last night." He glanced across to Chan for help here. "The show was a success," he repeated, but his own repeats sounded feeble and defensive after Laprisco's bold attacks. "No one can deny that."

Chan remained silent.

"Success on what terms, pal?" Tony Laprisco came back at him with lilting sarcasm. He leant forward, forcing Neil's attention his way. "On what terms? A jackass like you gets up and sings songs that are so good they can't miss, and a bunch of sailors get up and dance to rhythms people have danced to for the last thirty years? Any rookie can do that. Any asshole can do that. That's not Neil Diamond. Neil Diamond comes from some place else. Some place you've never been to, that's for sure."

How long was this going on for, Neil wondered, and to what end? He looked again at Chan, but Chan was sitting behind his desk with his chin resting on his knitted hands, in an attitude of sublime indifference now. He did not look at Neil. He only stared ahead at the wizened figure in the rattan chair, and stared as if Laprisco had an attraction and a reality for him nothing else in the room could match. As if he had found, in the puppet features, the waxy skin, the static mantle of hair, what he had been searching for at last. Here was the real thing, the definite article, the very perfection of the product he wanted. He looked at Laprisco as if he were beautiful, or as if he'd fallen in love with him. Neil could make no sense of that. Had Laprisco frightened him somehow? Had he already struck a deal? Was it conceivable that he, Neil, could be ousted, after just one night – and such a night of triumph! – by this puppet in the rattan chair?

"Look," Neil began, with very English reasonableness,

"I'm sorry if I offended you somehow, Mr. Laprisco. No doubt you have your own way of doing those songs that is just as successful. Maybe more successful. I don't want to argue with you about that. What I want to know is, what's the point of this meeting here today? I came to see Elbert."

"The point is," Laprisco announced, "I don't ever want to see you do what you did to those songs again, friend."

"Fine." Neil forced a smile, then glanced across to Chan for support. Who is this guy?

"Don't be cute, pal. Read my lips." Neil looked back, still smiling. Laprisco pointed at his lips, thinned by age and a life of song. "No more shows. Finito."

Neil frowned and looked to Chan again. Chan returned his look now, but there was no expression whatever in his eyes. Neil had at last come face to face with the oriental inscrutability revered and deplored throughout history. It was Laprisco who explained.

"I'm going to do some shows for Elbert, Mr. Atherton. We're letting you go. As of today. This morning. Period."

The sudden dropping of his surname into the proceedings stung Neil.

"I'll be doing all the clubs," Laprisco drawled, his manner lazy now the truth was out. "My band's already here. At The Excelsior. We're doing three days at The Excelsior starting Tuesday and then The American Club – " he glanced at Chan for confirmation; received it – "The American Club next weekend, then all the other clubs. All the major clubs. The best clubs. Then out to Manila, Bangkok, Singapore, the Mandarin Oriental, and so on. Elbert's fixing all the tickets next door . . ."

Neil was staring at Elbert Chan. This was quite a betrayal.

"My business manager's already faxed through a contract and Elbert's already signed it. The deal's done. It's all over, pal."

If Chan and Laprisco had expected some emotional scene where Neil stormed out of the room never to be seen again, it was their turn to be disappointed. A silence fell in the poky office, so that the hum of the air conditioner became obtrusive. Neil didn't look at either of them, these men who'd conspired, plotted and overthrown him before he'd even come to power, or even been paid. Instead he stared between them at the pretentious, lolling Anglepoise, whose unlit lamp was actually facing his way, like some defective instrument of interrogation. Then he stared at the opposite wall, at the laminated list of Entertainments Managers that had been the source of so much agitated dreaming and scheming. It was now suspended over July's girl, who stood in a long profile shot, bare-breasted, nipples erect, in a pert gymslip, reaching on tiptoe up a rack of chrome-plated weights.

June's girl had gone. Had quit him too.

The list of Entertainments Managers hung straighter on its treasury tag than it had when Neil had first stopped by, weeks ago. It must have been taken down this morning, or perhaps last night, while Chan discussed arrangements with Tony Laprisco and pointed out this name and that name, made this call and that call, those calls that Neil had never been able to persuade Chan to make, to Martin Wong at The Pacific Club, or Gavin Fan at The Clearwater Bay Golf & Country Club – *I've got a window here in the itinerary of Tony Laprisco, who's out here from L.A. playing The Excelsior this week, but you'll have to give me a quick decision because Tony flies to Osaka next Tuesday and I've promised The American Club Saturday, so –*

"I think we had better come to some kind of agreement," Neil said coolly, his eyes lingering on the list, the girl, her breasts.

There was a pause. Neil glanced first at Chan, then at Laprisco.

Chan's expression did not change. The poker player.

One of Tony Laprisco's droopy eyebrows lifted in surprise at Neil's note of challenge, and the wrinkled tissue from his eye-socket, his own original and untreated skin, very stained and mottled, very frail, was itself surprised by daylight.

Neil's voice was firm with Laprisco: "If you go ahead with these shows you can count on a number one fan, Mr. Laprisco. Every night. On that I give you my word."

Laprisco's eyebrow dropped. He grunted. Was that all? "You won't get past the door, pal. I'll fix that. Elbert'll fix that."

Neil looked squarely at each of them in turn as he continued: "Well, you better fix it good. Real good," Neil said, raising his voice. It was his turn to talk turkey. "Because I have nothing to lose, you see. Nothing at all." He gave Laprisco a long, hard stare. "And you know what will hit you, don't you? While you're singing *Cracklin' Rosie* and *Sweet Caroline*? Not food. Not fish-heads. Not chicken wings. I'm not talking about that. You know what'll hit you, don't you?" They all knew what he was talking about. He didn't need to say it. "Can you handle that?"

There was no big emotion but it was all clear, loud, matter-of-fact.

"Nothing will stop me doing that," Neil continued. "Not while I can eat and breathe and shit. You're going to have to kill me to stop me doing that."

Laprisco tried to laugh it off but it was obvious he was shocked.

"You really are a fucking kook!"

He'd shot his bolt though and everyone knew it. His insults were lame now. Neil had raised a practical threat to which insults were no match. His loudness and gravity of purpose had given everyone something to think about, including himself. Did he mean what he said? Yes, he meant what he said. And no one would want someone like him around, someone in his state of mind. Like having a highjacker or a terrorist in the crowd. And to get rid of him would be a real headache – he'd make sure of that. Oh yes. No one knew those streets outside better than him.

Neil looked to the floor. He sat on the cardboard boxes with his head lowered, his long, dyed black hair hanging loose around his face, and his hands tucked under his skinny thighs. It was an attitude befitting a much younger Neil Atherton, to be found backstage twenty years ago, sitting on a trestle or loudspeaker, perhaps. He was too old to be parked here on these boxes to one side of Chan's office. And yet just a few feet away there was Tony Laprisco, at least ten years his senior, who was quite at ease with what he had become in his struggle to wrest fame and fortune from a petty life. Whatever talents Laprisco had been born with he had used to the very last dreg. And when had he been born? Fifty-eight or sixty years ago? During the second world war, maybe? A Pearl Harbour baby, maybe? How had their lives, starting out from such different times and places, converged here in Elbert's office? How could such an intersection be made sense of? Only the songs of Neil Diamond could make sense of such a thing.

Chan, always the first to identify the decisive issue, was the next to speak. He cleared his throat.

"How much do you want?"

"Not much," Neil said, smiling wanly at his old partner. "The fare back to England, plus a couple of thousand to keep me going . . . Then I'll be off your hands. In half a day I'll be the other side of the world. You happy, me happy, everyone bubbling over with happiness."

Chan glanced at Laprisco, but his new man was looking only at his fingernails, leaving any concession to his agent. For Tony Laprisco, who had already sacrificed so much to his art, there could be no further loss of face.

Chapter Sixteen

Trabajan

Chan's haste was really quite unseemly. Within a few minutes his receptionists had organized a discount economy ticket for a stop-over flight with Singapore Airlines, five o'clock that afternoon. Just like that. Not even a night flight. It was as if the only thing in the world that mattered to Chan right now was to get rid of Neil. He'd become bad feng shui. He had to be disposed of before his bad luck spread and infected something else. The travel agency. The printing business. The sports franchise . . .

In ten minutes they were in the back of a cab taking a snakes & ladders route through backstreets to Neil's block. By cab it was no distance at all – no more than a five minute ride, even doubling back on themselves every other turn. Neil made an alteration to his imaginary street map, relocating *The Languages and Translation Services Ltd.* to a spot much closer to the central 'You Are Here' hole of Chan's office. Just for the memories.

Chan told the driver to wait double-parked in the street.

He'd said nothing to Neil in the cab, apart from demanding his address, and he said nothing to him in the lift either. While they ascended the only sound was the rattling fan above their heads sucking in foul air from the lift shaft. The same air the cabin pumped into the corridors and classrooms on the eighth floor, and that passed in and out of Mr. Cheung's unwholesome lungs. Well, here was a showdown, an exposure, the truth laid bare. What would Chan make of Cheung, and of Neil's 'home', his 'apartment', his 'bedroom'? And what would Cheung make of Chan, come to that?

Neil was in the habit of holding his breath in the lift but on this last journey, standing behind the grave and composed Elbert Chan, he found himself forced to breathe deeply to calm himself. The enormity of his disappointment this morning, together with the absurdity of what was now happening – and at such a pace! – had induced a desperate hysteria. The situation mocked itself and mocked Chan, robbed him of his businesslike formality and dignity. In the reflection of the cabin walls, in their filthy, stippled aluminium, Chan's face was pitted with acne scars, and his suit looked grubby and shapeless. Under the cabin light his face had the pallor of grave illness, of liver or kidney failure. It was a ghoulish reflection, and full of menace, a truer portrait of Chan, Neil considered, like something a painter or photographer might have achieved.

The extremity of the situation inflamed Neil's hysteria, he couldn't help it, and just before the end of the ride, as they passed the seventh floor, a burst of laughter escaped him. Worse, he broke wind, just afterwards. Both sounds were loud, brash, shockingly vulgar. The damp smell of his wind, a smell of half-digested hash browns, like rotting pastry, was harmless enough and soon dissipated by the fan, but to break wind in a lift was to break a taboo in Hong Kong. An unforgivable discourtesy. He apologized.

"I'm sorry," he said. "I'm sorry . . ."

Chan didn't even turn his way.

When they got out Chan rapped smartly on the door of *The Languages and Translation Services Ltd.* As if in response, vague sounds came from within. Chanting voices. Surging. Falling. Neil stood with his hands locked behind his back, trying to restore self-control, but of course the more he tried to keep the hysteria in check the more absurd things seemed, and the more irrepressible his mirthless laughter became. He remembered the choir in this attitude on the swimming pool patio, hands behind their backs, just last night. *Dai Aspora*. The choirmaster on the diving board. His jokes. Their version of *Wandering Star*. Such associations were difficult to deal with, but the real pressure of the hysteria came from the underlying, half-formed, very strange idea that it was he, rather than Chan, or the wretched Laprisco, who really held the power now. Neil had a heady feeling, an omniscient and omnipotent view of what was going down here. It was he, did they but know it, who was going to betray them – Oh yes, he was certain of it. It was inevitable. Fated. But unlike Chan and Laprisco he had no breathing space in which to conceive his deception, instead he had to think on his feet and invent his plan as he went along, and with everything happening so fast that wasn't easy.

The lugubrious Mr. Cheung opened the door, but only wide enough to see out, as if he were trying to keep the chanting behind him indoors, as if it were a cause of shame or complaint. Cheung glanced over Chan's shoulder to Neil. Neil stood very erect, hands behind his back, bolted together now with self-control. Behind his tortoiseshell glasses Cheung's eyes slid back and forth between his visitors with primeval wariness. Neil had never been allowed to come up here before 8 p.m. This was out of sequence, out of order. It didn't fit between the blue columns of his ledger, or his wife's ledger. He withdrew his head. He was going to close the door.

Chan's patience was spent. He barked out something in Cantonese, speaking in the same way to Cheung as he had to the taxi driver. After the blast of words there was a momentary pause, then the old man stepped aside, opened the door wide. Chan's presence, for someone so small and nondescript, was quite extraordinary.

Inside *The Languages and Translation Services Ltd.* there reverberated a chorus of old-fashioned rote instruction. It was distracting for Neil finally to see and hear the place at work. The sound was disturbing. It was religious, full of eternal dolour, or like a dismal labour-camp dirge in various keys and tongues. Mrs. Cheung was at work as usual, ruling out blue columns with the short wooden ruler.

In the classroom down the passage from her cubicle – in what had been, for over a month, his bedroom – Neil saw a lesson in full progress. The door was wedged open to allow some lift shaft air into the cell. A tall and heavy set man with sandy curls was sitting at the head of the Formica table. That table where Neil had flattened his stage outfit every night, ever since he'd bought it. The teacher, or instructor was in his mid-thirties. He wore a creased, plain white shirt, grey flannel trousers, and black socks with leather sandals. There was something unmistakably English about his slovenly dress and demeanour. He was conjugating Spanish verbs, of all things. In order to emphasise each new inflexion he slapped the table severely with his open palm. Despite that, not everyone was paying attention. Further down the table, keeping clear of the instructor maybe, an adult student sat hunched with his head in his hands, asleep or in despair. Sitting next to the teacher and in full view was a silent Chinese teenager, a bright and cheeky looking fellow with a floppy fringe, wearing an orange tracksuit top. Weekend clothes. He caught Neil's glance and stared back, wide-eyed with insolence. Ignoring his instructor completely the boy mouthed to Neil a single word, very slowly:

'Hel . . . lo . . .'

Neil gave him a frown of adult disapproval – Attend to your

class! – but the boy only did it again:

'Hel . . . lo . . .'

The instructor leant forward, his torso blocking the boy from view, in order to reprimand someone at the other end of the table, some laggard or sluggard who just couldn't keep up:

"*Trabajo!*
Trabajas!
Trabaja!
Trabajamos!
Trabajáis!
Trabajan!
Once more, after me!"

The instructor leant back for the repeat and the insolent student was there again, ready for Neil, staring up, smiling and wide-eyed. He might have been about to blow a kiss:

'Hel . . . lo . . .'

Neil scowled, thrust out his jaw – Get back to your work!

"*Trabajaba!*
Trabajabas!
Trabajaba!
Trabajábamos!
Trabajabais!
Trabajaban!
Once more! After me!"

Neil turned from the room. He had to think! He had to plan! But he sensed the boy behind his back:

'Hel . . . lo . . .'

Chan was about more important business. Oblivious to the noise all around he was pursuing some delicate negotiations with the devious Mr. Cheung. They had moved to Cheung's reception desk down the corridor. It seemed Cheung detected that, despite the forcefulness of Chan's manner, there was an underlying pressure that rendered his visitor vulnerable, and through some deceit he had persuaded Chan to part with money in exchange for Neil's passport and belongings. Neil frowned as he watched Chan shell out, note by note, what looked like a fortnight's rent in exchange for his worldly goods. Cheung then recounted the money, note by note, before surrendering Neil's goods over his reception desk, piece by piece. Finally, from a drawer in his desk, he took out Neil's passport, the heart of the deal, and handed it over.

Chan was fully laden as he came back down the corridor. Cheung didn't help or follow – he was busy recounting again Chan's $100 bills into the drawer of his reception desk. As Chan walked back down the wooden corridor, burdened with all Neil's luggage, his suitcase and guitar, his shameful bindle tucked underarm, as Chan walked towards Neil he stared at Neil with an expression of fierce contempt, even hatred, directed at Neil and at him alone. Because Chan had been right all along, of course, hadn't he – You are a tramp, a gypsy, aren't you, Mister? He'd known from the start and he should have known better.

But Neil just didn't care about that now. *That's why the lady* . . . It was his turn to be sublimely indifferent. He held up a hand, arresting Chan at the corner.

"Wait a minute," he said.

"Wait?" Chan snapped, standing there with all the gear.

"My case."

Chan handed over the suitcase. Neil knelt down and set it on the floor and opened it. Things seemed to be as he'd left them. His black stage outfit was neatly folded on top and strapped in under the elastic belts, then weighted further with his hardback book. This had slipped a little. Neil lifted the stage outfit at each corner, all the way round, checking that the rest of his stuff was untouched. No trusting Cheung, or Mrs. Cheung. Everything appeared to be in order. He was about to close the case when he had a change of heart about the

Michael Aspel book, the autobiography. Something was wrong. It was different somehow, altered in shape and weight and colour – altogether a lighter, cheaper, trashier thing, hiding there in his suitcase. Bad feng shui. Why let the past ruin the future? He took the book out. He closed the case then stood up, the case in one hand and the book in the other, and nodded to Chan – he'd carry the case, thanks. He stepped over to Mrs. Cheung's cubicle.

"For you," he said, reaching into the cubicle and leaving Aspel's life on her makeshift shelf, next to her ledger.

Mrs. Cheung looked at the book, at Aspel's smiling face, then over her shoulder at Neil. She seemed startled, frightened. By the book? The face? Her hair was drawn up in a tight bun. Neil noted for the first time that it was always that way.

Neil smiled and nodded to the book. "For you," he said, more warmly.

"Come on." He felt Chan step up behind him. "Come on . . ."

But Mrs. Cheung had picked up the book, the bad feng shui, in both hands, and was trying to offer it back to Neil. Her mouth was thin-lipped, her face drawn with anxiety. She had sensed it already. The bad feng shui.

"No," Neil said, still smiling. He shook his head. "It's for you. For you." He pointed at himself – "From me – " then to her – "to you."

Again Chan's patience was soon spent. He reached past Neil and snatched the book from Mrs. Cheung and slung it down the corridor towards the Spanish class, towards Neil's old bedroom. It lay cover up, with Aspel's face now grinning the other way, pointing its bad feng shui towards the open classroom.

At the smack of the book on the floor the teacher broke off his chant and looked out. He frowned grimly at the disturbance, at the book, and at Chan and Neil down the corridor. The teacher's face was much older than Neil would have expected. A bag of angry lines laced up under an effeminate, curly bonnet. He was pushing sixty, maybe, the man who had his room by day, in his black socks and sandals. Neil smiled to himself. Him by day, me by night. All sorts to make a world.

"Come on," Chan said. "The taxi."

From the comfort of the taxi's air conditioning Neil stared out at the pavements he had walked all day for the past few weeks. Pavements thick with touts and tourists and businessmen and businesswomen, and, running through the crowd like dye running through a current, that darker, smaller tribe in rags, intent on a million errands in the heat, pushing and pulling their rusty trolleys laden with fish, broken electric motors, blocks of ice . . . He passed by them all now in the cool taxi, on his way to the international airport.

But his plan! The plan . . .

They took a left turn down Waterloo Road towards Yau Ma Tei and the new roads out to Lantau Island and Chek Lap Kok. At Reclamation Street they were held up at the lights. Neil knew this street, though he had never known where it fitted into the labyrinth of Tsim Sha Tsui. He was surprised to find it so close to his daytime haunts. Half a year ago, half his lifetime ago, he had ventured down here on household errands for Angel, to buy paint, shelves, shower curtains, and more recently, those ceramic bedside lamps . . . Here they sold every conceivable fixture and fitting for the home, office or factory. The street was part of the old workshop of Hong Kong. Men squatted at platform saws on the pavement wearing nothing but shorts and sandals, slicing up lengths of rusty iron and aluminium, rods of copper or bronze. Their greasy bodies had been worked to such a leanness they looked diseased.

The lights changed and Neil turned away.

Not more than a couple of hours ago he had sat in McDonald's imagining that he was becoming part of the citizenry here . . .

The plan!

Their taxi was sucked up a concrete chute onto the expressway corridors to Lantau and the vast container terminals at Kwai Chung. Views of the harbour and the business district opened up on the left, and the ferries, Jetfoils and swaggering liners were pretty in their silvery wakes, under brilliant sunshine. Neil suddenly found himself able to look at and enjoy the spectacle as he had never been able to before. He did not have to worry, for the duration of this taxi ride at least, about keeping body and soul together. He sat on the right of Elbert Chan, the wrong side to enjoy the view, but he unashamedly leant forward and stared past his companion to the open sea. Chan looked stern and kept his eyes front, like a police escort, content to endure this awkward journey in silence.

The Tsing Ma Bridge swung into view. The scale of the thing was staggering. He'd read somewhere that the saddles for the suspension cables weighed 500 tonnes each. Hoisting them to the top and fixing them in place had been an unparalleled feat of civil engineering. And while the bridge-builders applied themselves to the physics of that challenge, what had he been doing here, in Asia's premier world-class city? Well, he'd been busy too. While they applied themselves to the physics of bridge-building, he'd applied himself to the lyrics of *Longfellow Serenade*, committing those lines to heart. Or maybe he'd been reading about interviews with Neil Diamond that had taken place around thirty years ago: *"This is a beautiful beautiful Tom Paxton song, very lovely, very delicate . . ."* Or he'd been gleaning what hard facts he could behind the composition of *Sweet Caroline* – or was it *Cracklin' Rosie*? – purportedly written in a Memphis hotel room one sultry evening and recorded the following day. And while he did that the bridge-builders worked to binding deadlines full of penalty clauses, and jacked their 500 tonne cable saddles up the stanchions of the Tsing Ma Bridge, and lifted into place sections of ready-made road and railway.

Ah well, it took all sorts to make a world, Neil thought again, wryly, leaning back into his seat next to Elbert Chan. But as they sped along the magnificent bridge at eighty kilometres an hour, high above the shimmering sea, it struck Neil that this was not actually true. His sort need not be taken at all. There was, self-evidently, a need of some kind for people such as Neil Diamond, though surely even they must find it hard to live with themselves after a while. But whatever case could be made for the pedlar of trash and illusion, there was surely no case at all to defend one who only followed, the counterfeit and impostor running along behind. Surely there was no room on the ark for such a stowaway. It was an inexcusable thing to do with a human life. Even if he had made a success of it, even if he had played The American Club and The Clearwater Bay Golf & Country Club, and had made a living, and had sat next to Petula Clark in Business Class, flying city to city, even if his most sublime fantasies of wealth and success and sexual fulfilment had come true, there was an inherent worthlessness about it all.

But as the Tsing Ma Bridge came to an end and the freeway opened up towards the airport, Neil's head rolled against the headrest and he shut his eyes. There it was again. That lofty view of the world. That glorious view. This time, from the Tsing Ma Bridge. Like any other view it was something you either could or could not afford. And he couldn't afford it. Not any part of it. He had to forget all that. He had to earn, or somehow to turn the tables on his erstwhile ally and cheat him for all he could get. The taxi was cruising at 110 k.p.h., on the speed limit, and once again his time was running out.

In the end subterfuge was the easy part.

Chan said, at the check-in desk, by way of farewell: "Here's your money."

Neil counted his money. He thumbed through the notes awkwardly because he had his passport and ticket in one hand, the new bank notes in the other, and his guitar strap was sliding down his arm. When he finished counting he shook his head, licked his thumb and forefinger, and started a recount. He rubbed and checked one by one each crisp, red, $100 bank note. Chan had handed him $1100, not $2000. $900 short. Nearly half missing. $900. Excuse me? Mr. Cheung? Mr. Chan? A mistake, here, I think, because . . . The act of robbing him like this was of as much consequence as the missing notes themselves. He felt some slippage in his bowels. Something poked and stirred deep down there. He broke wind again, softly, couldn't help it. A distress signal.

Chan shut his eyes and winced. "You're disgusting. You know that?"

"We agreed on two thousand dollars. To keep me going."

Chan opened his eyes. The film of deceit had not blinked away.

"I had to pay a fortnight's rent."

Neil held up his hands, full of notes and vital documents. Vital documents. The genuine dismay he felt about this – that swindling bastard Cheung! That utter bastard! – made his subterfuge at the check-in desk effortlessly convincing. What lay at the end of these eleven red bank notes? What came next, after each and every one of them had been broken up and squandered on his petty, piecemeal existence? Nothing. Darkness. Blackness. The unthinkable. The pit. The pipes and wires.

He pushed his guitar strap back up his arm. He needed more time. He had to correct this somehow. But how? The concourse of the brand-new airport fell quiet as if in sympathy. His gaze settled on one of the magnificent lifts that connected the Arrivals and Departures floors, set in a cabinet of shining steel and glass. His concentration became hooked up for a moment in its gliding mechanisms, its cogs and hydraulics and sliding doors, all the elegance of its engineering on display.

All sorts to make a world . . .

His eyes came back again to the bald, blank face of Elbert Chan, but before he could speak Chan made his move.

"Goodbye."

And he just turned about and walked away. Turned his back on Neil and walked away. Neil watched his diminutive figure until it bobbed and sank below the waves of travellers and well-wishers crowding the concourse.

"Hello . . . Can I help?"

It was the check-in attendant. In Girl Guide uniform. Silly hat and smile. She needed a response. Her smile and uniform demanded a response.

Neil adjusted his guitar strap and picked up his suitcase.

"Could you direct me to the toilets, please?"

Chapter Seventeen

Love in the Afternoon

By the time the Airport Express left Lantau Island the key decision was in place and there could be no going back on it. That gave some peace of mind. From the comfort of the brand-new air-conditioned carriage, with its expensively upholstered seats and its scented carpets, Neil absorbed the vistas of sea and mountains beyond the window: the sea traffic, the fishing junks and the tugs and dredging barges – *Those in peril on the sea* – and the dead mountains behind, blasted by quarries, blackened by fire, shabby and ruined.

By the time the train raced across Tsing Yi to the outskirts of Kowloon, where sea and mountain gave way to hamlets of apartment blocks, in their serried ranks of beige and grey, with their futuristic flyovers ending in mid-air, by the time Neil re-entered the hard, urban ambit of his prospects, he had narrowed things down to two possible scenarios. One was grim and unpleasant, difficult even to contemplate. The other was a touch soft and sentimental, warm and optimistic. Staring out the window at the changing view, Neil focused on the first, filling it with so many bleak and uncomfortable details that the second took on tones of realism.

There would be no end to her anger. She would resent bitterly what he had done, the breach of trust, and the way he had wasted her money and her time. She would hold him at the door, not even let him in. She'd shout him down, in the tiny, echoeless vestibule outside her apartment. And he'd just have to stand there and take it, surrounded by his ragged bits and pieces, his suitcase, bindle and guitar.

Yet, if he were patient enough to hear her out, and let the big emotion wash by, at last she might let him come in and explain. And then, whatever else she objected to, whatever else might shock her or even amuse her about his story, she had to respect his tenacity and determination. Key virtues, in her book, and that should buy him time. And the deal he would put before her now, on the low glass coffee table, the bottom line of the deal he would put before her now, was that: *He had quit all that crazy business!* – but he had definitely quit, and he was having nothing more to do with any of it, and all he was asking for right now, all he wanted from her, was another ticket home and a little time, a little grace time, as it were, in order to get back from Chan the money he was owed from The Mariners' Club engagement, and to settle his account there. In fact, Chan and he were about square by his reckoning, but it was a plausible line. One week. Just one week. For proper closure. The grace time to do that. A key line. Key virtues, key lines. Grace time. Like they gave you in the car parks before your parking ticket expired. And when the week was up she could follow him all the way onto the plane, if she liked. She could see him strapped in. She could have a word with the chief air steward, call him over to the seat – *Under no circumstances whatever is this man allowed to . . .*

In the somewhat more optimistic scenario, as Elbert Chan might have put it, Angel was actually very pleased to see him. She let him in straightaway. At first there was some indignation, of course, for show, for pride, but that gave way to the deeper feelings soon enough. She did things for him. Polite things. She made him a cup of tea and she gave him something to eat. Nothing special. Not a croissant or Danish –

just a plate of toast, biscuits, or even bread and butter, something easy and to hand. She called out to ask him which he wanted from the kitchen, hiding in there while she pulled herself together. When she came back with his toast, biscuits or bread and butter, while he sipped his tea, she asked more personal things. She asked after his health, about how he'd been looking after himself. In fact, he didn't have to say much in this scenario, because it was she that did the confessing. She told him she'd not enjoyed coming home to the empty apartment every evening. The quietness and solitude had begun to oppress her. She'd become irritable at work, especially towards the end of the day, and she wasn't performing so well. Colleagues had noticed: *'Hey Angel . . . Everything all right at home? . . .'* She just missed having him around – someone to rely on, someone who knew where she came from and understood the shape of her life. They'd been together a long time, after all, and they'd worked out their own way of getting by – a companionship, if you like, not like other people's, other couples', but no less valid for that – and it was so easy to take companionship for granted and to imagine you could do without it, but you really couldn't. It went much deeper than you knew . . .

By the time the Airport Express pulled in at Kowloon, Neil was ready for what lay ahead. His suitcase, bindle and guitar slipped easily from the rollers of the new luggage racks, and his worldly goods felt light in his hands. He decided to splash out on a taxi for the short journey to Kowloon Tong. There he'd pick up a KCR train back to Sha Tin. He'd take the courtesy bus to Pictorial Gardens and he should arrive at about half past six, he estimated, shortly after she'd got home.

According to the wristwatch of the man in the seat next to him, he arrived at Pictorial Gardens a few minutes ahead of schedule. His own useless Rolex still adorned his wrist at all times, too shiny to discard. It was one of the things he anticipated laughing about with Angel, once the ice was broken. He'd take it off and put it neatly before them on the glass coffee table, setting it out there as if on a jeweller's counter, chuckling at the silliness of it. His baggage he'd laugh at too, the pathetic bindle and trashy guitar, which he struggled to drag out now from the courtesy bus.

He'd quit all that crazy business – Oh yes, indeed – and he was definitely having nothing more to do with any of it.

He checked the car park before going up to her flat. The Mazda wasn't there. She wasn't back yet. Or something had happened to the car, maybe. It was too early for her to have gone out already. Of course the unimaginable crossed his mind. She'd moved apartment. She'd cut her losses on the lease, packed up and moved to some fancy studio flat on the Island. But that was unlikely. Angel was not one to waste money, and her expenses would have been redoubled with a move to the Island, even for quite a modest place.

He didn't think about what he had to do. There was still a chance she might be in so he had to get up there. He carted his case, his bindle and guitar into the lift and pressed the button for the twelfth floor.

As he removed his luggage from the lift an unmistakable sound penetrated between the noises of his movements, between the scrape of his suitcase against the door, the bang of his guitar case on the fake marble tiles, and the soft thud of his bindle, tossed into the airless vestibule. He somehow ignored it, this sound, put it off, was deaf to it, shunned its meaning, denied where it came from. But once everything was out in the vestibule and the lift door had shut and the lift car had slunk away, once all noise and movement had ceased, he could not escape the sound, nor his own understanding of it. To distract himself he listened out for those dull, inevitable clangs as the lift descended, as the counterweights passed by their floor.

There was only one other apartment door in their vestibule. He stepped across to that door and listened. Nothing. Silence. Empty. No one lived in that apartment. A speculative investment, the agent had said, to be re-floated on the next price tide.

He had nowhere else to go but their apartment door. There was only the lift door, and the door he'd already been to. The vestibule was no more than ten feet by twelve feet. The size of a single bedroom. A confined, windowless, claustrophobic space.

The unmistakable sound seemed to amplify, come closer to him, beckon to him, in this tiny antechamber. The lift came up again and passed by, ascending to the top apartments. He saw the cabin light come and go.

He stepped up to their door.

At the door, with his ear against the wood, he could hear the man's noise too. A tight, restrained noise. An animal noise, through clenched teeth. Coming and going. He was carrying her around the apartment, fucking her as he carried her around with him, causing her to groan, to pant, to cry out in ecstasy.

Thoughts of banging at the door or ringing the bell, of killing their pleasure, of killing them, lasted a moment only. Neil was defeated here, in the fake marble vestibule. There was nothing for him here, stuck in this tiny, airless, humid space, nothing for him but humiliation and despair. And on and on they went. Around the apartment. Knocking against things, holding onto things, coming close to the front door, only a few feet from where Neil stood, just the other side of this wooden panel. He had never been that kind of lover to her. He had no rights here. There had been nothing to come back to after all, nothing even to talk about. No tea and toast or bread and butter.

He summoned the lift and heaved all his luggage back into the car.

Once downstairs and outside he took a shortcut round to the bus stop. In doing so he crossed the visitors' parking spaces. There was the red Mazda, parked crookedly in the sun, the roof still down. They had been in such a hurry she hadn't even put her car away in its proper place in the shade.

He hitched the strap of his guitar case high over his shoulder and headed off, back on the road, under the rich evening sky. He tried to engage his mind on more modest business. The route he needed to Tsim Sha Tsui and to the dreadful Chungking Mansions.

Chapter Eighteen

No Reprise

The layout of The American Club was clear from the second level of the car park. The area for alfresco functions had been hewn out of the rock of the seafront itself, and the best tables looked down directly to the open sea, across the empty private beach. The members and their guests wore tuxedoes and evening dresses. There was a dress code here. There was decorum. Waiters all in white hurried between tables under the direction of a lean and mean head waiter. He pointed, snapped his fingers, and even clapped his hands with old-fashioned authority. Neil leant forward on the car park railing, coolly taking in the scene below. This was where the barbershop quartet performed each month, according to Chan, their harmonies underscored by the roll of the breakers, and punctured now and then by the claps and finger-snaps of the head waiter.

The razzmatazz for *Uncut Diamonds* was impressive, no denying it, and the first set had gone down well. The stage was broad enough to accommodate a sizeable line-up, but Laprisco had kept his musicians back, in the shadows, almost out of sight. He himself occupied a raised hexagonal platform downstage, lit all around by twined strands of multi-coloured fairy lights. Fairy lights were strung out all around the dining area, extending from a network suspended over the stage. The elevation of Laprisco's personal platform made him taller than his three black backing singers, who shared a lower platform, downstage right, with only a single string of plain fairy lights at its base.

It was a such a beautiful evening maybe the members of The American Club and their guests would have occupied every table with or without Uncut Diamonds. Elbert Chan was there, of course, keeping an eye on things, seated at a table for one close by the stage. There was a champagne bucket next to his table. Maybe that was complimentary, from the Entertainments Manager, via the head waiter, with a card for Elbert – *'Elbert, thank you so much. I think this guy's terrific. I really do. Terrific. I haven't seen the members enjoy their music so much since Manfred Mann came last year . . .'*

Now people kept turning in their seats and glancing back to the clubhouse, wondering when the band would return. At the end of the first set Laprisco had promised his audience he'd do requests and dedications after the break. Some people, the worse for a few glasses of wine, were impatient to make their requests and dedications known. They were writing things down for Laprisco on torn cigarette packets and paper napkins.

And Laprisco was making them wait, building it up, timing it right, the true professional.

Neil considered his position. The car park was on three levels. On the top were floodlit tennis courts whose powerful lights shadowed the levels below. Dressed all in black he was practically invisible, perfectly safe. He took in the vista that he'd studied earlier by daylight – over to the left were the lights of Turtle Cove, and across the bay a lighted path in Shek O Country Park, under the mass of Hok Tsui Shan mountain . . .

The time had come. He had to act.

He slipped away into the dim car park interior and walked down the line of Mercedes, BMW, Jaguar and Rolls Royce until he came to the far corner. Here a green Toyota sports car, some new but unwanted toy, sat on partially deflated tyres. The windscreen was thick with grime and festooned with valeting ads trapped under the wipers. Neil squeezed past the car, trying to avoid soiling his outfit on the dirty wings.

Now he looked down on the rock at the back of the stage. He could see all the way round to the steps that descended from the alfresco function area to the private beach.

His difficulty lay in gaining access to that beach. No doubt if he went through the club entrance it would be easy enough to find his way down to ground level, but he daren't risk that. If he were challenged in the club by anyone, anyone at all, his entire scheme would be blown away, and he had put too much into it, packed in tight too much hope and fantasy, to take a risk like that. If he had been intent on just abusing Laprisco somehow, creating a scene, ruining the performance, it wouldn't have mattered so much. But that wasn't quite what he had in mind.

He had to walk back to the coast road and find a way down to the beach through the rocks and foliage. But the road headed up and inland. Too steep. Too difficult. Besides, there would be no route through. There would be fences, gates, barbed wire, security, dogs – every precaution would have been taken to debar unaccompanied guests such as Neil Atherton.

Applause, rippling outward from the clubhouse, signified that Laprisco and his entourage were returning to the stage. Neil caught a glimpse of the short, bat-like figure stepping out jauntily between distant tables. He stopped after a couple of rows to pick up a request or dedication, which he slipped away in his cape without reading. Neil watched Laprisco smile and chat with the member or guest who'd given him the piece of paper. He leant over the table to say something about that particular song, or to ask something personal about the dedicatee. Watching this, a new feeling welled up inside Neil, and it complicated and confused his ideas about Tony Laprisco, and about what was going on here, about what he was doing here. He watched, fascinated, as Laprisco stopped and started between the tables, collecting more and more dedications en route to the stage. Then a member of the band stepped down and came forward to meet him with his radio mike, trying to hurry him up, hustle him – "Let's go, Tony!" – a rehearsed routine, without doubt, that only stalled things further, but very effective. On that cue Laprisco was suddenly obscured by his own audience, who unanimously stood and applauded, urging him on to the second set.

"Thank you . . ." He turned, pulling his arm from his friend . . . "Thank you . . . Thank you . . ."

The new feeling Neil had to come to terms with was envy. Green, bold, molten, overwhelming.

He tried to set it aside, along with all the other riotous feelings clamouring for predominance this evening. He had to act, make his move, that was all there was time for tonight. He had to get down there quickly and unseen. And now he got lucky. Halfway along the end of the car park there was a fire ladder. He looked about. This second level was like a deserted luxury car showroom. The attendant was on the ground floor in his air-conditioned hut, and very comfortable in there. The cars were parked for the long night ahead, if not for the whole weekend. Neil eased his way back between the dirty sports car and the wall and walked to the ladder. He climbed onto the wall and crouched there. Allowing no time for second thoughts he gripped the side of the ladder and shook it hard, making sure of its fixings, then put one thin black boot gingerly into the dark. He found a rung and worked his foot across until it locked against the other side. He took a breath, held it, and clambered out from the car park into the open air. Keeping himself tight and flat against the rungs, bracing himself there, he glanced up – nothing but the blaze of the tennis court floodlights – then down – the soft warm sand not thirty feet below.

Uncut Diamonds were tuning up. Without any preamble from Laprisco, far too quickly and without warning, they hit the opening rhythms of *Sweet Caroline*. The lead and bass guitars drew out those rhythms, gathering pace and volume as Neil descended, rung by precious rung, to the beach.

At the bottom of the ladder he hesitated, squatting in the sand, listening to *Sweet Caroline*. What confidence to leave this song until the second set! It made Neil feel amateur to remember how, in the shabby Compass Room of The Mariners' Club, he'd used up *Sweet Caroline* at the very start, sold out to the crowd, too uncertain of success to save it for when he might use it to best effect.

Under his boots the sand was just as soft and warm and powdery, just as luxurious, as he'd imagined it would be. He seemed to be sinking in it. He couldn't move himself. He stayed there, squatting at the foot of the ladder, clinging to the side bar. The sea breeze tousled his hair and filled his jacket. An awning flapped somewhere to his left, up the beach. The cover for a dinghy or jet-ski, perhaps, not tied down properly. He could hear the waves ahead lap and plash beneath the music. For a moment he could not stir himself. The warm breeze and the sounds of the sea were holding him back, fixing him there in the soft sand, on a level with elemental things. Then he rose, resolved, and ran, head down, his black hair bouncing on his shoulders, one hand clasping together the lapels of his jacket.

When he arrived at the foot of the concrete steps he had to stop a moment to catch his breath. He dusted the sand from his boots and removed some odds and ends of seaweed impaled on the stubby heels. He glanced up the sandy steps and began his ascent, but stopped again where the steps divided halfway up. To the right one flight led to the club pool, on a short pier over the sea. The pool was floodlit. Adolescent American voices were audible intermittently, shouting, shrieking, laughing in the pool, penetrating the night air with their hilarity and their obscenities – *"Over here! . . . Pass it over here, you fuckin' jerk! . . ."* There was a jungle cry, the smack of a belly flop, the sound of thrashing water. *". . . Hey motherfucker! Wadja doin'?!"*

Neil turned to the steps on the left that ascended to the alfresco dining area. *Sweet Caroline* was already in its second verse.

The sound of Laprisco's band was very good. Very good indeed. He had to admit that. In fact, it was excellent. It was so much better than what he had managed at The Mariners' Club with *Los Reyes*. This performance put that evening into perspective. For a moment he looked back upon Laprisco's vicious remarks in Chan's office as genuine, and not born of spite as he had supposed. Laprisco's band created a fuller and richer sound, much more a studio sound, and the backing singers made a huge difference – just as he'd known they would, when he'd talked through his arrangements with Chan. Chan had been wrong about that. He'd been wrong on so many counts, Elbert Chan, again and again and again. But now he sat up there, at his private table, keeping an eye on things, watching his new act, with his complimentary ice-bucket of champagne – *'Elbert, thank you so much. I think this guy's terrific. Terrific. I really do . . .'*

Success depended on the first few seconds up there. If things went wrong at the start there could be no recovery – he would face immediate humiliation, ridicule, laughter, expulsion.

And what if that did happen? What then?

Nothing. Neil had thought no further along those lines. Those lines converged in darkness at the back of his mind. A darkness that was at times terrifying, at times alluring.

He had spent so much of his life waiting like this, in abeyance, waiting his turn, that he'd become accustomed to taking a seat, as it were, and looking back at his life from a viewpoint of detached retrospection, as if it were part of a biography already written. Not his own biography, but a biography about someone more important in which he had a significant but not decisive role. And within this biography he just knew – somehow he'd always known – that there was a felicitous exit for him somewhere, near the end of some middling chapter, before the main life was fully explored. Tonight, though, at The American Club in Tai Tam, Neil had a sense that his middling chapter had taken a bad turn. If this plan tonight did not work, then – No, there was nothing else. Nothing at all. It was over. There was only the darkness, the blackness. The unthinkable darkness he had sensed, with a premonitory twinge, at the airport: the pit at the end of the trail of Chan's eleven red bank notes. If this did not work out tonight he might as well wait for high tide and wade out into the warm, forgiving South China Sea, under the moon and the stars, under the glittering waves . . .

So the timing had to be perfect. He took out his sunglasses, smoothed down his hair. He had no mirror to check how he looked, but he'd inspected himself as best he could in various wing mirrors in the car park, and was confident that in this light there could be nothing amiss about his appearance. His descent from the car park had been easy. His ascent up these steps had been easy. Maybe that was because tonight fate was on his side. Why should he not believe that? That tonight was *his* night, after all.

He put on the sunglasses.

He leapt up the steps two at a time and sprang onto the alfresco area. He was at the end of the line-up, ten feet or so from the backing singers. He stood there, in full view. The band was rising to the third refrain. In a moment he took in the sweep of white tables to his right and a blur of glittering dinner dresses and white tuxedoes, their brilliance subdued by his sunglasses. He saw the uplifted faces, all gazing at Laprisco's performance, and their uplifted smiles. And, yes, Elbert Chan at his single table, very close, staring up and smiling at Laprisco too . . . but starting now to turn, and to turn his way. Neil took a dash to his left and sprang onto the platform of the backing singers. Grinning wildly at the three black girls he plucked a radio mike from their centre stand. In just four more light and springy steps, in his thin black boots, he was out there, right out there, on the second hexagonal platform, with all its coloured fairy lights, out there with Laprisco himself, and simultaneously he was in full song, just like at The Mariners' -

Oh sweet, sweet, sweet Caroline. Would the band keep rolling? Would they keep it coming? Or would the sound behind him fade into discord and collapse, allowing the crash of the breakers, the sea breeze, the flap of an awning somewhere, the adolescent voices at the pool, to intervene and overwhelm –

Hey motherfucker! Wadja doin'?!

But no.

Just as he had foreseen, the audience loved his surprise entrance and Laprisco, quick as he was, could do nothing but go along with the pretence. The audience were already on their feet applauding this new enrichment of their truly great night out. Laprisco could only acquiesce to Neil's beaming smiles and theatrical gestures of warmth and friendship, and smile down to the audience himself, and try to keep up with the new power that Neil's harmony lent the act, and go along with the idea that Neil's appearance was actually part of a well rehearsed gimmick, his own idea, in fact, and now an established routine perfected between old showbiz friends –

the audience suddenly had double doublers, double Diamonds, duelling Diamonds!

Or did they? There were some who were applauding with such vigour it crossed Neil's mind that they thought the real Neil Diamond had turned up tonight, as part of a unique and freakish stunt. They thought the real Neil Diamond had stood up! From a nearby table Neil thought he heard someone say – *'No no no! The tall one is the real Neil Diamond! Which one? That tall one! That is Neil Diamond! I have all his albums!'*

Neil didn't neglect the band behind him: as soon as the pretence had caught he turned round to them, and to the backing singers, and he grinned knowingly at them, confirming this was all part of a surprise dreamt up between him and Tony. And because Tony had not stopped the show they swallowed this, or something like it, it didn't matter. They thought the whole thing was one of Tony's wacky ideas, perhaps, like coming out to Asia in the first place, or part of an idea that had been put to him and that he had taken on under pressure, for unknown, diverse reasons.

Neil knew Tony Laprisco could not stop the show now. There hadn't been one single moment when he could have stopped the show. Neil's manoeuvre had been so well timed and executed he'd caught the audience in the palm of his hand as securely as he'd caught the radio mike from the backing singers. For Laprisco to have brought things to a halt, to have protested in any way, would have turned the evening into farce. A performer went with the mood, he took the audience with him where he could, and he incorporated whatever surprises came along into his act. To go against the mood, the audience, was an unthinkable faux pas. It was professional suicide.

Neil's next challenge was to establish himself for the rest of the evening. He had to preempt any line from Laprisco that might force him off stage after just one number. Towards the end of *Sweet Caroline* he turned to the band and cut the song short, so that as the music died he was already there with his commentary, ahead of Laprisco.

'Ladies and gentlemen – Could I hear it once more for Tony Laprisco!'

He stood beside Laprisco and started the applause off himself, beaming down at the wizened figure from Los Angeles in his puffy cape. Laprisco could do nothing but bow graciously and receive the rich applause of his audience, and even as he bowed Neil seized more floor time to address the crowd:

'Tony and I go back a long, long way, ladies and gentlemen! I owe this man everything! I sing the songs the way Tony taught me, and no other way – Hey, there is no other way! – And there's no song he taught me better than our next number, so let's hear it for the biggest Neil Diamond hit of all time. I'm talking about a song that was four weeks at the top of the UK charts and went to number one in the land of the free. I'm talking about the song that launched Neil Diamond as a superstar! I'm talking about a song called Cracklin' Rosie, everybody! Let's move the tables – Let's dance! Let's LIVE a little tonight at The American Club, in Tai Tam!'

The band behind him, true professionals, hit those first and famous notes of *Cracklin' Rosie* even as Neil finished his introduction. As soon as some of the younger diners started to move their tables, a flurry of waiters all in white, under the direction of the head waiter, and what must have been the Entertainments Manager himself, scurried to and fro clearing space, so the members could swing out onto the patio and dance the night away, in the warm sea breeze, under the moonlight.

In some ways Neil was to blame, though not as much as he later blamed himself. The hexagonal platform that Laprisco used was not designed to be shared. Neil had never had any intention to take it over – in fact he had done everything he could to give due praise and preeminence to his host from the *Café Diamond*, but no matter how much he kept back and kept clear of Laprisco, the tiny puppet figure never quite had enough room. He took to moving around the hexagonal much more than he had in the first set, jiggling around, exhausting himself, blocking Neil, subtly detracting or distracting from Neil's performance in any way he could; and a couple of times he span about and, with his back to the audience, blasted angry abuse up at Neil, vicious abuse, right up in Neil's face, pretending he was singing back to him full throttle – *You fuckin' asshole! – I'll fix you! – I'll fix you, asshole! – You motherfuckin' asshole! – I'll fix you so good you never come back, asshole! . . . . I'll fix you, pal! . . . You fuckin' loser! . . . Don't you worry about that! . . .*

But Laprisco's attempts to outmanoeuvre Neil had limited success because the audience loved the new energy of Neil's singing, and loved quite as much the way it inspired Laprisco to greater and greater leaps and feats of showmanship. They loved the duelling Diamonds. Neil didn't at all mind being relegated to backing singer some of the time. He just delivered his harmonies to whichever sector of the audience Laprisco wasn't facing, so no one was left out. But such discretion only provoked Laprisco into more rash movement, as he tried to cut Neil off from every segment of the tiny platform. The more successful they were as a performing duo, the more risks Laprisco took to establish a preeminence Neil had never wanted to challenge.

It was during *Red, Red Wine*, appropriately enough, that Laprisco took what looked like a drunken step off the edge of the hexagonal. In a fast spin towards Neil, the toe of his country & western boot caught in the strands of fairy lights. He lurched, faced Neil a moment, then stumbled back, a wild

panic in his eyes. Neil saw it all. Laprisco went over the edge
in just the way he would have expected, like a marionette,
strings cut, as if he had no reflexes to defend himself. He
clutched his mike for balance, his head lolled to one side as he
went down, and the back of his skull met the stone floor first,
with all his weight, nothing to defend it but the mantle of
black hair. He came to rest just a few feet from where the more
adventurous dancers were striking out to the reggae rhythms
of *Red, Red Wine*.

The music stopped but before the band could disentangle
themselves from their instruments, or the backing singers
could step down in their high heels, several waiters in white
had already surrounded Laprisco. They stood shoulder to
shoulder, their hands folded in front, protecting the club
members and their guests from what might have been a
distressing sight. Within seconds the head waiter was on the
scene, hurrying ahead of a Chinese doctor. The doctor, a
plump, distinguished man in a stylish snow-white tuxedo with
silk lapels, followed calmly behind the head waiter, glancing
from side to side at the gathering crowd.

"*Let the doctor pass! Let the doctor pass!*" Panic crackled
now in the head waiter's commands.

Neil had broken through the inner guard of waiters. He
watched the doctor put on his spectacles and kneel by
Laprisco to examine his neck and shoulders. He worked his
way down the emaciated and surprisingly elderly frame,
enjoying his own moment in the limelight. When he looked up
to give his prognosis he spoke to Neil rather than the head
waiter, or the other dignitary now present, the Entertainments
Manager maybe, who stood by his head waiter's side, closing
ranks. The doctor spoke distinctly to Neil and to his assembled
audience. With the authority of his voice and his perfect
command of English, his fancy tuxedo was transformed into a
medical coat.

"He'll be all right," he said. "Nothing's broken. Some concussion, that's all. But we better get him to the hospital. Where are you parked?"

Fluent in deceptions this evening, Neil didn't hesitate.

"Top deck," he said. " . . . But my car's a two-seater, way too small . . ."

At that moment, delivering this petty lie, he became aware of the presence, in the pressing crowd, of Mr. Elbert Chan. Chan was standing behind and between the head waiter and the other dignitary. He was shorter than both of them and Neil met his eyes between their shoulders. It was a fleeting moment only but he took in from that meeting such a wealth of feeling he lost poise and concentration.

Whatever story, whatever lie lay behind Neil's reappearance here tonight – dropping by The American Club in his two-seater, parking on the top deck, indeed – it apparently had neither relevance nor interest to Elbert Chan. Chan's expression showed no trace of surprise or curiosity. His eyes had lost their protective film of deceit and were just cold now towards Neil, but very cold, deep sea cold, so that Neil could hear the waves again beyond the crowd. Chan's eyes were fathomless with blame, accusation, and disappointment, as if his soul were drowning under successive waves of these emotions. Now, after Laprisco's fall, it was all over, it really was all over, Neil understood. The king was dead. All the trawls around the karaoke bars of Wan Chai, all the calls to the Entertainments Managers, all the agitated dreaming and scheming – it was all finished, dead and gone forever, after Laprisco's fall. Neil had slain the king and there could be no return, no reprise, never, ever again. With the faintest shake of the head Chan turned away and disappeared into the crowd for a second time, a last time.

A stretcher and first-aid box had been brought from the pool by the American youths, four lithe young men of powerful build, still dripping from the pool. They'd taken over from the waiters, who trailed behind. The youths were enthusiastic volunteers, politely covering their excitement about the accident and the possibility of mortal injury, but stealing glances at Laprisco's body at every opportunity, while they laid out the stretcher. One passed the first-aid box to an attendant waiter.

The good doctor guided the young men in shifting Laprisco onto the canvas but they seemed to know well enough what they were doing.

With the stretcher raised and borne aloft, the head waiter took full control again. "*To Dr. Lam's car!*" he barked.

Neil followed the procession. He was surprised to see that beyond the immediate circle of the accident people were already seated again, and ordering refreshments. The lithe-bodied adolescents weaved by their tables as stretcher-bearers now, hair and costumes still dripping, padding in wet feet over the stony floor towards the club doors. Laprisco's weight was nothing to the young men and the procession moved swiftly. Too swiftly. Neil wanted their progress to slow, so that other members of the band had time to catch up and break through, so that he might speak with them, establish something with them. But none of the band caught them up. Not one. When Neil glanced back, he saw the high heeled black singers accepting drinks from a pair of young waiters. They were chatting with a group of dripping, full-bodied girls from the pool – deliciously shapely, healthy young girls. These girls were already sipping cocktails, running their hands through their wet blonde hair. And further round, further back, the instrumentalists were suddenly nowhere to be seen. They'd just melted away. The messy business of dealing with Laprisco's old and broken body was being left to Neil and the good Dr. Lam. So much for the loyalty and affection, the showbiz camaraderie of Uncut Diamonds.

Once inside the clubhouse Dr. Lam stopped the stretcher and had it lowered to hip height so that he could have another look at his patient in the light. He took Laprisco's pulse and moved his head gently from side to side. He drew up the brown lids and the eyeballs rolled skywards. Dr. Lam looked concerned.

"It could be worse than I thought," he muttered to Neil. "Quicker by car, though."

Neil had no reply. Silence seemed his best option. He had to keep down a rising panic – where was all this leading him?

Dr. Lam said, as an afterthought, just to himself: "Funny little chap . . . "

Pressed on by the head waiter, who seemed to fear now that Laprisco might die on the club premises, the procession continued with a new urgency through the club and out to the car park.

"Wait here," Dr. Lam directed, by the car park entrance.

Neil noted that the car park attendant, in his air-conditioned hut, had fallen asleep.

In just a minute Dr. Lam's car, a blue Bentley, nosed from the lower deck of the car park. A waiter opened the rear doors. One youth dipped inside the car and drew the stretcher along the seat. The others unscrewed the poles and pulled them out from both sides in four sections. The waiter closed the doors, but Dr. Lam directed Neil from his window – "You better come along and sit with him. Keep his head steady."

Escorted by a waiter, Neil went round to the other side of the car. The waiter opened the door again for him. Neil climbed into the back of the Bentley and drew Laprisco's puny shoulders up, so that the head and the mantle of black hair rested against his chest. The waiter closed the door behind him and Neil leant into the corner, against the armrest. He felt that rising panic, but stronger now – where was all this leading?

Dr. Lam hadn't moved from the driver's seat. With a touch to a stalk on the steering column he put the car into gear and they turned up the slope to the main road.

"We'll go to the Li Poon," Dr. Lam said, checking the road was clear. "It's a public hospital. There's a private one that's closer but it has no casualty department."

Again Neil said nothing. He had no opinions on the Li Poon or the private hospital to offer Dr. Lam. He was uncomfortable in the deep leather seats of the Bentley. Laprisco's head and shoulders were heavy and the door's armrest dug into his kidneys. The absolute silence in the car aggravated his discomfort and his self-consciousness.

"He took a nasty fall," Dr. Lam said, glancing at Neil in the rear view mirror. Neil caught the glance, and his gaze lingered on the polished mirror. It was an elegant, blue-rimmed oval, or opal, hanging like a fixed jewel to adorn the Bentley's walnut and calf interior.

"I hope he's okay."

"He may not be, you know," Dr. Lam replied, in a matter of fact way. He didn't even say, *I'm afraid* or *I'm sorry to say.* "He may not be," he repeated. "I think he's a sick man," he added. "Very thin and weak . . .You know him well?"

Neil's stage line slipped out again, but it seemed terribly true all of a sudden: "Tony and I go back a long way."

"Well, let's hope he pulls through," Dr. Lam said, and with that token professional optimism he brought the conversation to a close, much to Neil's relief.

"Let's hope so," Neil echoed.

Some music, soft jazz, a Miles Davis blues sound, filtered into the silence. Dr. Lam adjusted the volume from the steering wheel, relieving them both of any further need to converse.

Neil looked down at the short body of Tony Laprisco stretched along the rear seat on the canvas. His shiny slacks rode up clear of his boots. How skinny and puny his ankles looked under the creases of his country & western boots! Little wonder they had given way with one false step.

Suddenly, alarmingly, Laprisco's body tightened up. It curled and shrank on the canvas. Then his back arched in a death throe until, in one long, tight rasp, he broke wind. The noise of it, thin, insistent, like a fly buzzing on glass, lasted a couple of seconds or more. At the same time an appalling dog meat stench filled every cubic inch of the Bentley. All the nervous gases from Laprisco's performance had blown out in one go. The stink was so fierce Neil feared Laprisco had followed through, had shat his pants on the stretcher.

"Oh dear," murmured Dr. Lam, and he lowered all windows, flushing the car with warm sea breezes.

Laprisco's body relaxed once more and he tried to say something. He was trying to sit up so that he might be heard. Yet it wasn't quite like that. The movements didn't go so far. The eyes did not open. Some words did come, but his voice was faint and uncontrolled. Neil leant down to catch what he was saying.

"The Café . . ." Laprisco muttered. " . . . The Café . . ."

Laprisco seemed in a state of delirium. The words were floating out from his coma on the steady pulse of subconscious anxieties. The phrase grew, though, and became hoarser and stronger.

"The Café Diamond . . ."

Neil bent down to Laprisco's puppet head. The mantle of hair had stayed firm and intact, yet it was not a wig, Neil observed. Or if it was, if it was a wig, it was the best conceivable, the most expensive ever made.

"The Café . . ." Laprisco said again. *"The Café Diamond . . ."*

"Yes, Tony?"

"The Café . . . . ."

Neil frowned, concerned, and as if in response to his

solicitous attitude Laprisco continued, still with his eyes shut.

"I had to do something . . ." Then his voice became urgent, delirious, before fading again into faint repetitions – "It's bust . . . It's gone . . . So I had to . . . I had to . . . had to . . . I had to . . . "

Anxious that the urgency would return and Laprisco would work himself into some agitation, Neil said:

"Sure, Tony. Of course you did . . . You did what you had to do."

With this cliché from Laprisco's homeland, indeed from his home town, Neil hoped to seal up any need on Laprisco's part to explain what he'd had to do. He felt that whatever it was that Tony Laprisco had had to do, that troubled him so much just now, didn't really matter any more, and probably never had mattered very much, not in the general scheme of things.

After Neil's words, Laprisco fell quiet. Neil's gentle counsel, given to subdue rather than to console, had done the trick. Neil lifted his gaze and looked out the opposite window of the Bentley, still open, as was the window behind him. The rush of sea air around the gliding limousine tousled his hair from behind and blew strands around his neck and face, which he stroked back behind his ears. They were on a slow bend in the coast road looking out to sea. The moon was bright. The waves glittered. Colourful navigation lamps shone from yachts and junks moored in Turtle Cove, and a line of white lights illuminated the winding path through Shek O Country Park, up Hok Tsui Shan. The Miles Davis track was, appropriately enough, the very soft and beautiful, *Just Squeeze Me*.

How pretty it all was, Neil thought, just for the ride.

Chapter Nineteen

Tokens, Coupons

Chan's eyes were oddly bright and brimful of – what? – what was it, exactly? – certainly not gladness, not tidings, certainly not drunkenness, nor concern or sentiment of any kind – but what, then? Ah, Neil knew what it was. Precisely what it was. Nothing special, when all was said and done.

"Are you okay?" Chan asked, leaning down. "Has there been any news?"

It was optimism, that was all. Pure and simple. Distilled, liquefied, and dropped into Chan's tired eyes like Optrex.

"Can I get you something?"

Starshine, moonshine, the very blight of life.

"You don't look too good."

The worm that had eaten into every corner, corrupted every decent memory, ruined every honest hope and all ambition.

"Shall I get a nurse?"

The worm that had, at last, been drawn from Neil, been cast out, after such a long hot struggle, cast out like a biblical curse. And it had found a new host, it had eaten its way into the soul of this soulless man standing in front of him, with his blank and shining eyes, with his hands in his pockets and his dinner jacket in baggy folds. Impossible.

"Has there been any news, Neil?"

Neil rolled his head against the white wall.

"No news."

Chan seemed to be avoiding mentioning Laprisco by name, as if, after the accident, the name itself were ominous and infected: now it was Laprisco's turn to become bad feng shui. Neil's eyes left Chan. He looked ahead, at the opposite wall of the waiting area, at the posters there. The pink cross-sections and front-sections of pregnant women. Tubes, organs, in simple shapes, elipses, lozenges, figures of eight. Simple colours. Reds. Browns. Pale blues. Bold labels. Ectopic pregnancies, whatever they were. The business-end of lust, romance. Of the songs. The Neil Diamond songs. Chance, dance, romance. And he looked at the other posters, the grey posters, step-by-step, telling you what to do in the event of a cardiac arrest. It was all here. Lust, birth, death. He stared at those grey and pink posters, trying to think, in his exhausted and vulnerable state, trying to work out what was going on here.

"Where are the band?" he asked, without looking up.

Neil still had room for this very genuine concern. He had been waiting for those Uncut Diamonds, for one rough diamond at least, all through these early morning hours. Someone had to show a token respect.

"They went back to their hotel."

Neil looked up. "Their hotel?"

"That's right."

Neil was incredulous. "Back to The Excelsior?"

"No." Chan glanced about the waiting area. "Only Laprisco's at The Excelsior. The rest are Kowloon side at The Metropole." His bright eyes returned to Neil. "How about something to eat, Neil? Some breakfast, maybe."

Neil frowned to himself, and at the posters opposite, with that second use of his name: it compounded the disrespect to everyone.

Breakfast?

"You look like you could use some food. It'll pick you up," Chan continued. "I know a couple of hotels that do all-night breakfasts. We can talk. You can tell me what happened. All about it. Everything."

Neil lifted his dopey gaze again. It was quite an effort.

"Aren't you forgetting someone?"

Chan's mouth turned down at the corners, as if this direct reference to Laprisco's plight were in poor taste. Neil shouldn't have done that.

"Lam says there's no telling. Could go either way . . . But long term he's optimistic . . ."

Optimism. Optrex . . .

Neil was too old for all of this, too old for Chan's games and deceptions, whatever they were this time. Too old for sneaking around car parks, descending fire ladders, sprinting headlong across the sucking sand, and performing, posturing and pretending, making it all up as he went along. Too old for this lonely, silent vigil in the Casualty Dept. of the Li Poon Christian Hospital. The rows of orange seats in front of him were far too bright for his eyes, and their plastic was too sharp and hard for his lean buttocks. The air conditioning chilled him to the very bone. How he envied Laprisco his comatose state, several floors above, all responsibility surrendered to the medicinal drip.

"What about some breakfast, Neil?"

That third tug at his name – no one had used his name for a week or more – dragged Neil to his feet. The offer might not come round a fourth time, not in the same form anyway, and once again he had nothing left to lose.

"Okay."

"I can't see what you're driving at."

They were at the All-Night Breakfast-Bar of The InterContinental Hotel in Kowloon, having come by taxi all the way back to Chan's side of the harbour. At first Neil presumed they had returned here because this is where Chan's hotels were, and the hotels were cheaper here – and perhaps they were going to connect with *Uncut Diamonds* at The Metropole – but they were at the five-star InterContinental and they remained alone. "Breakfast here is better than at the Peninsula," Chan had informed Neil on the way in, as the doormen pulled wide the swing doors. Chan had actually guided Neil through the open doors, taken him by the elbow and guided him into the hotel. Neil Atherton was his friend, his guest, at the five-star InterContinental, at 4 a.m. "More expensive than the Peninsula, but better quality too."

From the All-Night Breakfast-Bar above the lobby, The InterContinental Hotel seemed to have no walls. For two whole floors this side of the building was just glass, without any frames or visible support. Diners up here, or drinkers in the various cocktail bars below, could look out over the harbour to Hong Kong Island and enjoy the movement of the sea traffic, and the twinkling office stacks across the water, without visual interference of any kind. To Neil, who had never been in a place like this in his life before, the view was quite literally staggering – his tired legs, tired not only from the night's exertions but tired with an accumulated fatigue, the weariness of several weeks walking the streets – his tired legs had buckled when he and Elbert came up the stairs from the lobby and he saw that view. Saw the other side of things. Life from this different vantage point. Elbert had taken him firmly by the elbow again – "You all right, Neil?"

Now, sipping his second glass of coffee, Neil came to understand what gave the view its power. It wasn't just the beautiful panorama itself, with all its gliding reflections and deceptions. It was the silence of the scene beyond the glass. The silence underscored it all, as it were. The wash in the harbour was heavy from the weight of traffic – the ferries, barges, crane barges and liners – yet they all went by without a sound, not a hundred yards away. In the closeness of the sea traffic to the massive glass walls there was a danger, a recklessness, but it was suppressed, silenced, there was not a word about that. The risk had been taken and forgotten, had sunk to the bottom of the sea.

And not even the softest Muzak, not even Mozak, to spoil that silence. Not here at The InterContinental.

Bacon and eggs, fried tomatoes and hash browns were sizzling on the griddle behind the bar. The chef wore a proper chef's hat. Just for bacon and eggs. He ground fresh sea-salt and fresh black pepper onto the eggs.

Neil could live like this. It wasn't bad at all. He could settle for this.

"It's obvious, Neil," Chan said, taking his plate. He looked up at the chef and rapped out some command in Cantonese. The chef turned and barked the same command at an assistant, a boy, and the boy dropped to his knees, swivelled, crouched, and snapped open a chunky steel door beneath the bar. Not a fridge. A cold-box. The boy fetched out for Chan a plate of peeled onions. The boy brought those onions from the cold-box, three peeled onions on a clean white plate, so fast it was as if his life depended on them. His life for three peeled onions. Service. Quality service. That's what it was.

"Onions?"

Neil didn't particularly want onions, but he didn't want to miss any part of the ritual.

"Thank you," he said.

"Don't mention it," Chan said.

What had got *into* Chan?

"It's obvious," Chan repeated. "What we have to do." He smiled and raised his glass of coffee. " . . . Isn't it? Don't you think? . . ."

Tired and awe-struck though he was, Neil became alert

again at that use of the royal pronoun, following hard on so many uses of his name. But he didn't reply. He had no answer to Chan's question and he didn't want to seem obtuse by coming up with the wrong idea. In all honesty, he couldn't imagine anything they had to do which was so very obvious, as Chan had said, and which could inspire all this sudden largesse, optimism and bonhomie, and which at the same time could be to his advantage. He could think of nothing that fitted such contradictory criteria.

And he had to get on with his breakfast. Neil took his time unfurling his cutlery from its linen napkin. When he cut into the hash brown, though it had only just been flipped from the griddle, it was crisp and dry. The egg was lightly cooked and slippery in a film of extra virgin olive oil. Neil was very hungry indeed, in fact he was ravenous, starving, but he took only a corner of the hash brown and a sliver of egg white on his fork, not wishing to appear the barbarian. Then, at last, he began to eat. Ah, how different a hash brown was at The InterContinental to a hash brown at McDonald's! How could such a difference be achieved with such humble ingredients? And how could Neil ever eat at McDonald's again? He'd rather starve to death! He drank some coffee and the attentive chef immediately replenished his glass.

But why was Chan trying to seduce him in this way, into the high life? What did he still have left to trade with Chan, that he didn't even know about?

Neil chewed, swallowed and gazed over Chan's shoulder at a passing crane barge, a huge, lumbering structure, a dredger for shifting tons of silt and rubbish, debris of spent risks, failed risks, off the sea floor. He thought a moment of those men inside the barge, buried in its bowels, in its engine room and its stowage quarters, the stevedores who laboured to keep body and soul together with tarry ropes and greasy hawsers, without hope of anything better than another day's toil in the fetid heat, and the buffetings of bad weather.

Those in peril on the sea . . .

He thought also of a certain bench seat out there, very close but out of sight – thank the Lord – on the esplanade. Maybe that bench was only fifty yards away. That solitary bench, among all those benches of young lovers, that he'd chosen after his visit to The Cosmopolitan. It must have been around this time, 4.00 a.m., that he'd settled down out there.

Good God, Neil wanted this InterContinental breakfast so badly! He wanted this life of which Chan had given him a tiny taste – just a corner of hash brown, a sliver of egg white – so very, very badly. It was so reviving! He would do anything for it. He would sell his soul for it right here and now – going, going, gone! – for just one more glass of the delicious Columbian coffee.

"Tony's out the frame, of course."

Evidently Chan was at ease using Laprisco's name now. At the five-star InterContinental it had no power. It lost its ominous overtones. Chan ate a forkful of egg and bacon, the bacon in a tidy, bulky fold.

"Tony's out the frame," he repeated, still eating. He wiped his mouth with his napkin and glanced away, avoiding Neil's eyes. "And that lets you back in."

Neil raised an eyebrow, but he wasn't really following Chan that closely.

"A new start. A fresh start."

Neil glanced up, more quizzical this time.

"You pick up from last night, Neil. From where you left off."

Chan cleared his throat, wiped his mouth with his napkin once more.

Neil still couldn't see what Chan meant. He frowned. "Laprisco's not here, remember." He waved his knife. "He's in the Li Poon Christian Hospital. On the third floor . . ."

"No no no." Chan dipped his head and sipped more coffee. He was uncomfortable with what he had to say and it came out too loud: "You stand in for Laprisco."

Neil chewed, swallowed, frowned. "Stand in for him?"

"That's right."

"I stand in for him? . . . What do you mean? . . . What do you mean, I stand in for Tony Laprisco!" Neil laughed. He broke a croissant and dipped it in his coffee. He laughed again. "You're joking, aren't you? . . . You mean I pretend to . . ." Nothing moved in Chan's face. His eyes could have been made out of mica. "You mean I . . . I impersonate him? I impersonate Laprisco? But he's already impersonating someone!" Neil laughed again, for a third time, but thinly now, and for too long. "I'd be an impersonator of a Neil Diamond impersonator, for goodness' sake!" he said desperately. "What's happening to me?"

He stared around the breakfast bar. The idea was like a punch line, throwaway and inevitable. Here, once more, he was up against that block in understanding Chan had, that cultural failure of the imagination. The same as when he couldn't see what was wrong with playing The Mariners' Club in the first place, in front of a bunch of sailors, following a Welsh male voice choir. He just couldn't see what was so wrong about it, why it jarred. Here it was again, only this time that failure of imagination was too much.

"Do you know who I am?" Neil dusted flakes of croissant from his hands, trying to dust off his dismay. He leant towards Chan and whispered, his voice hoarse with feeling, his eyes filling: "Hey . . . Do you know who I am?"

Neil sat back again. Chan returned his watery stare and let Neil's emotion roll by, disappear into the seascape over his shoulder, beyond the glass.

The breakfast was ruined.

"I know who you are, all right," Chan answered. "But that

doesn't matter. The point is, you've got to be someone else, haven't you?" He went back to his meal. He ate more egg and continued with his mouth full. "Because no one wants Neil Atherton." He chewed and swallowed. "Do they?" He had no feeling. No mercy. He was soulless. "So you've got to be someone else. Yesterday it was Neil Diamond. But things have changed, moved on. So we move on too, move with the times. Today's another day. You're not Neil Diamond any more. You've been downgraded. Today you're Tony Laprisco."

"Tomorrow I'm Sammy Davis Jnr." Neil snapped his cutlery together in disgust. He'd had enough. "Do you want me to black up?"

"Look," Chan lowered his head, driving the point home. "The bottom line is – no one wants you. Do they? I mean, do they?"

Neil looked out at the water beyond the wall of glass. The vessels. The silent waves. The warm, glittering waves, under the moonlight, and the office block light. "No," he admitted, more to himself than to Chan. "I suppose they don't."

"But they do want Tony Laprisco. They've all signed up for him. That's a fact, no matter what you or I might think about Tony Laprisco. And I told you at the start – what you or I think doesn't matter. Golden rule. All the clubs want Tony, and that's that. Osaka, Bangkok, Manila, Singapore . . ." Chan sipped his coffee. "This is quite an opportunity here, and it's on the table. More coffee?"

Neil hesitated, then nodded.

"And don't worry about *Tony* – " Chan shook his head, wanting to be rid of this nagging, tenacious concern – "because he'll probably never know anything about any of this. He's well out of it. For the moment, anyway. I spoke to Lam, like I said."

What was that supposed to mean – 'I spoke to Lam'? What

was that about? What was Lam going to do? Knock off Tony Laprisco? Shoot him up with something? *Excuse me, nurse, while I give this patient a couple of shots* . . . Just so Neil could take over his crummy act?

But why did Chan's idea stick in the throat so much, like the bacon and egg, and the hash brown, slippery though it all was with the richest virgin olive oil?

"Look . . ." Chan pressed on again, lowering his head and his voice, as if they had to keep all this from the chef. "There's a string of dates already fixed, and I can arrange more at my clubs . . . "

My clubs? It was the first time Neil had heard Chan refer to them as his clubs. They weren't his clubs. Iannis had told him that. *He buys his stuff with coupons!* Iannis's scorn echoed in Neil's mind . . . *With coupons! . . . With coupons! . . .*

Chan continued, almost sotto voce, his tired eyes alert, flicking now from side to side.

"The itinerary's wide open. We walk right in. You travel on Tony's passport. I can fix that. No problem. From now on you *are* Tony Laprisco, out from L.A., owner of *The Café Diamond*."

"You're going to call me Tony, now?"

"If you like." Chan shrugged. "It doesn't matter. What I call you now doesn't matter. The point is, this tour gets us started. Tony's tour. Your tour. The whole Star Tributes concept. It's perfect. The show must go on. Simple as that."

Neil let his eyes stray over Chan's shoulder to the view again. The crane barge was going back the other way. Could it be the same one? Going back? Ah, the endless merry-go-round of commerce. Once on board you just couldn't get off. With or without *Cracklin' Rosie*.

Neil's eyes came back from the view to Chan's face. Something had occurred to him.

"Laprisco's at The Excelsior, you said . . ."

Chan smiled a new, benign smile. Very worrying. "And the room's covered by his credit card. Nice room. Twelfth floor. Harbour view. And you get all the trimmings, too." He raised his coffee glass. "Cheers."

What did that mean? Trimmings?

"Everyone's a winner here."

"Yeah," Neil said, looking over Chan's shoulder into the night. "Except Tony Laprisco."

Chan nodded, conceding that.

"Except Tony Laprisco."

He wiped his mouth with his napkin and nodded again, as if to say, You're right there. You could say that. "Except Tony Laprisco," he repeated. He studied the deposits on his napkin. "You're right. He's not a winner here. Not in this scenario. He's a loser. But then – " he raised his coffee glass – "maybe he always was."

Neil drank more coffee himself. His fourth glass. The chef refilled it without a word. Service. Quality service.

Chan broke his croissant. "It's a nice suite . . . I've been up there. Harbour view." He nodded over his shoulder to the view behind him and smiled a smile that entirely overreached itself.

After eating half his croissant Chan dusted his hands and took out a long roll of fax from inside his dinner jacket, then a gold ballpoint pen. He re-folded the fax until it exposed the part he wanted Neil to see. "You need to practise his signature." With his napkin he made sure the marble breakfast bar was free of any grease or coffee spillage, and then he set out the last page of the fax for Neil's inspection.

Neil did not take Chan's proffered gold ballpoint. Instead he took up the fax itself, removing it from under the slight pressure of Chan's fingertips.

Here was the contract that Laprisco had boasted of a week ago, back in Chan's poky office, at that fateful meeting. *The deal's done. It's all over, pal.* Neil undid Chan's careful folds and let the document unravel between his legs. Laprisco's contract, faxed in from L.A., was over three feet long. Neil squinted at the faint and tiny print. It was full of dense legalese: *Notwithstanding disbursements already accredited on account of the aforementioned all shall be held in escrow in the name of the undersigned* . . . In escrow? Paragraph after paragraph in escrow. The earnest striving, by the lawyer who drew up the contract, working late in an office tower somewhere, in downtown L.A., on the twenty-seventh floor, perhaps, the earnest striving by that lawyer to seal up any fissure of ambiguity, through which might drain any portion of the humble profit from Laprisco's enterprise. Neil was perplexed by the idea that, suspended from the bottom of this flimsy fax, there were weighty consequences – punitive fines and charges, the curtailment of personal liberty, the bloody book of the law, for anyone daring to defraud – as he was going to defraud, in Elbert Chan's new scenario – the sick, comatose, fifty-eight or sixty year old, Tony Laprisco.

"Why're you reading it?" Chan asked. "You don't have to understand any of that. You're not signing it. It doesn't matter. Doesn't mean a thing. Never did."

"I'm just interested . . ." Neil squinted at the paragraphs, skimming and scanning by the clauses, sub-clauses, minutiae.

"It's bogus," Chan said. His words were clipped. "Just get on with practising the signature. You need it in the hotel."

Neil came to the bottom of the document. He folded it up, taking his time, so that it lay as it had lain on the counter a couple of minutes before. He treated the contract with respect, even reverence. Whether it was bogus or not, whether it could ever stand up in a court of law or not, the scroll of fax represented a life, all the ambition, determination, and creativity of a life. Here it all was, on this slippery roll of fax paper, Laprisco's shot in the dark at fame and fortune. Neil remembered the Tony Laprisco of just six or seven hours ago, smiling and chatting with his fans before the second set, folding a dedication and slipping it away in his cape without even reading it.

Laprisco's signature was a long, loopy, showbiz thing. Still Neil hesitated, didn't copy it, didn't sign up.

Chan was losing patience. "It's toilet paper," he said.

There was Chan's signature too, in Chinese: just dashes, strokes, pokes and spokes. Probably a made up thing. Didn't mean anything. Never did. For all Laprisco knew, and Neil knew, Chan's signature might have said, 'Fuck you, Jack!' In fact, it probably did. Neil patted his pockets. Chan offered his gold ballpoint again. Both Chan's and Laprisco's signatures were in blue ink. The very same.

"Practise there," Chan directed. "Beneath his signature."

Neil did as he was told, at first laboriously, then with increasing ease and confidence, duplicating again and again the showbiz signature of Tony Laprisco, full of whipped up flourishes. Soon the bottom of the fax was covered in signatures. The contract, stitching up its various parties clause by clause, was signed twenty or thirty times over by Tony Laprisco.

"You've got it. That's enough."

But Neil was carried away. There was a satisfaction in tossing off Laprisco's signature faster and faster and with increasing ease and contempt.

Chan leant forward and took hold of his gold ballpoint. Their eyes met. "That's enough." Both his hand and his voice were firm.

Neil gave up the pen and Chan replaced it inside his jacket.

"What about the band?" Neil asked. "What about Uncut Diamonds? And the singers?" He was suddenly most concerned about them all, thinking in particular of the lovely black backing singers, sipping their cocktails on the terrace of The American Club.

Chan tore off the signatures from the fax and gave the scrap to Neil. "Keep that in case you need to practise some more." He shoved away the rest of Laprisco's contract, crumpling it, stuffing it into his inside pocket as if it didn't matter any more, it had served its purpose. In answer to Neil's question he held out his hands. "What d'you think I've been doing all night? I've been to The Metropole. I've seen everyone. They're all on board. They're actually very grateful to me. And you."

"Grateful to me?"

Chan nodded. "I told them you'd do it. I knew you would. And they can see it's all for the best. The show must go on."

Chan's eyes shone again, like the office lights across the harbour, brash, confident, brimful of optimism.

Chapter Twenty

At The Excelsior

Chan had paid the expensive taxi bill from Tai Tam back into town. He had paid for the very expensive breakfast, and now he was about to pay for this other taxi on The Excelsior forecourt. They'd come back beneath the harbour again to Hong Kong Island, and they'd taken the scenic route as well, via the Eastern harbour. Another $100. All this criss-crossing and shelling out . . . *I'll pick up the tab . . . This one's on me . . . I'll get this . . . Don't worry, Neil . . .*

"Tonight I pick up all the tabs," Chan said, pulling out his wallet one more time.

But every payment left a pocket of silence, and at the bottom of the pocket the short change of suspicion. Neil knew he was being lured into a trap. The whole proposition was a trap, baited with the all-night breakfast. That was perfectly obvious. It didn't bother him. What did bother him was that he also knew Chan was corrupt. He had dubious connections. Neil had always assumed the corruption was just petty and personal, that it didn't lead far, not far underground, anyway. He'd assumed it was nothing much to worry about because that was the easiest thing to do. There had never been any thugs or hoodlums waiting in Elbert's anteroom, after all. Only Iannis, flicking through his brochures. And who could be more innocent than Iannis? Or himself?

But at this hour on Sunday morning, tired and wrung out, half dreaming already, Neil's imagination became inflamed with other possibilities. Maybe Chan's connections did lead underground, to where the bad people lived. The kind of people who, in a recent newspaper story, had chopped up a young girl, a teenage prostitute, for not paying her dues. Chopped her up alive with machetes in front of her flatmate, then burned her severed body-parts, stuffed the remains into a mannequin, and left the mannequin on a sofa in her apartment, watching tv. After a week in hiding the flatmate went to the police, just as they wanted – a message to the rest. The flatmate's sleepless face and haunted eyes were spread all over the inside pages, along with shots of the smeared mannequin slumped on the sofa. Neighbours had blamed the smell on the drains.

Chan escorted him into The Excelsior, actually taking his elbow again and guiding him, steering him, as he had at The InterContinental. He was making sure everything went smoothly, every step of the way. But to what end? He stood around at reception, a step or two behind Neil, hands in pockets, dinner jacket in baggy folds, while Neil picked up a key to Laprisco's room.

Neil began with an apology to the night clerk, telling him he had left both his keys inside the room, but his apology was quite unnecessary. The clerk, a dandy with a blown dry bouffant, gave him a warm smile and swiped another key straightaway, no questions asked. Offering the key to Neil he smiled again, and Neil sensed him looking him over as he bent down to sign for the key. The clerk had taken a shine to him, with his died black hair, his fancy black clothes and boots. Neil didn't need this complication right now.

"No problem, Mr. Laprisco."

Neil winced inside. "Thanks . . ."

As he walked away from the desk with Elbert, across the

marble floors, he was struck by what the clerk would think of them from behind, walking so close together towards the lift lobby, beneath the chandeliers, he in his show outfit and Chan in evening dress.

"What's happening to me?"

"Calm down," Chan said, taking his elbow again. Neil snatched his elbow back. He stole a look over his shoulder at the night clerk, who was indeed watching them, and who nodded to him, to them, and smiled.

Once they'd turned into the lift lobby, Neil remarked on the ease of the deception about the key: "Anyone could have done that," he said, and on saying it aloud the thought occurred – When did that clerk come on duty? Anyone could be up there. Already. Waiting in Laprisco's room . . .

"They've got your credit card number," Chan answered shortly. Neil was being obtuse again. "That's all that matters. Besides, to a Chinese all foreigners look the same. Try to hang on to that."

Despite the early hour on a Sunday morning, the first lift down was occupied.

A Nepalese looking gentleman with a shaven head, quite elderly, very tall, stepped out of the lift, and as he did so he graciously wished them both good morning. The greeting was odd, staged, it drew attention to itself. And there was something phoney about the man's dress as well. It had an old-world colonial quality. He wore a dogstooth jacket with white shirt and red silk cravat. It was the leisure wear of yesteryear's gentlemen. It looked like a statement, a bizarre homage to a bygone era.

Chan evidently knew the man. He held the lift doors open while they watched this elegant figure sweep on, with proprietorial stride, across the lobby of The Excelsior. Chan beckoned Neil into the lift, released the doors, and stepped inside.

"That's Khan," Chan said, finishing the tacit introduction. Pleasing scents lingered in the lift from Khan. Jasmine. Rosewater. Coconut. "He's been here since it opened in seventy-six. From bellhop to deputy. Old school. Knows everything. Probably knows every guest in the hotel on any given day. Watch him. Avoid him if you can."

After the tip about Khan, which seemed to Neil a touch exaggerated and dramatic, like the man himself, both he and Chan remained silent during the ride up to the twelfth floor. They stared into the polished brass plates of the cabin interior and allowed the elevator music to take the strain. Neil's suspicions eased. How different this ascent was, he thought, to the last lift they'd shared up to *The Languages and Translation Services Ltd.*, in that rattling cabin of stippled aluminium, with the fan sucking in the foul lift shaft air. Just one week ago to the day. Neil felt no desperate hysteria now. No burst of laughter came rushing from him as they passed the seventh floor. No break of wind. Not this time. This time he felt he was about to arrive, not depart. And yet, what had really changed, at the bottom of things, at the bottom of the lift shaft, from that lift to this lift? Nothing at all.

Elbert didn't want to get out with Neil. Something had unsettled him.

"Okay. I'll leave you here. Get some sleep. We'll talk later."

Elbert shut the doors of the cabin, cutting off an already abrupt farewell, and Neil stood alone in the corridor of the twelfth floor, the key to Laprisco's room in his hand. The corridor carpet was very deep and thick. In its rich pile there were odours of musk, pine, lemon, lavender, a fusion of fresheners that lent the corridor the scent of a place well tended to, watched over day and night by the likes of the dandified night clerk and the mysterious Mr. Khan. Neil felt safer still. The wild thoughts were silly here. Polished plaques with embossed numerals directed him right, to the even numbers. 1202. Harbour view. Laprisco hadn't stinted himself on his trip to the Far East. This puzzled Neil, given his mutterings about the *Café Diamond*'s demise. *It's gone . . . it's bust . . .* This tour must have been Laprisco's last roll of the dice too, his own pearl of great price.

Turn and turn about.

Tony and I go back a long way . . .

Neil came to the door of 1202 but hesitated before swiping the key. His fears returned.

What if Chan had got it all wrong? What if the good Dr. Lam had made a faulty diagnosis? What if Laprisco had been only lightly concussed, and he'd woken up while Neil and Chan had breakfasted at The InterContinental, woken up fresh as a daisy, sat up in bed, top-of-the-morning, 100%, and had called a nurse, got himself dressed, and discharged himself from the Li Poon Hospital? What if he'd hailed a taxi and was already back here in his hotel – what if he was right now taking off his country & western boots, then lying down to ease his headache and to listen to the radio, to the early morning news roundup? . . . Neil frowned. In his exhausted state he couldn't stop these wild fears taking shape, couldn't bat them away. He saw right through the door of 1202 into the suite beyond. Laprisco was padding around in his socks, fixing himself a drink from the mini-bar, humming to himself soft Neil Diamond tunes . . . *Longfellow Serenade, Song Sung Blue* . . . Or he was already undressed, sitting naked on the bedside with a whisky and soda in his hand, or rather bourbon on-the-rocks, his mantle of black hair across his white shoulders, broken up in tails and strands. His aging body slumped on the bedside, the tumbler at the end of his hairy arm. Or he was standing by the window in his hotel dressing gown staring down at the harbour view . . .

Why had Chan stayed in the lift? Why had he abandoned Neil like that? What did he know? If not Laprisco, who else might be in the hotel room, behind that door? Who else might be with Laprisco, waiting for Neil to call?

I'll fix you, pal! . . . I'll fix you, asshole! . . .

Had Chan's breakfast been ceremonial in some way? Last rites?

Two or three ghoul-faced Chinese, in evening dress, hair tied back. One stops his mouth as soon as he opens the door – a fist or plug straight in his mouth, smashing his teeth – while the others bundle him inside, drag him kicking into the bathroom. Strangle him. Twist his neck, break his neck, crack it on the side of the bathtub. Chop up his body in the tub, fully dressed. Body parts in polythene bags. Suitcases. Two suitcases. Rinse the bath. They walk him out the hotel, in the suitcases, pulling him along as if nothing's in there but suits and shirts. But nipped in the bottom corner of the second case is a telltale red bubble of polythene. The doorman doesn't notice, or doesn't care. They walk free.

Small fishing boat, engine running, at the quay. Out into the harbour. Suitcases over the side . . . Under the glittering waves . . .

The unburdened boat lists, rocks, turns back to the shore lights . . .

All gone. All over. Finito.

Neil backed away from the door and stood a moment in the empty corridor, listening, afraid. He tapped the key card on his fingernails. Nothing. Not a sound. Just the quiet hum of the air conditioning and the rattle of a room-service trolley far away down the corridors. He pulled himself together, took a deep breath, stepped up to the door and swiped the key. A green light shone on the lock. He pushed the door open.

"Hey there! How're you doin'?"

He span around to see two guests – heavy, middle-aged Americans, late-night revellers – exchanging greetings at the lifts. The one who'd spoken, very fat, moustachioed, turned away from the lifts and started down the corridor towards Neil. He smiled and nodded.

"How're you doin', friend?"

"Fine," Neil answered. "Just fine."

"Great. Terrific . . ."

Neil slipped into the room and closed the door, but then found himself in the dark. He opened the door again and rammed the key in the holder that operated the power. The lights blinked on, the air conditioner hummed to life, and behind him the door closed softly on its spring.

No other sounds. No sleepy breathing or snoring from inside the suite. No, "Hey there! How're you doin'?"

No fist in the mouth – *Take that, motherfucker . . .*

This was the right room, that much was certain, because immediately ahead on Neil's left, glittering under the entrance spotlight, was an open wardrobe filled to capacity with Laprisco's sequinned outfits: his suits, his jackets, his capes, and two very striking long silk scarves – yellow, blue – delicately draped over padded shoulders. On separate hangers at the end were his flared black 'pants'. Three pairs of buffed country & western boots, side by side, stood to attention on the floor. There was a card round one boot from *Excelsior Shoeshine*. Quality service.

Opposite was the bathroom. Neil poked his head in, checked behind the shower curtain, then pressed on to the bedroom. An empty bed. The curtains were drawn. He scanned the room. On the bedside table was a courtesy chocolate, put there for Tony Laprisco. The cover of the bed had been turned down for him too. Neil checked under the bed and in the walk-in cupboard. He was alone in room 1202.

He stared at the courtesy chocolate and the turned down bed cover, and the starched white sheets. All to welcome back Tony Laprisco, and to wish him a good night's sleep after his show at The American Club, Tai Tam. Well, too bad, Tony,

Neil said to himself. Too bad. Neil was toughening himself up. Away with guilt and false sentiment. Away with waking walking nightmares. Here was a lucky break and he had to seize it with both hands.

The red message light on the telephone was blinking hotly but Neil ignored that. He wasn't bothered about Laprisco's personal messages right now. He sat on the bed and called reception and asked them to find the number of the Li Poon Christian Hospital in Tai Tam. They found it while he waited. He called the hospital and asked after his friend Mr. Laprisco, admitted about six hours ago, about 11.30 p.m. last night . . . Mr. Laprisco's condition was stable, he was told. Nothing more. Neil left a message. They were to call him immediately there was any change in Mr. Laprisco's condition. "Immediately," he repeated. "I'm at The Excelsior. Room 1202. Leave any messages for Mr. Diamond. Got that? Mr. Diamond. Room 1202 . . ."

With that job done Neil sagged on the side of the bed but he would not let himself lie down. Not just yet. This was a moment to be savoured. It was a moment with quite a history behind it when one looked back over the last six hours, or over the last six weeks, come to that.

Had he arrived, at last? Had he? Neil thought he had, or at least that he was as close to arrival right now as he was ever going to be. It was time, then, for that Martini, the one he'd promised himself at the Star Ferry terminus, in another lifetime, should the moment come when he had surefire prospects here. He should be taking his Martini in the cocktail bar downstairs, the one overlooking the harbour, and staring across to The InterContinental, the mirror image. But that didn't matter so much just now. He'd manage all right on his own. He found the mini-bar and raked through the spirits, beers and juices.

There were lots of options, lots of ready-mixed cocktails

and liqueurs, even some advocaat, but unfortunately there was no Martini. Again, it didn't matter. He poured himself a whisky with ice, then went to the window and drew back the curtains. Before the glass was a low, curved window seat of a rather sensual design, carpeted and cushioned. He rested a knee there.

Another view across the harbour but to Kowloon now and from twelve floors up. Giant handfuls of light were strewn all over the place. Down to his right, on his side of the water, was the Eastern corridor, built on stilts in the sea. It was flushed with traffic queuing for the crossing. Long, angry lines of red lights. There was a hold-up down there, a police block or an accident. Not twenty minutes ago he and Chan had sped along that corridor above the sea without let or hindrance, hardly a vehicle in sight, breaking all the limits. Chan talking on and on with his new optimism about the fixtures, the clubs, the band, the tour – Osaka, Bangkok, Manila, the Mandarin Oriental in Singapore – while destiny swept them on their way.

Neil sipped his whisky. At five a.m. it made a strange but satisfying rinse to The InterContinental breakfast.

Life, Neil thought, sipping his whisky again, and then again, came down to a question of vicious circles, or virtuous circles. One could talk about Life in this way, looking down at the harbour view, with a large whisky in your hand that you didn't have to pay for. Things were either spiralling up or they were spiralling down. There was nothing at the centre to take hold of, nothing around which things revolved, no handle or lever there to stop the world – *'Stop the world! I want to get off!'*, as Tony Newley would have said – no axis or handle so you could steady yourself, find a spiritual bearing, get a fix on things. No axis – only taxis. Life came to a halt when you stopped at the lights, or when you sat on the toilet, or when you fell asleep, or when you died. Otherwise, there was just the endless spiralling up or down, and you were expected out there all the time, oh yes, as a duty, on the wires and gyres, going up or down.

As if to confirm his new hypothesis the telephone rang and for the second time in five minutes Neil span around on his stubby heel. He nearly spilt his free drink.

The Li Poon? Laprisco? Before he'd finished *one* drink from the mini-bar?

He went back to the bedside and set his whisky by the low dome of the night-light. He picked up the receiver.

"Hello?"

"Tony? . . ."

The voice was young, female, and thickly Chinese. Neil looked at his feet on the carpet. His black boots. They were not as small and mean as Laprisco's. Neither were they as well polished.

"Tony here. Speaking."

"Tony Laprisco?"

"Speaking."

There was a pause. She didn't recognise his voice. Or she expected him to ask her a question. But what was it? He didn't know what the question was, the password, and his mind froze.

" . . . Do you want me to come up? It's kina late, or early . . ." She chuckled.

Neil's heart began to race. The *trimmings* . . .

"Sure," he said, slipping into his soft, warm American. "Come on up. Doesn't matter. We'll have some fun."

She hung up.

Neil put his receiver down, then picked it up again and read through the voicemail instructions. He tapped in the keys to pick up Laprisco's messages. There was just one. It was this girl. "Hello Tony. This is Myrna – " or was it Mona? – "Elbert told me to call, but you weren't in. Do you want to call me back on this number?" She ran off a number far too quickly for anyone to write down. Why did people do that? Neil hung up the phone but didn't delete the message. The hot red light still blinked. He might get back to that number later, but for the meantime he took the phone off the hook. He didn't want to be disturbed for a while.

He went through to the bathroom and checked his appearance in the mirror. There it was again – the friendly blue-rinsed glass that flattered so. His stage outfit looked good. In fact, in the soft spotlights of the bathroom it was rather special, he considered. He began to see why the night clerk had taken a shine. His face was tired and haggard, yes, and his long black hair still cast its shadows, but it was that look of the aging rock star, stylish in its own right. A lived-in face, older and wiser now, and very wary of being double-crossed one last time. All in all, not a bad prospect. Back out on the streets of Tsim Sha Tsui in the midday sun, or searching out a spot of shade on the esplanade, or sitting in McDonald's with a Fillet-o-fish half bitten and forgotten on its damp tissue – what a distant memory that was right now! – back in those places, this person was a very poor prospect indeed, just street-trash waiting for the lights to change. But here in room 1202 at The Excelsior, Hong Kong Island, there was a very different story. Neil flipped the cap off a bottle of Excelsior body lotion, took a fingertip of the rich white cream, and, leaning closer to the glass, moistened and flattened his eyebrows, and the hair at his temples. He narrowed his eyes, trying to bring some firmness to them in their slack sockets. He tried a warm and welcoming smile but it went too far, exposing high gums, dark roots, the shadows of age, of mortality. He let the smile retract in stages, setting it right, then stood back and raked through his black hair and straightened himself up –

And the bell rang.

Neil opened the door and waved the girl in without a word. It was a performance, like stepping up on stage, taking the mike from its clip. For moments like that you had to fake the confidence, always. Before closing the door he glanced furtively either way down the empty corridor.

When she took off her shawl in the hallway and turned to him he recognized her straightaway: she was last month's girl, June's girl, the girl on the exercise cycle. Her top had no straps, just as the bikini had had no straps in the photograph in Chan's office – that's what triggered the memory once the shawl was off. She was no more than seventeen or eighteen years old. She'd lost weight and her hair was different, short and spiky now, but it was definitely the same girl. She was smiling a well-trained smile and she was made up in that doll-like way Chinese men preferred. Her face was round and pretty, but there was hardly any bridge to her nose, Neil noticed. The protrusion started too late, a blemish that had been invisible in the shot for the calendar. She kept her well-trained, acquiescent smile, hoping to please, while he stared down at her and inspected her. She was meant to be unshakeable and unshockable, of course, an unshakeable and unshockable doll.

"What would you like to do, Tony?"

No holding back, then. But this appointment was meant to have taken place hours ago, on Laprisco's return, and she must have re-arranged her schedule to fit it in. So there was a time pressure. She'd called on the off-chance, just taken a little risk here, because she already had a wake-up call at The Excelsior, at six or seven o'clock, perhaps, and that's why his call could be worked in now. She had another client just along the corridor, or right next door, maybe, a wake-up call to see some businessman from the mainland, or Europe or America, to suck off some businessman before he took a sauna and had breakfast.

She had a shopping bag with her, a red and gold one from Esprit. She lifted the bag.

"I have some things," she said, still smiling.

Neil said nothing. His throat was dry. He went back to the bedside and picked up his whisky. He took a sip and stared at her over the rim of the glass. Her green top was cut short, exposing her navel. There, bared for him, was the skin of her belly, so smooth and white in this light it looked as if it had been brushed with talcum powder. It was the skin he'd so often ached to touch from across the street, across the malls, McDonald's . . . There was a red jewel set in gold in her navel, to draw down the eye. Her skirt, in the same dark green, but covered in some lighter green glitter, was tight, but not provocatively short. It was a stylish outfit, and very sexy, but in hotel lobbies and expensive night-clubs she would attract attention rather than suspicion.

Sipping the whisky calmed Neil, gave him something to do.

"You decide," he said. Then added, remembering his social graces, "How about a drink?"

She didn't answer for a moment but instead went to the controls at her side of the bed. Without any fumbling for the right switch she dimmed the main lights. Then she said:

"Advocaat, please, Tony."

So polite. Service. Quality service.

Chapter Twenty-one

Tracksuits

When he awoke the next day, very late, very much revived, in room 1202, Neil felt as if some long held dread had been lifted from his life. He couldn't quite name the dread, but without it he felt at ease with himself in a way that he could never remember feeling before, never in his entire life. He stretched in the clean white linen of Laprisco's bed. Fresh linen for a fresh start, a new start. It was as if God Himself had visited Neil in the night, while he slept, and He had told him that he was all right now, home and dry, there was nothing more to worry about ever again. Neil spied Laprisco's courtesy chocolate on the bedside table. He reached out, took it and put it in his mouth without a second thought.

For some time he did not lift his head from the starched pillow. He ate and swallowed the chocolate, enjoying its clammy sweetness, and then lay listening to the hum of the air conditioner. Eventually his eyes slid to the drawn curtains. He remembered Myrna-or-Mona drawing those curtains in the dark, one knee on the window seat. He remembered her from behind, her white back. The blue thong, a cord, that divided her teenage buttocks, and, when she turned from the curtain, the wonderful bra that had no material, that was just a few blue cords across her breasts, just tight enough to indent her flesh. She came back to him again, in his memory, and sat on the bedside, close to him, and began to cover herself in aromatic massage oil. She had warmed the oil in a phial over an aromatherapy burner. The oil and the burner and the special underwear were some of her 'things' from the red Esprit bag. Some of the nicer things. Neil hadn't wanted any of the nasty things. The burner was a pretty, delicate piece of glazed clay. By this stage its candle was the only light this side of the bed. She took off her fancy bra, poured some of the warm oil into Neil's coarse, cupped hands, and allowed him to anoint her breasts. The only breasts he had so anointed, apart from Angel's, for twenty years. And such different breasts. Small and round and firm.

Thus he had drifted, finally, quite by chance, into the calendar picture in Elbert's office. He had arrived. The girl's slippery indifference had actually come within his lecherous grasp. The Chinese skin he'd fantasised about touching and caressing for so many months, he touched and caressed – until impatiently she stopped him, and insisted they get on with the act itself.

Lying alone between the starched sheets Neil closed his eyes and felt his erection. The memory should neither be resisted nor wasted. He went to the bathroom and enjoyed a long, hot, onanistic shower.

Breakfast was another cooked English breakfast, with croissant again, and a sticky Danish too. Neil had it set out on his table by the window. He signed quickly, snapped the room-service wallet on the bill, and handed the wallet back over his shoulder. The boy was rushed and brusque as well, once it was clear that there would be no tip. Neil would have liked to tip him, a tip would have created a distraction and some useful goodwill, but he had no tip to offer the boy.

And that caused him to frown once he was on his own again. He sat by the window, the view, in his hotel dressing gown, his long dyed hair still wet from his shower, his breakfast before him, and with all this he should have been content. Yet he frowned. Outside it was a grey and heavy day. He tried to take an interest in it, the grey view, an amalgam of greys – water, sky and concrete – and to enjoy the world for what it was this early Sunday afternoon. But his focus weakened as inner worries took hold and pushed and jostled him against the hard edges of his problems.

The difficulty of being broke, again. The difficulty of the forthcoming meeting with Elbert Chan. The uncertainty of his tenure here at The Excelsior. The possibility of Laprisco's return to room 1202. Lam was optimistic, Chan had said. A professional opinion. That was a vicious, unruly worry, the thought of Tony Laprisco returning here – angry, in pain, head in a white bandage, a white turban – to discover him sitting by the window, sated with the luxuries Laprisco had ordered for his own delight on his Asian tour, on his last roll of the dice. In Laprisco's suite, in *his* chair, *his* dressing gown, eating *his* breakfast – he'd explode! – *Not you again! I'll fix you asshole! I'll fix you this time!* He'd call Khan. Hotel Security. He'd call the police. Every time the phone rang the panic and pressure of that anxiety would come back. Thinking of that, Neil went to put the phone back on its hook.

Funny how quickly, then, he considered, taking his seat at breakfast once more, funny how quickly, after all, the astounding good fortune of the early morning hours had leaked into insignificance. Again the two eternal questions held him in their pincers:

Who was going to foot the bill? If it was him, how was the bill to be footed?

The silver Excelsior cutlery felt heavy and old-fashioned – Khan's cutlery – and the breakfast had cooled. The first sip of coffee was both tepid and acrid.

While he breakfasted he considered the minor but very

demanding problem of what he was going to wear today. To put his stage outfit on again, which had seen such hard use over the last fifteen hours, would be unpleasant and unhygienic, and to go out in it, into the hotel corridor, into the lift and the lobby, would draw the kind of glances – from the desk clerk, for example – that he didn't want today. Or any other day, as it happened. The wearing of his ambitions on his sleeve for all and sundry to stare at and peck at was part of his old life, part of the endless tramping of the streets, the supplicatory visits to Chan's offices, part of being teased and humiliated by the receptionists, and all of that had to be over and done with now. It was finished, that chapter, that phase. But he needed to fix it somehow, put in a full stop and end it most definitely, so there was no slipping back.

Chan had promised him something at The InterContinental last night.

A new start. A fresh start.

Neil looked up from his breakfast. He stared a moment at the grey view. Above all, today, he knew, above all, he just wanted to appear a normal citizen, one who had paid his bills, who was going about his business, looking in shop windows, breezing by, on his way somewhere or other, maybe to meet someone for coffee or for lunch, or just window-shopping for his own diversion. It didn't matter. But in order to begin the day as a normal citizen you had to get dressed.

His baggage – underwear, bindle, guitar, suitcase, everything he owned apart from wallet, watch and passport – was not here. It was at ChungKing, where he'd been holing up all week until the American Club engagement. He still had some bills to pay at ChungKing. Neil shifted in his seat at the thought of those bills and sipped some more of the tepid coffee. He could have paid those bills. He could have gone back to ChungKing today and settled his bills and picked up all his things, if it hadn't been for Myrna-or-Mona. Her little invoice had taken away every cent he had. Within five minutes of slipping out of bed she'd cleaned herself up in the bathroom, and then cleaned him out. She'd stood there at the bedside, her Esprit carrier bag on the bed, while he'd counted out the notes. And he'd kept counting out the notes. Oh, such a lot of money! All he had, and it still hadn't been enough. Her fee was two thousand dollars. About a hundred and sixty pounds. He'd paid her less than half. It was okay, she'd said, folding up the notes, dropping his wad in her Esprit bag – she'd collect the rest from Elbert Chan. But would she? No, she wouldn't. He'd been duped there, of course. She'd collect the entire fee from Chan and pocket his cash. She'd say he'd never paid her. A helpless shrug and smile, her hands up, palms out, palms up. He didn't have a bean, Elbert. So then Chan would demand the entire fee back from him, and demand a tip for her too, which he'd pocket for himself, of course. So he'd pay 200%, 300%, 400% by the time they'd finished with him. Of course, of course. That's how it would work.

So there lay another difficulty in his forthcoming meeting with Elbert Chan.

But it occurred to Neil that he needn't return to ChungKing at all. He had his outfit here, and his wallet, watch and passport. Why not just abandon the rest and forget about the debt? There was nothing of any value. Why cling to any of it? What's past is past. Let the grasping Pakistani landlords of ChungKing do what they liked with his underwear, his suitcase, guitar and bindle. They could burn the lot and dance in the flames for all he cared.

In turn that idea inspired something more mischievous. He rose with a start, upsetting his plate and knocking his half eaten Danish onto the carpet. In the walk-in wardrobe was the room safe, on the chest of drawers. It was closed. A good sign. He read the instructions and tried a couple of random combinations – wild guesses at Laprisco's birthday – then he called Housekeeping. He told them he'd forgotten his code for the safe.

They'd be right up.

Neil poured himself more coffee and drank it standing, waiting around, staring out the window at the grey and heavy day.

It was the same boy. Neil hung back in his dressing gown while he opened the safe. Unless there were some loose change in there he would have to go away untipped a second time. Laboriously the boy punched in the master code from a plastic card. The lock whirred and the door sprang open.

There lay inside a large, black, leather flight wallet. Neil felt his heart begin to race on seeing this. But why? He was tripping on the slightest chance into headlong over-excitement. Why? Survival reactions. Fight or flight. Animal reflexes kicking in when he couldn't even see the danger.

Laprisco's flight wallet didn't sit flat on the safe floor. It looked swollen, distended. Neil wiped some crumbs of Danish from his mouth and led the boy back to the door.

"Thanks," he said, seeing him out.

He returned to the safe and seized the swollen flight wallet and brought it out into the bedroom light. He weighed it in both hands and felt its skin. Real leather. Soft. Worn. A chunky steel zip. Strong. Unfailing. An old friend. It was like having some vital organ of Laprisco's here in his hands. Something big. His liver. His pancreas. Neil slit it open and spread it wide.

In the main compartment was an American Airways ticket and a printout of some flight information. That was all. Neil put these back in the safe. There were internal flaps, folds, valves in the flight wallet. In one he found $64 U.S. in notes. Not bad. In another a large wedge of receipts, retained for tax purposes, presumably. And in another more receipts, masses of receipts. These gave the wallet its bulk. He double-checked all the flaps, folds, valves. No cards. Then in the back of the wallet, zipped up in its own compartment, he found Laprisco's American passport. This took him by surprise and made him feel a flush of foolishness. Of course it would be here, in the flight wallet, in the safe. Tossing aside the wallet on the bed, he went to the window to study Laprisco's passport in the grey daylight. He held it to the window and felt it, bent it, rubbed its cover, making sure it was for real. Then he flicked to the back, to the photo page.

Here was a shock from the world outside room 1202. The first of the day. Neil flinched, stepped back. An ugly genie had flapped out from the passport, brushing his face with its wings, flapped free into room 1202, never to be shut up in those pages again.

The picture was in stark and grainy black and white, with a sepia tinge from the weathered seal. It was Laprisco's face, no doubt about that. There were the sagging black eyebrows. But the face was so gaunt and drawn, the mouth so sagging and down-turned, it was like a mask, a theatrical mask, representing eternal sorrow, eternal tragedy. Or like a crude, carved African mask. Eyes hooded, blind, half dead. The dome had no hair at all. Nothing. Shaven. Death's-head. It felt like something from a different era. It was not a picture of a living person at all. It was part of a historical document from the dawn of photography, from an anthropological study that had gone horribly wrong, some jungly research about cannibals on a faraway archipelago . . .

He'd been caught in the camera flash, that was all, but the picture was so bad it was as if his eyelids had been drawn down on his corpse. The death's-head stared back at Neil from beyond the grave, with hooded and vindictive malice. A voodoo curse now pervaded room 1202, harbour view, darkening the room with ill omens.

A wig.

The best, the most expensive wig ever made, perhaps, but a wig, after all.

There was the date of birth. 31.07.39. Laprisco was fifty-nine at the end of the month. Fifty-nine years old and still singing *Cracklin' Rosie* and *Sweet Caroline* with such artistry and passion.

Neil took up the discarded flight wallet from the bed and went through it again, through all the slack flaps and valves and folds. There was nothing else. The $64 U.S. was not the gold strike he needed, but it was a start. The passport went back inside its zipped compartment, out of harm's way, and the wallet back in the safe. Neil reset the combination for his own birthday. The money could be spent on some clothes, but he'd only use it for that purpose as a last resort. To have some cash in hand was the main thing. He could change a few notes at reception and start the day's business.

After breakfast, still in his dressing gown, he set off for the 18th floor. The fitness centre and the male and female Spas were on this floor, and adjoining them was a sports shop. It was hardly more than a glass kiosk but it had a fair range of sportswear on display. Neil signed for a couple of pairs of swimming trunks, some ludicrously expensive sports shirts, three pairs of tennis shorts, four pairs of white socks, some smart white trainers, and, to cover it all up, a blue-black tracksuit. It was the only tracksuit they had. They had to unpin it from a display board in the window.

To keep up appearances he dropped in at the Spa Jacuzzi. He spent no more than ten minutes in there, pleasant though it was, and then left the Men's Spa as he'd come in, still wearing his hotel dressing gown, but now carrying a very full Excelsior carrier bag. The carrier bag, in gloss white and gold, lent immediate assurance.

Once back inside 1202 he checked the phone messages again. There was a new one, from Chan. Nothing from the Li

Poon Christian Hospital. He thought of giving the Li Poon another call, but he didn't. A complacency was setting in about Laprisco's helpless condition, and it was thickening with every invasion of his privacy, every theft of his personal property. Neil noted the complacency and he resolved to guard against it. Nonetheless he didn't call the Li Poon.

Chan wanted him at his office after lunch, between two and two-thirty. Neil deleted that message, then went back to Myrna's-or-Mona's and took her number down. He fetched the flight wallet from the safe and tucked her number away in an inner compartment, then deleted her message too. He was brisk and businesslike in attending to these details, as if with that manner he could impose a sense of order and normality on what he was doing, and on all those other things that were going on, he suspected, just beyond his control.

That manner imposed a mood. Rather than change just a few U.S. at reception, where the rates were so poor, he changed all $64. It was raining outside and without even thinking about it or doing any sums at all, Neil took a cab from The Excelsior forecourt all the way to Tsim Sha Tsui. Today was a winner-takes-all, no-holds-barred, go-for-broke day. New chapter, new phase. No going back.

Tall and confident in his blue-black tracksuit, still feeling fresh and supple after his Jacuzzi, his hair wet on his glossy shoulders, his belly full of his five-star breakfast, he breezed into Chan's travel agency. He carried his flight wallet nipped by one corner between thumb and forefinger. He entered with the assurance of one who would be seeing Mr. Chan immediately, no questions asked. Anyway, the facetious receptionists wouldn't be there, not on a Sunday afternoon.

But they were there. And there was someone else there too, already waiting in the anteroom. Someone had an appointment ahead of him to see Elbert Chan this Sunday afternoon.

Iannis, his old, forgotten adversary, was perched on the cushioned bench seat behind the door. He sat on the very edge of the seat in a tight and upright posture, as if holding indoors some ungovernable wind from McDonald's. Or as if keeping in check a sports injury, a lumbar sprain or slipped disc. He was so stiff and upright he might have been bound up in a medical corset, beneath his shabby Mizuno tracksuit. Despite his obvious discomfort, Iannis was coolly flicking through one of his holiday brochures as usual, about to pick another five-star vacation. On Neil's grand entrance he stopped his flicking and looked up, and the pages of his brochure came to rest at the centrefold. A smiling, bikinied Asian girl lying on a brown sugar beach.

Neil, who'd stopped dead in his tracks in front of Iannis, stared down at this man whom he'd cut out and discarded from his life. There was a painful silence. The door flapped shut behind him on its spring. Neil's gaze shifted to the bikinied girl on the sugar beach, and he thought: I have tasted that, and you have not.

Behind him, the supercilious receptionists, the harpies, in a weekend mood, began to titter openly. Their laughter locked Neil in a tableau with Iannis.

New York? Paris? Montreal? First class? Business Class? Club Class?

But who shared the joke today? Certainly not Iannis. Iannis glanced round Neil's legs to the receptionists, and his face was heavy with menace. Neil unfroze too and turned, glanced back over his shoulder at these girls, from whom he had taken so much punishment, so much humiliation. They'd had a lot of fun, a lot of laughs at his expense, over the last few weeks. Oh yes. *Would you like a ticket to Guangzhou? First class? . . . So you can meet him there? Find him in the street?* Oh, too much fun, too many laughs. Neil tried to silence them with a glance both haughty and severe, chin thrust out over the shoulder of his glossy tracksuit, but they kept tittering at him all the same, hands raised to their mouths, and he gave up, turned back to Iannis. Then they stopped. Abruptly. The bold and ugly menace of Iannis's expression and the naked aggression in his eyes, the hatred even, the violence there, a murderous violence, had silenced the girls. Neil glanced back again to see one of them slip away from the reception counter and go to rake through a filing cabinet.

Iannis continued glaring at the receptionists, pinning them down, making them squirm. He hadn't shaved for a few days and under his bristles there was an eruption in his complexion. The follicles goose-pimpled in a pustular and feverish way. Neil could hear him breathing, a faint wheeziness chasing his breath. His eyes were shot and heavy. They lifted at last, turning up slowly from the reception counter to settle on Neil, and Neil too felt trapped by their menacing glare. Evidently he had done something wrong as well – something very wrong, something quite unforgivable. But what?

On this go-for-broke, no-holds-barred, winner-takes-all Sunday afternoon, it seemed unfortunate in the extreme that Iannis was sitting here on the bench in the anteroom, in such poor shape and so filled with antipathy. From where Neil stood he could smell stale sweat coming off Iannis. With every wheezy breath the smell wafted from the zips and vents of his worn-out tracksuit. And Neil could smell booze. Strong booze. Spirits. Even as he stood there absorbing these odours Iannis rose up against him from his cushioned bench and stepped close, keeping his back-braced, his arse out. He furled his brochure tight in his muscular grip, making it into a truncheon or cudgel, which he now used to push in Neil's shiny new tracksuit, till he met his ribs -

"You laughing at me?"

It was whisky talk. Or worse, whisky mac talk. Neil could smell the ginger. He didn't want to deal with this. It wasn't why he'd come here today.

"You fucking with me, pal?"

Out the corner of his eye Neil saw the second receptionist return to her position at the counter, but there was no superior tittering now.

"You laughing at me?"

There was high tension in the air. There was fear, created by the squat and brooding, boozy black guy. There was a static charge in the air, as if the synthetic material of the two black tracksuits had been viciously rubbed together.

"Because if – "

"I am not laughing at you," Neil interrupted softly, seriously. He repeated that, his voice very low, making downward, calming gestures with his free hand. "I . . . am . . . not . . . laughing at you."

"So what's the big idea?" Iannis poked at the baggy front of Neil's tracksuit again. There was so much puffed out material around Neil's skinny frame, so much puff to poke at with his truncheon or cudgel.

Neil shook his head. "It's just a coincidence. A crazy coincidence. That's all. Nothing personal."

Iannis cocked his head. His mouth was open and his dry tongue now stuck to the roof of his sour mouth. Ginger. Whisky mac. He tilted his head, lowered his eyelids. It seemed theatrical, the posturing of cool, black indifference – Sammy Davis Jnr. – but Neil could tell it was a sincere attempt at that, not a game at all. Neil was reminded of the films of the late Sammy Davis, the wiry, tiny black guy making it through, somehow, against all the odds. But Iannis wasn't making it through, wasn't getting anywhere at all. The odds were stacked too high against him and he couldn't lift them. There were pallet-loads of odds. There were sixteen tons of odds, the same sixteen tons the flat-footed Tennessee Ford couldn't lift, in the dockyard song that Sammy Davis immortalized –

You lift sixteen tons and what do you get?
Another day older and deeper in debt.
Saint Peter, don't you call me 'cause I can't go,
I owe my soul to –

But to whom did Iannis owe his soul?

As if he could hear the song too, as he searched Neil's face, and could understand how it spoke for him, Iannis's eyes filled with emotion. The swollen, sports-ball eyes slid sideways in a film of water, glancing back at Chan's office door -

"He's fucking busted me!" he said, and with these words his emotion welled up and the pressure behind his eyes was finally released. It was not toughness, after all, not tenacity or resolution: it was just water pressure, years of tears of frustration, loneliness and unhappiness. "He's fucking busted me!" he repeated, and swallowed hard, checking the quaver in his voice. "That fucking Chan."

Neil frowned. He couldn't help seeking some clarification. "What do you mean? Busted you? He can't do that. He can't bust you."

"Can't get no work!" Iannis answered, his voice cracking. He lowered his eyes, shook his head. He glanced over his shoulder at Chan's office again. "He's fucking burned me, pal. I'm broke. Flat broke." He looked up at Neil: "Say, you couldn't – "

"Burned you? How do you mean, burned you?"

"All the clubs. The clubs. He's – " another glance over his shoulder to Chan's door – "He's put out the word . . ."

Busted. Burned. The word. Neil was too much obsessed by his own prospects with Chan to see what Iannis was getting at.

"What word?" Neil queried. "Do you mean . . ." He took a breath and blinked, reluctant to bring this up . . . "About your act?"

A frown crossed Iannis's brows.

"You mean, your Sammy Davis act?"

Iannis said nothing. He shook his head in bewilderment.

"Has he told them . . . that it's no good?"

Iannis's chin retracted on its goose-pimpled neck – now Neil had said something quite astonishingly tactless, quite beyond belief – and Iannis shook his head in a different way, exasperated, weary, hopeless. Oh dear, oh dear . . .

"You fuck off," he said, pushing past Neil with his furled brochure. "You fuck off now, you hear me?" At the door, without looking back, he added: "You're just another loser. Another fucking loser."

He left, the door flapped shut again on its spring, and Iannis was gone.

Quiet.

Neil looked to the closed door of Elbert's office. He could hear Elbert's voice. He was on the telephone, sitting behind his melamine desk. He was having one of those odd, bilingual conversations, mainly in Cantonese, but with sudden bursts of English thrown in. The English parts were accompanied by ripples of phoney laughter. The call closed in English:

"Sure, sure . . . Never again, Harry. No problem . . . You have my word. Hahaha . . . He won't, he won't . . . no problem at all . . . What? . . . He better not! . . . Be seeing you, then . . . Look forward to it . . . Hahaha . . . . . . Bye for now . . . Bye . . . Bye . . . . . . Bye . . ."

Chapter Twenty-two

Last Respects

"He was the best."

Chan sat poised in his office chair, in a new dark suit, white shirt, and plain red silk tie, with his hands lightly clasped across his waist. From his attitude and his dress there came an air of propriety and gravity this Sunday afternoon. The lightness and bonhomie of the early morning hours had evaporated. That was something they both had to move away from, Neil sensed. The breakfast at The InterContinental was so much washing-up now.

That's what it looked like, but Neil also sensed there might be more to it.

"He was the best."

Chan was talking about Iannis. His pronouncements were made with some reverence, as if, sitting there in his dark suit, he were addressing a hushed and private audience at Iannis's funeral, as if he were paying his last respects. Across the poky office Neil sat in attentive silence in the rattan armchair, one new white trainer pulled up on his knee, his flight wallet in his lap. Rain clattered on the air conditioner unit in the window. Neil's attentive attitude and the lonely clatter of the rain added to the funereal ambience.

"But – and it was a big but – " Chan continued, leaning forward and squaring his Compaq on his desk – "He had no manners, you see." He looked up at Neil confidingly. "Iannis had no manners. Now, the Chinese won't put up with that. Not at these clubs."

Neil nodded. Of course not.

"So I had to let him go."

Neil had made a passing enquiry about Iannis, just mentioned him by way of conversation as he took his seat, and Chan had responded with this unexpected seriousness, as if he had been called upon to explain himself, to offer extenuating circumstances about why he'd busted and burned Iannis and put out the word.

"We have to talk through our engagements." Chan sat up. They had to move on again. They had been wasting time on Iannis.

And with the change of subject Neil knew Iannis really had made his last exit. He'd disappeared. Just like that. So complete was his disappearance he might actually have died. The guard on the ground floor would be told not to let him up any more. He would be pushed back onto the street, with his cumbersome sports bag. And he'd fall back, after being pushed, stumbling, swearing, drunk, into the street, into the taxi rank. That was it. No more Iannis, sitting on the cushioned bench behind the door, flicking through travel brochures, staring at the beaches. The next bench for Iannis was the park bench.

These thoughts did not excite pity in Neil, more an acute awareness of the vulnerability of his own position. He was sitting here in the rattan armchair in place of someone who might come back any time, according to Dr. Lam, and usurp him. Maybe at any moment. But the way Chan was talking about their engagements, 'our engagements', going over all the things he'd said in the taxi last night as they sped along the Eastern corridor, but in a different way now, more firmly and decisively – the way he was talking it was if Tony Laprisco, like Iannis, were no longer with them, were no longer a cause for concern.

" . . . next Friday it's The Clearwater Bay Golf & Country Club . . ."

People passed through Chan's hands like water. If Neil hadn't made his bold and reckless move last night to join forces with Laprisco, he too would have passed through Chan's hands, and Tony Laprisco would be sitting here, where he was sitting. And last night Myrna-or-Mona would have called on the real Laprisco. *Sure. Come on up. We'll have some fun.* It would have been Laprisco's body, his fifty-nine year old body, sitting naked on the bedside, his wig of black hair resting on his white shoulders, his belly a sac of wrinkles. It would have been Laprisco's body, pear-shaped, balanced there, a bourbon at the end of his hairy arm, and Myrna-or-Mona's head in his lap, working, working . . . . *We'll have some fun . . .*

". . . Saturday is Deep Water Bay and maybe we could extend that by one night . . ."

Your life was swiped like a charge card. There was a debit and then the human transaction was over. That was his life, Neil's life, that's what it would be like from now on. A life swiped through other people's lives, over and over – through Chan's life, Iannis's life, Neil Diamond's life, Laprisco's life, Myrna-or-Mona's life – swipe, swipe, swipe – and no real human contact was ever made, nothing substantial ever happened, nothing you could even talk about with anyone.

". . . The Discovery Bay Golf & Country Club on Lantau Island . . ."

Which was where the difference lay between the music Neil used to play and love and the music he was now obliged to play. The old songs had been about something human, about individual people and their trials and triumphs – a tapestry woven by the artists and passed down from generation to generation. That's why so many folk albums had that word – Tapestry – woven in the title or in the songs. And the performers all knew and shared and respected that . . . bullshit.

" . . . Osaka, Bangkok, Manila, Jakarta, and we'll finish in Singapore, at the Mandarin Oriental . . ."

Neil wouldn't drift up again in his hot air balloon, high above the sea and city. When all was said and done he had to earn: he had to earn, or, like Iannis, to burn. That's what he was doing here. It was simply a matter of keeping his concentration and playing along with Chan for a mutual benefit. It wasn't just a debit. He was buying into something here. It could be big, but if there were any possibility at all of gain, of profit, of a dollar and a cent, he had to stick with it. Laprisco's passport was in his flight wallet. He felt for it through the leather.

"I want to show you something."

He unzipped the flight wallet and removed Laprisco's passport. He leant forward and pushed it across the melamine desk.

Chan took the passport with a curious frown. He handled it delicately, that attitude of reverence, gravitas, returning. For the first time in all Neil's visits Chan pulled down the pretentious Anglepoise and switched it on.

"Since you've found this – " he began, thinking aloud, flicking through the passport under the light – then he broke off. He'd already reached the back, the photograph. He stopped, but no shock registered on his flat features. There was no flinching back or sharp intake of breath.

"It was a wig, you see," Neil said, with some satisfaction. The truth about the man Chan had given preference and favour to, over him, had at last been exposed.

Staring at the photo Chan's eyes narrowed and his expression became meditative, as if he were recognizing

Laprisco in a new way, or as if there were some interest in the photograph beyond its immediate ugliness, something pitiful about it.

Chan said quietly: "Makes a difference, doesn't it?"

He closed the passport and set it to one side, then switched off and folded away the Anglepoise.

"A good find," he said. "We'll use that. We'll take out his photo and put in one of your publicity shots. Easy. No problem. Pick it up tomorrow. Then you can use it at the hotel. Hey – " he looked up brightly at Neil, realizing something – "that saves us some hassle and some money." The thought cheered Chan. "Well done, Neil. Terrific find."

With this casual talk of adulterating Laprisco's passport, Neil pulled his new white trainer further up and gripped both hands on the sole. There was something wrong here. Something obviously and desperately, pitifully wrong. Either he was missing it, he just couldn't see it, or Chan was missing it – that failure of the imagination again.

"Er . . . Hold on there, Elbert," he began. "Don't we need to exercise a little caution about this?"

Chan looked confused. "What do you mean?"

Neil shut his eyes a moment. He tried to remain detached, ironic. "Well, let's see now . . . If Laprisco recovers – and Lam's optimistic, remember – he'll want his passport back, for a start, and with his own photo at the back, not my photo. So what happens to me then, Elbert? That's what I want to know. What happens to my tour? What about that scenario? What happens then? Hmmn?"

"If Laprisco recovers?" The old cartoon lines of puzzlement deepened and darkened Chan's forehead again.

What did Chan really expect, Neil asked himself, in the event of Laprisco's return? That he would just go away? Fade out? Disappear? With a couple of thousand dollars? Take a flight back to England, for a third time? While Laprisco resumed his itinerary? Did he really believe that could happen? That was not going to happen. Neil wanted to make it very clear to Elbert Chan that his disappearance was not an option. He wasn't going to be busted and burned, and no one, least of all Elbert Chan, was going to put out the word on him and his act.

"What happens then, Elbert? Would you like to explain that?"

"Don't you know?"

"He just slots back in, right?" Neil laughed sarcastically, eyes to the ceiling. He was asserting himself now against Chan. He shifted in his seat, in his slippery tracksuit. He laughed again, at Chan this time, consolidating his point. "I'm not going to walk away, Elbert. If Laprisco comes back I'm not going to just disappear. Fly off. Buzz off. Piss off back to England. I want you to understand that. We would have to re-negotiate – "

"Now you hold on there – "

Elbert raised a hand, but Neil had no time for any more bluff and bull – he was in full flow –

" – There would have to be a new deal. There would have to be a two-way split. A double act of some kind. Like last night. Something of that order. I mean it." Now it had come up, Neil wished he had thought through this other scenario more carefully. He'd run ahead of himself and had to pause.

"Sure," Chan stepped in. "Of course there would. But since Laprisco isn't coming back – "

"But how do you know that? Have you talked to Dr. Lam again?"

"Didn't he call you? He said he'd call you personally at the hotel."

"Well, he didn't call me!" Neil raised his arms in exasperation. What the hell was going on here? "Lam didn't call me. I know nothing. I don't know what's going on."

Chan leant across his desk to explain. He lowered his voice:

"Neil, Tony Laprisco isn't coming back. Not unless he dusts himself off and walks out the furnace." He shook his head. "He isn't going to do that."

Neil scowled. "Furnace?"

Chan nodded.

For the second time today reality was breaking through in a shocking way. "He's been burned?"

Busted, burned . . .

"Tomorrow noon." Chan checked his watch, as if remembering a train or plane. "By tomorrow this time he'll be cremated."

Neil looked away. "Then he's dead . . ."

"Of course he's dead! You think they're going to burn him alive? He wasn't that bad. It's all over for Laprisco. He's history. Soon he'll be cinders. I was at the Li Poon this morning paying my last respects."

Neil said nothing. How could he be so blind? So dumb? Chan's manner, his dress, all his talk about 'our engagements', to which Neil had hardly listened, being so preoccupied, as always, with loftier and weightier matters.

"A fellow in the band has organized it all," Chan informed Neil. "The bass player. Very sharp guy. He's picked Tony clean. Got the cards, the cash, arranged all the details. By tomorrow Tony's gone. Out the frame. Puff of smoke. No announcements, no family, no friends – just disappears. So what's happened doesn't actually change anything at all – not for us. It's a misfortune, and we move on. The tour rolls on. Otherwise the band can't even pay their hotel bills. They're stuck here. Band, singers, everyone. So they agreed the show must go on. That's show business, they all said."

Chapter Twenty-three

His Own Agenda

"Oh! Mr. Laprisco! . . ."

Neil stopped and turned. He was in the middle of the lobby, on his way to the lifts. The dandy was coming out from Reception, from behind the desk flap, and there was Khan too, behind him, the bald fellow in his out-of-date dogstooth, staring straight at him, trying to fix him to the marble with his stare.

It was Tuesday, three days before the first engagement at The Clearwater Bay Golf & Country Club, and he had just been to *Ask For Toni's* to have his hair re-straightened and re-dyed. Some grey twists had been creeping back around the crown. Toni had fixed that and he looked good right now, and felt strong. He stood his ground, in his black tracksuit, in his white trainers, with his white and gold Excelsior carrier bag at his side, and let the dandy glide up to him across the marble.

"I'm sorry, Mr. Laprisco, but would you mind coming this way, please?" His blown dry bouffant trembled with nervousness. Something was up.

Neil frowned down at the dandy, didn't move or speak. He was quite at ease now, strolling around The Excelsior Hotel. He flicked a glance back at Reception. Khan was still staring, trying to hold him there. No need.

"Just a routine check, sir."

"What's the problem?"

"No problem, sir. We just require your confirmation of some purchases from the Spa Shop. No problem at all. Just routine."

Neil had been hitting the men's Spa Shop pretty hard. On Monday he'd bought two top of the range tennis racquets, which he'd just resold in Mong Kok for petty cash. Hence the carrier bag. He'd also bought more swimming trunks. There was an expensive style he found comfortable as underwear, so he'd bought a few pairs. So what?

"Some tennis racquets, sir?"

"What about them?"

"And some other things . . . Some other things, sir."

Neil took a breath, hesitated. He couldn't sustain this conversation in the middle of the lobby, with people passing by, glancing back, lifting their sunglasses, but he didn't want any negotiations with the elderly, lizard-eyed Khan either. He heard Chan whisper in his ear: *'Watch him. Avoid him if you can . . .'* Already it seemed to be the other way around: it was Khan who was watching him, after just a couple of days.

Neil refocused on Edward, the dandy. His name was embossed in silver on a black badge. Edward Reception.

"I'm in a bit of a hurry right now, Edward . . ." Neil left a pause for the fellow to back off, but Edward said nothing. Neil sighed and glanced at his broken Rolex. The hour hand had come loose now. Even as he consulted the watch the chunky golden hour hand slipped round the face and six hours went by, just like that. Time out.

"Can we keep it brief? I'm in a hurry, like I said."

"Of course, sir. Very brief. It's just a routine check."

Neil followed him to the polished mahogany of the Reception desk. Khan lifted the flap for his minion and they stood together behind the desk. His inquisitors.

"Sorry to trouble you, sir." Khan said, stripping a rubber

band from a roll of chits. Neil looked down. All his chits were here, in rolls, on the mahogany. Meal by meal, drink by drink, snack by snack. And his chits for the swimming trunks, sports shirts, the tracksuit, the tennis racquets, trainers, they were all there too, rolled up in colourful rubber bands. There were so many of them. So many rolls. Really an awful lot of rolls and chits.

Khan flattened the Spa chit for the tennis racquets and Neil stared down at the loopy, egotistical flourishes of Laprisco's signature, at which he'd become so expert.

"We generally double-check all purchases over five thousand dollars made in one day, sir."

Neil said nothing.

"So if you wouldn't mind counter-signing these. Just for our records."

Neil took the proffered pen.

He dashed off another Laprisco signature, identical to the one already there on the chit.

"Thank you so much, sir." Khan smiled.

"That's okay." Neil smiled back for a moment and held his stare. The lizard eyes softened. The old man was relieved, pleased. No aggravation, then. Not on his watch.

"Now, if you'll excuse me . . ."

"Of course, sir. Sorry to have bothered you."

"We're very sorry to have bothered you, sir," Edward echoed.

"That's okay."

Neil left them and resumed, at measured pace, his journey across the marble to the lift lobby, walking tall in his black tracksuit, empty carrier bag at his side.

He sat on the bed, directly beneath the air conditioning, which he'd cranked up to maximum. The telephone cradle lay on the bed beside him.

"Well? What is it?"

"They're asking about my chits."

There was a long pause and some crackling from the other end of the line, as if the receiver were being passed from hand to hand, from person to person, among lots of uninterested parties. Anyone want to deal with this?

"Are the police involved?"

"No . . . no!" Neil reassured Chan. "Of course not. No police! Just the fellow from reception."

"Khan?"

Neil realised too late – oh, what a mistake! – how vital it was not to inform Chan about this development, to keep him at a safe distance at all costs. He'd telephoned Chan on a reflex, in a panic, because there was no one else to look to for reassurance, for help, if he needed it. What if things became serious? What if he found himself on the run, like a common criminal? He'd need a bolt-hole of some description. But of course the last thing he was ever going to get from Elbert Chan was reassurance, help, if he needed it, or a bolt-hole of some description. He should never have picked up the phone.

"He was fine!" Neil laughed, trying to dismiss what he'd just said. "I dealt with it. No worries. They just wanted a counter-signature, that's all." Neil laughed again. He had to pretend quickly that he had another, more important reason for calling: "Look, I was wondering – "

"So the police are not involved."

Chan's tone was demanding.

"What? . . . There's nothing like that! No police! Stop panicking! Forget about it. Look, I think we should get the band together to rehearse, because – "

"You haven't seen or spoken to a policeman or a policewoman?"

"I just told you, Elbert!"

"But what do you *know*?"

The question was entirely rhetorical.

"We really need to rehearse, Elbert," Neil continued, "and we need to go through exactly – "

"No one needs to rehearse," Chan cut him off. There was something very different in Chan's voice now. Something flat and final. "No one needs to rehearse," he repeated, and with that, before Neil could say anything else, Chan put down the receiver.

Neil sat on the bedside, the receiver in his hand, mulling over that last line, and on what he might have messed up with one stupid call . . . and with all his swimsuits and tennis racquets . . . There was a resonance to Chan's line. It kept going, repeating itself between the purrs of the receiver in his hand. No one needs to rehearse, to rehearse, to rehearse . . . Chan couldn't drop the whole thing now, surely, just because of this? He couldn't just abandon him here! In The Excelsior? Leave him to his fate! Could he?

Of course not. Paranoia again. But understandable, forgivable, under the circumstances.

Neil looked up. The sensual window seat, which had actually become sensual since Myrna-or-Mona's visit, was cut so low that even from the bedside you could stare down at the harbour view. That stale old harbour view, under a grey sky. But he did not see the view. His eyes lost focus. He was remembering that he already had Laprisco's passport. He'd collected it from Chan yesterday, with his own photo in it, a good photo, cropped from one his publicity shots at The Mariners' – an excellent job by some shady Chan connection. That passport, his passport, was back in Laprisco's flight wallet, his flight wallet, safely zipped up, in his room safe. He realized how far he'd already come, how deep he'd already walked into the shadows of Chan's new 'scenario'. And the tickets were already prepared at Chan's agency, and Chan had said he'd confirmed all the engagements on Laprisco's itinerary, the whole Far East tour. The switch was complete. On Sunday Chan had run through all the dates, listed each Hong Kong club, one by one, and then the Far East tour, the whole itinerary. There it all was. On a plate. Starting Friday. Nothing could go wrong from here. Khan didn't matter, Edward didn't matter. He just had to show them his passport. No arguing with that, for goodness' sake. Elbert wasn't going to drop this whole project now, just because of that call! He was brusque because he was busy and had to get off the line. No way would Elbert drop all this now . . . But even if he did, even if he'd got cold feet – *Are the police involved?* – even if he betrayed Neil and abandoned him here in his hour of need, even if he did that, with everything so well fixed and organized, why shouldn't he – they, Neil and the band, *Uncut Diamonds* – drop Elbert Chan? Drop Chan himself? If he copped out. It was just an intimation, just the beginning of an idea. Why not betray, if he were betrayed? If Chan didn't want a piece of this any more – fine. Bye-bye.

The harbour came back into focus, under the grey sky. There were two liners down there, one coming, one going. He had often stared down at the decks of those liners from the Ocean Terminal car park, just a pier away from The Pacific Club. Many afternoons he'd spent watching the sunbathers on the liners' decks through his wraparound sunglasses. And he'd stared, fascinated, at the ships themselves, those dedicated leisure cruisers, floating casinos, and peered through their portholes into their cabins – he'd been like a child, covetously peeping at some vast white model at an exhibition. Star Line Cruises. Star Pisces and Star Leo. Local tours to Hua Hin and Vietnam. They had live entertainment on those liners. Comedy acts. Tribute artists. To console the losers. Every night. His kind of entertainment. From the Ocean Terminal car park you could see into the ballroom and see the restaurant tables, the dance floor. You could see into the gaming rooms.

You could see right into some of the luxury cabins. Neil could remember every detail of the liners from those long, wasted afternoons. They were the same ships that were down there right now, twelve floors below. In his mind's eye he could see, on Star Pisces, the tiny medical bay, and the hairdressers' salon, side by side, on the top deck. The red cross of the medical bay – He lost everything he had! – and the black and white tiles of the hairdressers' salon. The client's chair facing out to sea. You could have your hair washed, cut and styled facing out to sea, watching the pink dolphins, the distant islands, the first mountains of Vietnam coming into view . . . Neil was surrounded by prospects, whichever way he looked. He had the passport, the band, the bookings, the entrée. He could have his hair re-dyed and re-styled – curled, chopped, frizzed – a new look, on the way to Vietnam. Who needed Elbert Chan? The way he had called Chan, as if that were all he could possibly do, go to Chan for help, as if Chan were his only access to work and survival – that may have been true once, but over the weeks he'd allowed Chan too big a role in his life. He'd made Chan into a prima donna, curtaining off his own initiative behind the scenes. If Chan tried to betray him now he'd turn the tables on him.

He'd betray Chan and all his worthless kind.

He sat alone in the sauna of the Men's Spa with his eyes shut and with a thick white Excelsior sheet towel around his waist, imagining the ballrooms of Star Pisces, Star Leo, imagining the tiny stage, hexagonal perhaps, with fairy lights, and imagining plugging a new acoustic-electric into the ship's current there. He was sitting on his hands in the sauna, cushioning his lean buttocks from the pine slats. He opened his eyes a moment to glance at the egg timer on the opposite wall. The Excelsior egg timer wasn't filled with sand but with glittering coloured crystals that shone in the red, underwater light. They teased the eye as they slunk through the waist of the glass. The timer was running low. Neil closed his eyes and inhaled deeply, taking the heat down into his lungs. It was no longer uncomfortable, the heat. He had reached the point when he could surrender to it. The pores of his skin were opening wide and giving up their dirty, boring secrets of the street. All the grime that had accumulated over the last weeks, while he tramped the highways and byways of Tsim Sha Tsui, was running out and draining away. From the Men's Spa of The Excelsior Hotel that life seemed as many months distant as he was floors from the street. His sweat trickled down into the thick white sheet towel. The intense humidity and the copious sweat from his scalp made his new hair dye run, so that faded black lines slipped down his shoulders and chest, leaving smudgy deposits in the towel fold.

It was heavenly. He had never understood the attraction of saunas before The Excelsior. How easily a whole day could slip by at The Excelsior Hotel. It began with a late, luxurious breakfast. When that had settled, some light exercise in the gym. Then a shower, sauna, steam bath and Jacuzzi. By the time all that was done he would need a glass of cold white German wine before lunch. And after lunch came the main business of the day.

Thinking of it made his gut tighten, pull in from the smudged towel.

His call to Myrna-or-Mona.

A smiling fat man came through the changing room door. He was so gross, so layered and creased with fat, that he couldn't fasten his sheet towel but had to nip it around his waist with one hand. In his other hand he carried a mobile phone. In a jokey way he fumbled and cursed as he tried to close the door behind him, phone in hand.

"There you go . . ." He chuckled. "Gotcha now! . . . Phew!" He turned to face Neil directly. "Hey there! How're you doin'?"

It was the moustachioed American from the wee small hours of Sunday morning. The late night reveller. In the underwater light of the sauna, as he stooped and loomed across the slats, he looked like a giant sea slug, a giant whelk nosing across the sea floor towards Neil. Foraging, menacing. But when he closed on the bench the wet and greasy impression slipped away. There was a dryness about his brown hair and his thick moustache that suggested treatments, dyes, preservatives. He looked mid-forties but could have been ten years older, or even more. The hair on his chest was pure grey in patches.

The man seemed to notice Neil's inspection, and to resent it.

"You're leakin' a bit. You know that?" he said, pointing at the streaks of black dye on Neil's chest. He parked himself along Neil's bench and Neil felt the slats give, heard them bend and creak under the weight.

Neil looked down at his streaks of dye, at their inky smudges in the sheet towel. Had Toni shortchanged him on the dye? When the treatment was so expensive? Oh, Toni. You too. Of course.

Everyone's a conman.

The man chuckled again. "Happens to all the mainland Chinese, you know? The old guys. Bad dye. We have to clean this place out every day. Mop and bucket. Takes a couple of hours. Every day. Really."

Old guy's dye.

Neil raised an eyebrow in polite surprise, but said nothing.

"I'm GM, or Mr. Jim, as the Chinks have it. General Manager." The fat man held out his hand. "Pleased to meet you . . ."

Neil shook the GM's hand but couldn't think of what name to offer in return. Which was safe? Atherton? Laprisco? Diamond? Or something new? He was saved by the mobile phone buzzing on the pine slats. The GM jabbed it silent and pointed to the No Phone symbol on the wall, next to the glittering egg timer.

"Can't break my own rules!" He laughed again. "So . . . d'you like it here?" He had a professional need to start a conversation.

"It's a great hotel."

"No!" The GM laughed loudly, genuinely, this time. "Sure it is. Of course it is. It's The Excelsior. No. I mean, Hong Kong."

"Yeah," Neil said, nodding, smiling. "It's a lot of fun."

"It's a hell of a lot of fun . . ." the GM confirmed. He sighed and threw off his towel, exposing himself beyond his layers of fat. Big white whelk, in a bed of coarse grey weed. He looked down at himself. "Best nightlife I've ever known. Ever. That's for sure. I love it here. I love Hong Kong, don't you? . . ."

Now Neil had the GM all rolled up: just another cock-slave, another whoremaster and addict of the Wan Chai girly bars.

The phone went off again and this time he picked it up and squinted at the number on display in the red light. He scowled and took the call.

"What is it?"

He pressed the phone tight into his hairy ear. The caller spoke very fast, in a garbled panic.

"Whooah . . . Slow down, slow down . . . Start over . . ."

During the repeat Neil caught a name. A rather important name. He leant a little in the GM's direction, but couldn't make out what was coming through. The GM had the phone butt tucked so tight into his ear the wisps of sound were unintelligible.

The GM frowned and looked concerned. He glanced across at Neil, who was still leaning his way. He covered up his sex with the sheet towel again.

"What d'you mean? . . . What d'you mean? . . . There's some joker . . . That can't be right . . . Surely not . . . "

The GM glanced across again. "Excuse me . . ." He pointed at the phone. "Sorry about this, but . . ."

Neil nodded, smiled back. Of course. No worries.

"What d'you mean? . . . What other guy? . . . What other guy? . . . But this other guy . . . . You said this other guy . . . The same one? . . . Wait a minute, now . . ."

Neil had to move. He knew he had to. But he could not move, as in a nightmare.

"What? . . . What's that? . . . No! . . . Where? . . . Well, so what? Maybe he plays a lot of tennis . . . No way! . . . That's a lot. That's a hell of a lot! . . . How many swimsuits? . . ."

Neil tightened his towel, preparing to exit.

"Okay, but how d'you know . . . I see, I see . . . And the other guy? . . ."

Neil hung his head.

"The other guy . . . Come on . . . Let's have it . . . "

He shut his eyes.

"Oh no no no . . . This is a weird one, I mean really weir . . . Weirdo . . . Khan, the way I read this is . . . This joker . . . What? . . . But he must have his own agenda, right? . . . Must have. Hidden agenda. Don't you think? To do that . . . Freak . . . Weirdo . . . Loser . . . What's that? . . ."

Some long blast from Khan. The GM slapped the bench in exasperation.

"Oh, for Christ's sake, Khan . . . If you've got this wrong – Christ! – if you've got this wrong, Khan, you know what I'm gonna do? I'm gonna bust you back to fuckin' bellhop, d'you hear? I surely will. Because this is just too weird. Too weird. Doesn't make any fuckin' sense to me . . . I don't need this . . . Dead? . . . You're kidding . . . I can do without this . . ."

Neil got up from the bench and the GM covered the mouthpiece to speak to him.

"Hey, I'm sorry . . . Real sorry about all this . . . I spoilt your sauna . . . Give me your room number. I'll have something sent up . . ."

"Doesn't matter," Neil said, waving away the GM's concern and exiting via the Spa, as if he were moving on to the Jacuzzi now.

Chan.

Only Chan. Only Chan knew how fast it would slip away.

And suddenly there were people standing talking in front of all the doors. And outside the Spa, in the corridors, there were abandoned service trolleys. All the cleaners were busy in the suites. He had to move the huge trolleys himself and squeeze past. And then the lift would not come. All the lifts were at the top of the hotel, at the beck and call of some conference up there, and when the first one finally came it was too full and didn't stop.

He took the emergency stairs. Still hot from the sauna he now worked himself into a filthy sweat running down a dozen flights of dusty, concrete steps. There was no air conditioning in the stairwell, no windows of any kind. It was bare and empty and shadowless, in a white concrete light.

Back in 1202 he began to calm down. Nothing had been disturbed, nothing touched or taken. His flight wallet was still in the safe, and in it his new passport. He went back to the door of the suite and slipped on the 'Do Not Disturb' sign and the safety chain. Just a thought.

He sat on the bedside and picked up the phone. It had to be done.

His call was blocked by one of the receptionists. They too, now, were back in play. The harpies.

"I'm sorry, Mr. Atherton, but Mr. Chan is unavailable right now. But can I help you? Do you need another flight to London? Economy? Or super-economy?"

"I have to speak to Mr. Chan."

"Or do you need a ticket to New York, sir? First class, Club class, or Business class, sir?"

"Listen, lady . . ." Neil really wanted to let her have it, but knew that was not the way through. "We have no time for that joke right now, hilarious though it is. I need to speak to Elbert Chan and he needs to know what I have to say – for his own safety. The police will be up here any minute and I'll send them straight over."

The call was transferred.

"Chan here."

"Elbert?"

"Chan here."

"Elbert, they've rumbled me at the hotel. I don't know how or why, but they have. They may be on their way up to the suite this very minute. I need a bolt-hole."

There was a pause, and those crackles again, as if the receiver were being passed from hand to hand around the room. Er . . . Anyone want to deal with this?

"Excuse me, but who is this?"

"It's Neil, Elbert."

"Neil who?"

"Elbert, I want to meet you somewhere and – "

"But I don't want to meet you, you see. Not anywhere. I don't want to meet you."

"Then I'm coming over to your office."

"No you're not."

"I'm coming over."

"They won't let you up."

"What?"

"I've told them. I've already told them not to let you up."

Neil had never felt so helpless. "Not to let me up?"

"Not to let you up."

"Elbert – "

"You can't come up."

"But you can't just – "

"Please don't tell me what I can and cannot do, Mr.

Atherton. It's time to move on now. Goodbye. I mean that."

And he hung up.

Neil replaced the receiver, then lifted it again, set it aside. He sat there on the bed, very still, very low, suffering another lapse in concentration. He stared beyond the window seat at the view and his mind slipped back to those earlier thoughts. The band at the Metropole. The black backing singers. The white liners down there. Hua Hin and Vietnam. The restaurant and ballroom. The medical bay and the hairdressers', side by side. Top deck. Black and white tiles. The mountains of Vietnam coming into view, while he had his hair re-styled and re-dyed, with good dye this time . . .

A sharp knock at the door.

Those images tumbled to the floor and fragmented, like locks of hair under the stylist's scissors, disintegrating on the black and white tiles.

He stood and went to the door. He opened it on the slip chain.

There was the dapper figure of Edward, squeezed in the narrow gap, his bouffant bedraggled, strands of it floating in the currents from the air conditioning. He was on his own. He had a newspaper in his hand and he looked apologetic.

"I didn't order a paper."

"I'm sorry, sir," Edward began. "But we have to discuss something. I have to come in."

"No you don't."

"Sir, I have to – "

"You don't have to come in. I don't want you to come in."

Edward held the folded newspaper up to the chained gap.

Just a small article, just a filler towards the back of the paper, before the 'What's On' section, but with a picture too. The picture was from a distance and from below. A publicity shot. It could have been anybody up there on stage, in the glittering sequins, with the long black hair. A Rolling Stone.

Johnny Cash. Neil Diamond . . .

Entertainer Dies.

When he read that subheading, took it in, *Entertainer Dies*, Neil felt something dying in him too. He felt the finality of Chan's words echo again in his mind – *No one needs to rehearse, rehearse, rehearse . . . I don't want to meet you, you see. I don't want to meet you, meet you, meet you . . .* And he felt, behind him, beyond room 1202, in the grey day outside the hotel, some celestial movement taking place, the movement of destiny, it must have been, within which the movement of those liners in the harbour, gliding along at their stately pace, was a part, as was the movement of the planes ascending from Chek Lap Kok at their impossible angles, and, closer to home, below, at the door, the humbler movement of taxis wheeling out of The Excelsior forecourt, one after the other. Neil knew now that he would never get on board the boats or planes, or get inside the taxis – never, ever, ever get on board, with or without *Cracklin' Rosie*, or Elbert Chan.

Entertainer Dies.

In a slow, defeated way, Neil unslipped the chain and opened the door wide.

"You better come in."

His shoulders rounded as he led Edward into the suite, and he sat down on the end of the bed because he had to. He felt weak and he felt a sudden chill, a chill to the bones. The superficial glow lent by the sauna and his panicky flight down the emergency stairs had passed. The air conditioning in 1202 was a cold, ill wind blowing through the suite. He zipped up his tracksuit top.

"Let me have a look at that," he said, taking the paper.

Edward surrendered the paper, then stood dutifully by the dressing table, hands behind his back.

"I'm sure everything can be explained, sir," he said.

Neil stared down at the article, unable to read it, his

concentration slipping fast again. It was only a few paragraphs but he needed a full two minutes to go through it, and to grasp some idea of what he could do about it. He needed a story here. A counter story for this bit of cub journalism. Had they nothing better to write about?

When he looked up at Edward again his expression was set. He knew how he looked. He knew the shadows his damp black hair cast, that made his face so worn and lined, so bedevilled and betrayed. But he knew also that there was a tightness, a defiance in his eyes now, and in the grim set of his mouth. He was going to see this through. He had to. No other option. But he needed to make it up as he went along and it wasn't going to be easy.

"Okay . . . So, you really want to know about this? Let me tell you . . . Okay . . . You see, this guy – " he pointed at the picture of Laprisco – "this guy was – " Neil shrugged, and he winced at the difficulty, the tedium of this endless sham, of trying to explain this to Edward and find the right words for him. But actually he had no idea what to say at all. He was tempted just to fetch his new passport from the safe and thrust it under Edward's nose and tell him to *fuck off*, but he couldn't. The passport wasn't enough any more.

He looked up again at Edward. "You see, this guy . . . " He gave a tight-lipped smile to Edward, standing there above him by the dressing table, arms behind his back, mock-military, at ease . . . "Let me tell you about this guy, okay? Since you're so interested. D'you really want to hear it?"

Edward looked increasingly suspicious. "Yes," he said. "If you wouldn't mind, sir."

"This guy – " Neil hung his head and squeezed his temples with his long, musician's fingers, as if he were trying to remember this guy, to recall just what had happened with this guy, for Edward's benefit, but just stalling for time and desperately trying to work out what should come next – "This guy was some kind of showman, you know?" He looked up again. "But strictly small-time." He avoided Edward's eyes and focused above them, on the fallen, bedraggled bouffant – and as he did so an angry, helpless voice cried out inside him – *Why should I be at the mercy of a fop like you? Or anyone like you?* But he was. He always was. Chan, Cheung, Laprisco, even Wong, and now Edward Reception. All short men, each shorter than the last, like Chinese dolls within dolls. He'd been supplicant to them all. And still was. Yet he had to press on, nothing else for it: "This guy was just a small-time entertainer, you know? In fact, he was very, very small-time. A small-time loser, if you want my opinion. Are you with me?"

Edward nodded curtly. They weren't making much progress.

Neil poked Laprisco's picture: "They've got it all wrong here," he said – and suddenly he'd found it, the way forward, the story, it was obvious – "This guy came to the American Club on Saturday night – " he poked the picture again, irritated, impatient, insulted by all this muddle and confusion – "that bit's right, the date and everything – Okay. But then he tried to – I don't know what you'd call it – he tried to – to muscle in on my act? He actually tried to climb up onto the stage? . . . " Neil laughed, shrugged, looked to the picture again, and the heat of his impatience cooled to regret. He brushed a long hair off the picture. Where had it come from, that hair? It was coarse, long, black – not his. Was it Edward's hair, from the bouffant? No. Myrna-or-Mona's? No – too long. It had to be a hair from Laprisco's wig. The very same. Housekeeping wasn't so good here after all. How many more hairs from the wig had moulted here? The wig that was now ashes, cinders, and had been for a whole day now, more than a whole day, like the whole man. Ashes. Cinders. "Of course it didn't work out," Neil continued, "and there was an accident, and – " he brushed the photograph again, but gently now, all irritation spent, "it's all here. They just got the wrong guy. They muddled it up. The name, I mean." He looked up at Edward. "Because we both impersonate the same star, you see? We both impersonate the same superstar. That's why they got it muddled up. Neil Diamond. You know? . . . You know Neil Diamond? . . . Don't you?"

"No."

"What? . . . Hello? . . . Edward? Anybody in there? I'm Tony Laprisco, remember? Hello? I did a show here last week!"

"What show?"

"Uncut Diamonds. Tuesday, Wednesday, Thursday. You didn't see it? Hear about it?"

Edward shook his head, still suspicious. "I was graveyard shift but – "

"Graveyard shift!" Neil grunted. "You know nothing, Edward! You don't even know what's going down in your own hotel! For Christ's sake! No wonder you're confused! Anyway, Neil Diamond was a superstar twenty years ago, back in the seventies." Neil took a tone of weary superiority now with Edward, as if he were explaining to him something he'd had to explain to many others like him before. "You see, it is very, very competitive out there. Everyone thinks they can do it. This guy, for instance. He thought he could do it. But he couldn't. There was just no meaning in the songs, not the way he sang them. It was just a travesty. They all think they can cut it but they can't. Only the best survive. I mean, this guy . . ." Neil frowned down at the picture and appeared sympathetic a moment, but then he raised his eyebrows, changed his mind about what he'd been going to say. "But he's dead now," he concluded, with a touch of pathos. "And it's all over for him, and that's sad. Very sad." Neil looked up at Edward again. "Or is it? I don't know. It's not much of a life. On the road." He added, anecdotally: "He played a gig at some poor man's club here. The Mariners'?"

Edward nodded.

"Tsim Sha Tsui?"

"I know that club."

"He played there. But it didn't go so well, I heard. Then he came after me, trying to team up, a sort of double act, trying to muscle in on my show. He was – " Neil broke off yet again, and looked down at the paper one last time, and gave the photograph one final, tender brush, but this time genuine sympathy, involuntary sympathy, no affectation, welled up in his voice, as if he'd faked it too well for his own good, fallen for his own sham – "He was just a sad and lonely guy, you know?" he said to Edward. And saying this, Neil thought not of Laprisco at all, but of Iannis, and that look in his eyes, under the sick film of water, that swollen, backward, sliding glance toward Chan's office; and he thought of himself too, he couldn't help it, and he felt his own eyes tear up. "Just one of those guys who are like that." He had to blink back his emotion. "Who wind up like that, for one reason or another . . . Just a sad and lonely guy, trying to get by. Earn a living. Keep body and soul together. D'you follow me?"

Edward nodded.

Neil stood. He faced Edward at the end of the bed. He gave the paper back.

"Now I'm going to show you something." Neil led Edward to the walk-in cupboard and the safe. "Turn away," he said, while he tapped in his birthday. The safe opened. "Look at this." Neil took out Laprisco's passport and flicked it open at the photo page, which now showed his own face, slightly offset, chin up and proud, neatly cropped from a publicity shot at The Mariners' –

"Here's my passport – "

"It's all right, sir – "

"YOU LOOK AT IT! YOU LOOK AT ME!" Neil demanded, holding it in front of Edward's eyes, rudely close. "Take a good look. A good look. That's me, right? And there's my name, right? Anthony Laprisco. I am alive and well, thank you very much. You see that? And here's my return ticket. Open ticket, see?" He let the printout of flight details drop down for Edward's inspection.

"It's all right, sir – "

"YOU LOOK AT IT! LOOK AT ME!"

Neil stood there for a full five seconds, trying to hold the moment steady but trembling too, with a depth of emotion that surprised him, that he didn't have to fake at all. Then he returned the documents to the safe, pushed the door to, and the lock whirred shut.

"Now," he said, turning back to the defeated, chastened Edward. "I have told you the story, I have shown you my passport, I have shown you my return ticket. Anything else, Edward?" He began to usher Edward out the suite.

"I'm sorry, sir, I – "

"But if you're still not satisfied, I'll tell you what you can do. But you won't like it, and I'd rather not do that. I'd rather keep it civil. Okay?"

They were at the door.

"I'm sorry, sir – "

"I don't want to hear any more about this, okay? I'm feeling a little anxious now about the way I'm being treated at this hotel, particularly by you and that tall guy. The bald fellow. Tell him to back off too."

"Please accept, on behalf – "

"A bottle of champagne? Sure. Send it up. But not another word about it, okay?"

Neil began to close the door.

"Sir – "

"Bye."

"Sir?"

"I have to move on now."

He shut the door.

Chapter Twenty-four

A Martini

He had dealt with Edward, sent him on his way, and Edward would not be coming back, but that did not mean someone else wouldn't come back in his place. Khan or Mr. Jim, or more likely both together. Sooner or later his alibi, for all its spontaneous wit and ingenuity, would be unpicked. The chase had begun. The countdown.

Neil sat on the end of the bed, head bowed, hands in his lap. This was his call, and his alone. He had to quit. That much was clear. He looked up out the window. Such a grey day.

But where could he go?

He thought of Angel. But no. Impossible.

He thought of meeting the band, but those thoughts – of *Uncut Diamonds* and the clever bass player and the beautiful backing singers, and of the tour, the liners – those thoughts, those options, residue of evaporated fantasy, slipped away in a few moments, like the last crystals slinking through the sauna egg timer. There had been no future in any of it. No more future than in an egg timer.

That was the realization he faced squarely, at last, sitting on the end of the bed in room 1202, after he'd sent Edward on his way. There had been no future in the wile, the ruse, none at all. It couldn't work. It was all a game. An idle game. And he began to appreciate, reluctant to admit Chan had got there before him, that this was the realization Chan had faced during their phone call just an hour or so ago. Chan's whole scheme, his resuscitation of the grand tour – *The show must go on!* – spawned on some exuberant optimism of the early morning hours, and the pleasures of a cooked breakfast at The InterContinental, Chan's whole scheme had depended upon him lying low for just a few days, these last few days before the bookings started. Then Laprisco checked out of The Excelsior and they were on their way. It had all fitted into place. But Neil hadn't lain low. Not low enough, anyway. Maybe if he'd lain a bit lower, then maybe . . . But if you thought about it for a moment, Elbert, it was a bad plan. It was a lousy plan, Elbert. Just the slightest complication unravelled everything, Elbert . . .

After reckoning up all he had, all that he could physically lay hands on, he found there was still one option, one last bit of crystal, that turned and shone with a certain lustre, and slunk through the waist of the glass – as indeed, he noted, there always had to be.

He could go home.

Homeward Bound, full reprise.

He could return to his roots. Where it all began. Like some long forgotten pioneer finding his way back. And to make the gamble real and true, when he went to the safe to retrieve his open ticket, in a moment of pure, light-headed recklessness, he left behind, locked in the safe, the British passport of Neil Atherton. He locked it up in there and left it behind. Something for Edward and Khan to puzzle and worry about. Let them play cops and robbers. They'd love to. Who cares?

Dressed in his blue-black tracksuit, wearing his heavy wraparound sunglasses, Neil took the emergency stairs from the twelfth floor. He came down the twenty-four flights at a steady pace – no hurry, take it easy, on the home run now. It was very hot and stuffy in the dusty stairwells again, and echoey, but clean and well lit all the way down. He carried his smart Excelsior carrier bag, white and gold, at his side, filled with his show outfit, his swimming trunks and spare sports clothes, and on top, his swollen flight wallet. It was a long, hot, slow descent. When at last he came through the fire door into the back of the lobby, the blast of the air conditioning froze him a moment in the doorway. Then he was on his way.

He kept up a good pace across the lobby – dodging, ducking, weaving, knocking someone with his carrier bag – "Excuse me, I'm so sorry – " and was more than halfway to the doors when the first call came -

"One moment, sir!"

It was Khan himself.

But Neil kept on going. There was enough space between him and the reception desk. Plenty of space. Khan would have to run to catch him, and he wouldn't do that.

"One moment, sir!"

He was only yards from the door. The doorman hadn't noticed Khan. He was too attentive to his duties, a true professional. Neil smiled benignly to him and held his attention by reaching deep into his empty tracksuit pocket for a tip. He must keep smiling, must not wipe his sweating, itching brow, just keep digging for that tip that wasn't there. Behind his sunglasses his eyes were tight and full of panic.

"One moment, Mr. Laprisco!"

Neil was through, outside, where another doorman already held open the taxi door. Quality service. Every time. He slipped into the back of the cab.

"Airport," he said.

The door was shut and the taxi started off, but then the driver hesitated. He hesitated! Khan was on the forecourt, approaching, gesticulating.

"Let's go," Neil said. "Forget about him."

And to his relief and surprise the driver did what he was

told. He pulled out into the traffic. Perhaps it was his outfit, Neil thought. His hair. The wraparound sunglasses and the blue-black tracksuit. Perhaps these things had the look of a criminal disguise, a man on the run, someone desperate. His hair might have been mistaken for a wig. Quite easily mistaken for a wig, in fact. In a second the driver had tossed up between the elderly, elegant Khan, in his outmoded dogstooth and red cravat, and his fare all in black, in his big sunglasses, travelling incognito, and he'd decided the latter might be the more dangerous man to cross.

Good call.

Neil met the driver's eyes in the rear-view mirror. He said again, with an imperceptible backward glance: "Forget about him." He lifted a hand from The Excelsior bag in his lap and dismissed the incident.

"He's just another loser."

It turned out the late & great Tony Laprisco had not travelled with his band, nor with the pretty black backing singers. His entourage flew in the belly of the plane while Tony travelled Club class. He'd spared himself no expense on his Asia tour, his last throw of the dice. Neil was directed up the carpeted gangway into the mega-top of the 747. Hostesses, in their discreet, immaculate uniforms, smiled at him brightly everywhere he looked. Well, of course they were used to all sorts up here. All sorts of rich folk. Aging rock stars were nothing new, on their way back to L.A.

"Welcome aboard, sir," said one close by, attentive, hands behind her back. This was the top job, working up here, away from the ceaseless demands of the masses in economy. These girls would be keen enough to stay in the mega-top, would do anything to stay up here.

Another one, shorter but prettier, much younger, was actually waiting by his Club class chair. A personal attendant.

"Welcome aboard, Mr. Laprisco."

Neil nodded, took it all in his stride.

She put her hand out for his Excelsior bag and he let her take it and stow it overhead. Neil watched her stretch her short, full body until her blouse parted from her skirt, exposing her jewelled navel. Once she'd stowed his bag, she moved aside and straightened up her uniform. Neil settled into Laprisco's puffy Club class armchair. The chair was too fat and set too far back. It was, one might say, too laid back. Out the corner of his eye Neil tried to absorb the meaning of the controls, described in a stainless steel diagram on the arm.

But the hostess was by his side again. She bent down to him. She was so close she might have reached forward and taken off his sunglasses. She was so close he could feel and smell her peppermint breath. She was so close she could have kissed him.

"Would you like something to drink, Mr. Laprisco?"

"Yes, I would," Neil replied.

He knew exactly what he wanted to drink.

"I would like a Martini," he said.

"With ice?" The word extended into her ice-white smile.

"Yes, with ice . . . and . . ."

"Yes?"

It was as if she wanted him to say it.

"An olive," Neil said.

"An olive?"

"Yes."

He returned her smile with a smile she could not possibly understand. It was so broad it exposed his high gums, the dark roots of his teeth, it lifted the heavy arcs of his dusty, dated, plastic sunglasses.

"I like an olive in a Martini."

Printed in the United Kingdom by
Lightning Source UK Ltd., Milton Keynes
138583UK00001B/8/P